Out of the Crowded Vagueness

also by Brian Dyde

Antigua and Barbuda: Heart of the Caribbean
Islands to the Windward: Five Gems of the Caribbean
St Kitts: Cradle of the Caribbean
Caribbean Companion: The A–Z Reference
The Empty Sleeve: The Story of the West India Regiments
of the British Army
A History of Antigua: The Unsuspected Isle
Where the Sea Had an Ending: A Caribbean Travel Miscellany

with Robert Greenwood and Shirley Hamber
Caribbean Certificate History Book 1: Amerindians to Africans
Caribbean Certificate History Book 2: Emancipation to Emigration
Caribbean Certificate History Book 3: Decolonisation and Development

Out of the Crowded Vagueness

A History of the Islands of St Kitts, Nevis and Anguilla

Brian Dyde

MACMILLAN
CARIBBEAN

Macmillan Education
Between Towns Road, Oxford OX4 3PP
A division of Macmillan Publishers Limited
Companies and representatives throughout the world

www.macmillan-caribbean.com

ISBN 0-333-97598-7

First published 2005

Designed by Mike Brain Graphic Design Limited
Typeset by EXPO (Holdings) Limited
Maps by TechType, except page xi, by Brian Dyde
Cover design by Mike Brain Graphic Design Limited
Cover: Methodist Chapel, Charlestown, in 1802. Courtesy Museum of Nevis History.

The authors and publishers would like to thank the following
for permission to reproduce their photographs:
Author's Own Collection – plates 4, 16, 30, 39; *Brimstone Hill Fortress National
Park Society* – plates 8, 20; *Commonwealth Office, Department of Library
Information Services* – plates 18, 29; *Corbis* – plate 37; *Coville L. Petty* – plate
26; *Getty Images / Hulton Archive* – plate 10; *Museum of Nevis History* – plate
11; *National Archives of St Kitts* – plates 19, 27, 28, 31;
National Portrait Gallery London / Carl Fredrick Von Breda – plate 7;
RCS (1800–1889) – plate 24; *RCS / Photograph by Jose Anjo, c. 1900* – plate 21;
Popperfoto.com – plates 33, 34, 35, 36, 38, 40; *Royal Geographical Society* –
plates 1, 25, 32; *Royal Maritime Museum, Greenwich* – plate 9;
St Kitts Heritage Society – plates 2, 3, 5, 6, 12, 13, 14, 15, 17, 22, 23

Printed and bound in Thailand

2009   2008   2007   2006   2005
10 9 8 7 6 5 4 3 2 1

To the memory of
Sidney and Edith Dyde
and
Enid Joseph

Contents

Plates

Maps

Acknowledgements

I would first like to thank my beloved wife, Veronica, for her support and patience during the writing of this book, and for her invaluable help in the preparation of the final manuscript. I am equally thankful to Nick Gillard at Macmillan for asking me to undertake the work in the first place, and to Anstice Hughes for her expert copy-editing. In response to my enquiries for material and information, I must also thank Jacqueline Armory, David Druett, Jane Grell, Raymond Haynes, Cicely Jacobs, Victoria Borg O'Flaherty and Colville Petty.

In searching for the bulk of the material needed I received a great deal of help from the staff of the Cambridge University Library, the Foreign and Commonwealth Office Library, the libraries of the Institute of Commonwealth Studies and the Institute of Historical Research at the University of London, the St Kitts Heritage Society, the Basseterre Public Library, the Nevis Historical and Conservation Society, and, last but far from least, the Anguilla Library Service. No one, knowing the size of Anguilla and even vaguely aware of the unimportant role it has played in Caribbean history, can fail to be surprised to learn that the island's public library now houses what is undoubtedly the finest, and probably the most extensive, collection of books, maps and documents about the English-speaking West Indies anywhere outside North America and Europe. Although housed and freely accessible to researchers in the public library, the collection is the property of the Anguilla National Trust, to which it was donated in an act of unparalleled generosity by Don Mitchell, QC.

Brian Dyde
Pembroke
August 2003

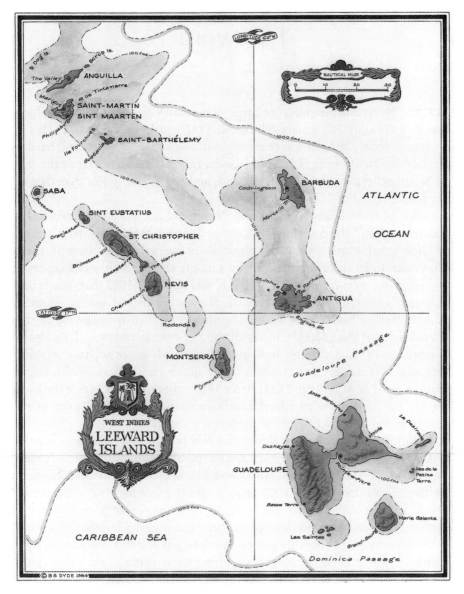

The Leeward Islands

Foreword

St Kitts, Nevis and Anguilla are three very small Caribbean islands, which together are only 365 square kilometres (141 square miles) in size. This is an area precisely the same as that of Lanai, one of the smallest (and hardly the best-known) of the Hawaiian islands, slightly less than that of the Isle of Wight off the south coast of England, and considerably less than that of the Greek island of Naxos.

Two of the islands, St Kitts and Nevis, are no more than two miles apart. In spite of the constant interchange between them, the intermingling of their inhabitants, and the duplication in everything to do with their administration, all brought about by this proximity, each was a separate British possession for over 250 years. It was not until 1883 that, with considerable misgivings in both islands, they were placed under a united administration based in St Kitts. Together they then formed one of the presidencies of the Federal Colony of the Leeward Islands which had been formed in 1871. Although it is out of sight of the other two islands, Anguilla lost its separate colonial status much earlier than Nevis, being made a ward of St Kitts in 1825. After 1883 it became very much the least significant part of the tri-island administration, its name not even being incorporated into the title of the presidency until 1952.

Nothing changed very much in the relative status of the three islands until 1967, when the by then once again separate colony of St Kitts-Nevis-Anguilla achieved full internal independence as a 'State in association with Britain'. Soon after this the 6000 or so Anguillians, rather than allow themselves to be ruled directly by St Kitts with no recourse to any other authority, staged a revolt. Under an inept and illegal administration, and with little regard for the difficulties which might accrue from possessing a virtually non-existent economy, an attempt was made to set up an independent state. The long interregnum which followed the failure of this attempt ended in 1982 with the return of Anguilla to its original colonial status, then dignified under the title of a British Overseas Dependent Territory. This success of the Anguillians in detaching themselves from St Kitts had a profound effect on the people of Nevis, as was demonstrated the following year. When the sovereign state of St Kitts and Nevis, with a total population of a little over 45,000, entered the community of nations in 1983, it was with a federal form of government and what amounted to full internal independence for the 10,000 people of Nevis within the federation.

Many aspects of life among the people of all three islands – all speaking the same language and nearly all springing from the same stock – have in recent years been studied and written about in great detail, and individual histories, of a sort, have been compiled for all three islands. But out of all this material there is next to nothing which gives an overall picture of how things really came to be as they are for the present inhabitants of any one of them. The many books and articles listed in the bibliography have all helped in the writing of this book, but at the same time they can be seen as adding to – in the words of the Trinidadian-born intellectual and historian C.L.R. James – 'that crowded vagueness which passes for the history of the West Indies'.[1] It is hoped that what follows will go some way to lessening this obscurity in one corner of the Caribbean at least.

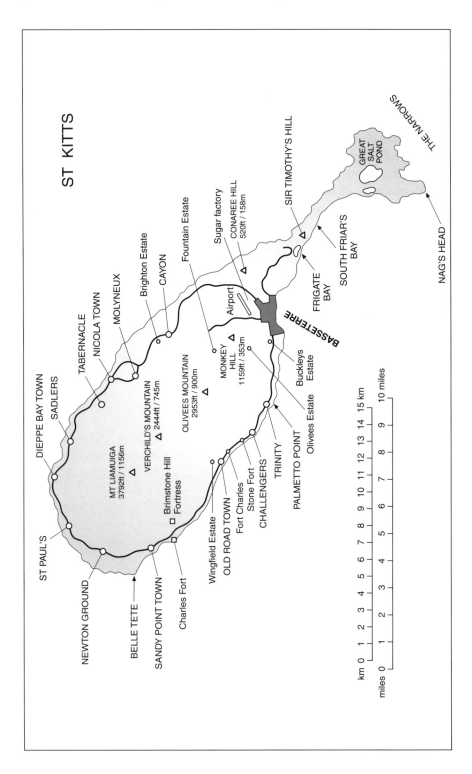

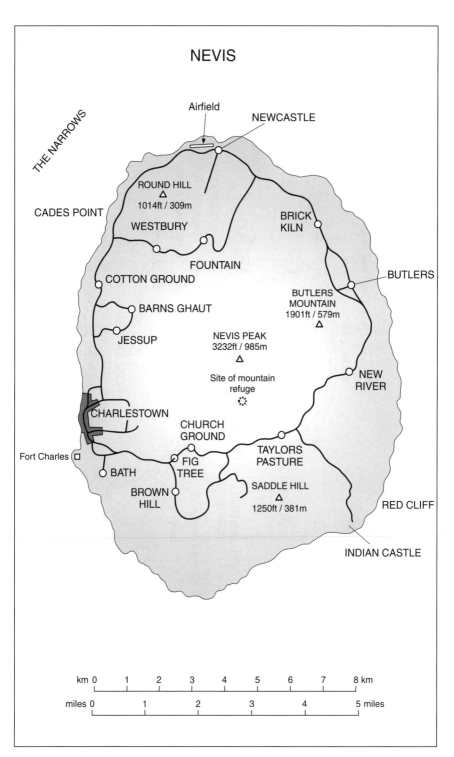

NEVIS

THE NARROWS

Airfield

NEWCASTLE

CADES POINT

ROUND HILL
△
1014ft / 309m

WESTBURY

BRICK
KILN

FOUNTAIN

BUTLERS

COTTON GROUND

BUTLERS
MOUNTAIN
1901ft / 579m
△

BARNS GHAUT

NEVIS PEAK
3232ft / 985m
△

JESSUP

Site of mountain
refuge

NEW
RIVER

CHARLESTOWN

CHURCH
GROUND

Fort Charles

BATH

FIG
TREE

TAYLORS
PASTURE

BROWN
HILL

SADDLE HILL
△
1250ft / 381m

RED CLIFF

INDIAN CASTLE

km 0   1   2   3   4   5   6   7   8 km

miles 0   1   2   3   4   5 miles

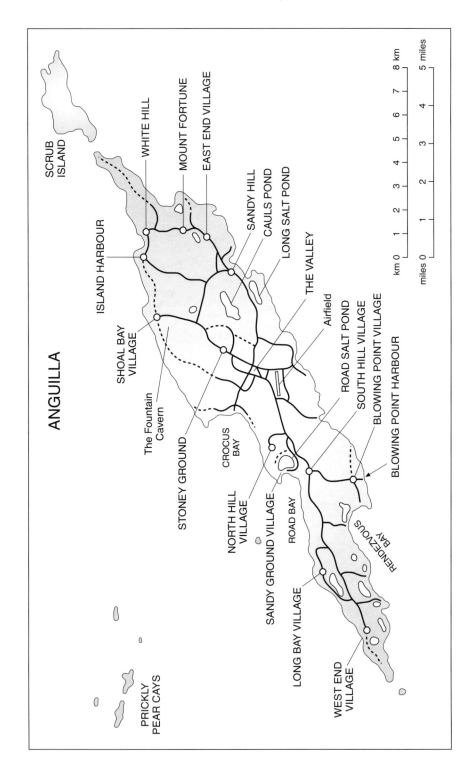

1

The Islands

The eastern end of the Caribbean Sea is separated from the Atlantic Ocean by the Lesser Antilles, the long chain of islands which stretches from Trinidad in the south to Puerto Rico in the north. Situated in the northern half of this chain, generally referred to as the Leeward Islands, St Kitts, Nevis and Anguilla are about 800 kilometres (km) (500 miles) north of Venezuela and 2000 km (1240 miles) south-east of Florida.

The Lesser Antilles lie along the edge of the Caribbean tectonic plate, a zone of great geological instability caused by the underthrust of the Atlantic plate – a movement which takes place at the rate of perhaps 2 centimetres (less than one inch) a year. Although tiny, this movement has been enough to create persistent geothermal and volcanic activity for the past 40 million years. As a result the main part of the Lesser Antilles, between Grenada and Anguilla, is made up of two parallel arcs of islands.

The outer arc consists of volcanic islands raised during the earlier half of the 40-million-year period, which are all now greatly eroded and consist largely of coral limestone over a volcanic base. All are fairly flat or low-lying. Anguilla is at the northern extremity of this arc, which also contains the islands of St Martin, St Bartholomew, Barbuda, Antigua, Grandeterre (the eastern part of Guadeloupe) and Marie Galante. St Kitts and Nevis are both part of the younger, inner arc formed during the last 20 million years stretching from Saba southwards to Grenada. All of these islands are high and steep, having been built up around one or more volcanic cones. Many of these cones, including Mount Liamuiga in St Kitts, are either still active or have been in historic time. Because of their position on the inner arc, St Kitts and Nevis are both completely surrounded by the Caribbean Sea, the boundary of which is some 80 km (50 miles) to the north-east. This is something which cannot be said of Anguilla, where the north coast faces directly on to the Atlantic. All the islands, particularly those on the inner arc, are prone to earthquakes of varying intensity. These have been a feature of life throughout their recorded history, and have not infrequently caused loss of life, much damage to property, and acute distress.

The islands are located in that part of the Caribbean region which enjoys what must be considered a virtually ideal climate. Although at around 17 degrees north of the equator they are well within the tropics, the almost constant north-easterly or easterly trade winds have a great moderating influence, producing a mild uniform climate with a mean air temperature which ranges from about 24°C in January to 27°C in July; only very rarely does it exceed 32°C or fall below 16°C. The trade winds are also responsible for bringing moisture from the Atlantic, but the amount of rain in each island is very much determined by its relief. The droughts which have been experienced regularly in Anguilla, and occasionally in Nevis, are uncommon in St Kitts. The only major change to this pattern occurs when one of the low pressure waves which occasionally interrupt the trade wind and bring rain turns into the violent storm known as a hurricane. Such storms have from time to time throughout their recorded history affected all three islands, often with disastrous results in the days before modern forecasting and monitoring techniques became available.

Although earthquakes and hurricanes must have ravaged their landscapes for countless thousands, perhaps millions, of years before the arrival of human beings, it was not until the islands began to be inhabited by man, perhaps 6000 years ago, that any major change to their flora and fauna took place. Since then, with the most drastic changes taking place during the last 500 years, the original vegetation and animal life has all been transformed.

The native forests – luxuriant on St Kitts and Nevis if nowhere as prolific and dense on Anguilla – were exploited from the time the first people reached the islands, but it was not until after the arrival of Europeans that they began to disappear altogether. In the early years of the seventeenth century it was still possible for a transient English adventurer to record that in Nevis 'the wood groweth close to the water side, at a high-water mark, and in some places so thick…you cannot get through it, but by making your way with hatchets'; and for one of the first settlers in St Kitts to describe that island as 'all overgrown'. All three islands now have vegetation which only too clearly shows the disturbance wrought by man. Intensive land use in all of Anguilla, and over all the lowlands of St Kitts and Nevis, has removed all trace of natural vegetation. The mountains of the latter two islands are still covered with tropical forest, but most of this has been greatly modified by man, and completely undisturbed original rainforest is rare in either island. The long south-east peninsula of St Kitts, the low hills of Nevis, and virtually the whole of Anguilla all support nothing but scrub woodland.

Because the Eastern Caribbean islands were never connected by a land bridge to either South America or the Greater Antilles it is considered that their original fauna could only have developed from life forms transported quite fortuitously over water or through the air. St Kitts, Nevis and Anguilla are all situated at the northern end of the island chain, and so far from any mainland that none of them could ever have supported anything but a very limited number of animal species. Anguilla, belonging to the outer and much older arc of islands, is thought at one time to have been part of a very much bigger island, incorporating its neighbours St Martin and St Bartholomew. As such it undoubtedly had a greater range of fauna, including species unknown elsewhere. One of these, a huge rodent called the Anguilla Heptaxodont, *Amblyrhiza inundata*, whose fossil remains were found in 1968, was the size of a small deer.

What animals existed in any of the islands when man arrived very soon began to disappear. Today, other than bats, there are no truly indigenous mammals to be found in any of them. The only other indigenous terrestrial creatures are lizards and iguanas, although there is a possibility that even the latter were not native, but brought from the mainland by the early Amerindian settlers. The same people certainly introduced into St Kitts, and probably Nevis, the agouti and the guinea pig, but these too have long since been hunted to extinction. The agouti held out longer, but none has been seen in either island since the early years of the twentieth century.

The present animal wildlife of all three islands is extremely sparse. In Anguilla it consists of nothing other than bats, lizards and a small population of iguanas. In St Kitts and Nevis, where iguanas are now virtually extinct, lizards and bats are joined by two animals introduced at widely separated times during the colonial period. Specimens of the West African green monkey, *Cercopithecus aethiops sabaeus*, began to be brought to the islands as pets within 25 years of the first European settlement. By about 1670 some had escaped and entered the wild, and within a hundred years they had become so plentiful that their population could no longer be controlled in either island. The number has always been greater in St Kitts, where it is believed the monkey may well by now be a distinct sub-species. The Asian mongoose, *Herpestes auropunctatus*, was introduced into the same two islands in the late nineteenth century, in order to control rat and snake infestation in the sugar-cane fields; something it did only too well. With no natural predators, mongooses multiplied rapidly and now, rather like the monkeys which raid and damage fruit trees and smallholdings, they are considered a pest.

St Kitts

St Kitts is 176 square kilometres (sq km) (68 square miles) in area, and in shape has been compared variously to a kite, a guitar, an Indian club, a paddle, or a pear with an elongated stalk ending in a knob, with its main axis running north-west (the base of the 'pear') to south-east (the knob at the end of the 'stalk'). The island is some 30 km (19 miles) in length, with a maximum width of 8 km (5 miles). It is 3 km (2 miles) from Nevis in the south-east, and 10 km (6 miles) from St Eustatius in the north-west, separated by channels 9 metres (m) (30 feet) and 55 m (180 feet) deep respectively. At some time in the past, all three, together with tiny Booby Island in The Narrows between St Kitts and Nevis, would have formed part of one large island. The central range of mountains forming the body of the 'pear' is separated by cols into three distinct parts: Mount Liamuiga, Verchild's Mountain and Olivees Mountain. Offshoots of Olivees Mountain are Monkey Hill, which overlooks the capital of Basseterre, and the Canada Hills to the north of the town. Plains (one containing a salt pond) and low hills separate Basseterre and the Canada Hills from the neck of the stalk-like peninsula. This long, rugged extension of the island terminates in a group of steep scrub-covered hills surrounding a very large salt pond.

The peninsula and the Canada Hills are older than the rest of the island, and probably have not changed greatly during the past two million years. In the main mountain mass Mount Liamuiga (called Mount Misery until 1983) is the largest and youngest volcano. The top of the jagged pinnacle rising from the edge of its crater on the eastern side at 1156 m (3792 feet) is the highest point of the island. The crater it overlooks is over 200 m (656 feet) deep and one kilometre (1100 yards) in diameter. It contains a small pond, together with a group of active fumaroles and boiling water outlets. Brimstone Hill, on the lower south-western flank of the mountains, is the most important of several subsidiary cones. It has been determined that volcanic eruptions, with pyroclastic flows and mudflows, took place at around 1600 BC, again between 1000 and 250 BC, and most recently in about AD 250. These were all major events which, as well as affecting the whole of St Kitts, must have had an impact of one sort or another on the surrounding islands – all of which probably had been inhabited since well before 2000 BC.

Most of the island is well-watered, with an average rainfall of about 1270 millimetres (mm) (50 inches) a year around the coasts, and up to 3810 mm (150 inches) a year in the mountains. The south-east peninsula, however, is very dry, with a mean annual rainfall of probably only half that of the rest of the coastal area. Due to its volcanic origin, the soil in the main body of the island is loamy, fine-grained, extremely fertile and very friable. As a result it soaks up much of the rainfall and prevents drainage by rivers and streams. A significant feature of the island is the number of steep-sided guts running from the 300 m (1000 foot) contour down to the coastline all around the mountain range. Small streams flow constantly above this contour, but the ghuts – as guts are called for some unknown reason in St Kitts – fill up and flow only during periods of heavy rain. One or two rivers, like the Wingfield, Cayon and Stone Fort, flow a little more readily but still fail to reach the sea in more than a trickle for a large part of the year.

Nevis

A smaller island than St Kitts, Nevis is 93 sq km (36 square miles) in area. It is ellipsoidal in shape, about 13 km (8 miles) in length from north to south, and 10 km (6 miles) in width. It is of entirely volcanic origin, built up around an almost symmetrical central volcanic cone called Nevis Peak. Saddle Hill to the south, Round Hill to the north, and Butlers Mountain to the east are the three most prominent of the subsidiary volcanic cones which helped form the island.

Nevis Peak is 985 m (3232 feet) in height. It has not erupted in historic times and may well have been dormant since before mankind first entered the Caribbean. This does not mean that all volcanic activity on the island has ceased: there are small deposits of sulphur and gypsum and a hot spring not too far from the capital Charlestown, and a fumarole has been active near Cades Bay in the north-west since 1953. Although Nevis Peak and Mount Liamuiga are similar in age and structure, their most recent volcanic activities were very different. The last eruption of Nevis Peak must have been in the form of a colossal explosion, sending a massive amount of material into the air, as the whole island has been littered with volcanic rocks and boulders ever since. These have seriously affected the cultivation of the island, making it necessary to repeatedly clear and drain each field, and have rendered ploughing impossible. Such volcanic activity has also produced soil quite different from that of St Kitts, its far greater clay content making it less permeable and very susceptible to erosion.

Nevis Peak deflects the rain-bearing winds and makes the rainfall very unpredictable. As a result, while the island suffers from periodic droughts, it also means that heavy rain storms can be experienced at any time of the year. An average annual amount of about 2500 mm (100 inches) falls on the peak itself, but no more than about 1000 mm (40 inches) in the lowland areas. The rain drains off Nevis Peak into the sea through the same sort of steep-sided guts (ghuts) that are found in St Kitts, but the only constantly flowing water is the Bath Stream which is fed by the spring inland of Charlestown mentioned above.

Anguilla

Anguilla is over 80 km (50 miles) to the north of St Kitts, separated from it by water over 600 m (2000 feet) in depth. As a long, low, narrow limestone island it bears no resemblance in outline or formation to either St Kitts or Nevis. It also differs from its closest neighbour St Martin, about 10 km (6 miles) to the south, which is hilly and more rounded in shape. The island runs in a roughly north-east to south-west direction and is 91 sq km (35 square miles) in area. It is about 25 km (16 miles) long and no more than about 5 km (3 miles) wide in the middle, with either end being much less than this. Another aspect differentiating it from either St Kitts or Nevis is the presence of a number of satellite islets and cays, of which Scrub Island off the north-eastern end is the largest. Other than Anguillita at the south-western end, all the others lie at varying distances off the north-west coast. The furthest, Sombrero, is nearly 55 km (34 miles) away.

The island is made up of basal volcanic rock, overlaid by coralline limestone of varying thickness with an undulating surface. The limestone is fissured and contains extensive cave systems. A ridge overlooking the main harbour at Road Bay on the north-west coast is the highest point at 65 m (213 feet). A long, wide valley running through the centre of the island to the south of this ridge is not very much above sea level. Distinctive features of the island are the salt ponds which have been created by sand and coral beaches forming across some of the bays. The largest, at Road Bay, was of great economic importance for many years.

The central valley is the only part of the island suitable for extensive cultivation as it is the one area where there is a decent depth of the distinctive Anguillian soil – formed from the ferruginous constituents of limestone, and red in colour. Elsewhere the soil is thin and poor, with only modest pockets suitable for cultivation, or the surface is little more than bare rock. What agriculture has ever taken place has always been hampered by the lack of fresh water. Anguilla has an average rainfall of about 1000 mm (40 inches) a year, but due to its low elevation and the permeability of the limestone it has no surface streams and all well water – because wells have to be sunk below sea level – is saline. The consequent, constant shortage of water has been a major impediment to economic development.

2

The Early Inhabitants

How, why and when the first people arrived in the northern islands of the Eastern Caribbean are questions that cannot be answered. What can be stated with some conviction is that the long-accepted theory – that the first inhabitants, unsophisticated aboriginals known as the Ciboney, were followed in turn by a more highly developed peaceful people called Arawaks, who in turn were in the process of being displaced by an even more developed but warlike race called Caribs when Columbus arrived in the Caribbean – is not only greatly over-simplified but very misleading.

'Ciboney' is merely a term used at the time of the Spanish conquest by the missionary Bartolomé de las Casas to describe a slave class among the people who then occupied Hispaniola. It has no relevance whatsoever to anyone who ever lived in the islands of the Eastern Caribbean. Evidence has been found of human occupation in Trinidad to the south, and Hispaniola to the west, dating back to around 5000 BC, but nothing in any of the Lesser Antilles earlier than a site in Antigua which was occupied in about 3100 BC. It is assumed that the sites in Trinidad and Antigua were inhabited by a race of hunter-gatherers, now categorized by archaeologists as the Ortoiroid people (after the name of the site at Ortoire in Trinidad) who gradually spread through the island chain from South America to reach as far as Puerto Rico by about 1000 BC. As people to whom pottery was unknown they are considered as belonging to the Pre-Ceramic or Archaic Age. They can have had no connection whatsoever with the people then inhabiting the islands further to the west, who it is believed originated in Central America.

Arawakan is a language group found among the people of South America living in and between the Orinoco and Amazon river basins, and it was successive groups of Arawakan-speakers who, from around 400 BC moved into the islands north of Trinidad. Whether the first such migration displaced the earlier inhabitants, or the migrants found the islands unoccupied is not known. These were the forerunners of people who, ever since the European discovery of the Caribbean, have been called 'Arawaks'. The names by which they were known to themselves or others at the time are of course unknown. The Saladoid people (as they are called after a style of pottery found at Saladero in Venezuela) were more advanced than the earlier inhabitants, with a more settled way of life marked by a slash-and-burn type of agriculture and the use of pottery. By AD 1000 they had spread through the entire region as far as Cuba and the Bahamas. They had also evolved a far more advanced social organization and way of life, leading in modern times to their being given a new identity as the 'Taino' people with a distinctive Tainan culture. They were divided into three distinct groups. The smallest of these, confined to the islands east of Puerto Rico, was already under pressure from the next wave of Arawakan-speakers (the first of such people whose name or an approximation of it – the Igneri – is known to us) who had entered the Caribbean some centuries earlier and by AD 1000 had already occupied all the islands south of Antigua.

Within another century or two yet another group of Arawakan-speakers began their Caribbean odyssey. By 1493, when Columbus sailed for the first time through the Eastern Caribbean, these newcomers – again with a name known to us as something like Calina, Kallipina or Kalinago – already controlled all the Lesser Antilles and were making bride-capturing raids on Puerto Rico. Columbus later became aware of the fear they created among the Taino of the Greater Antilles as a result of their warlike activities, but unfortunately for the Kalinago (the term generally adopted) and their descendants, completely misinterpreted the tales he was told involving words like 'caniba', 'carima' and 'carib'.

Once reports using these words – all of which are akin to the Spanish word for the bloodthirsty man-eater – appeared and were misspelt in print in Europe, the myth arose that the Taino had described a tribe called the Caribs who practised cannibalism. As a result, from 1493 until very recent times the world at large considered a Carib and a cannibal as virtually synonymous. In fact there is no evidence whatsoever that they ate human flesh as a matter of course or as part of their diet, although it is very possible that, as happened in other societies at the same stage of development in other parts of the world, small parts of slain opponents may have been consumed by warriors in rituals designed to impress potential enemies.

Even so, once the people encountered by the Spanish in the Eastern Caribbean had been identified in this way they became a race apart. From then on it seems to have been generally accepted that when Columbus arrived they, the bloodthirsty Caribs, had already disposed of the previous inhabitants of the islands – a peaceful people given the general name of the Arawaks – by killing and eating the men and taking the women for concubines and slaves. In fact, there never were people in any of the islands who knew themselves or each other as 'Caribs' or 'Arawaks', and nor was there such a clear-cut division between successive inhabitants of the islands – all of whom it is from now on more appropriate to refer to as Amerindians. It seems far more likely that when any newcomers moved into the islands from the mainland, although some warfare must have taken place, the majority of those already living in any one island would have been assimilated or forced to migrate. After all, both lots of people sprang from the same roots, spoke closely related languages, possessed not dissimilar societies, and shared much the same culture. Today 'Carib' is accepted as the official name of a group of people living in Dominica and a much larger group in South America. Those who were in the islands during the European contact period are now generally referred to as 'Island Caribs'.

The Amerindians of course had no written language, and very little, except hearsay, was recorded about their way of life before the seventeenth century, when the French settled islands such as Dominica and Guadeloupe where the 'Caraibes' lived in large numbers. Some of what is known comes from a *Dictionaire Caraibe-François* compiled by a French missionary, Father Raymond Breton, who was sent to Guadeloupe in 1635 and spent the next twenty years or so either there or in Dominica. The dictionary contains a transliteration of the name supposedly used by the Island Caribs for each of the islands, although it is difficult to see how Breton, who never visited any other island, could have indicated those out of sight of either Guadeloupe or Dominica. Even if he had possessed a map – something most unlikely – this surely would have been incomprehensible to anyone he interrogated. Regardless of this, and of the lack of any English edition of the dictionary, unscholarly anglicized versions of Breton's Amerindian names have been used freely in modern times, even leading to the odd call here and there for some island to adopt such a name officially.

According to Breton the Carib names for St Kitts, Nevis and Anguilla were *Liamaiga, Oualie* and *Malliouhana* respectively. Only in St Kitts, where for some unknown reason it is spelt 'Liamuiga', does the name now appear in any connection other than with boosting the tourist industry, the island's highest mountain having been renamed in 1983. Meanings have been given to the names for St Kitts and Anguilla, but these, like the names themselves, have never been verified and the information on which they are based appears nowhere other than in Breton's dictionary.

Evidence concerning the early Amerindian occupation of the three islands is very generalized and lacking in any detail concerning the length of time any particular group of people inhabited them. None of the islands held a great deal of interest for archaeologists much before the last quarter of the twentieth century, and the results of earlier, mostly amateur work, involving little more than the collection of surface artefacts, probably only served to make the later work more difficult. Stone implements such as grinding stones, hammers and hatchets, as well as objects made of flint and shell, were collected from the earliest days of the European settlement, but no record was kept of how and where they were found.

Pre-Ceramic Settlement

Although nothing remains other than middens and shell piles to prove it, all three islands were inhabited during the pre-ceramic period, probably from around 2000 BC. One such site has been located in St Kitts, with two each in Nevis and Anguilla. The site in St Kitts, in the vicinity of the present deep-water port, was found to contain two middens dating from about 2000 BC and 200 BC. It is of particular interest that both of these middens were located underneath a stratum of volcanic tephra, and therefore could be linked with the last known eruption of Mount Liamuiga, an event which took place around AD 400. As the site is nearly 14 km (9 miles) from the crater the presence of this layer provides startling evidence of how violent the eruption must have been. If there had been no warning signs from the volcano to allow evacuation beforehand, it is doubtful if anyone at this site, or anywhere else on the island except possibly the south-east peninsula, would have remained alive afterwards.

Saladoid and Taino Settlements

St Kitts, Nevis and Anguilla all possess numerous archaeological sites containing pottery sherds, from which it has been possible to establish their very approximate dates of occupation by Saladoid people and their descendants. These range from the first century AD to about AD 1400. Those in St Kitts and Nevis, found anywhere around their coasts where there was a water supply, mainly date from after about AD 500. This is perhaps not surprising, given the nature of these two islands and their nearest neighbours. The volcano called The Quill in St Eustatius erupted in AD 400, at much the same time as Mount Liamuiga. Whatever tectonic activity induced these events may well have had a similar effect on both Nevis Peak and Chance's Peak in Montserrat, perhaps causing them to erupt at about the same time. Major volcanic eruptions, even if they were confined only to St Kitts and St Eustatius, would have been a major deterrent to earlier large-scale settlement.

It seems that once any danger from volcanic activity had passed, St Kitts offered more to the Taino people than Nevis, and its population increased accordingly. Rock carvings, the petroglyphs which are a feature of Tainan culture, have been discovered at four sites around the island. The best-known of these, at Wingfield Estate, has been called 'The finest example of rock carving in the Lesser Antilles'.[1] In the Stone Fort River gut, a mile or so to the east, there are 300 or more human faces and figures cut into the sandstone sides of the ravine containing the upper reaches of the stream. Another mile to the east of this there are two large rocks on the waterline at Harts Bay, on which yet more human faces and figures were discernible at the beginning of the twentieth century, if no longer. The fourth petroglyph is in the north of the island, behind the manager's house at Willett's Estate, but the first archaeologist to see it in the early 1900s considered that it 'may have been brought to its present position in recent times', adding: 'in these utilitarian days the stone has been found convenient in washing the clothes and in grinding the chocolate for the family, and in consequence the petroglyphs are almost effaced'.[2]

In Nevis only a handful of sites, all on the east coast, have been found with artefacts which can be dated earlier than around AD 500. There are far more, all around the island but mainly along the east coast, that were occupied after this time. Three of these east coast sites, because of the amount of surface evidence left behind, had been recognized as belonging to the pre-Columbian period long before any archaeological work was carried out, and probably from the earliest days of the European settlement. Two in the south-east, about a mile apart on either side of Red Cliff, were each known as an 'Indian Castle'. The larger, which is probably the most important of all the Amerindian sites on the island, is at the mouth of Fountain Ghut on 'Indian Castle Estate'. The third site, several miles to the north at Butlers, has always been known as 'Indian Camp'. No Nevis petroglyphs have yet been discovered.

The first people who made and used pottery in Anguilla seem not to have arrived there before about AD 600. From artefacts and potsherds recovered from sites all around the island it is believed that by about AD 1000 it may have had a population of anything between 1000 and 3500 people living in a dozen or more villages. For each of these villages, given Anguilla's lack of streams, access to a source of fresh water must have been of prime concern. Apart from that in shallow surface ponds, which were prone to drying out, the only other supply had to be looked for below ground, in the fissures and caves of the limestone base of the island. Two such sources are to be found on the north coast, each with ample physical evidence of the importance that the Taino attached to them. These are the Fountain Cavern at Shoal Bay, and an opening called the Big Spring about two miles further east at Island Harbour, both of which contain petroglyphs. Those in the Fountain Cavern are particularly impressive, and have led to the supposition that the cave was used for religious rituals, possibly even serving as 'a major regional Amerindian centre for worship and religious activity' with the largest petroglyph supposedly representing 'the Supreme of the Arawaks, *Jocahu Bagwe Maorocan*'.[3] Such theories belie the realities of life as it must have been lived towards the end of the first millennium on a small, virtually waterless island on the edge of the known Taino world, and strain credulity.

The Island Caribs

Whether the Taino had been replaced by the Island Caribs in any of the three islands by the time the first Europeans arrived is open to question, as the settlement pattern of all the Leeward Islands after about 1000 AD is poorly understood. While it is known that the Caribs occupied all the islands from Guadeloupe southwards by the time Columbus arrived, it remains unclear whether the Leeward Islands were then inhabited by the Taino, by the Caribs, by a mixture of both, or by no one at all. From the relatively modest amount of archaeological research which has been carried out in St Kitts, Nevis and Anguilla it seems most likely that by the end of the fifteenth century each island either was still supporting a dwindling Taino population or had been abandoned altogether.

3

The European Discovery

Originally called Liamuiga (the Fertile Isle) by the native Indians who lived here before the arrival of the Europeans, the island was renamed 'St Christopher' by Christopher Columbus after the Patron Saint of travellers.

Columbus called what he saw 'Nevis' because of the snow on top of the one dramatic peak which constitutes the island. In fact he was quite wrong. He saw clouds and believed it was snow, 'Nieves' in Spanish.

In 1493, Christopher Columbus sighted the island of Anguilla and named it for its eel-like shape: Anguilla means 'eel' in Spanish.

These accounts of how the three islands acquired their present names were all garnered from the Internet on the same day in the year 2002. All were nothing more than website versions of explanations which had been generally accepted and widely circulated for many generations. Not one of them is true.

The islands which in due course were to be known as Nevis and St Kitts entered recorded history – in that order – on 11 November 1493, eight days after Columbus on his second voyage to the New World had entered the Eastern Caribbean for the first time. Leading over 1000 men in a fleet of 17 ships, he was anxious to return to the settlement on Hispaniola he had left behind on his first voyage, and to continue his search for the route to the riches of Asia. He had little time for any of the small islands, and two weeks after making its transatlantic landfall on the north coast of Dominica on 3 November the fleet had reached Puerto Rico. Although the journal and charts made by Columbus have been lost it has been possible to trace his route across the Eastern Caribbean from accounts written by others who accompanied him on the voyage. Unfortunately, these differ about the names given to some of the islands sighted on the way; a situation made even worse by the misplacing and misspelling of many of these names, and the inclusion of others, on the first maps of the Caribbean.

The route followed by the fleet from Guadeloupe, where it had remained for a few days to replenish water supplies, was to the north-west, passing to the south-west of all the other islands between there and the Virgin Islands. It is generally accepted that Guadeloupe, Montserrat, the uninhabited islet of Redonda, and the Virgin Islands (as a group) all bear the names given to them by Columbus. Tales such as those that open this chapter have all arisen as a result of the uncertainty about the names he gave to the islands he saw in between. Having sailed past Redonda on 11 November, the fleet anchored overnight in the lee of the next island, to which it is fairly certain Columbus gave the name San Martin. This then became the name by which Nevis was known to the Spanish for the next twenty or thirty years.

To determine from the early accounts and maps the name he gave to the island immediately north of San Martin is far more problematical. It could have been San Jorge (the name proffered by Columbus's biographer, the American historian Samuel Eliot Morison), or La Gorda (Fat Island) or – if we are to accept accounts which almost undoubtedly were inspired by Columbus's own records – another name altogether. The Italian historian Peter Martyr Anglerius published the first account of the discovery of America in 1516. In this he records what happened after the fleet left Guadeloupe:

> they passed not far from another island which the captives
> seized in [Guadeloupe] said to be very populous and
> replenished with all things necessary for the life of man.
> This they called Mons serratus because it was full
> mountains....

> The day following they saw another island, which, because
> it was round, they called Sancta Maria Rotunda. The next
> day they found another island which they called Sancta
> Martini which they let pass also because they had no time
> to tarry. Like-wise the third day they espied another,
> whose diametral side extended from the east to the west,
> they judged to be 150 miles.... This last they called Sancta
> Maria Antigua.

The explorer's son, Ferdinand, in a biography of his father written around the same time, after recording the naming of Guadeloupe, Montserrat and Redonda states:

> Next he came to St. Marie la Antigua, which is above
> twenty-eight leagues in extent. Still holding his course

NW. there appeared several other islands towards the
north, and lying north-west and south-east, all very high
and full of woods, in one of which they cast anchor and
called it St. Martin.[1]

If we take into account that both writers – even if they had access to
the original records of Columbus – could only have been working from
hastily written field notes and rough sketches, and ignore the ridiculously
exaggerated lengths they quote, together they make a convincing case for
Columbus having given the island to the north of San Martin the name of
Santa Maria la Antigua. However, even if this is what he called St Kitts in
1493, the name did not stick for very long, as confusion about it and others
arose very quickly.

The earliest map showing the discoveries of Columbus was drawn in
1500 by Juan de la Cosa, the chief cartographer of Columbus's second
voyage, and must have been based on the observations he made at the time.
The maps shows Guadeloupe, Montserrat, Redonda, Nevis (as San
Martin), and then five more islands lying in a line to the north-west. The
largest of these, separated from Nevis by two unnamed islands, is called La
Gorda. The other two islands are named: the one nearest to La Gorda
indistinctly as something like *S. de Lanrebe* or *S. delanebo*, and the outer
one quite clearly as San Cristobal. Assuming the two unnamed islands
were in reality the hills of the south-eastern peninsula seen from some distance offshore, then we have to accept that St Kitts was given the name La
Gorda, and the island which subsequently became Saba was the first
St Christopher. There is a slight possibility that the island between,
St Eustatius, was the one Columbus called Santa Maria la Antigua, it
having been suggested that *S. delanebo* might be a corrupt abbreviation of
the name.[2]

Further confusion arose as other islands were found and other maps
began to be published in the early years of the sixteenth century. St Kitts
must soon have acquired its permanent name, as it appears as San
Christophoro on a map made in 1513. At much the same time the name of
St Martin was transferred from its near neighbour which, doubtless
because of the snow-like clouds almost always covering the peak, then
assumed the name Las Nieves (an abbreviation of *Nuestra Senõra de las
Nieves*, Our Lady of the Snows). In the early 1520s the Spanish carried out
a complete survey of the region, in order to determine the true extent of
their new possessions, and it was as a result of this that many of the original names were changed or given to other islands. After about 1525 the
names of all the islands were very much as they are today, although one or
two maps still managed to label the St Christopher-Nevis group with the

name of St Martin as late as 1570. The name St Christopher, or St Christopher's as it frequently appeared, was not abbreviated until the beginning of the eighteenth century. In view of this it is appropriate from now on not to use the shortened version, St Kitts, in the text until that date is reached.

Columbus himself never set eyes on any of the islands to the north and north-east of St Christopher, but all had been located and named by 1520. They all, including Anguilla and Sombrero, are shown on a map drawn between 1523 and 1525.

Sombrero, which was then a low, flat islet with a pronounced hump in the centre, was named because of its outline. The much-repeated story that Anguilla received its name because of its long, narrow shape – similar to that of an eel – can be discounted. Very few islands in the world have ever been named after the shape of their surface area, and it is difficult to believe that that of Anguilla could have been immediately apparent to the person who named it. It seems far more likely that, as the island has always provided a very suitable habitat for lizards of all sizes, these were responsible for its name. The appearance and movements of some species could easily lead to their being confused with snakes. In 1631 a visitor to St Christopher saw nothing wrong in describing an iguana as 'a kinde of serpent', and nearly twenty years later the French historian Charles de Rochefort was able to report seeing lizards in Nevis that had 'four feet which are so weak that they can onely crawl along the ground, and wind their bodies as Snakes'. As Anguilla has always provided even better living conditions for lizards than either St Kitts or Nevis, the first Spaniard ever to step ashore there would very quickly have become aware of their presence. It seems far more likely that a myriad black tails wriggling noisily through the undergrowth, rather than measurement of the length and breadth of the island, gave Anguilla its name.

Eroding the Spanish Monopoly

None of the small islands of the Eastern Caribbean was of much interest to the Spanish: something shown only too well by Columbus's quick dash through them in 1493, and the confusion which arose about many of their names. Once the Spanish were in control of the larger Caribbean islands and the conquest of the mainland had begun, they paid no more than passing attention to the Lesser Antilles. As the main entrance point into the Caribbean was the passage between Dominica and Guadeloupe, Spanish ships used these islands to obtain water and provisions. Hogs were released there and on some of the other islands in order to breed in the wild and provide an emergency source of food. A captain-general of all the islands between Barbuda and Martinique was appointed in 1520, but it was very much a titular appointment as he was never able to establish a permanent settlement on any of them. Slightly more interest was taken in Trinidad, but even there Spanish authority was not established until 1584. With regard to all the islands to the north and west of Guadeloupe, Spanish interest lay only in trying to remove the native population to work as slaves in Hispaniola, and in denying the use of the islands to any other European power. Whether any Taino were still living in these islands by this time remains open to question, but even if there were it seems unlikely they could have survived in any of them much later than about 1520.

The Spanish were less successful in preventing other Europeans from using the islands. The French corsairs who appeared in the Caribbean early in the sixteenth century were soon joined by like-minded pirates and privateers from England and the Netherlands, and all needed somewhere well away from any Spanish base where they could replenish water and food supplies, rendezvous with allies, or just lie up in safety. As the century progressed, most of the islands were used in this way by assorted English, Dutch and French seaborne raiders. St Christopher and Nevis, which each had a safe anchorage and a reliable source of fresh water, became particularly popular. In 1585, a fleet of over 30 English vessels under the command of Sir Francis Drake, on its way to attack Santo Domingo and Cartegena, anchored off St Christopher 'wherein wee spent some dayes at Christmas to refresh our sicke people, and to cleanse and ayre our ships. in which Island were not any people at all that we could heare of…'.[3]

Nevis became even more popular once it was realized that it had valuable stands of timber. In 1598 the master of a ship named the *Anne Francis* sailed for the Caribbean 'with intent to cut wood at Nevis', and returned to England with a cargo of logwood and lignum vitae. Two years later another English ship, the *Antelope*, collected a similar cargo, and other ships soon followed. Both St Christopher and Nevis had an additional attraction for the English after 1607, when Virginia was established as the first permanent English colony in North America. Because of the prevailing wind system the fastest route from England to the new colony took ships across the Atlantic to the Caribbean. As a result, ships supplying the new colony regularly called at the islands in order to replenish their water supplies. This was not without its perils, as other people, such as the French corsairs who were operating out of St Christopher in 1609, were just as keen to use the islands.

The Spanish authorities in Hispaniola and Cuba of course wished to prevent the islands being used at all, but had too few resources at their disposal to bring this about. Each year two fleets from Spain passed through the Caribbean, one bound for the Isthmus of Panama, and the other onwards through the Gulf of Mexico to Veracruz. The warships accompanying these were also supposed to keep the Eastern Caribbean islands free of intruders, but as the timing of the fleets was fixed and well-known this proved an impossibility. In February 1621 the Governor of Havana complained to the Crown that corsairs were operating out of 'the islands of Nevis and Virgin Gorda, which are the enemy's safe places and anchorages, where they winter, preparing and careening their ships and fortifying their spirits'.[4] The two warships he eventually managed to obtain and despatch to the region achieved very little. Other than capturing the odd vessel and causing a short-lived general alarm they brought about no lasting change to the situation.

The Arrival of the Caribs

By this time, and apparently regardless of the increasing use being made of them by Europeans as replenishment and repair bases, most of the islands either, like Nevis and St Christopher, supported a Carib community or, like Anguilla, were occasionally visited by roving bands of Caribs. There are no reports of them in either St Christopher or Nevis before the early years of the seventeenth century: Drake found the former uninhabited in 1585, and no sighting of 'Indians' was recorded in the latter by the first wood-cutters in the 1590s. However, there is every reason to believe that Caribs must have moved into both islands soon after this.

In Nevis in 1603 they are reported as having sold tobacco to Bartholomew Gilbert, the master of a ship called the *Elizabeth* which had called to cut lignum vitae. Four years later, when Captain John Smith, on his way to establish Virginia, spent five days at Nevis, the Caribs were rather more wary and had no dealings with him or his men. How many there were, then or at any other time during the short period they were destined to inhabit the island, it is impossible to know.

It is equally impossible to know how many Caribs lived on St Christopher at any one time, other than that almost certainly there would always have been more than on Nevis. But, regardless of whether their numbers ever amounted to many hundreds or were just a few dozen, they were doomed – like their fellows in Nevis – to no more than a brief occupancy of the island. Although none of them would have realized it at the time, this was foreshadowed with the arrival of an English ship in 1622. On board was a man who was on his way home after having been on an unsuccessful expedition to Guiana which had left England two years earlier. When Thomas Warner stepped ashore, looked around and 'well viewing the Island, thought it would be a very convenient place for ye planting of tobaccos, which ever was a rich commodetie',[5] the muffled death knell of the Caribs sounded.

The Arrival of Warner

Thomas Warner was well into middle age when he first saw St Christopher, having been born in Suffolk in about 1575. As the younger son of a gentleman farmer he had had to make his own way in the world, something he had achieved through long service in the army. This had eventually led to his finding a place at Court as a captain in the king's bodyguard, and to his introduction to various men of wealth and influence. It was with one of these, Roger North, that Warner had taken part in the attempt to establish an English colony in Guiana. This had no hope of success, as the Spanish were determined to keep other nationalities away from the mainland, even if they were unable to prevent the islands from being used, and after many vicissitudes it was abandoned in 1629. Warner obviously saw the writing on the wall soon after the colony had been established and in 1622, at the instigation of one of his fellow settlers who had some knowledge of the Eastern Caribbean, he set off to look for a better prospect somewhere among the islands.

St Christopher, with its mountains, running streams and clear blue seas, could not have presented Warner with a greater contrast to the low, swampy landscape and muddy waters that he had left behind. It was not of course uninhabited but, as he would soon have discovered during the months he seems to have spent on the island, the Caribs were there in no great numbers. Their leader, the first Island Carib whose name is known to history, was Tegreman (Tegremond or Tegramond), a man who by this time must have been very familiar with Europeans and their ways. There were already several Frenchmen living on the island, and growing tobacco. Who these were, or how and when they arrived, are questions that can never be answered. Over the years many Europeans had deserted, been shipwrecked or stranded among the islands inhabited by the Caribs and, with no desire to return to the sort of lives they had left behind, had 'gone native' and been absorbed into Carib communities with complete success. With regard to the Frenchmen on St Christopher there is nothing to suggest they had not done exactly the same.

With his assessment of the overall Carib numbers, his appreciation of the friendly attitude of their chief, and possibly even inspired by the efforts of the French growers, Warner had no trouble in persuading himself that the island was indeed 'a very convenient place for the planting of tobaccoes' and the establishment of an English settlement. All that remained was for him to return to England, obtain the necessary financial backing for his scheme, and to find other people willing to settle on the island. It is not difficult to believe that some of the Caribs and one or two of the French tobacco-growers may have watched as he left: the former with no idea of how short a time they had left in possession of the island, and the latter with no inkling of the events which were to take place there between the French and the English once the Caribs had gone.

4

The Settlement of St Christopher

After Warner had returned to England, although it did not take him too long to find financial backing for his project, he seems to have had difficulty in attracting prospective settlers. A syndicate of London merchants, led by Ralph Merrifield, was prepared to put up the money, and a friend from Suffolk, John Jeaffreson, offered his support, but not too many other people were interested. As a result, when Warner left England again in 1623 in the ship *Marmaduke*, he was accompanied only by his eldest son and a handful of men. He arrived at St Christopher with a total number of settlers variously recorded as being anything between 13 and 19 in number, on 28 January 1624.

The *Marmaduke* anchored about halfway along the south-west coast of the main part of the island, in a sheltered indentation in the shoreline which soon came to be called Old Road Bay. The settlers disembarked to establish their first settlement between the Wingfield and East rivers, a part of the island which by this time must long have been familiar to many ships' crews as a watering place. As it was also, because of the unfailing water supply, the main Carib settlement, the new arrivals were not immediately welcome:

> At their arrivall they found three French-men who sought
> to oppose Captaine Warner, and to set the Indians upon us;
> but at last we all became friends and lived with the Indians
> a moneth. Then we built a Fort and a house....[1]

The erection of a fort – which could have been no more than a wooden palisade around a few primitive, thatched huts – caused some concern to the Caribs and Tegreman 'did aske what theire loopeholes and flanckers were for'. He was fobbed off by being told 'it was made that they might looke after those fowles they had about theire houses',[2] but from then on relations between the Caribs and the settlers were never quite the same again.

Once the settlers had somewhere secure in which to retire if necessary, they began clearing enough land to start growing tobacco. The first planting had hardly been completed when everything was ruined by a hurricane in September, and they had to start all over again. In March 1625 the ship *Hopewell* arrived with much needed supplies and a few more settlers, including John Jeaffreson. The additional men and material must have given heart to the original band of settlers, but can have done little to allay Carib suspicions. The second planting of tobacco was a success and by the time the *Hopewell* was due to leave there was a reasonable quantity ready to be shipped. Warner took this back to England himself, leaving Jeaffreson in command of the settlement.

The Arrival of the French, 1625

Throughout most of the sixteenth century by far the greatest number of privateers in the Caribbean were French. By the early years of the next century, although their numbers had decreased considerably, they were still very much in evidence and corsairs were sailing regularly from ports such as Dieppe and La Rochelle. In 1625 one such privateer out of Dieppe, under the command of Belain d'Esnambuc and with a man named Urbain du Roissey on board, attacked a Spanish galleon off Cuba. Being much smaller than the galleon, the French ship ended up being so badly damaged that d'Esnambuc's only hope of making her capable of recrossing the Atlantic was to find a safe place in the Caribbean out of reach of the Spanish where she could be careened and repaired. As such places could only be found among the small islands to the east, the ship slowly made her way in that direction. D'Esnambuc had the choice of several suitable islands at which to carry out the work, but headed for St Christopher as word had already reached France before he left that there were Frenchmen living there.

D'Esnambuc and du Roissey (the relationship between them is uncertain) with 80 or so crew members reached the island towards the end of the year, probably soon after Warner had left in the *Hopewell*.[3] They were reasonably well received by Jeaffreson and the rest of the English, who by now were well aware that their settlement was causing an increasing amount of resentment among the Caribs, and left to get on with repairing the ship. It was obvious that she was so badly damaged that it was going to take months of hard work to make her fully seaworthy.

This gave d'Esnambuc ample time to size up the situation with regard to the English and the settlement they had created on an island which was still nominally a Spanish possession. It could not have taken him long to realize there was nothing to prevent him from doing the same thing, particularly after he had heard from his fellow countrymen who were already living there when he arrived. But, like Warner, he first had to return home to raise the necessary capital and sell the idea to prospective settlers. All he needed was a reasonable amount of tobacco to take as a sample of what could be produced, and this was something the French growers were only too willing to provide.

In the meantime however, the addition of over 80 more Europeans to those already on the island raised the total to an alarming level as far as Tegreman and the Caribs were concerned. Word was sent out, and in early November several hundred Carib warriors began to arrive in canoes from other islands, prepared to join in with Tegreman in an attempt to get rid of the European interlopers. Unfortunately for the Caribs, as one of the settlers indicated later, numbers meant little when opposed by firearms: 'We bade them be gone, but they would not; whereupon we and the French joyned together, and upon the fifth of November we set upon them and put them to flight.'⁴

It is doubtful if those who were not killed left the island, as a second attack soon took place at the end of December. This too was successfully beaten off, but after it the English – to the great detriment of their planting activities – had to maintain a constant guard around the settlement. These conflicts also delayed work on d'Esnambuc's ship, and he was not able to leave for France until the middle of 1626.

A Clash of Commissions

Warner's return to England the previous year was made in order to obtain official government sanction for his settlement, preferably in the form of proprietary letters patent. Unfortunately, as he soon discovered, such grants were no longer being given to untitled men but only to favoured titled courtiers. With the help of Merrifield and one or two men who had entrance to the Court, all he could obtain was a commission from Charles I. Although this was merely something issued while the proprietorship was being sorted out among members of the peerage, and could be revoked at any time, Warner must have found its wording very satisfying to read:

> Whereas We have byn crediblie informed by our well-
> beloved subject Raphe Merifeild of London, Gentleman,
> for and on the behalf of our well-beloved subject Thomas
> Warner, Gent. That the said Thomas Warner hath lately
> discovered fower several Islands in mayne ocean toward
> the Continent of America, the one called the Island of St
> Christopher's, alias Merwar's Hope; one other the Isle of

Mevis; one other the Isle of Barbados; and one other the
isle of Monserate, which said Islandes are possessed and
inhabited only by Savage and Heathen people, and are not,
nor at the tyme of the descovery were in the possession, or
under the gouerment of any Christian Prince, State, or
Potentate…by these presents doe give and grant the said
Thomas Warner…the custodie of the aforesaid Islandes,
and of everie of them together with full power and
authority for us & and in our name & as our Leuitenant to
order and despose of any landes or other things within the
said Islandes….[5]

The commission was signed on 13 September 1625. Why Warner considered Barbados, an island 340 miles (550 km) to the south-east of the
other three, as one of his 'descoveries' is far from clear. Although it was
found by the Spanish early in the sixteenth century and had appeared on
maps from 1513 onwards, Barbados had not been visited by any
Englishman until five months before the commission was first issued. It is
thought that Warner may have heard of this visit and, even though he can
have known nothing of the island, decided to pre-empt any other
claimant. The suggestion which is often made that the commission was
meant to refer to Barbuda, the island only 56 miles (96 km) away from
St Christopher, is untenable. Warner was just as aware of this island as he
was of its neighbour Antigua. If he considered the latter not worth
claiming because of its lack of water, it is hardly likely he would have
been interested in the former, which was smaller and even drier.

If the fourth island listed in Warner's commission was indeed Barbados
it was not included for his benefit, but rather for that of the nobleman who
was even then already negotiating for the proprietary rights to most of the
islands in the Eastern Caribbean. To list it together with three other
islands, all within sight of each other hundreds of miles away in another
part of the Caribbean, and to consider all four could be governed by one
man, made no sense otherwise. At the same time, it also gives some idea of
how poorly the layout and extent of the region must have been compre-
hended by those in authority, from the King downwards, in London. It is
doubtful if the officials who drew up the commission, the Privy
Councillors who signed it or Charles I himself, in whose name it was
issued, had more than the vaguest notion of the whereabouts of any of the
islands.

Such ignorance, if that is what it was, was not confined to London. In
France, d'Esnambuc and du Roissey returned from St Christopher with
enough tobacco in 1626 to excite considerable interest. After living it up

for a while they managed to gain entry to the court of Louis XIII, and to make their case for establishing a settlement in St Christopher.

The Minister of State, Cardinal Richelieu, was soon persuaded and on 21 October 1626 issued a commission even more fanciful than that which had been given to Warner the previous year:

> Be it known that Sieurs d'Esnambuc and du Rossey...have for fifteen years spent vast sums on the crews and armour of ships and vessels in search of fertile lands in a good climate which may be taken possession of and settled by Frenchmen. They have been so active that some time ago they discovered the islands of St Christopher and Barbados...and other neighbouring islands all situated at the entrance to Peru...forming part of the West Indies, which do not belong to any Christian King or Prince. They landed and stayed for one year....They even learned from the native Indian inhabitants of the islands that there are some gold and silver mines, which would have been sufficient reason for numbers of Frenchmen to settle the islands....Wishing to spread the Catholic Faith and to establish as much trade and commerce as possible, and considering that the inhabitants of the islands are not friendly people, we have given Sieurs d'Enambuc and du Rossey exclusive rights to settle the islands of St. Christopher and Barbados and the surrounding islands.[6]

At the same time Richlieu set up the Compagnie de Saint-Christophe in order to meet the needs of the new colony. Its charter called upon d'Esnambuc and du Roissey

> to leave in the islands of St. Christopher, Barbados and others located at the entrance of Peru a number and quantity of men that they deem necessary to work there, trade; grow tobacco and all other sorts of merchandizes to barter and trade money and merchandize that it will be possible to gather and extract from the said islands and neighbouring places.[7]

In return they were to receive 10 per cent of the profits made on all business transactions, and to be provided with three ships. Just as with Warner's commission, the equal prominence given to the name of Barbados in the charter was for some ulterior motive. Like Warner, d'Esnambuc and du Roissey had no conceivable interest in an island so far away from St Christopher, and about which they knew nothing.

The Massacre of the Caribs, 1626

Warner returned to St Christopher in August 1626 with three ships. All three brought much-needed provisions, and in two of them were 100 or more new settlers. The third ship carried a much less propitious cargo, consisting of 60 slaves. It is not known how, when or from where these unfortunate individuals were acquired. All that is certain is that they were the first of the countless thousands who were going to be brought to the island over the next two centuries.

Once Warner had re-established himself as governor and learned of all that had taken place, both with the Caribs and the French, while he had been away, he must have been doubly thankful for the new settlers and the additional men-at-arms they represented. He had not been back on the island very long before being warned that the Caribs were once again preparing to attack the settlement. A Carib woman 'that did often frequent amongst ye English, who it seemes they had used courteously' told him that

> ye King [Tegreman] & ye rest had made theire drinking as
> it is theire custome to make a drinking 3 or 4 dayes, and to
> be druncke before they goe vpon theire designes, And that
> ye King did intend to kill them all....[8]

As this would make the third attempt by the Caribs to drive out the people they must have realized by this time were all set to take over the entire island, Warner decided to act first:

> Like a wise man and a good Souldier he tooke ye
> advantage of theire being druncke and fell upon them by
> night & did kill & slay a great many of them. Amongst ye
> rest they slew King Tegreeman in his hammacco & runing
> him with theire rapiers through ye hammacco & into the
> body....[9]

This attack, which took place a mile or so to the south of the settlement near the mouth of Stone Fort river, has over the years been inflated into a hideous massacre of several thousand Caribs.[10] Although undoubtedly a terrible and tragic event, it is most unlikely that it involved a bloodbath of anything approaching this magnitude. There simply were not enough English to carry out such carnage, and nor were the Caribs, even if some were drunk, the kind of people to submit meekly to destruction on this scale. Another reason for questioning the extent of the massacre is that the Caribs continued to live on the island for many years afterwards, surely something they would never have done after an attempted annihilation of their entire community. Five years after it had taken place a newly arrived English settler in 1631 noted 'St. Christophers hath many naked Indians, & although ther bellyes be to great for ther proportions, yet itt shewes ye plentye of ye Iland in ye nourishing of them.'[11] It could well be that one or two hundred Caribs were slain, but even if the figure ran into only a few dozen it was still a massacre, a disgraceful episode in early European colonial history. The place where it happened was never forgotten, as the names Bloody Point and Bloody Bay (near the present-day village of Challengers) still testify today.

The Division of the Island, 1627

In France, as soon as the Compagnie de Saint-Christophe had been established, d'Esnambuc and du Roissey wasted no time in leaving Paris for the coast in order to obtain the three ships promised by Richelieu, and to find the necessary prospective settlers. By the beginning of 1627, one vessel, *La Catholique*, at Le Havre, and two others *La Victoire* and *La Cardinale*, at ports in Brittany, were hurriedly being prepared to carry several hundred men and all the supplies they needed to the Caribbean. D'Esnambuc in Le Havre and du Roissey in Brittany were both extremely anxious to get back to St Christopher as soon as possible, and as a result none of their ships was fully prepared for the voyage by the time they sailed. D'Esnambuc left Le Havre at the end of January to join up with du Roissey, and all three ships, carrying between them about 500 crewmen and settlers, set off across the Atlantic on 24 February. The lack of adequate preparation for a voyage which was to last over ten weeks became apparent long before land was sighted. No ship carried enough water or provisions to sustain so many men over such a long period, and disease soon broke out. By the time they reached St Christopher on 8 May, less than half of the original total complement remained alive.

We have no way of knowing how they were received by Warner, or of what he thought when he was shown the commission given to d'Esnambuc and du Roissey by Richelieu. All that is known is that five days later he and d'Esnambuc signed a treaty, formally dividing up the island between the English and the French. Under its terms, as the English were already occupying the central part of the island, planting on either side of the mountains, the French were confined to the areas north and south of this (see Plate 2). The borders were largely determined by convenient river guts. That of the northern part, which was soon known as Capesterre, ran from somewhere close to Belle Tete north of Pump Bay, eastwards over the mountains, and down Lynche's Ghut to Sandy Bay.

The border with Basseterre to the south ran from the mouth of Frontier Ghut, northwards over Olivees Mountain and along the Cayon river from its source to the sea. The salt ponds on the south-eastern peninsula were declared to be common property. Other clauses in the treaty covered such things as the extradition of runaway slaves, the free use of roadsteads and highways, and joint action against both the Caribs and the Spanish if necessary.

Another feature of the treaty was the provision made that St Christopher and S. Christophe – as the two settlements now became known – would remain neutral in the event of England and France going to war, unless expressly directed otherwise by their sovereigns. Expedient as this may have seemed when the treaty was signed on 13 May, it represented little more than wishful thinking. There was never to be any love lost between the people of St Christopher and S. Christophe, and once each had a flourishing economy, neither side would waste any time before joining in whatever conflict took place between their mother countries.

Having established their rights on the island in this way, the two French signatories departed from Old Road, d'Esnambuc to land men and supplies in Capesterre and du Roissey to do the same in Basseterre. Most of the settlers who had survived the crossing were in poor condition, and the materials and provisions they needed were in short supply. As a result nothing very much could be done at either end of the island except to build thatched huts for accommodation and to make a slow start on clearing land for planting. Once this was under way d'Esnambuc sent du Roissey with the empty ships back to France for more aid.

Had the French but realized it as they began the struggle to survive, the English settlement was also in distress. The previous September a hurricane had not only caused much damage ashore, but also wrecked two of the three ships which had accompanied Warner's return to the island. Provisions were running very low at the time the treaty was signed, and the English settlers were anxiously awaiting the return of the third ship, which had left for England with a large cargo of tobacco some time before the French arrived.

5

Establishing Proprietary Government

The distress among the English settlers, brought about by the ravages of the hurricane of the previous year, was relieved in October 1627 by the arrival of the *Hopewell* with a cargo consisting of provisions, arms and ammunition. She also brought out Warner's wife and several other women, but whether these were as welcome as the rest of the cargo remains open to question. Warner by this time was living with a Carib woman (possibly the one who had warned him of Tegreman's 'designes' in 1626) and was soon to father a son by her. As many of the other settlers must have followed his example, this could well have been one of the main reasons why relations between the Caribs and the English broke down as they did.

The *Hopewell* was followed before the end of the year by several other ships, all with more supplies and more men (accompanied perhaps by a few more women) anxious to make their fortunes as settlers. Whether any of these vessels also brought more slaves is not known, but some of them certainly carried the first groups of white labourers, contracted as indentured servants, to the island. The majority of these were Irish, driven out of Ireland by a combination of population growth and the establishment there of English and Scottish plantations. Most, if not all of them, were Roman Catholics. In as much as they added to the overall size of the English settlement they were welcomed by Warner. However, as he was soon to discover, their loyalty lay with their co-religionists rather than the English Crown. Also among the passengers in one of these ships was Warner's main backer, Ralph Merrifield, bringing new instructions about the running of the settlement.

The Carlisle Patent

The negotiations about the proprietorship of the islands, which had begun in London before Warner had received his commission as governor, continued long after he had returned to St Christopher. In the end it was granted to James Hay, the first Earl of Carlisle, in the form of letters patent signed on 2 July 1627. By this time Charles I or his advisers must have decided that, regardless of the Spanish, the French, or any other nation, the eastern part of the Caribbean was an English sea. Those responsible for drawing up the document must also have managed to obtain a detailed map of the region, as the grant gave Carlisle

> St. Christopher's, Grenada, St. Vincent, St. Lucia,
> Barbados, Mittalanea [Martinique], Dominico,
> Marigalante, Deseada [Desirade], Todosantes [The
> Saintes], Guadeloupe, Antigua, Montserrat, Radendo
> [Redonda], Barbuda, Nevis, Statia [St Eustatius],
> St. Bartholomew, St. Martin, Anguilla, Sembrera
> [Sombrero], Enegada [Anegada], and other Islands, before
> found out to his great cost....

All these were to be

> brought to a large and copious colony of English, to be
> hereafter named 'the Carlisle or the islands of Carlisle
> province', reserving a yearly rent of £100, and a white
> horse when the King, his heirs and successors, shall come
> into those parts.[1]

Carlisle, of course, had had nothing to do with settling any island, and neither had he incurred costs of any sort. Nor had he any intention of ever visiting his 'Province'; his proprietorship being merely an easy way of making money through the 'priveledges, Jurisdictions, prerogatives, Royalties, Liberties, Freedoms, Regall Rights and Franchises whatsoever, as well by Sea as Land within the Limits of the said Islands', all of which were given to him by the grant. As 'absolute Lord' he had the right to choose his own governors, make laws, set up courts, appoint judges, lease land and impose taxes.

In informing the settlers of all this, Warner played it safe by stressing that even though they would now have to lease their holdings from Carlisle they would be allowed to send cargoes to England free of duty. Even so, the news still 'begott some disturbance' among those who had been hoping to profit at some time from the sale of freehold land. This was quelled by Warner easily enough, but from then on he began to be viewed as a despot very much in league with Carlisle. This opinion must have been greatly reinforced the following year when news was received of a second grant having been made to Carlisle. This gave him the right for ten years to collect customs duties on island imports and exports, whether levied in the West Indies or in England. Not too long after this became known, Warner found it prudent to return once again to England, leaving his son Edward in charge of the settlement. He spent the next 18 months in London, working with Carlisle to better both their fortunes and in supporting the Earl's claim to Barbados, a subject then under investigation. He was amply rewarded for his efforts. On 21 September 1629, largely as a result of representations by Carlisle, he was knighted by the King, and a week later Carlisle appointed him governor of St Christopher for life.

The Settlement of S. Christophe

Du Roissey, who had been sent back to France the previous year for more settlers and provisions, returned to the island in May 1628, after another disastrous crossing. His ships had been just as poorly outfitted and supplied as they had been in 1627, and once again many people had died from disease and hunger before reaching land. Those who survived added to the overall French population of the island, but this still remained far too low to enable S. Christophe to become properly established – or to keep the English from taking advantage of the situation. Off the coast, where they considered the provisions of the treaty did not apply, English privateers plundered French ships that were at anchor. Ashore, regardless of the treaty, English planters knowingly extended their activities into both Capesterre and Basseterre. If this situation was to be rectified, d'Esnambuc needed far more settlers and a strong display of force, and later in the year he returned to France to get both.

Not long after he had left, the settlers obtained some material assistance from the arrival of a Dutch ship, one of many then trading throughout the Caribbean. The captain of the ship, 'finding the tobacco most excellent, traded with the French, even letting them have some merchandise on credit'. He was so delighted with the cargo he obtained that he agreed to return with more supplies six months later. The arrival of this one vessel seems to have had a regenerating influence on the settlers, who

> seeing themselves thus succoured by foreigners in the
> midst of their necessity, regained their courage and began
> straightway to clear their lands, to plant crops which
> would furnish them food, to cultivate tobacco and to build
> houses.[2]

Their courage increased even more the following year when d'Esnambuc returned with three ships filled with provisions and 300 settlers, and a squadron of six warships under the command of François de Rotondy, Sieur de Cahuzac. While the settlers and supplies were being landed at Basseterre, Cahuzac proceeded with his squadron to Old Road, where Edward Warner was acting as governor in the absence of his father, and demanded the English withdrawal from French lands. When Warner prevaricated Cahuzac responded immediately by attacking the ships which were lying at anchor in Old Road Bay, blowing three out of the water and driving another three aground. This was more than enough to bring Warner to his senses, and he quickly gave orders that the offending settlers were to withdraw from the poached areas.

The achievement of this, although very much welcomed by the settlers, was not the main reason why Cahuzac's squadron had been sent to the Caribbean. During the time d'Esnambuc had spent in France it had been discovered by Richelieu that in 1629 the Spanish were planning to use the warships accompanying the second of the annual treasure fleets to drive all intruders out of the Eastern Caribbean. The main aim of the French squadron was to prevent the Spanish from attacking S. Christophe. Unfortunately, Cahuzac either wilfully misread his instructions or received some misleading information. Having finished his business with Warner, he disregarded the threat posed by the Spanish fleet and acted as if it had already passed through the region. In this he was much mistaken, and in dispersing his squadron by giving permission for each ship to set off on an independent privateering voyage he left his shoreside compatriots defenceless.

The Settlement of Nevis, 1628

One of the early settlers on St Christopher was a trader and ship's captain named Anthony Hilton, who probably arrived there early in 1625. As he had obtained financial backing from some Irish merchants, and so was not beholden to Merrifield or Warner in any way, the latter would only allow him and the men he had brought with him to settle on the opposite side of the island, somewhere along the north-east facing coast. Once a suitable site had been found, Hilton then became, as his brother John recorded 40 years later, 'ye first that did settle that side of ye Island'. The new settlement did not survive for very long:

> He and others having cleared ground, built houses,
> & fooloved planting, it came to pass that ye Indians
> betimes in ye morning came upon them & did fire theire
> houses and Slue divers of his men. He with some others of
> his household, making theire escape into the woods, gott
> to ye leeward to ye rest of ye English....[3]

Warner then had little option but to let Hilton join up with the rest of the English, 'where he did Settle another plantacion & with ye companie he had, made what tobaccos he could'. He obviously fitted in, as in due course he became one of the signatories to the 1627 treaty with the French. He must also have been successful with his planting, as immediately after signing the treaty he left, first for Ireland, and then for London where he found a ready market for his tobacco.

Inspired by this success, he now became more interested in founding his own settlement on another island than in continuing under Warner's authority on St Christopher. Early in 1628 he joined up with a merchant named Thomas Littleton, who, as was recorded two years later, 'with some others got a Pattent of the Earle of Carlisle, to plant the Ile called the Barbados, thirty leagues Northward of Saint Christophers.' The island referred to was of course Barbuda, whose name still caused confusion and about which very little was known. In the spring, with a ship outfitted by Littleton and his partners, and accompanied by 100 settlers, Hilton departed for an island 'which by report of their informers and undertakers, for the excellencie and pleasantnesse thereof, they called Dulcina'.

Barbuda turned out to be a different kind of place altogether, so much so that 'when they came there, they found it such a barren rocke, they left it'. There was then no alternative for Hilton but to head for another island. None of the small islands to the west, or Antigua to the south, appeared to offer any better prospects so, 'At last because they would be absolute, they came to Mevis, a little Ile by Saint Christophers; where they seated themselves well furnished with all necessaries'.[4]

Hilton and his men landed on the west coast on 22 July 1628. With ships able to anchor reasonably close to the shore in a calm and sheltered stretch of water, their landing place was ideal for a settlement. The clearing of the land began, and their first crude shelters laid the foundations of what was to become Charlestown. The opening of the island in this way soon began to attract people from St Christopher – presumably those who either were not satisfied with the amount of land they could obtain there, or were anxious to escape Warner's increasingly autocratic rule. By the end of the year nearly 150 had moved across Nevis. This caused so much resentment in St Christopher that, when Hilton went there to revisit his original plantation, an attempt was made by one of Warner's close associates to have him murdered. Another man who turned against Hilton, once he had been informed of the settlement of Nevis, was the Earl of Carlisle, who wished to install a relative named George Hay as governor. He issued orders for Hilton to be replaced, and in August 1629 Captain Henry Hawley, in command of a ship appropriately named the *Carlisle*, arrived off the new settlement to effect the change by landing Hay and taking Hilton captive. Before this could happen Hawley's intentions were betrayed, and Hilton managed to board another ship which was just about to sail for England. The ensuring contretemps, which involved the Nevis settlers threatening to use force to prevent Hay taking over as governor, was brought to an abrupt end on 7 September by the sudden arrival of a huge Spanish fleet.

The Spanish Attack, 1629

The outward-bound Spanish treasure fleet, under the command of Don Fadrique de Toledo, consisted of 14 merchantmen, escorted by at least 20 galleons. When it sailed into view, all of the settlements – in Nevis, St Christopher and S. Christophe – were caught by surprise, and none was in a position to mount more than a token defence.

On Nevis this consisted of firing a single cannon, as John Hilton, the brother of the fleeing Governor, recalled many years later:

> Wee had but one great gune, which we had placed vpon
> pellicn point, & wee Shott soe long as wee had either
> bullett or powder, & brought one of theire Shipps vpon
> the carreene to Stopp hir leakes, we had Soe battered hir.[5]

This gave the *Carlisle* chance to cut her cable and escape, but instead of heading out to sea, Hawley, with both Hay and the man Anthony Hilton had made deputy governor, merely sailed across to St Christopher and ran the ship aground. The rest of the English ships off Nevis were captured. The firing of the 'great gune' ended when the ammunition ran out, and all resistance was brought to a halt after the Irish indentured servants had 'proved treacherous, runn away from vs & Swimed aboard and told them where we hid our provisions & in what cae our Islands stood in'.[6]

John Hilton, who had assumed the leadership in the absence of both the Governor and Deputy Governor, was then obliged to board de Toledo's flagship and negotiate the terms of surrender. These were simple and surprisingly generous. All the settlers, except for four kept as hostages, were embarked in Spanish ships which immediately sailed for England. The four hostages, among them John Hilton himself, were retained to ensure the safe return of the vessels involved. Once the settlers had been removed in this way, the Spanish systematically destroyed all the crops and burnt all the houses.

De Toledo then descended on S. Christophe and the defences du Roissey had managed to establish, mostly in front of the few buildings which formed the rudiments of the town of Basseterre. When troops were landed after an initial bombardment, they were met by a force made up from among both the French and English settlers. As there was no one in overall command of this force, and no concerted plan of action, it offered little resistance before being dispersed. Du Roissey, d'Esnambuc and about 400 of the French settlers managed to make their way to Capesterre, and were taken off the island by two or three French vessels. They were then taken to Antigua, via St Martin and Anguilla (where in both islands a few may have settled or remained for a while at least). The remaining French settlers were shipped back to France under the same conditions as those given to the English in Nevis.

Edward Warner, whose high-handedness had lost his settlers any chance of escape when their ships had been destroyed by Cahuzac, was forced to surrender also on the same terms as those given in Nevis. Except for five hostages, everyone was to be shipped to England. Since well over a thousand people were involved, this turned out to be not so easy to arrange as in Nevis and, while waiting to be embarked, between two and three hundred of them escaped into the mountains. As the arrival of the treasure fleet at its loading port in Central America could not be greatly delayed, de Toledo had little time to devote to their recapture and they remained at large until after he had left. It was fortunate for Edward Warner that he was not taken as one of the hostages; otherwise, because the English refused to return the Spanish ships, he would have spent the next five years in gaol. George Hay, the man sent by the Earl of Carlisle to be governor of Nevis, was not so fortunate as he was taken in place of Warner. The Earl himself lost not only his relative and governor-designate, but also his ship the *Carlisle*, which was refloated by the Spanish and taken as a prize.

Recovery in St Christopher

The English who had taken to the hills in preference to deportation came out of hiding as soon as the Spanish left, and began the task of rebuilding and replanting. They were alone on the island, except for the residual Carib population, until the French under d'Esnambuc returned at the beginning of 1630. More English settlers soon began to appear, and in May the Governor, now of course Sir Thomas Warner, returned from England and reimposed his authority. He came back not a moment too soon. The Spanish had devastated the provision grounds as well as the tobacco crops, food was in short supply, and there was a great deal of unrest. The settlement required firm and capable leadership, just as much as it needed more people and provisions, in order to survive. Warner provided the necessary authority and, by the middle of 1631, after a period of great hardship bordering on famine, St Christopher was well on the way to full recovery.

At the same time, however, the Governor remained a servant of the Proprietor, and both men wanted to enrich themselves out of the island. Warner had not been knighted for nothing, and his rule, which was now even more autocratic and arbitrary than it had been before the Spanish attack, was carried out with the help of men he himself appointed. There was no freehold land; and the settlers, or planters as it is now more appropriate to call them, could only obtain land by taking out leases and paying rent. Carlisle accepted no responsibility for their protection, and all were expected to bear arms and pay for their own defence. Each planter bound himself to pay an annual rent, per head, of 50 lb (pounds) (23 kilograms (kg)) of tobacco. Out of this 20 lb went to Warner, 'for the maintenance of the governor and the good of the Island', and 10 lb to the Captain of Militia he had appointed. The remaining 20 lb went to the Proprietor. Collection of the rent and other taxes was ruthlessly enforced, with those who failed to pay having their houses destroyed.

Regardless of all this, life in St Christopher, whether as a planter or merely an indentured servant, remained highly attractive. The population rose so rapidly that, only three years after the Spanish attack, Warner was in a position to consider new settlements in the other islands over which he had been given authority in his original commission of 1625. With a settlement already in place on Nevis, this left Antigua and Montserrat, to both of which he sent people from St Christopher some time between 1632 and 1634 (with the former date being the one generally accepted).

Those sent to Antigua were led by his son Edward, who became the first Governor, while those he sent to Montserrat were mostly Irish Catholics who had reached the end of their time as indentured servants. While working out their indentures all such people were considered to be disloyal, as was recorded in 1631: 'these seruants of ye planters rather desyer ye Spaniards might come, yt by itt they might be freed, then any willingnesse they shew to defend their masters'.[7] This had been borne out only too clearly when de Toledo had arrived two years earlier. Once their indentures expired they stood little chance of becoming planters under Warner, and he was only too pleased to be able to ship some of them to the neighbouring island, where an Irishman, Anthony Briskett, had just been granted the governorship by Carlisle.

Carlisle must have welcomed the opening up of two new sources of wealth, but he was never to benefit from them. He died in April 1636, heavily in debt, leaving an heir, his son, who was not yet legally of age, and his proprietary rights in the hands of three trustees. As the second earl was by no means favourably disposed towards these trustees, this left scope for considerable confusion about the Carlisle patent once he came of age.

D'Esnambuc and S. Christophe

Following the Spanish attack on S. Christophe, the settlers who had escaped with d'Esnambuc and du Roissey, after seeing how little the small islands to the north had to offer, ended up on Antigua. Before they reached there du Roissey decided he had had enough and took one of the ships back to France. This act of desertion was not appreciated by Richelieu, and he ended up as a prisoner in the Bastille. The rest of the settlers under d'Esnambuc, after a short time on Antigua and an equally brief period on Montserrat, and having discovered that the Spanish were no longer in evidence, returned to S. Christophe. By then they were no more than about 350 in number.

These were so disheartened by what had happened, and by the lack of assistance from France, that they decided to grow one more crop of tobacco and then quit the island altogether. As a result of this, not enough food crops were planted, and by the middle of 1630 they, like the English next door, were suffering from famine. This was relieved by the belated return of the Dutch trader who had first visited early the previous year. His arrival, with all the provisions they needed, and his readiness to buy the entire tobacco crop, completely altered the situation. The French, far from wanting to give up and leave, then 'thought of nothing else than to produce merchandise in order to attract the Dutch. They no longer took the trouble to send anything to France'.[8]

Putting the major part of the economy of the colony in the hands of the Dutch in this way contributed greatly to the demise of the Compagnie de Saint-Christophe which took place five years later. It was replaced by the Compagnie des Iles d'Amerique, which was chartered in February 1635 and given the monopoly of trade with S. Christophe and the other islands which by then had been settled by the French. This company revitalized S. Christophe, increasing the population by shipping out more colonists and gradually building up its trade. By the time d'Esnambuc died in December 1636, the population had already expanded enough to permit the sending of settlers to Martinique, and the level of trade was almost on a par with that of St Christopher.

The Reoccupation of Nevis

Anthony Hilton returned to the Caribbean with Sir Thomas Warner in 1630. Having made his case to the Earl of Carlisle in London he had been confirmed as governor, and with George Hay in Spanish hands there was no danger of being supplanted. He arrived in May to find 'a considerable campanie' of the displaced settlers had already found their way back, and not all were pleased to see him:

> amongst which there was one Mr. James Russell whom ye
> people that was there had made choise of for theire
> governor, betwixt whome & Capt Hilton there was some
> difference on that night att Hiltons first coming there
> about theire government.[9]

What then took place during the night is unknown, 'But ye next morning it was soe agreed vpon that Capt. Antho. Hilton should be governor.'

He did not remain so for very long. Among the many people who came to the island once planting had restarted and the settlement was flourishing again was his partner Thomas Littleton, the man who had largely financed the original settlement in 1628. None or very little of his outlay had ever been repaid, and in April 1631 Littleton brought a Bill of Complaint before the Court of Chancery in London, naming all those who owed him money. Their combined debts amounted to £5000 (the equivalent of about £500,000 at the beginning of the present century). As most of these debtors, led by Hilton, were back in Nevis by the time the complaint was heard, Littleton had no option but to go there to see what he could recover. What took place after he arrived there, probably towards the end of the year, is, like much else to do with the early history of these islands, unrecorded. All that is known is that Hilton fairly rapidly decided that life at sea was preferable to life ashore, even as a governor, and departed for Tortuga to resume his career as a ship's captain among the buccaneers who used it as a base. Once he had gone, Littleton, presumably having obtained the sanction of Carlisle before he left England, then took over as governor. He remained in office, overseeing the gradual development of Nevis, although at odds with many of the planters, until at least 1634. Sometime afterwards, in order it seems to pursue Hilton and others of his debtors, he too decamped for Tortuga, leaving a planter named Luke Stoakes to act as his deputy while he was away. Stoakes remained in office for only a few months before news was received that Littleton had died on the way to Tortuga: he was then replaced in 1636, on Warner's instructions from St Christopher, by another inhabitant of the island named Thomas Sparrow.

6

Proprietary Rule and its Demise

Warner was in a position to choose a new governor for Nevis in 1636 because, following the death of the first Earl of Carlisle, he had taken the Earl's place as lieutenant-general of all the islands covered by the patent, having been appointed to this position by the trustees. He was probably very pleased by his new title, but it never allowed him to exercise very much more than nominal control anywhere other than on St Christopher. There, he continued to govern in a purely arbitrary fashion with the help of a council to which he nominated all the members, and without any consultation with the rest of the ever-increasing population. It was a situation which was deeply resented but which, until something seriously disturbed the tobacco-based economy, remained unchallenged.

The making of such a disturbance began in the late 1630s, when a glut of tobacco on the European market brought about a fall in price. In May 1639, in order to raise the price again, Warner entered into a treaty with the Governor of S. Christophe to ban all tobacco cultivation on the island for a period of 18 months. Once this was in place, he was able to exercise his authority as lieutenant-general and extend the ban to both Nevis and Antigua. By October 1640 the ban had had the desired result as far as the French were concerned, and planting resumed. Warner thought otherwise, and extended it by another 12 months for the English planters, much to their chagrin.

The Beginning of Representative Government

The annoyance of the planters in St Christopher increased alarmingly after the ban was lifted in October 1641, when a prolonged period of bad weather prevented them from planting, and Warner began to press for the payment of the rents which had not been collected while the ban was in place. What later became known as the 'First Rebellion' broke out in early December, when one planter went around urging others not to pay 'his Lordships rent for the vacation yeares' and a protest committee of sorts was formed. The demands made by this committee were rejected outright by Warner, and in January he declared martial law and imprisoned those members he considered to be the ringleaders of the revolt. All might then have been well, had Warner not decided to hang another protestor for insulting a member of his Council.

When this unfortunate individual was executed at the beginning of February, about 1500 men immediately took up arms, and a second rebellion broke out. On 8 February a list of grievances was drawn up and given to Warner. In this the rebels asserted that, as they lived in 'a free Colony' which was not a garrison and therefore subject to English law, no laws could be passed without the people's consent obtained through a representative assembly. Until Warner agreed to the creation of such an assembly and to meet various other demands, they intended to remain under 'armes'. With only his Council and a few dozen others to back him, Warner had little option but to agree. On 11 February he granted a general pardon, and within a month or so an Assembly of 24 members had been elected.

However, Warner was not a man to accept any diminution of his authority without seeking revenge. His first act took place when four members of the Assembly went to England in April in order to clear the setting up of the Assembly with the second Earl of Carlisle and the trustees. He wrote ahead of their arrival, saying 'I had rather bee a poore Souldier...then to bee a Governor over all those that will not bee obedient to lawfull Commannd', and asking for them to be given 'Condign punishment' as rebels. It seems very likely that the four men may have been executed as a result, as there is nothing more about them in the sparse records of the time that still exist. He later had several other members banished or prosecuted as the occasion arose. Even so, and whether the Assembly was able to function continually from then on or not, representative government must be dated from this time.

The uprisings in St Christopher, as might be expected, did not go unnoticed in Nevis, or indeed in any of the other Leeward Islands, where the planters were equally without any say in the way they were governed. There were protests of some sort in Antigua, Montserrat and Nevis in the spring of 1642. That in Nevis, from the scanty information available, seems to have been the most troublesome. In April, following a report of the island 'being much perplexed with Some Rebbells', four 'Mutineeres' were deported to be imprisoned on St Christopher. The exact year of the establishment of the Nevis Assembly is unknown, but it seems very probable that, along with the one in Antigua, it came into being in the mid-1640s.

The Proprietorship under Parliamentary Rule

The beginning of the English Civil War period in 1642 brought about a situation in which the governors of the various West Indian colonies became virtually independent. The royal chain of authority, through which the proprietorship operated, was broken, and for the first year and a half of the war the Parliamentarians had little time to interest themselves in colonial affairs. As their innate loyalty to the Crown was offset by their dislike of the proprietary rights, this suited the planters very well. It suited them even more when, at the end of 1643, they were given exemption from all taxation other than that needed to support their own government. This had been authorized by the 17-member Parliamentary Commission for Plantations which had been set up under the Earl of Warwick in November to oversee colonial administration. There was very little else the Commission could do for the time being, having no forces available anywhere in the Caribbean to enforce acceptance of Parliamentary rule or bring about changes in administration. In 1645, when the Earl of Warwick wrote to Warner in St Christopher stressing that he had to put himself under Parliamentary authority, he had no means of making him obey. Warner, who was particularly adept at keeping both sides happy, refused to commit himself to either the Royalist or Parliamentary cause, and retained his independent authority until his death in 1649.

In 1647 Carlisle took it upon himself to lease his proprietary patent for a period of 21 years to Francis, Lord Willoughby of Parham, for a peppercorn rent and on condition that they divided the gross revenue derived from the patent between them. Willoughby was then made lieutenant-general of all the islands. His subsequent actions, which were to lead to far-reaching changes in the running of the islands, began in February 1648 when he deserted the Parliamentary cause and fled to join the exiled King Charles II in Holland. Two years later and with the King's approval he sailed for Barbados, established his authority as lieutenant-general and proclaimed a Royalist government. This made Parliament take positive interest in the West Indian colonies at long last, and in 1652 an expeditionary force was sent to Barbados. Troops were landed and the island was soon surrendered by Willoughby, who then departed to attempt a new settlement on the South American mainland in Surinam. This led to annulment of his lease of the proprietorship, suspension of the Carlisle patent, and overall control of the islands covered by the patent being assumed by the Parliamentary Commission for Plantations. Trade between the colonies and England was of prime concern, and a year earlier Parliament had passed the first Navigation Act, incorporating measures primarily designed to take such trade away from the Dutch. After the Act came into effect all trade between England and the West Indies could only be carried in ships built in England, owned and commanded by Englishmen, and with a majority of Englishmen in the crew.

St Christopher and the 'Western Design'

With the islands under direct control, and their trade out of the hands of the Dutch, Parliament now became much more interested in the West Indies. By 1654 this interest had developed into a grandiose plan known as the 'Western Design', under which it was envisaged an English colonial empire could be created by seizing all the Spanish possessions in the Caribbean. In order to put the plan into effect, an expeditionary force, carried in a fleet under the command of Admiral William Penn, left England at the end of the year. It sailed with a mere 2500 troops, with the intention of acquiring at least as many again from among the colonists in Barbados and the Leeward Islands. Penn arrived at Barbados at the end of January, quickly recruited some 3000 men, and sailed for St Christopher at the beginning of April. Commissioners had gone ahead, and another 1300 men (300 of them from Nevis) were embarked on arrival. Penn then departed on his mission to put the Western Design into effect by attacking Hispaniola. This failed ingloriously, mainly due to very poor planning and the equally poor quality of the men recruited in the West Indies. Penn afterwards complained to the Governor of Barbados:

> We are ashamed of the cowardice of our men which yet
> continueth, and were not the enemy as cowardly as
> themselves, they might with a few destroy our Army, or
> else the Officers must leave their charges, and charge the
> enemy in a body together; nor will they be brought to go
> on again...and to say the truth your Men and the men of
> St. Christophers lead all the disorder and confusion...these
> People will never be brought to March up to that place
> again. This hath made us to take up a new resolution...to
> attempt Jamaica in the next place....[1]

The attack on Jamaica that followed was more successful, and the Spanish surrendered the island the following month. Its capture was the expedition's only achievement.

It is perhaps not surprising that the men who were recruited from St Christopher did not perform well on the battlefield. The majority of them must have joined the expedition in desperation, mainly in order to leave the island and start life again in another part of the Caribbean. Few could have signed up for any other reason. By the 1650s St Christopher had become overcrowded, and with most of the land already leased and being worked by the lessors with white servants or black slaves it was not capable of supporting a large landless population. One of Penn's recruiting officers early in 1655 had noted 'This island is almost worn out by reason of the multitudes that live upon it.' The problem on Nevis was not so acute, but the island still had a surplus of landless people. In 1657 about 1200 of them went with Luke Stoakes (see p. 38 above) to found a new settlement in Jamaica.

The Settlement of Anguilla

While many of the poor and dispossessed in St Christopher and Nevis were prepared to venture, either as soldiers or settlers, to the other end of the Caribbean, others took their chances closer to hand. Amongst these were the individuals who left in 1650 to establish the first settlement on Anguilla. Almost nothing is known of the early years. The first settlement was probably at Sandy Hill Bay on the south coast, although it is possible it could have been at Crocus Bay or Road Bay on the opposite coast. The inhabitants, who probably never numbered more than 100 at any time during the first decade, soon got down to work planting tobacco. Although in 1658 it was reported that Anguillian tobacco was 'highly prized by experts', it was not a crop with any future, and the settlers soon had to be content with being little other than subsistence farmers. The island's close association with St Christopher was first officially recognized in 1660 when William Watts was appointed governor of both islands.

The End of Proprietary Rule

Parliamentary rule ended in England in May 1660 when Charles II was proclaimed king. He returned from exile determined to exercise, through Parliament, closer control over the colonies. In July he wrote to Lord Willoughby in Surinam, directing him to surrender the unexpired term of the lease he had obtained from Carlisle, and to assume the government of Barbados and the Leeward Islands under royal command. Later the same year the Parliamentary Commission for Plantations was replaced by a committee of privy councillors known as the Lords of Trade and Plantations, and another Navigation Act was passed. This Act elaborated on that of 1651 with the addition of an 'enumeration clause' specifying that cotton, sugar, tobacco and various other named products grown in a colony could only be exported to England or to another English colony.

It took until September 1663 for Willoughby to reach Barbados, but once there he wasted no time in making the planters aware of the changes needed as a result of the establishment of Crown rule. Within a month he had persuaded the Council and Assembly to agree to pass an Act imposing export duty of $4\frac{1}{2}$ per cent on all the island's products, in return for cancellation of all proprietary rents and dues, and for confirmation of all existing land titles 'in free and common socage of the Crown'. Minor tenants would be granted permanent leaseholds, and any land from then on could be bought, sold or passed on as the owner saw fit. Half of the $4\frac{1}{2}$ per cent tariff was to go to Willoughby, while the other half would be used for the maintenance of royal authority in the upkeep of forts and public buildings. In March of the following year he left for the Leeward Islands, and during the summer obtained a similar agreement from the Council and Assembly in each of them. With the passing of these Acts, proprietary rule came to an end.

S. Christophe under de Poincy

Following d'Esnambuc's death in 1636, S. Christophe was administered by his deputy, Pierre du Halde, for another two years before a proper replacement was appointed. The new Governor, who was also made Lieutenant-General (or Governor-General) of all the French islands, was the Chevalier Philippe de Lonvilliers de Poincy. He left France in February 1639 and, having first called at Martinique and Guadeloupe, arrived at Basseterre in April.

He was already a rich man who had been knighted by Louis XIII but, in keeping with the attitudes which were common amongst all the prominent men, of whatever nationality, in the early days of West Indian colonization, he was only too keen to acquire more riches and prestige. Once he had established himself, he began to govern in a way even more authoritarian that that of Warner next door. His Ordinance concerning the ban on tobacco planting (entered into with Warner), which was issued within a few weeks of his arrival, makes this only too clear:

> All planters and householders...whatever their rank and
> condition, are ordered and enjoined to uproot all the
> tobacco on the islands of their plantations, without
> reserving a single plant, at the end of October next...and
> are forbidden to replant or make tobacco in any sort or

form, on any pretext whatsoever, for eighteen months thereafter...on pain of confiscation of the plantations where any tobacco is found...confiscation also of all servants, men and women, whether whites, Negroes or Indians, together with an arbitrary fine...and a year's imprisonment....[2]

At the same time, he not only continued to tax the planters but made every effort to put all their trade in his own hands by becoming the colony's only wholesaler. By forbidding individual planters from boarding trading vessels, he became the only purchaser of the ships' cargoes which he then resold at a profit. None of this did much for the turnover of the Compagnie des Iles d'Amerique, but de Poincy 'and his clerks grew very rich at the expense of the poor planters who groaned under the monopoly'.[3]

By 1644 de Poincy was doing so well out of being governor of S. Christophe that he decided he could afford to leave the colony in the care of his nephew, Robert de Lonvilliers de Poincy (hereafter referred to as de Lonvilliers to avoid confusion), and concentrate on seeing what benefits he could accrue elsewhere. As governor-general he did, after all, also have overall responsibility for Guadeloupe and Martinique. Unfortunately he had already interfered too much in the running of these islands for this to be acceptable to their Governors, and the following year they were able to persuade the Company to revoke his appointment as governor-general. His replacement, Noel Patrocles de Thoisy, was appointed in February 1645.

De Thoisy arrived at S. Christophe in November, having previously been well received in Martinique and Guadeloupe, only to find that de Poincy refused to recognize his authority. After some sort of skirmish, which forced him to leave Basseterre, de Thoisy called at Old Road to try to persuade Sir Thomas Warner that he was now the lawful governor-general, and to find out if he could depend on English assistance or neutrality in the event of a conflict between himself and de Poincy. This got him nowhere, as Warner, who was on very good terms with de Poincy, 'would not permit Du Toisy nor any of his Company to Land on the English ground, neither to refresh themselves to bury the Dead nor to deliver a letter to himselfe from the Queene of England'.[4] Following this blank refusal to acknowledge his authority, de Thoisy then had no option but to return to Guadeloupe.

Early the following year he tried again, mounting an invasion on Capesterre with armed men under the command of the Governor of Martinique which succeeded in capturing de Lonvilliers and another of de Poincy's nephews. If he then considered that, by sending these to

Guadeloupe to be held as hostages, de Poincy would admit defeat he was much mistaken:

> when Toisy's partey had surprised a french Forte by the
> Seaside and taken two of Poincy's Nephewes Sir Thomas
> with some Companies of English tooke the feild with
> Poincy and by the Countenance of the English disbanded
> the French....[5]

After that it took another year for the situation to be resolved, something only achieved after the release of the nephews by the appointment of de Thoisy as governor-general of Martinique and Guadeloupe only. De Poincy was allowed to remain as governor-general of S. Christophe.

Such events did little for the standing of the Compagnie des Isles d'Amerique, or to make it a profitable organization. By 1648 it was virtually bankrupt and had largely lost control of the various governors who, like de Poincy, were all running their islands very much to their own advantage. Two years later, when it was decided to wind up the Company and sell the French Caribbean possessions, Martinique and Guadeloupe were immediately bought by their respective Governors. De Poincy took a different approach and, as a Knight of the Order of St John of Jerusalem, decided to try to interest the Grand Master of the Order in acquiring the remaining colonies. As a result, in May 1651 the Knights of Malta agreed to buy S. Christophe, along with the newly settled islands of St Martin, St Croix, and St Bartholomew, for 120,000 *livres*. The change of ownership made little difference to de Poincy. He remained in charge of S. Christophe, where he was now called the Bailiff, until his death in 1660.

Le Chateau de la Montagne

When he took over as governor of S. Christophe, de Poincy moved into the house d'Esnambuc had built on the eastern slopes of Olivees Mountain, a little over two miles inland of Basseterre. It must have been a modest building, well below the standard he considered befitted his wealth and status, because in 1642 he decided to replace it with something much grander.

What he built was described thirty years later by an English author as 'a stately castle...most pleasantly seated, at the foot of a high Mountain, not far from the Sea, having spacious Courts, delightful Walks, and Gardens and enjoyeth a curious prospect.' The only trouble with this is that the author, Richard Blome, who never set foot on the island (indeed, probably never ventured out of England in his life), was merely cribbing from a book published 12 years earlier in France. This was the *Histoire naturelle et morale des iles Antilles de l'Amerique,* compiled by Cesar de Rochefort, who was a minister of the Protestant Church and one of de Poincy's supporters in Paris. Although an important book, a lot of it was pirated, and it is doubtful if much or any of the contents was based on his personal observations.

If anything bears this out it must be the book's elaborately detailed illustration of the 'Chateau de Mr le General' in S. Christophe (see Plate 3). This illustration, showing a four-storey, four-square mansion, surrounded by walled courtyards and formal gardens, and approached by a tree-lined avenue through pastoral surroundings, was accepted as a true representation of de Poincy's residence, not only by Richard Blome in 1672 but seemingly by most people ever since. In fact, the illustration can show no more than an artist's very fanciful impression of what de Poincy would have liked to build; either that, or what, on the opposite side of the Atlantic and working from hearsay and sketchy reports, de Rochefort imagined he had built.

The site on which de Poincy's new residence was built, and the period when this took place, together provide enough reason for dismissing the construction of a 'stately castle' or 'chateau'. The situation of 'La Fontaine', as de Poincy called his new residence, is known precisely, as the present Fountain Estate house was built on the same foundations. The site, on the side of a fairly steep slope, with no flat land anywhere in the vicinity, bears no resemblance whatsoever to that of the illustration. Nothing even approaching the layout of the walled gardens shown in the drawing could ever have been attempted. Nor, in the 1640s, barely twenty years after the settlement was founded, is it possible to believe that enough men with the necessary skills – architects, quarrymen, masons, carpenters, landscape gardeners – could have been found living on, or induced to come to, the island to carry out such a grandiose project.

Very few buildings anywhere on the island were made of anything but wood before the last decades of the seventeenth century. A Swedish military engineer, who visited both the English and French parts of the island in 1654, recorded:

> The houses on this Island are, on account of the great heat,
> built only of boards on square posts, the walls as well as the
> roofs, and the wall boards not closer together than one can
> pass a hand out and in between each board, in order that the
> air may be able to blow in to cool the people staying within.[6]

As the same man called on de Poincy at his residence, but had nothing to record about his visit other than that he was 'sumptuously entertained', the house must surely have been nothing, literally, to write home about.

The West India Company

Following its acquisition by the Knights of Malta, the colony continued to prosper, being described by a visitor in 1655 as so well cultivated 'that I thought I was in the French gardens, every acre accordingly a family subsistence, noe corne wasted'. Whether the Order itself derived much benefit as a result of this prosperity is open to question. De Poincy and his successor, Charles de Sales, exercised complete authority, controlled much of the internal economy, and were quite content to let trade with Europe become a virtual monopoly of the Dutch. In 1663, when a serious fire broke out in Basseterre, no less than 60 of the buildings destroyed were warehouses belonging to Dutch traders. As a result

> The island suffered very much during four or five months, because all the salt beef and bacon, wine, oil, brandy, flour, cloth, and other goods were entirely burned, so that the planters were deprived of all those things in a single day and were forced to await aid from Holland, which had always proved their refuge in time of necessity.[7]

In the same year the Chief Minister of France, Jean Baptiste Colbert, decided that the time had come to end this situation by reorganizing the way the colonies were administered and by taking their trade out of the hands of foreigners. In May he set up a state-aided concern called the Compagnie des Indes Occidentals (West India Company), giving it a monopoly on West Indian trade and the authority to take back the various islands through compulsory purchase. In 1665 S. Christophe, St Croix, St Martin and St Bartholomew were bought back from the Knights of Malta for 500,000 *livres*. The new company did no better than the previous one, and ceased to exist after it had become bankrupt in 1674. From then on the king of France and his ministers took direct control of all the country's West Indian possessions.

7

The Beginnings of a Plantation Society

By the 1660s in both St Christopher and S. Christophe, and also in Nevis, more effort was being put into the growing of sugar-cane than any other crop. Having been introduced into the region probably by the Dutch from Brazil, it had begun to be planted in S. Christophe in about 1640, and in St Christopher two or three years later. Nevis lagged behind in its introduction, but by the 1650s sugar had become the island's staple product. In 1652 it was reported that Nevis was 'the best island for sugar: it makes little of any other commodities, only some tobacco to windward, which is valued more than any of the English plantations'.[1] This view ignored the place of sugar in S. Christophe, where more was then being grown than in Nevis or St Christopher. Before he died in 1660 de Poincy alone had six mills at work on two of his plantations.

Although sugar rapidly became the main product of both islands, other crops continued to be grown commercially until well into the 1670s. Peter Lindeström, the Swedish military engineer who visited St Christopher in 1654 (and was 'sumptuously entertained' by de Poincy (p.47 above) when he went across the border into S. Christophe) was most impressed by what was then being grown, recording a view of the island which puts to shame the output of its present-day agriculturalists:

> This is a very fertile island, there grow oranges, lemons
> sweet oranges, potatoes, bananas, sugar, tobacco, nutmegs,
> walnuts, chestnuts, grapes, red, blue, white and brown,
> pepper, ginger and innumerable quantity of all kinds of
> valuable and rare fruit. Ginger lay there in the fields in
> large heaps, like tumbled-over houses thrown together; if
> it was not carefully looked after and dug out in the fields,
> it would become so firmly and strongly rooted in, that it
> prevented all other fruit and roots from growing. On the
> ground all over, the fields were covered with oranges,
> lemons, pepper and all other kinds of fruit, which had
> fallen from the trees, like hail.... We threw oranges and
> lemons, like snowballs, at one another.[2]

As sugar took over, crops such as tobacco, indigo and ginger, mostly grown on smallholdings by former indentured servants who possessed neither capital nor slaves, became less and less economical to produce. These small farmers were particularly affected by the Navigation Acts, as was made clear in a petition from the Council and Assembly of Nevis sent to the King in 1664:

> whereas they formerly enjoyed freedom of trade with all
> nations in amity with His Majesty, they are now debarred
> from same…. Many of the meaner sort were wholly
> employed in the manufacture of tobacco, whereon they
> lived comfortably, but now that supplies come only from
> English ports where tobacco is no commodity, and not
> being able to produce sugar, they are forced daily to desert
> the island.[3]

Those who did not flee continued as best they could for another decade or so, but after 1677 tobacco ceased to be a commercially grown crop in either St Christopher or Nevis. The 'meaner sort' who were growing other crops found it just as difficult to continue. In 1676 one of the richer planters of St Christopher, Christopher Jeaffreson, noted: 'indigo of late has yielded…but small profit… and I see everybody that is able, working upon sugar, which is certaine gaine'.[4]

Working on Sugar

Only the wealthiest planters could afford to convert their estates from the production of tobacco, indigo, ginger or raw cotton to the manufacturing of sugar. Commercial quantities of all of the former could be produced by a few people working a few acres, using few tools and employing only basic land husbandry techniques. The manufacture of marketable quantities of even the lowest grade of unrefined sugar, on the other hand, required lots of land, lots of skilled and unskilled labour, proper estate management, buildings and a range of expensive equipment. In an age long before the industrial revolution began, a functioning sugar plantation was the nearest thing to an industrial concern; a 'factory in the field' according to one modern historian.[5]

The operation of a sugar plantation, which had been perfected by the 1670s, was to remain virtually unchanged for the next two hundred years or more. Because sugar-cane takes between 14 and 18 months to ripen, planting had to be staggered so that it could be harvested over a period of several months. Account needed to be taken of the climate, to ensure planting took place between June and November, when rain was most likely, and to produce full-grown cane ready for harvesting during the driest months between January and May, when the sugar content was at its maximum.

The best results were achieved by dividing a plantation into similar-sized 'pieces' which were then planted to mature at intervals. As each piece was cleared, cuttings from the harvested cane, each about two foot long, were planted in large holes under a mixture of soil and manure. Provided the entire operation of clearing and replanting a piece was completed between October and December one year, and given the right weather conditions in between, harvesting could begin in January two years later. During the whole of the growing period each piece had to be weeded, fertilized and as far as possible kept free of vermin. Harvesting was just as laborious as planting and weeding. The cane was cut with bill-hooks, stripped of its leaves – the 'trash' – before being made up into bundles, and then carted to a mill for grinding. The trash was collected, either to be dried and used as fuel or to become litter in animal pens.

Very early on it was found that the planters who had switched to sugar were presented with a problem not faced by those who grew other crops, caused by 'idle wandering and illdisposed persons who make it common use and practice to wander, and with lighted torches to go a crabbing in and about the plantations of several persons where sugar canes are growing'.[6] The Act which was passed in 1672, prohibiting the carrying of such torches near the cane fields, was the first of many such decrees. None ever succeeded in stamping out deliberate cane-burning, and fire-raising in the fields was to remain a problem as long as sugar-cane was grown on the island.[7]

To begin with, all the mills were powered by animals, and even though wind-driven versions based on the standard European model began to be built before the end of the seventeenth century, animal-powered mills were still to be found on St Kitts, Nevis and Anguilla until the early years of the nineteenth century. Close control was needed over harvesting and delivery to the mill, as the cut cane had to be crushed as quickly as possible in order not to lose any of the sugar content. The cane juice produced as a result of the crushing, having been piped to an adjacent building, then had to be boiled immediately to avoid fermentation. The boiling process was repeated in a series of different-sized copper kettles with the impurities being skimmed off between each transfer, until in the smallest of them the juice had been turned into a thick, dark brown sludge. This was then tempered with lime in order to promote granulation, before being run into earthenware pots which were then taken for curing into a heated drying shed. After two days each pot had to be drained of the accumulated molasses, and after a month emptied completely. The resultant blocks of golden-brown muscovado sugar, less the top and bottom bits which were removed and re-boiled, were then packed into huge wooden barrels called hogsheads. Each hogshead, holding a nominal 1000 lb (450 kg), somehow then had to be transported to a suitable place for shipping.

The operation of a sugar plantation, from the planting of the 'pieces' to the shipping of the final product, required an enormous amount of labour with almost every aspect of the work under close supervision. As such plantations came into being in the seventeenth century, their owners had to address their minds to how the necessary labour was to be acquired, and how the required supervision was to be provided.

Indentured Servants

In the early days of the settlement of both St Christopher and Nevis, before sugar became important, most plantation workers were white indentured servants. These were recruited by individual merchants or ship masters in the British Isles and taken to the islands, where their indentures for a period of years were each sold for around 500 lb of tobacco (this then being the accepted medium of exchange). For the first few years this provided a workforce of reasonable quality, people who were prepared to work hard during the period of their indentures and keen to better themselves afterwards. As such they generally were not badly treated, but this changed as the demand grew. Ireland became a prime source of servants and their overall quality decreased. As many planters then ended up with people who had no knowledge of agriculture, or had no great interest in working, or were disaffected Roman Catholics, or who combined two or all of these drawbacks, their treatment suffered and many ended up little better than slaves. The situation became worse after the start of the English Civil War, when servant numbers were made up by political prisoners, felons 'and other incorrigible rogues' deported to the West Indies by the Parliamentarians.

As a result of this, and also because Jamaica and the North American colonies then offered much better prospects, by the 1660s all of the Leeward Islands found it difficult to attract servants. The indentures of any who were brought to the islands were now each worth anything up to 2000 lb of sugar. In 1664 the Lords of Trade and Plantations reported that such servants were transported for about £6 a head and 'after certain years they are free to plant for themselves or take wages for their service, and have the value of £10 to begin planting for themselves'. In St Christopher and Nevis, where a servant over 16 years of age had to work for four years, and one under that age for seven years, 400 lb of sugar was fixed as the equivalent of the £10 bounty.

Although the amount of a servant's bounty was fixed at £10, the price that had to be paid for his indentures in the first place made some planters not prepared to consider even 400 lb of sugar as the equivalent of this amount of money. In 1677 Christopher Jeaffreson in St Christopher wrote to a cousin in England:

> I confess all servants are very acceptable here; and if any laborious and industrious men would transport themselves, I should gladly receive them and allow them the customs of the country, with meate, drinke, lodging and clothing, as are necessarie; but it is not the custome to promesse any more than three hundred pounds of sugar at the end of their term of four years.[8]

This then was the going rate for an unskilled labourer, a man prepared to work as a field hand. That for skilled craftsmen, the men essential for the proper running of a sugar plantation, was quite different. Four years later Jeaffreson sent another letter to England asking for 'some white servants, especially a mason, carpenter, taylor, smith, cooper, or any handy craftsman', pointing out that these were 'the trades most necessary here', and adding:

> I would allow to such a one, when a good workman, a thousand pounds of sugar wages, for each yeare that he should serve me, with what must be paid for theire passages, tools or instruments....

In the same letter he indicated that the bias against servants from Ireland remained as strong as ever: 'Scotchmen and Welchmen we esteeme the best servants; and the Irish the worst, many of them being ever good for nothing but mischief.' He also left the recipient in no doubt about the place such esteemed servants now occupied in plantation society:

> slaves live as well now as the servants did formerly. The white servants are so respected that, if they will not be too refractory, they may live much better than thousands of the poor people in England, during their very servitude, or at least as well.[9]

By the end of the century, white indentured servants as members of an unskilled labour force had disappeared. They had moved into the class of artisans and overseers, and their place as plantation labourers had been taken over by black slaves from Africa.

Slaves

The first of these slaves were those brought in 1626 to St Christopher (p.26 above), where they would have been bought by the wealthiest of the original English settlers. The first shipment of slaves received by the French on S. Christophe were landed in 1635 from a Dutch ship which had taken them from a captured Spanish slaver. Many more must soon have followed to both sides of the island, but very little is known about the numbers, or the rate at which they were shipped, before the last quarter of the seventeenth century. What is known, however, is that throughout this period the great majority of slaves were carried to the island in Dutch ships. The French probably bought more than the English, and by 1646 slaves were being imported regularly into S. Christophe. A male slave at this time cost 4000 lb of tobacco, and a female 3000 lb. Only rich men like de Poincy could afford to buy at these prices, and it is believed that he may have had over 600 slaves at work on his various plantations by 1654. These probably represented about one-fifth of all those owned by the French planters, who at the time were reported to employ 'in tilling their land neither oxen nor horses, but only slaves'.

After the transfer from tobacco to sugar had begun and brought about an increased demand for slaves, the English suffered in comparison with the French by the restrictions imposed by the Navigation Act of 1651, which made it illegal to trade with the Dutch. An attempt to supplant the virtual monopoly in slaves held by the Dutch was made at the end of 1660, the year in which the second Navigation Act was passed. King Charles II gave a patent to the Company of Royal Adventurers Trading in Africa, granting it a monopoly which included the supply of slaves to the West Indian colonies. Unfortunately, as the Company set the price of a slave at £17, a figure well over twice as high as that of the Dutch, it found few buyers for the relatively few slaves it managed to ship across the Atlantic. This left the English in St Christopher, Nevis and the other Leeward Islands at a severe disadvantage, compared with the French. In September 1666 Willoughby complained to the King that all the islands were short of slaves, arguing that 'these settlements have been upheld by negroes and cannot subsist without supplies of them'. The difference between the development of St Christopher compared with that of S. Christophe caused by the shortage of slaves soon became much worse. Brought about by the events connected with the Second Dutch War related in the next chapter, the expansion of the sugar industry of S. Christophe progressed very much at the expense of the English planters and their slaves. By 1671 the difference between the two sides of the island was very marked: in S. Christophe the French numbered over 3600 and owned nearly 4500 slaves, while in St Christopher there were no more than 1000 English in possession of about 900 slaves.

The Company of Royal Adventurers, which had shipped no slaves for the previous five years, went out of business in 1672 and was replaced by the Royal African Company. This took a far more positive attitude towards supplying the colonies with labour and established depots to handle the sale of slaves in Jamaica, Barbados and the Leeward Islands. The last, which was to supply all four islands, was based on Nevis as this was the one which had suffered least during the war. The Company bought slaves at around £3 each and, provided the entire cargo had previously been contracted for in London, sold them in Nevis at £16 a head. If the cargo had not been contracted for first – and few planters in any of the four islands were rich enough to afford this – then slaves were sold individually at an average market price of £20 a head.

The first shipment arrived within a year of the Royal African Company being chartered, and over the next ten years a total of around 5500 slaves were landed in Nevis. They were sold for a total of about 18,000,000 lb of sugar, which remained the normal currency throughout this period. As might be expected, the planters of Nevis had first choice of all the slaves landed. This inevitably led to complaints from the other islands, concerning both the quantity and quality of the slaves that remained. In 1680 the Council of St Christopher asked for a more regular supply or to be allowed to arrange direct shipments, giving as the reason 'it being as hard a matter altogether and as great a bondage for His Majesty's subjects to cultivate his Plantations here without negro slaves as for the Egyptians to make bricks without straw'.[10]

At the time of the Council's lament St Christopher had a total population of about 3900, of whom just over half were slaves. This compared very unfavourably with S. Christophe, where there were 4300 slaves in a population of 7300, and even more so with Nevis, where a population of about 8500 contained some 5000 slaves. Poor Anguilla at this time supported a mere 550 people, of whom over half were children and none was a slave.

The number of slaves in St Christopher increased slowly but their situation, and that of their owners, was not improved when they were caught up in another conflict, King William's War, which broke out in 1689. As a result of events connected with this war, and which are related below, the development of the sugar industry of St Christopher was seriously disrupted once again. After the war, and although the Royal African Company's monopoly had by then been broken, the shortage of slaves continued and sugar production suffered accordingly. At the end of the century there were still no more than 3000 slaves in St Christopher, where they represented about 60 per cent of the population, compared with the 6000 who formed 80 per cent of the population of Nevis. Society had also changed in Anguilla by this time: the white population had risen to around 500 and between them they had acquired slightly more than this number of slaves.

Besides being less troubled by the wars of the seventeenth century, the main reason why Nevis was able to make the transition from tobacco to sugar and prosper so rapidly was because of the presence of a mercantile community larger and more go-ahead than that on any of the other islands. While three members of this community, as agents for the Royal African Company, provided the planters of Nevis with the pick of the slaves sent to the Leeward Islands, others supplied all the goods and services needed to produce sugar. Some of them, once they had made enough from such trading activities, bought land or took over existing estates and became planters themselves.

Among these merchants, and probably leading the rest with their business acumen, were a number of Jews of Sephardic heritage who had arrived around the middle of the century. They were descended from families who had gone to the early Dutch settlements in Brazil after the expulsion of Jews from Spain and Portugal in the fifteenth century, and then been forced to leave when Brazil was claimed by Portugal. Some of those who had moved to Barbados, eventually finding life too restricted or business prospects too limited, had sought better opportunities in a less-crowded island like Nevis. There they were not made unwelcome, and by 1690 were so well established that Charlestown possessed a synagogue and a Jewish school. The earliest tombstone in the still extant Jewish cemetery dates from 1679.

Religion

It is not known what the Established Church thought of the presence of a synagogue on Nevis, as the Church of England had only a marginal role in the society of any the Leeward Islands during the seventeenth century. Religious fanaticism dominated in every island, as many of the settlers had left England – and France – to escape persecution or to be able to follow their own method of worship.

The first Church of England clergyman in St Christopher was the Reverend John Featley, who arrived in 1625 and became the rector at Old Road. He was followed about five years later by the Reverend John Lake, whom Warner installed at the small settlement which had grown up at Palmetto Point, a couple of miles to the east of Old Road. A third clergyman, named Palmer, was later sent to minister to the settlers on the opposite, windward, coast. All were licensed by the bishop of London, were supported by tithes (paid to begin with in tobacco, and later in sugar), and had churches which were no more than wooden structures. None of these three, nor their successors, stayed for more than a few years, and it seems unlikely that the presence of any of them was widely welcomed. In 1642 one of the demands made by the men leading the 'Second Rebellion' (p.40 above) was

> The division of Keyon [Cayon] doth desire to have their minister put out, and to have Mr Palmer againe, the new incumbent being a contentious man, and one that hath sowed muich discord among his parishioners by his scandalous tongue.[11]

No proper parishes were established until 1655, by which time there were three churches on the leeward side and the two on the windward side. Whether there were then, or at any time in the next twenty years, five parish priests in residence seems most unlikely. Nor is it likely that Nevis or Anguilla were better served. Although Nevis was divided into five parishes around 1670 it is very doubtful if more than one or two clergymen were present at any time during the next thirty or forty years. No minister is reported as ever visiting Anguilla before the closing years of the seventeenth century. In 1671 the Governor-in-Chief of the Leeward Islands reported sourly and with great exaggeration that, although by then there were some 40 parishes in the islands under his authority, all he had to man them with were 'one drunken orthodox priest, one drunken sectary priest, and one drunken person who had no orders'. Nine years later the Council of St Christopher felt compelled to write asking for more clergy 'of riper years and better read in divinity than the last young graduates that came hither'. It is not known how many of these 'young graduates' there were, when they arrived, or how long they stayed, but the Council demanded replacements because they measured up so poorly against the 'many Roman priests on the French part of the island who are questionless men of great learning and parts'.[12]

In S. Christophe the spiritual life of the settlers was taken more seriously, and Capuchin friars were at work at either end of the island within a few years of d'Esnambuc's arrival. A small church was built at Capesterre, somewhere in the vicinity of the modern village of Newton Ground, and another in Basseterre in the embryonic town of the same name. Members of another mendicant Order, the Carmelites, came to the island a little later. The friary they established on the lower slopes of Monkey Mountain was probably on or close to the site of the present-day St Peter's Church.

All was well between church and state until 1645, when the Capuchins became involved in de Thoisy's struggle to take over the governorship from de Poincy, choosing to side with the former. This led to the Capuchin friars being expelled in 1646, and de Poincy inviting the Order of Jesuits to take their place, The Jesuits subsequently built a church in Basseterre town, very close to the site now occupied by St George's Church, and established their college about a mile to the north.

An Irish Jesuit, John Stritch, arrived in 1650 and built a chapel in Capesterre very close to the border with St Christopher. This was deliberately sited in order to attract his fellow countrymen – both free and indentured – in the English settlement to cross over and attend the services he held. Stritch later moved to Montserrat, but continued to return to S. Christophe from time to time until he was replaced by another Irish priest, John Grace, in 1660. Whether either of these priests actually preached sedition is open to question, but there is no doubt that they did little to foster loyalty among those attending their services to anything but their faith and co-religionists. The result was that, throughout the troubles which afflicted the island during the last four decades of the century, the Irish invariably sided with the French.

By about 1670 a small congregation of Quakers, as members of the Religious Society of Friends were commonly called, had been established on Nevis. As they refused to participate in Church of England services, to bear arms or to swear oaths, their presence was greatly resented, and they were forced to live and worship under a variety of restrictions. When two missionaries accompanied by a Quaker planter from Barbados arrived in late 1671 they were welcomed by 'several honest tender friends', but refused permission to remain on the island by the Governor. After this, being prevented from proselytizing and frequently victimized, the Quakers on Nevis had no future and by the end of the century had largely disappeared. This was a great pity as theirs was the only Christian denomination at the time able to see African slaves as fellow human beings and prepared to do something to improve their condition.

8

The Loss and Recovery of St Christopher

The Second Dutch War which began in March 1665 was largely brought about by Dutch resentment of the English Navigation Acts which restricted certain trades to English shipping. Once the news reached Lord Willoughby in Barbados he ordered the Governor of St Christopher, William Watts, to seize the neighbouring Dutch possessions of St Eustatius, St Martin and Saba, while he himself attacked their settlements in Tobago and Guiana. Watts succeeded in St Martin and Saba, but as far as St Eustatius was concerned, the order had reached him too late, the island having already been captured by a force of English buccaneers led by Colonel Thomas Morgan. Later in the year, when it seemed likely that France would enter the war in support of the Dutch, Willoughby received instructions from London to attack S. Christophe as soon as the news of French participation in the war was received. For this reason when Watts and the new Governor of S. Christophe, Charles de Sales, renewed the Anglo-French treaty in January 1666 Willoughby refused to give it his ratification.

News of France's entry into the war in January reached the Caribbean at the beginning of April, and was first heard in Nevis. The Governor, James Russell, immediately sent word to Watts and followed it up by sending 400 armed men to Old Road as reinforcements. A little later another 270 men, buccaneers under Thomas Morgan, arrived from St Eustatius. This gave Watts a total of about 2200 men. Half of these he sent to guard the border with Basseterre in the south, in order to protect his rear, while he made preparations to march north with the remainder in order to seize Capesterre. This would then allow him to move clockwise around the island, picking up more men from among the English plantations on the windward side as he went, and attack the town of Basseterre from the rear.

Such movements did not go unnoticed by the French, and, once news was received that France and England were now at war, de Sales decided to pre-empt an attack, making best use of his limited forces. These consisted of about 550 men under Robert Lonvilliers de Poincy in Capesterre, and another 800 under his own command in Basseterre.

On 21 April, de Sales began an anti-clockwise march around the island with his men, leaving just 100 of them to maintain a presence in front of the English at the border. They had to fight their way along the coast but met no serious opposition until somewhere near what is now Nicola Town, where a more bloody skirmish took place and de Sales was killed. This did not stop the advance, and later in the day the force, now under the command of the Chevalier de Saint-Laurent, joined up with de Lonvilliers and his men in Capesterre.

Once the news of what was taking place on the opposite side of the island reached Watts at Old Road he moved quickly, and he and his troops, including the buccaneers, probably entered Capesterre from the south at much the same time as the French under Saint-Laurent entered from the north. The pitched battle which followed was particularly bloody, and led to Watts being killed outright, and the buccaneer leader, Morgan, being fatally wounded. Their loss left the English without any proper leadership, and the French under Saint-Laurent, although outnumbered, soon had them on the run. The battle then ended and formal surrender terms were agreed the next day.

Under these, all the English who did not own property were to leave the island immediately. Of the remainder, those who wished to stay could only do so after swearing an oath of allegiance to the French king and the West India Company; those not prepared to do this could sell their plantations to French buyers and would then be allowed to leave with their slaves and personal property.

The expulsion of those judged to be vagabonds began shortly afterwards. Nearly two-thirds of the 1300 or so people shipped off the island were Irish, and most of these were taken to St Bartholomew. Where the rest ended up is unknown. It seems unlikely that any of the people they left behind in St Christopher, the planters and their families, ever changed their allegiance. The 400 land transfers which took place under the terms of the surrender treaty were followed by an exodus of around 4000 people. Many of these went to the American colonies or Jamaica, but around half of them remained in the Leeward Islands. About 1500 of them crossed to Nevis, although the island could hardly cope with such an influx, and another 300 went to Montserrat.

One or two hundred more ended up in Anguilla, dramatically increasing the population and reinforcing its status as an English possession. This increase in the population together with the loss of the administrative control which the governor of St Christopher had exercised over Anguilla, led to the need for someone to take over leadership of the community. Well before the end of 1666, as a result of some sort of election, Captain Abraham Howell announced that he was now the governor, and would remain so until some other lawful authority was appointed. The situation was eventually regularized in 1673, when he was confirmed in office, with the title of deputy governor, by the Governor-General of the Leeward Islands.

The Attempt to Recapture St Christopher

A fleet of ships, sent by Lord Willoughby from Barbados with 600 armed men to assist Watts, arrived at Antigua, where it was intended to collect more men, a few days after St Christopher had fallen to the French. Henry Willoughby, one of the Governor's nephews who was in command of the force, then had no option but to land half of his men on Antigua, take the rest over to Nevis, and send the bad news back to Barbados. This resulted in 1000 more Barbadian settlers being impressed, and in another eight ships being commandeered in order to carry them to Nevis, from where an invasion of S. Christophe would be launched. With Lord Willoughby himself in command, the expedition left Barbados at the end of July. This is a particularly dangerous time of the year in the Eastern Caribbean and, a few days after sailing, the fleet was caught and overwhelmed by the full force of a hurricane off Guadeloupe. Only two ships survived. All the rest, together with Willoughby and virtually the entire invasion force, were never seen again. This disaster not only left St Christopher firmly in French hands, but also gave the opportunity for attacks to be mounted against Antigua and Montserrat with impunity. In Barbados William Willoughby, the brother of the drowned Francis and the father of Henry, who was acting as governor-general, could only wait for assistance to be sent from England.

A small squadron of warships under Captain John Berry was deployed among the Leeward Islands during the early months of 1667, but could do little other than prevent further French attacks on the islands. Berry's main achievement was to deter the French from any thought of invading Nevis. More offensive operations only began after the arrival of a relief expedition. William Willoughby, who had gone to England to make sure of his confirmation as governor-general, returned to Barbados in April. He came with two frigates, several merchant ships loaded with arms and ammunition, and a regiment of foot, under Major-General Sir Tobias Bridge, which had been raised specifically for service in the West Indies. In May the two warships, together with ships carrying half of the regiment under the command of Lieutenant-Colonel William Stapleton, were sent under the overall command of Henry Willoughby to Nevis, from where it was intended to mount the operation to recapture St Christopher.

The invasion, which began in the early hours of 7 June, failed dismally. All surprise was lost when the English ships became separated in the dark and ended up at daylight off Basseterre. The chosen landing place about three miles to the west of the town, in Palmetto Bay between Bloody Point and Palmetto Point, could not have been more inappropriate. Neither Willoughby, who remained offshore directing the operations from a boat, nor Stapleton, who led the invasion, had ever been to the island before and so had little idea of difficulties the landing place presented. The only way for the troops to leave the beach was by means of two steep and narrow defiles, up which they could only climb one at a time. The French under Saint-Laurent, who were able to observe from above all that was taking place below, had no difficulty in mounting their defence. The climbers in the gullies were picked off one by one as they reached the top, while those waiting on the beach below for their turn to climb were bombarded with rocks. Stapleton and his men persevered for six or seven hours, but eventually were forced to surrender. From the safety of one of the ships Henry Willoughby watched Stapleton and about 500 of his men, many of them wounded, being taken prisoner, and then departed for Nevis.

A few days later the remainder of the relief force, consisting of several warships under Rear-Admiral Sir John Harman and the other half of the regiment commanded by Major-General Bridge, arrived from Barbados. This ought to have been enough to have inspired Willoughby to try again, but:

> At a Councell of Warre held in Neavis Roade, on board
> His Majesties Shipp *Lyon*, by Sir John Harman, Knight,
> Leuit. Genll. Henry Willoughby, Governor James Russell,
> Sir Tobias Bridgge, and seuerall other officers, It was
> concluded and agreed upon, That the Souldiers & Seamen
> vnder Theire seureall Comands were In no wise Capeable
> off Re-attacqueing The Island off St. Christophers by
> Reason off the greate Nomber of the French Souldery &
> seuerall New Fortifycations lately made vppon that
> Island.[1]

As a result, even though the war ended a month later, several years were to pass before St Chistopher was restored to English rule.

The Treaty of Breda

The Treaty of Breda, which brought the Second Dutch War to an end on 31 July 1667, provided for the restoration of all captured colonies to their original owners. With regard to St Christopher it was agreed it would be returned to English rule at the end of January 1668. Six months in which to complete the hand-over must have seemed a sufficient length of time to those drawing up the treaty in Europe, but for those on the other side of the Atlantic involved in implementing the cession it was totally inadequate.

The return was delayed by long legal wrangling and many quarrels, mostly arising out of complications caused by the terms of the treaty under which St Christopher had been surrendered to the French in 1665. The planters who sold out at the time had agreed that they could not reclaim their plantations without repaying the full purchase price but now, in 1667, as many such properties had changed ownership, been greatly improved or left to depreciate while in French hands, there were disputes about the current ownership and value of many plantations. These disputes as well as disagreements over the return of slaves and guns which the French had seized in 1665, led to endless legal arguments and prevented any possibility of a swift English re-occupation of St Christopher.

The French were not only in no hurry to share the island again, but were anxious to keep the English out altogether if possible. In 1668 they went so far as to offer the island of Grenada in exchange for being allowed to retain St Christopher. Lord Willoughby in Barbados considered this would be 'no ill bargain', but the exiled planters in Nevis refused to consider such a move and petitioned the King accordingly, declaring that as far as they were concerned St Christopher 'was one of the flourishing colonies, the first and best earth that ever was inhabited by Englishmen amongst the heathen cannibals in America'.[2]

The Creation of the Colony of the Leeward Islands

Willoughby's reaction to the idea of allowing the French to retain St Christopher was seen by the Leeward Island planters as another example of how their islands were undervalued by the Governor-in-Chief in comparison with Barbados. His failure, and that of his brother before him, to provide them with adequate help during the war had already led to requests for a separate administration. In October 1667 a Nevis merchant and planter named George Marsh had raised a petition to the King, asking:

> That Your Majesty will be graciously pleased to send over some person as Your Majesty's lieutenant for the islands of Nevis, St Christopher, Antigua and Montseratt and that they may be no longer under the government of Your Majesty's lieutenant of the Barbados.

The petition reasoned that as the four islands were all in sight of one another they could give each other mutual support, whereas 'Barbados being a 100 leagues distant and many times 5 or 6 weeks before a ship can gain the Barbados from the Leeward Islands is rendered incapable of giving any sudden relief'. Even though this might well have been reason enough, the petitioners could not resist complaining that they believed the planters of Barbados did not want the Leeward Islands to recover from the effects of the war and restart sugar production: 'we can prove that several of the Barbadians have wished these islands sunk declaring it would be better for them, for now there was so much sugar made, that it was a mere drugg'.[3]

Although Willoughby visited the Leeward Islands the following year in an effort to counteract these views and retain control, his inability to hasten the return of St Christopher to English control worked against him. In November 1670 the Lords of Trade and Plantations established the Leeward Islands as a separate colony, and two months later appointed Sir Charles Wheler as the first governor-in-chief. He was instructed to take up residence in Nevis, and to make his prime concern the return of St Christopher to English rule, something which by this time was three years overdue.

The Recovery of St Christopher

Wheler arrived at Nevis in June and immediately opened negotiations with the French in Basseterre. These did not get very far, as S. Christophe was awaiting the arrival of the Governor-General from Martinique and nothing could be agreed without his presence. This delayed proceedings for over a month, and clearly upset Wheler. So much so that when the Governor-General, soon after reaching the island in July, issued an invitation to Wheler to visit Basseterre in order to resume the negotiations it was pointedly refused. Wheler reported afterwards:

> Then he and all the company with extraordinary
> importunity invited me to dine the next day with M. de
> Baas [the Governor-General]; but they got no answer than
> to this effect, that when the business was over M. de Baas
> should command me what he pleased, but that I would not
> set my foot upon St Christopher upon any occasion
> whatsoever but to regain possession.[4]

This had the desired effect and on 15 July, after Wheler had been received with all due ceremony at Old Road, a formal surrender document was signed and sealed. St Christopher was restored to English rule and Wheler was able to report to London 'I hope I may with modesty promise the

King, it shall be hardly lost as it has with difficulty been regained'.[5] Shortly afterwards he appointed a soldier, Captain Abednego Matthews, as the governor and returned to Nevis.

It was unfortunate for Wheler that he did not spend more time studying the terms of the surrender document before giving it his approval. Once the English planters had begun to return, it quickly became apparent that he had been completely outwitted by his French counterpart. None of the problems connected the current state and value of the plantations, or with the missing slaves and other property, had been properly addressed, and the returning English were soon at odds with both the French and their own Governor-General. The situation, which was to take well over another decade to resolve, was so bad that in the spring of 1672 Wheler was recalled.

He was replaced by William Stapleton, the officer who had led the troops in the misbegotten attempt to recapture St Christopher which had taken place five years earlier, and who, after his release from being a prisoner of war, had been made the governor of Montserrat. He was ordered to live in St Christopher when he was appointed, but disregarded this after a short while. He had married a niece of the Governor of Nevis the previous year, and so preferred to make his headquarters there. In any case, the society which was being re-established in St Christopher was hardly to his liking.

He arrived in St Christopher to find it still had a large French population. The plantations that had been bought in 1665 were either being worked by their new owners, or had been let out by absentee proprietors in S. Christophe, and squatters had moved on to the plantations which had not been sold. He began clearing the squatters, cancelling all existing claims to the vacated lands, and offering them to new settlers. This was followed in June by the passing of an Act to force all French servants and non-landowners to return to S. Christophe. The French who remained, those in legal possession of estates, were then required to take an oath of allegiance. These moves went some way to improving the situation, and two years later Stapleton was able to report that '299 of the old Proprietors of St Christopher's have claimed their estates, of whom 195 are possessed... and 104 are not possessed... and 139 of the old Proprietors have not made their claims'.[6]

One of the 'old Proprietors' who did return to claim his estate was Christopher Jeaffreson. When he arrived in June 1676 there were still no more than about 1000 English in St Christopher, and he was immediately made aware of how much the several hundred French who lived among them were disliked and mistrusted:

> it is miserable to see how the French insult us, and how
> they must be humoured upon all accounts to maintain a

faire correspondence between us. There is order for a fort
to bee built; but the inhabitants are soe wretchedly poore,
that it is feared they will not be able to goe through with
the designe, without some supplies and assistance from
England....[7]

By this time the situation with regard to land titles was very confused.
This was largely as a result of the French occupation, but made worse by
Stapleton's cancellation of claims attached to those estates which had been
abandoned by the 'old Proprietors'. The confusion affected even the
wealthiest among the returning planters, as is made clear in a letter
Jeaffreson wrote to a cousin a few months after his return:

I have never had nor seene any deed, by which my father
held this manor of Wingfield, but only that from the Lord
Carlisle, which nominates only [*sic*] a thousand acres.
After he had made choice of which plantation, I suppose
there was (or ought to have beene) some deed...setting
forth the bounds of the said plantations...alsoe concerning
a plantation which my father had on the windward side of
the island, called the Grange, which my cousin Robert
Jeaffreson, as some say, solde to Mr. Watkins, and that the
money was payd. Some call it mine. Soe many people are
buzzing these things in my eares, I would gladly know as
much as they; not that I have any intention of being
troublesome. It is now in the hands of a Frenchman....[8]

The circumstances gradually improved, and disputes over ownership
lessened as old claimants died or disappeared, and more and more of the
French-owned plantations were sold or leased to new English settlers. In
1678 there were about 130 French planters, making up 20 per cent of the
white male population of St Christopher. Ten years later only six French
families remained. Such a presence during this time did little to lessen
mutual mistrust, or to improve relations between St Christopher and
S. Christophe in general. It had become obvious to the English and French
alike that the island, with its great potential as a sugar producer, was too
valuable to be shared, and that sooner or later all of it would have to be
under one flag.

9

The French Wars and the End of S. Christophe

The French seizure of St Christopher effectively ruined it as an English colony, and once it had been reoccupied the economy had to be completely rebuilt. Up until 1665 it had been the most important of the Leeward Islands, but from 1667 until the early part of the eighteenth century it was very much overshadowed by Nevis. Before 1700 the annual sugar exports of St Christopher never exceeded 1000 tons, a figure often less than a third of that of Nevis. Sugar production was limited by the long drawn-out problems connected with the ownership of many of the plantations, but even more by a shortage of labour. This shortage delayed the economic revival of St Christopher, as it was something which could only be overcome by those planters with the means to buy substantial numbers of slaves, and such men were in short supply for many years after 1671.

In addition to labour, something else that was lacking when the English returned to St Christopher was a suitable and realistic means of deterring any future attack. At the time of the colony's return to English rule such deterrence depended on three small forts, Fort Charles at Old Road, another on a point at the southern end of Old Road Bay, and the third covering Pump Bay from Sandy Point. All were useless, having been stripped of their cannons by the French.

Wheler, shortly before he was recalled in 1672, complained of the way the French, who refused to return the guns, then took contemptuous advantage of the situation when passing Old Road:

> Their men of war sail under the King's fort (if so pitiable a durt pye may deserve the name of the King's fort) his pavilion up, and never strike till we have made a shot or two (and we can never hit because we have no platforms, nor no guns), and when demand was made for payment of the shot, a French Captain said he was sorry he did not duck the officer that came to ask it.[1]

Nothing was done until after Stapleton had taken over, when two of the forts – Fort Charles and Sandy Point – were abandoned. Fort Charles was replaced by a more substantial structure at a higher elevation about one hundred yards away from the original. At much the same time a new fort was begun on a headland known as Cleverley's, about a mile to the south of Sandy Point. It was of such a size, and funds were in such short supply, that the King had to contribute towards the cost. It took over 12 years to build and on completion was confusingly (in view of the existence of Fort Charles at Old Road) given the name of Charles Fort. Sycophancy in those days knew no bounds: the fortification erected on Nevis in 1670 to guard the anchorage off Charlestown was also called Fort Charles.

Such forts were of little value unless they were manned, and were not sufficient by themselves to prevent an invasion. For its overall defence St Christopher depended on the militia, drawn from among the planters and their white servants, backed up by a small number of professional soldiers.

The latter had originally belonged to Bridge's regiment which, after the Treaty of Breda, had been left to garrison the Leeward Islands. Following the disbanding of the regiment which took place after Wheler arrived in 1671, discharged soldiers were induced to settle in St Christopher with the offer of grants of land, ranging from 400 acres for a captain to 35 acres for a private. With the further inducement of a continuation of their pay from England, without which they had no means of buying what was needed to start working the land, enough men were attracted by the offer to form two companies. Unfortunately, as they rarely or ever received the promised pay, it was found very difficult to keep the companies up to strength. In 1675 Stapleton was compelled to write to London, begging the Lords of Trade and Plantations

> on behalf of the officers and soldiers of His Majesty's two standing companies…to move to His Majesty to be pleased to pay their arrears and to establish some fund for their future subsistence: they live in a most miserable condition among the poor inhabitants…who are not able to give them any subsistence: it is a disparagement rather than an honour to the nation, to have soldiers naked and starving in the eyes of the French who be mixed with us upon that island; they have officers and soldiers in good equipage and very well paid.[2]

As it is doubtful if the two companies together ever mustered more than 100–125 men, the defence of St Christopher rested mainly on the men of the militia. However, as many of these were 'the poor inhabitants' amongst whom the unpaid soldiers lived, all with little time to spare for anything other than eking out a living, they were poor fighters and generally unreliable. When asked to report on the state of the militia in November 1676, Stapleton had no option but to reply that, as 'in the exactest disciplined army unless it be to receive pay or bread, the third part of the number listed does not appear, what by sickness, cowardice or false musters, [so] much less may be expected from militia upon service'.[3] There was little that could be done to improve matters. At the time and for many years afterwards, the majority of the people in St Christopher were probably more interested in working out where their next meal was coming from than in worrying about a possible invasion.

Even Christopher Jeaffreson on his 1000 acres at Wingfield had his worries, as he expressed in a letter to his father-in-law in May 1677:

> I am something cautious of running too hastily into debt,
> considering our condition in this island, where we have
> scarce five hundred able English men, comprehending the
> two thin companies his Majestie is pleased to maintaine
> here. The French are three or foure tymes the number (if
> not more)....[4]

Jeaffreson was right to be cautious. Under-populated St Christopher, with its struggling economy, serious labour shortage and poor defence capability, was out-matched in every respect by S. Christophe. The English and French managed to rub along together and even, in April 1678, began discussions about a renewal of the treaty of neutrality. Although Matthews and Saint-Laurent soon met and agreed the terms, the days when the signatures of the two governors were all that were needed were long gone. It was now necessary for the draft treaty to be ratified in London and Paris, and this was something it was likely to take years to achieve. In the interim, as it had now become obvious to everyone that it no longer made sense to continue with the division of the island, each side made an attempt to buy out the other. The French offer to buy St Christopher was rejected, as the English hardly wanted to end up with a totally French island so close to Nevis. In 1679 Stapleton suggested to London that the French be offered Montserrat in exchange for S. Christophe as 'our neighbours and we can never cordially agree', but this too got nowhere. The two sides continued to live in mutual distrust, and by the time the treaty of neutrality was eventually ratified in December 1687 both Stapleton and Matthews were dead.

Matthews died in 1682 and was succeeded as governor of St Christopher by another military officer, Thomas Hill. Four years later Sir Nathaniel Johnson was appointed governor-general of the Leeward Islands soon after Stapleton's death. Johnson lived on Nevis to begin with, but in 1688 moved the governor-general's headquarters to Antigua, where they were to remain from them on. He was not to remain in office for very long, as later that year the 'Glorious Revolution' took place in England, replacing the Catholic King James II, to whom he had sworn an oath of allegiance, with the joint Protestant monarchs William III and Mary II. The deposed monarch was then welcomed in France where he set up court in exile. Even though the change was widely welcomed among the inhabitants of the Leeward Islands, and Johnson himself was a Protestant, his conscience would not allow him to accept the change. He resigned from office in July 1689, having nominated the leading planter of Antigua, Christopher Codrington, to take his place.

The Surrender of St Christopher, 1689

Codrington took over as governor-general at a crucial moment, as England had declared war on France in May, because of the support being given to the deposed James II. It took a month or more for the news to reach the Caribbean, but as soon as it did all the Irish in St Christopher declared their support for the exiled James II by crossing over the border into S. Christophe.

Shortly afterwards, with the eager assistance of the Irish defectors and in contravention of the treaty of neutrality, the French set out to destroy 'all that belongs to the Protestant interest' in St Christopher. This attack caused an immense amount of damage and the loss of many lives. The English militia and the 'two thin companies' of troops led by Matthews were no match for the French. Their only response was to ship their families to Nevis, and to retreat into the safety of the newly completed Charles Fort at Cleverley's Point, where they were immediately besieged.

The siege came to an end soon after the Governor-General of the French islands, the Comte Charles de la Roche-Courbon-Blenac, arrived from Martinique with more troops at the end of July. Two weeks of being bombarded from both land and sea was enough to convince Governor Matthews of the hopelessness of the situation. He capitulated on 15 August on the understanding that he and his men would then be allowed to leave for Nevis. This was quickly arranged, and within a day or two the whole island was once again in French hands.

The sudden influx of virtually the entire population of St Christopher was far from welcome on Nevis, where there was limited accommodation, insufficient stock of provisions and few charitable feelings for the distressed. This resentment was made worse later in the year when epidemics of smallpox and fever broke out and were blamed on the presence of the refugees. The deaths of about 700 people, including 200 slaves, which followed fuelled a series of disturbances. These were so serious that Codrington was compelled to send troops from Antigua to restore order. These troops, under the command of Sir Timothy Thornhill, had arrived from Barbados just too late to prevent St Christopher falling to the French. He later complained in a report to London of the barbarity which had been shown to the refugees by the people of Nevis: 'I can only call it a most wicked and unchristian contrivance to ravish from these poor creatures what little they have saved from their more merciful enemies the French'.[5]

The situation on Nevis was made worse still in November, when virtually the entire population of Anguilla arrived as refugees. This followed a French invasion, against which Howell and the few dozen men he had at his disposal could offer no resistance, and which had led to a general evacuation of the island. It is hardly likely they received a warm welcome from either the resentful inhabitants of Nevis or the bedraggled refugees from St Christopher. The misery which abounded from then on was exacerbated in April when Nevis suffered a severe earthquake. This caused landslides on Nevis Peak, all of the stone and brick buildings in Charlestown to drop 'of a sudden from the Top to the Bottom in perfect Ruines', and a tidal wave in which the sea withdrew 'a furlong' from the town for several minutes. Perhaps the only consolation left for all on the island was to learn later that the effects of the earthquake had also been felt in S. Christophe. There, not only was the governor's residence – the 'chateau' erected by de Poincy – ruined, but 'The earth opened nine Feet in many Places, and buried solid Timber, Sugar-Mills, & it threw down the Jesuits College, and all other Stone Buildings'.[6]

The Capture of S. Christophe

The Governor-General of the Leeward Islands, Christopher Codrington, could make no attempt to recover St Christopher without assistance from England. This arrived at Antigua in June 1690, in the form of a squadron of warships under Captain Lawrence Wright and about 2000 troops. On 23 June these troops, formed into six regiments, were shipped across to Nevis, where they joined up with Sir Timothy Thornhill's men who were already there. Codrington assumed overall command, and began to make preparations to invade S. Christophe by means of a surprise landing on a beach to the south-east of Basseterre.

The invasion force arrived in what is now known as South Frigate Bay on 29 June only to find that the French, having been forewarned by two traitors from Nevis, had 1000 men in place on the beach to prevent a landing. As Codrington was not prepared to take the risk of overcoming this force, he made a rapid change to his plans. In order to increase the chances of a successful landing by drawing off some of the defenders, Captain Wright and several of his ships were sent to feint a landing in Basseterre Bay. This had the desired effect, and later in the day about a third of the French troops were seen leaving the Frigate Bay defences. Codrington waited until after dark before making his next move, which was to land Thornhill and about 550 men on a beach in what is now called South Friar's Bay, immediately to the south of Frigate Bay and separated from it by a high, steep hill (see Plate 4). This eminence, known ever afterwards as Sir Timothy's Hill, presented a major obstacle to Thornhill's progress and he and his troops, once they had overrun the small French outpost they found at the beach, spent the rest of the night finding a way over it. Their route, which more than likely followed the line of the present road, brought them to the rear of the French defences in Frigate Bay at daybreak on 30 June. Their appearance behind the French lines was the signal for Codrington to land another 600 men directly on to Frigate Bay beach. Attacked from front and rear, the French defence crumbled after an hour or two, and was quickly turned into a rout.

Later in the day, after the remaining English troops had been landed, the entire force formed up in two columns to march on Basseterre. A rearguard action mounted by the French on the low hills to the north of Frigate Bay only served to delay entry into the town, and to make the English troops all the more ready to plunder it when they got there on 1 July. They met no opposition in the town as all the leading citizens had already left, with the remaining French troops, to take refuge in Charles Fort, the island's main stronghold at Cleverley's Point.

Heavy guns were needed if the fort was to be captured, and over the next three days a number of cannon were brought ashore from Captain Wright's frigates in Basseterre Bay. To haul these and their ammunition up the coast for ten miles, slaves were rounded up from among all those who had been deserted by their owners, and on 4 July Codrington set off to begin a siege. This began six days later after two of the guns, with an immense amount of labour, had been manhandled part of the way up Brimstone Hill only half a mile to the east of the fort. At the same time a number of Wright's ships took up position to seaward of Cleverley's Point. The French defenders were then in precisely the same situation as the English had been a year earlier but, because of the advantage the attackers had acquired by mounting guns on Brimstone Hill, in far more danger from the artillery bombardment which soon began. Six days of being pounded from both land and sea proved to be more than enough, and the French capitulated on 16 July.

The recovery of St Christopher, as far as Codrington was concerned, also meant the end of S. Christophe. In his view the English and French had fought for possession of the entire island, and as the latter had been comprehensively defeated it followed that full ownership went to the English as the victors. The French were disarmed and shortly afterwards shipped away from the island, some to Martinique and St Martin, and others to a new colony in the western half of Hispaniola known as Saint-Domingue.

The English success, although it brought an abrupt end to the French occupation of Anguilla and an equally quick resolution of the Nevis refugee situation, also caused some problems, not the least of which were those connected with the island's future development and defence. Codrington was much concerned about both, and in September 1691, by which time he was back in Antigua, he wrote to London outlining what he saw as the solution. He proposed that the arable land be divided in such a way as to attract a wide range of settlers. A quarter of the island, or about 15,000 acres, would be offered in lots of between 5 and 20 acres, 'so as for each ten acres there may be a fighting man', while the other three-quarters would be divided into much larger estates. These would be granted

> according to the ability of the setlers with due regard to make no plantation too large, and that they in general run between a 100 to 200 acres, which in these parts is a competent estate, and as much as ye generality of setlers will be in a capacity to improve and manage.[7]

Each of these planters would be required to employ one man suitable for serving in the militia for every 20 acres. In Codrington's estimation, if his proposals were accepted and all the land grants taken up, the island would then have a defence force of well over 3500 men.

The Governor-General's scheme was all very well in theory, but was not put into practice with any enthusiasm by his deputy on St Christopher. Neither Thomas Hill, nor the man who succeeded him as governor in 1697, James Norton, made much effort to reserve a quarter of the island for smallholders, or to restrict the amount of land granted to wealthier planters. No attempt was made to maintain a quota of white men on the larger plantations. The less well-off, such as servants who had served out their indentures, were actively discouraged from remaining on the island, ignoring the need for such men to act in its defence. As a result, by the end of the century the militia, instead of being the sizeable force envisaged by Codrington, was less than 400 strong.

The Return of S. Christophe

The war between England and France ended with the signing of the Treaty of Ryswick in September 1697. Shortly afterwards, those planters who had taken up grants on the French lands in the belief that the whole island was now an undisputed English possession were dismayed to learn that the terms of the treaty contradicted this assumption. The French demand for the restoration of S. Christophe, which followed the end of hostilities, was greatly resented by the planters, and met some resistance from London. The Board of Trade and Plantations, which had taken over the functions of the Lords of Trade and Plantations a year earlier, initiated efforts to persuade the French to accept some other island in lieu, but these were to no avail. In January 1698 Codrington was told to restore S. Christophe to its former owners. The slow rate at which the French settlers returned, and the delay in appointing a new governor, prevented the formal transfer from taking place for another year, by which time Codrington was dead and had been succeeded by his son who was also named Christopher.

The new French Governor, Comte Jean-Baptiste de Gennes, took possession of S. Christophe on 23 January 1699. Having arrived the day before to find the disgruntled English settlers had destroyed as much as they could before vacating the properties they had occupied, one of his first actions was to present the English Governor with a demand for reparations. In addition he asked for restoration of the original boundaries, the return of all slaves seized during the war, and renewal of the treaty of neutrality. Needless to say, neither Codrington nor Norton were in an hurry to accede to any of these demands, and did all they could to delay settlement. Two years later, with the dispute still no closer to being resolved, Codrington explained in a report to the Board of Trade and Plantations how he had been able to drag things out for so long:

> I have a very gallant but a very stupid man as President [of the Council in St Christopher], who deals better with Monsr. des Gennes than any Politician in Europe would do, for he confounds him with bad Latin and good Scotch, debauches away his soldiers, and then blunders on with eclærecssaiments that M. de Gennes knows not what to make of.[8]

The reason why such 'eclærecssaiments' (*éclaircissements*) or explanations were in the hands of the President of the Council at this time was because he was then acting as governor. In September 1700 a commission of inquiry, set up after Codrington had been petitioned by the planters of

St Christopher, had found Norton quite unfit to continue in office as governor. The many incidents of arbitrary arrest, extortion, greed and violence he had been accused of in the petition were substantiated, and after spending some time in gaol he had been dismissed early in 1701. He was succeeded by Lieutenant-Colonel Walter Hamilton.

The End of S. Christophe, 1702

The matters of contention between the French and the English, stemming from the state in which S. Christophe had been returned in 1697, had still not been resolved by the spring of 1701 when Codrington received warning of the possible start of another war with France. He immediately left Antigua for St Christopher, in order to spend the time before war was declared in getting the latter's defences in order. He remained there for several months, organizing the forts and drilling three standing companies of the militia, after persuading the Council and Assembly to agree to pay to keep them under arms. 'I can safely tell you', he reported to the Secretary of State in London in June after returning to Antigua, 'I have been not onely General but Engineer, Serjt. and Corprall.'9

The war of the Spanish Succession, as it came to be known, started in May 1702 with England and the Netherlands allied against France. Because it was so long expected, by the time the news reached the Caribbean in July Codrington had already returned to St Christopher. His preparations had all been made, and with armed men from Nevis and Antigua in addition to the three companies he had trained he was in a position to take immediate action. On 14 July, with Hamilton in command, troops were sent to present a show of force in both Capesterre and Basseterre, and Governor des Gennes was presented with a surrender demand. To the surprise of the English, and to the great chagrin of the inhabitants of S. Christophe, des Gennes showed no inclination to fight and signed articles of capitulation the following day. His supine response even gave Codrington pause for thought, causing him in his report to London to comment that the French did 'that over night which they were very much ashamed of next morning'. Under the terms of the surrender the French were once again all forced to leave for other French possessions. The disgraced des Gennes was summoned back to Paris to be court-martialled, but was taken prisoner by an English ship on the way and died before he could be tried.

This victory brought about the end of S. Christophe. After 1702 the English, having taken over the entire island twice in little over a decade, were no longer prepared to consider the possibility of ever sharing it again.

That they could no longer live in amity with the French on what from now on can be referred to as St Kitts was made very evident less than four years later.

The French Attack St Kitts, 1706

At the beginning of 1706 a fleet of 30 warships carrying about 2500 troops under the command of Comte Louis-Henri de Chavagnac, left France to carry to the Caribbean the sort of warfare which was then raging in Europe. On 13 February the fleet arrived off Nevis and began a bombardment of Charlestown in preparation for a landing. Fortunately for the inhabitants of the island, the return fire from Fort Charles, the prevailing sea conditions, a certain amount of confusion among the ships, and indecision on the part of de Chavagnac all conspired to prevent any troops from getting ashore.

Five days later, and presumably after de Chavagnac had had a chance to exert a little more authority, the attempt was abandoned and the fleet moved over to St Kitts. The ships and the troops were divided, and on 21 February simultaneous landings took place at Frigate Bay, Basseterre and Sandy Point. Despite the amount of warning the inhabitants must have had, all three landings were successful. As the Governor-General reported later, Hamilton and the militia were given 'such an amuzement as the enemy thereby without little or noe bloodshed on either side, soon became Masters of the Island except the Fort and Brimstone Hill'.[10] Brimstone Hill now came into its own. Following its use in the 1690 recapture of the island, it had been fortified and prepared as a refuge in the event of just such an invasion. It had filled up with the planters' families and other non-combatants soon after the French ships had been sighted off Nevis. When the same ships reached St Kitts, and put some 2000 troops ashore, Hamilton and his 700 or so defenders had little option but to seek refuge themselves, some on Brimstone Hill and the rest in nearby Charles Fort.

This left St Kitts completely at the mercy of the invaders, and for the next week the island was ravaged from end to end. The French stripped and burned the plantations, plundered Old Road and rounded up about 600 slaves. Over 300 plantations were affected, and it was later estimated that damage to the value of £145,000 had been caused. One plantation that was perhaps singled out for attention was that belonging to Joseph Crisp, the 'very gallant' and 'very stupid' President of the Council Codrington had used to bamboozle des Gennes with his 'eclærecssaiments'. The French not only destroyed his sugar works and 100 acres of cane, and went off with his slaves and livestock, but looted and then burnt down his stylish £1500 mansion. At the end of February de Chavagnac received word of the arrival in the Caribbean of another squadron of French ships, under the command of Pierre le Moyne d'Iberville. As de Chavagnac was subordinate to d'Iberville he quickly re-embarked his troops, forcing them to leave behind some of their booty, and left to join up with his superior at Martinique. There they combined their forces and planned the next invasion of an English possession.

The Attack on Nevis, 1706

The choice of an island to attack was not difficult to make: Nevis was still the most prosperous of the Leeward Islands, and de Chavagnac was able to supply more than enough information about its defences. When the combined French fleet of around 50 ships arrived there on 21 March no attempt was made to land at Charlestown or anywhere within range of Fort Charles. Instead, after confusing the inhabitants by sending ships to feint landings on other parts of the island, troops were put ashore on the south coast. Their landing was unopposed, as nearly all who were capable of offering any resistance were either in Fort Charles, or had withdrawn with their families to a fortified refuge halfway up the southern side of Nevis Peak (see Plate 5).

Later the same day, after a short three- or four-mile march from the landing place, the troops took possession of Charlestown and rounded up all the inhabitants as prisoners. D'Iberville was then able to demand the surrender of both Fort Charles and the mountain refuge by threatening his prisoners with death or being taken into slavery. His demand was met, and two days later a treaty of capitulation was signed. Under its terms the population of the island surrendered everything but the clothes they wore and the houses they lived in. All other property, including their slaves, was forfeit and to be seized as booty. The surrender was afterwards condemned by many both on and off the island. The officer in command of the militia, Colonel Thomas Abbott, was particularly put out by the number of his men who had taken themselves off to the refuge on Nevis Peak: 'Platforms will not fight themselves, [and I] could not pretend to fight their whole army myself. There was ne'er such an immorigrous [rebellious] people ever hatcht'.[11] The only men who did fight were those slaves who managed to avoid being captured by taking to the hills. They fought, not out of any loyalty to their owners or to the flag, but because they had no desire to repeat the whole trauma of being imprisoned, transported and then enslaved in an unknown place. In the end even their resistance proved no more than a futile gesture. When the French withdrew on 10 April they took with them well over 3000 slaves and a signed agreement from the planters to provide 1400 more or pay an indemnity of £42,000.

As well as seizing the slaves and a vast amount of plunder, the French also, as they had earlier in St Kitts, did an immense amount of wanton damage. Cane fields were burned, and nearly all the sugar works were destroyed after their mills and coppers had been dismantled and removed. It was later reported they had destroyed 'not only several boyeling houses, but the very dwelling houses themselves, not leaving at their going away above 20 standing on the whole island, the town excepted'.[12]

These French attacks on St Kitts and Nevis in the spring of 1706 proved to be turning points in the fortunes of both islands. The invasion of Nevis, which afterwards was calculated to have caused damage and losses to the value of £500,000, brought about the end of her supremacy. From then on, the island declined in comparison with St Kitts which, as a larger island with more fertile land and better resources, had more to offer investors and so recovered from the attentions of the French far more rapidly. But neither island was able to recover without assistance, and in 1711 Parliament voted £103,000 to indemnify those who had suffered. This represented only a fraction of the sums claimed: a total of £28,000 in St Kitts and £75,000 in Nevis.

The Condition of Anguilla

Both St Kitts and Nevis suffered greatly from the French invasions. Even though they had enough resources to ensure a fairly quick recovery, for some time in each island life for everyone, white and black, rich and poor, free and unfree alike, must have been very hard. For a time in both islands, conditions would then have resembled greatly those which had existed in Anguilla for the previous 50 years and which, to those living there, seemed set to continue indefinitely.

Most of the Anguillians had been forced into temporary exile following the French take-over in 1690, but before that life was so hard that many had wanted to leave permanently. The islands to the west were the most attractive, and in particular the one closest to Puerto Rico, now called Vieques, but then known as Bicque or Crab Island. In 1683 Stapleton had reported to London:

> I have been solicited by the inhabitants of Anguilla to let
> them settle Crab Island.... I refused for I feared that the

Spaniards and cow-killers of Puerto Rico might go and cut
them off in one night; but if two or three hundred men
could be found to put on it and build a redoubt there
would be no question of this settlement, for Anguilla is fit
for little but goats. But I was unwilling to scatter and
weaken the people.[13]

In spite of this a party under Abraham Howell went to Crab Island in the
same year, only to find they had left it too late. By the time they reached
the island it had already been claimed by the Danes, and they were forced
to leave.

Conditions on Anguilla deteriorated, if that were possible, after the
return of the refugees from Nevis in 1691. Cotton, by this time their only
commercial crop, suffered as a result of prolonged droughts, and from the
market being ruined by the war. Petitions sent to the Governor-General
asking to be re-settled somewhere other than Antigua, St Kitts, Nevis or
Montserrat were ignored. All that was left, other than subsistence farming,
was to turn to trading and smuggling – two activities with which Anguillians
were to be closely associated for the next 250 years or more. In 1701 the
younger Codrington complained to the Board of Trade and Plantations
about both Anguilla and Tortola, whose inhabitants he considered were

perfect outlaws and work together for the Danes and
Dutch which is impossible for me to prevent. Besides this
they serve for an intermediate mart or repository of
prohibited goods from St Thomas and Curaçao. I know
two or three little scoundrels have got ten thousand
pounds a man by the trade and still continue it through the
laziness, fearfulness or corruption of the Customs House
Officers, and I cannot be a searcher nor a watcher myself.[14]

One of these 'little scoundrels' may well have been the man who took
over from Howell as governor of Anguilla, George Leonard. It is hardly
likely that activities such as illegal trading, smuggling or the establishment
of even one warehouse full of prohibited goods could have taken place
without his involvement in some way. If so, he had more than sufficient
reason to want to enrich himself. Two or three years earlier he had left
Anguilla and, under circumstances which are far from clear but presumably
had much to do with the state of his finances, signed an indenture as a
servant to James Norton, then the Governor of St Christopher. 'After
which', as the court of inquiry looking into Norton's misdemeanours heard,

he was forced to work in the fields as a slave, almost naked
and half starved. Once or twice a week Col. Norton

caused him to be whipt in the pillory and the pickle of beef
brine to be put on his sores.[15]

What he had done to deserve such treatment, or how and when it ended,
are questions that – as with so many others to do with the early history of
Anguilla – are unlikely ever to be answered.

Under the sort of leadership provided by George Leonard, and considering the circumstances that prevailed in the island at the beginning of the
eighteenth century, it is hardly surprising that Anguilla was largely ignored
by the rest of the Leeward Islands, and its inhabitants considered to be no
more than poor, backward peasants. This view was made very apparent in
a report sent to the Board of Trade and Plantations in 1709 by Daniel
Parke, who had been appointed governor-general four years earlier:

> The Island kept no records whatever and no Ministerial
> Officer, Deputy Secretary or Council. Indeed there is a
> Deputy Governor, but they regard him not. They live like
> wild people without order or government and have neither
> devine nor lawyer among them. They take each others
> word in marriage, they think themselves Christian because
> they are descended from such, but I have got a parson to
> go to them lately out of charity, to make Christians out of
> them.[16]

1 Nevis from Mount Liamuiga, St Kitts

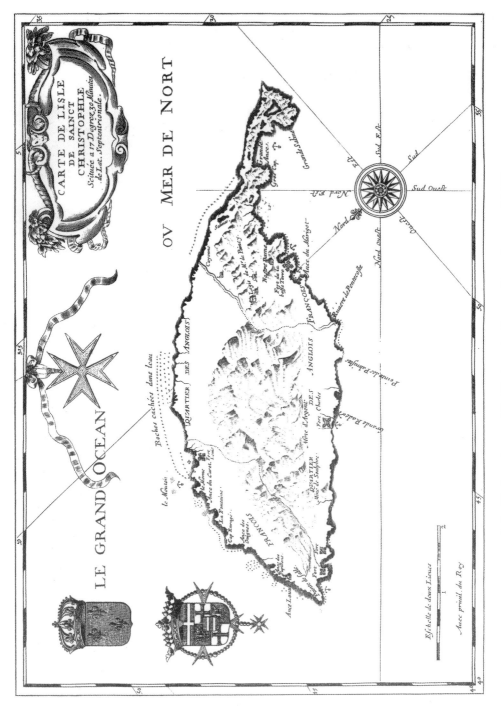

CARTE DE LISLE
DE SAINCT
CHRISTOPHLE
Scituée a 17 Degrez, 30 Minutes
de Lat. Septentrionale.

LE GRAND OCEAN

OV MER DE NORT

Eschelle de deux Lieues

Avec privil. du Roy

QUARTIER DES ANGLOIS

QUARTIER DES FRANCOIS

Mont de Soulphre

2 St Christopher: 'La S. Christophle' from a French map of 1657

3 The 'chateau' that never was: a European artist's fanciful impression of how de Poincy was supposed to live in S. Christophe

4 Frigate Bay and Sir Timothy's Hill, St Kitts, c.1950

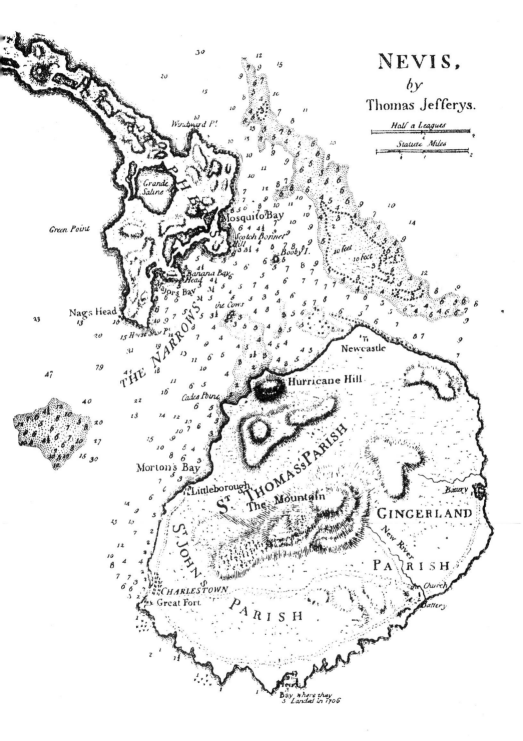

5 Nevis in the early eighteenth century

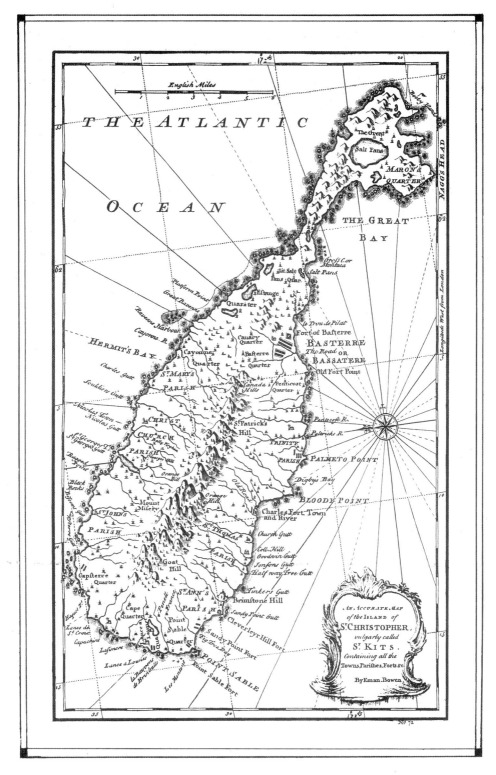

6 St Kitts in 1752

7 James Ramsay (1733–1789)

Published 31 Aug.ᵗ 1812, by Joyce Gold, Naval Chronicle Office, 103 Shoe Lane, London.

Brimstone Hill Island of Sᵗ Christopher

8 Brimstone Hill, St Kitts, in 1812

9 The Battle of St Kitts, 1782

10 Frances Nelson, née Woodward, who, as a young widow, met and married Horatio Nelson on the island of Nevis in 1787. The picture dates from around 1795.

11 Methodist Chapel, Charlestown, in 1802

12 Labourers' cottages in St Kitts, c.1920

13 Village life in St Kitts in the early twentieth century

15 Pall Mall Square, Basseterre, c.1900

16 Government House, Basseterre, 1904

17 The Court House, Basseterre, in 1920

18 Treasury Pier, Basseterre, 1955

19 Treasury Building, Basseterre, 1959

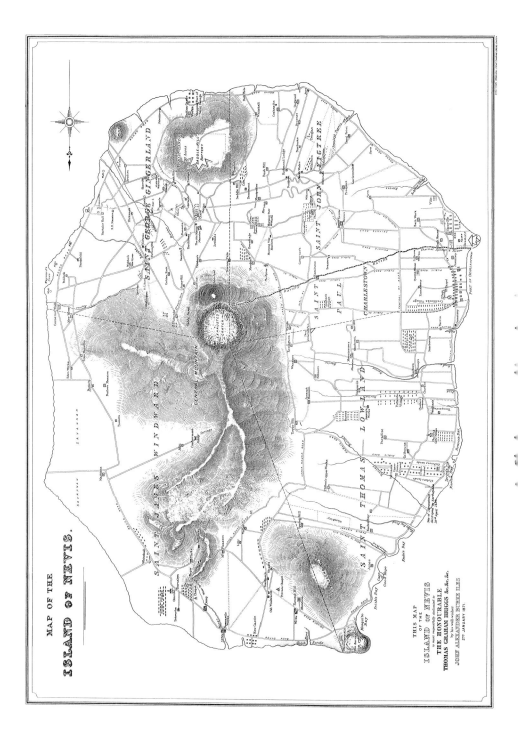

MAP OF THE
ISLAND OF NEVIS.

THIS MAP
OF THE
ISLAND OF NEVIS
is most respectfully dedicated to
THE HONOURABLE
THOMAS GRAHAM BRIGGS &c.&c.&c.
by his well wisher
JOHN ALEXANDER BURKE ILES
2ND JANUARY 1871.

10

Constructing a Plantation Society

Negotiations to bring the War of the Spanish Succession to an end took place in Europe in 1709 and again in the following year. Although on each occasion they broke down with nothing achieved, they did serve to indicate that the end of the war was in sight. This was of particular importance to the planters of St Kitts, who in April 1711 petitioned the Queen, stressing how much the island would be able to contribute to the Exchequer in the way of customs revenue after the war ended, provided the French were not allowed to return. Queen Anne, who had succeeded to the throne nine years earlier, was very sympathetic and recognized that the division of the island had been the cause 'of the effusion of much blood in the past'. When peace negotiations began at Utrecht in January 1712 the English delegates were instructed to demand retention of the whole of St Kitts as a condition of any settlement. This was eventually accepted by the French and, following the signing of the peace treaty in April 1713, St Kitts became an unequivocal British possession.[1]

Disposal of the Ceded Lands in St Kitts

This immediately raised the question of the disposal of the ex-French lands, which it was calculated amounted to 30,000 acres. Out of this the Board of Trade and Plantations, 'having discoursed with several planters and other persons well versed in the nature and state of St Kitts', considered all but 5000 acres were suitable for growing sugar. In 1714 the Board proposed that this be divided and sold in such a way as to attract the maximum number of new settlers. Most of it, 'divided into plantations...none exceeding 300, some of 250, 200 and 150, 100, 50 and some of 25 acres', would be sold only on the understanding that 'each grantee be obliged to cultivate the said lands in a certain limited time'. As for the remainder:

> it would be to the advantage of the settlement of that
> Island, that the poorer sort of inhabitants may have some
> parcels of the worst land near the seaside given them gratis,

> not above ten acres to ye most numerous family which will
> be a considerable strengthening of the island and a
> comfortable support to such poor people.[2]

In order to carry out the division of the land and to sell the lots, the Board proposed to send out 'Commissioners of known probity and ability not exceeding three with Surveyors under them'. In the meantime the former French quarters of Capesterre and Basseterre were to be divided into parishes, and membership of the Assembly increased accordingly.

The Board's proposals about disposing of the land were accepted in principle, but nothing was done about appointing the Commissioners or the necessary surveyors and, almost by default, the handling of the whole business fell to Walter Douglas, the man who had been made governor-general of the Leeward Islands in 1711. He made so many provisional grants to men who already owned large plantations that his successor, Walter Hamilton, complained in April 1716:

> I now come to the island of St Christopher's strictly in
> relation to the former French ground where I find that
> most part of the land has been granted by my predecessor,
> the former Governor, to several people but chiefly to the
> inhabitants of that island. This way of settlement will very
> little add to the strengthening of that island....[3]

These views were echoed the following year in letter sent to the Board of Trade and Plantations by a resident using a pseudonym. He complained:

> According to the present method of the Possessors (the
> richest Persons having large Quantities of Ground) they
> plant as long as the Grounds will bear without Husbandry,
> then leave them in a poor Condition, and proceed to take
> up Fresh Grounds, & by being in Favour with the
> Governours, they frequently got grants of what People of
> less Substance had made fertile.... There are few Families
> can manage above 200 Acres. Tho' some at present enjoy
> thrice that Quantity; And from thirty Years Experience I
> have observed; that Grants of large Quantities of Lands to
> Favourite Families have been the greatest Detriments to
> the Leeward Islands.[4]

If allowed to continue this would eventually lead to depopulation by driving the poorer people away. As it was 'the Tempers of the Suffering People have been so sour'd at this Usage, that above a hundred of them, have already left the Island'. Very little notice was taken of this or any similar complaint, and more and more smallholders, denied the prospect of bettering themselves while seeing rich men becoming richer yet, decided to sell up and leave. A visitor touring the island in 1719 observed how few remained: 'now and then we passed a small Cotton Settlement, whose humble and temperate Possessor, Hermit like, lived by virtue of his own and three or four Slaves labour'.[5] By 1721, when just over a third of all the land available had been distributed, only 19 out of the 134 provisional grants which had been made were for lots of less than ten acres. Out of all the other grants 45 were for anything between 200 and 523 acres.

The final disposition of the ceded lands did not take place for another five years, until after the appointment of the long-awaited three Commissioners. They promptly cancelled all the provisional grants and, with the use of a map which had been made for them by the Surveyor-General of Montserrat, began to auction the land in lots of not more than 200 acres. Most of it was sold in large 100–200-acre lots, and to planters who already owned estates in St Kitts or one of the other islands. The successful bidders for the areas which had been held under the provisional grants were, with very few exceptions, the same men who had held the grants. Three thousand acres, available in lots of ten acres or less, were set aside for the 'poorer sort of inhabitants' but not, as originally proposed, to be given away free. As a result only a fraction of this land found its way into the hands of the people it was intended for, and eventually most of it became incorporated into larger estates. The work of the Commissioners lasted nearly two years, finally coming to an end in March 1728, when they were able to inform the Board of Trade and Plantations 'that the sale of the French lands of St Christopher is just completed'.

A year earlier the government of the island had been transferred from Old Road to Basseterre, which then became the capital. It was still very small in extent, stretching no more than about a quarter of a mile along the shore, and a little more inland, but soon began to expand. The acquisition in 1750 of a large pasture immediately to the east assisted in the growth. The area around what was soon transformed into Pall Mall Square became desirable building land, and the town quickly doubled in size. Old Road's loss of status in 1727 did not immediately lessen its importance. It remained a busy port for at least another 20 years, and the legislature continued to meet there from time to time until around 1760.

At the time of the transfer there was no church in Basseterre, as the one which had been built in the previous century by the Jesuits (p.58 above) had been accidentally destroyed by fire in 1705. In 1730 the rector of the nearest church, Holy Trinity at Palmetto Point, complained to the Bishop of London:

> At Basseterre again is no place for ye public worship of
> God but a small hired room belonging to a private house,
> not sufficient to contain ye 3rd. part of ye audience and so
> exceedingly hot by reason of its smallness and ye lowness
> of roof that several persons are nearly ready to faint
> away…. The Church in Basseterre in ye French times is
> said to have been one of the fairest and best in ye West
> indies and it appears to have been so by ye walls and ruins
> yet remaining.[6]

His complaint did not go unheard, as within four years St George's Church had been erected on the French ruins and its first rector appointed.

In the opening years of the 1730s, with the entire island including the cultivable areas of the south-eastern peninsula now divided up into about 350 estates, St Kitts entered its golden age (see Plate 6). The white population stood at nearly 3900, a figure higher than it would ever be again, and the number of slaves had increased dramatically to well over 17,000. Sugar was the only product of any importance, and it was being exported at a rate of nearly 9000 tons a year. The planters were supported by rich merchants in Britain, and felt secure in the knowledge that with the aid of a powerful lobby in Parliament they also had the backing of the British government. No wonder in 1734 Sir William Mathew, who had taken over as governor-general two years earlier, felt called upon to remark that 'The improvement of this Island within Twenty Years past is very Extraordinary.'

The Prince of Orange Incident, 1737

Something else which Mathew might have considered 'very Extraordinary' was the most unfortunate incident which occurred three years later, soon after a slave ship, the *Prince of Orange,* had anchored off Basseterre. As was the usual practice, the cargo of slaves was brought on to the upper deck in order to let them recover from the transatlantic crossing for a few days before being offered for sale. The master of the ship, Captain Japhet Bird, later recorded what took place:

> on the 14th of March we found a great deal of discontent
> among the slaves, particularly the men which continued till

the 16th about five o'clock in the evening, when to our great amazement above an hundred men slaves jumped overboard....

This panic, it was later discovered, had been caused by a local slave, presumably accompanying his owner on a visit to look over the new arrivals. For no known reason, other than possession of a perverted sense of humour, he had managed to convey to the unfortunates on deck that after being landed they would have their eyes put out and then be eaten. The result was, in the captain's words: 'out of the whole we lost 33 of as good men slaves as we had on board, who would not endeavour to save themselves, but resolved to die and sunk directly down'. However, as far as he and the ship's owner were concerned, it could have been worse. They lost 33 slaves, but such was the demand that all those who were rescued, 'taken up almost drowned', were quickly sold. Although some of these did not last very long, their deaths, according to Bird, were 'not to the owner's loss, they being sold before any discovery was made of the injury the salt water had done them'.[7]

Contraction in Nevis

Mathew would have been hard pressed in 1734 to have said the same about Nevis as he did of St Kitts. In fact six years earlier, when he was still only the governor of St Kitts, he had reported to London 'that Nevis has quite lost its Trade, & is a desert Island to what it was Thirty Years ago', and nothing had taken place in the interim which would have changed this opinion. Very little else but sugar mattered by this time, and, in comparison with its neighbour as a producer, Nevis suffered from being much smaller and more prone to drought. In addition, as Mathew did remark in 1734, the island was 'Prodigiously Rocky and Stony': something which, even though 'the Earth between these Stones is Mostly Rich, and does not wear out and grow Barren as the Soil of Antigua or St Christopher's does', made the land very difficult to work.

Even though Charlestown had largely been spared from the ravages of the French in 1706, great harm was done to the life of the town, as the local minister recorded nearly twenty years later. In 1724 the rector of the parish church of St Paul's, the Reverend Robert Robertson, informed the Bishop of London that Charlestown consisted of

> About 70 Householders, with their Families, being in all (children included) near 300 Whites, whereof one 4th are Jews, who have a Synagogue here, and are said to be very

acceptable to the Country Part of the Island, but are far
from being so to the town, by whom they are charged with
taking the Bread out of the Christians' mouths. And this,
with the encouragement said to be given to the Transient
Traders above what is given to the Settlers, is by many
thought to be the true cause of the strange decay of this
place. At present there is not above 3 or 4 Christian
Families of Note in my Parish.... Formerly, I used to have
a congregation of 150 or more in the forenoon; now
seldom above 60 or 70, and many of the Seafaring or
Transient Persons....

Robertson provided this information as part of his reply to a question-
naire from the Bishop of London, which asked for information about
religion and church life from all the parish priests in the West Indies. With
regard to a question concerning the means used to convert the slaves it is
worth noting two of the replies he received from Nevis. Robertson said his
parish contained

Near 1000 Negro Slaves, and no means (or none fitted to
such an end) used for their conversion. Some attend their
Masters to Church. I have baptiz'd a few, and frequently
discoursed with some of the most sensible among them.
But that is nothing to what a work of this nature requires
– a work the difficulty whereof can hardly be credited by
any one who has not seen these Negroes, and conversed
with them for a competent time. And yet, hard as it
seems here, I know some Clergymen in these parts
tremble at the thoughts of what they own to be much
easier, how they shall be able to account at last for the
Christians, their chief (if not their sole) cure.[8]

At least he had given the matter some thought, and even if he had not done
very much for the souls of the slaves his reply betrays some sign of his
having this on his conscience. This was not something which bothered the
Reverend Henry Pope, the rector of St George's Gingerland on the opposite side of the island. His answer to the Bishop's question ran to a single
and not altogether rational sentence: 'We have a great Number of Slaves,
but most of them uncapable of the means of Conversion being natives of
Guinea'.[9]

The consolidation of smallholdings into large sugar estates which had
taken place in St Kitts had begun in Nevis even earlier, and by 1700 there
were no more than about 100 plantations on the whole island. The white

population, which had been around 3500 in 1660, by 1710 had fallen to about 1300, a figure which rarely if ever would be exceeded again. At the time of the French invasion in 1706 the slave population had been about 6000. Although those who were removed began to be replaced almost immediately, this figure was not reached again before the 1730s. Sugar production, which had been in excess of 3000 tons a year immediately prior to the French invasion, took even longer to recover and did not reach this figure again for the rest of the eighteenth century.

Struggling in Anguilla

Meanwhile, as the planters of St Kitts boomed and those of Nevis attempted, some more successfully than others, to catch up with them, the inhabitants (hardly planters) of Anguilla struggled along as best they could. As the eighteenth century progressed, the less was the interest taken in their affairs by the administration of the Leeward Islands, and the more they sought their own salvation. By 1716 the white population had increased to over 530 spread among nearly 90 households, and there were well over 800 slaves on the island. Only five householders did not own slaves; the rest had anything from one to 33 each. It is not without interest that those who owned the larger numbers bore names such as Howell, Hodge, Gumbs, Lake, Rogers and Richardson, all of which are still common in Anguilla today. The hankering to try life elsewhere was probably not as widespread by this time as it had been in the previous century, but for some the attraction of Crab Island (Vieques) had not decreased since Howell's failed venture in 1683 (p.79 above). The Anguillians who left to settle there in 1717 were no more successful. The Spanish, who long before had ended the Danish attempt to colonize the island, destroyed the settlement within a year.

Conditions on Anguilla at this time, and for many years to come, remained hard and very basic, and for the majority of the people life cannot have been too dissimilar for master and slave alike. Those who were not fully occupied in trying to scrape a living from the land went to sea, where a livelihood was to be obtained from fishing, trading or smuggling. The sort of society which developed was well summed up in 1734 in a report sent by Mathew to the Board of Trade and Plantations, in which he described the inhabitants as living 'like so many bandits, in open defiance of the laws of God and Man'. In order to try to improve matters, the following year he divided the island into three districts, The Valley, The Road and Joanshole (all three names reflecting the backwardness of the inhabitants), and introduced government in the form of a Council made up of two members nominated from each district. It was given none of the powers enjoyed by the Councils of St Kitts and Nevis and had no function other than to act as an advisory body to the governor.

Ten years later Anguilla became the only one of the three islands to be directly affected by the next conflict between Britain and France. This was the War of the Austrian Succession, which began in 1744. As far as Britain was concerned, this was a continuation of a war with Spain, the War of Jenkins' Ear, which had started five years earlier. In the Caribbean the outbreak of war in 1739 opened up the opportunity for rich pickings for privateers, and many local seafarers applied for and obtained the letters of marque necessary if they were not to be treated as pirates. Those sailing out of St Kitts did particularly well, as a merchant reported in 1744: 'We have ten Privateers already at Sea, and are fitting out four more; we flow in Money; a Division being lately made between one or two Privateers each man had £200.'[10]

During the same year two of these privateers sailed over to Anguilla, embarked the Governor, Arthur Hodge, together with most of the white male population, and from there launched an attack on the northern, French, half of neighbouring St Martin. Whether this achieved very much in the way of spoils is not known, as few details of the exploit were ever recorded. In any event it did the inhabitants of Anguilla very little good, as in May of the following year the French retaliated by invading the island. Fortunately for Hodge they landed on the leeward coast at Crocus Bay, which was overlooked by a high bluff. From this dominant position Hodge and his men, although greatly outnumbered, were able to repel the invasion. The French eventually withdrew, after having had more than 100 men killed, wounded or taken captive.

After the battered French invasion force had departed, Anguilla remained undisturbed for the next fifty years, a period during which only a slight improvement in the way of life took place. The first year in which sugar was produced was 1752. The amount must have been very small as in the same year it was recorded of the Anguillians that 'their chief product is tobacco, which has not enrich'd them, but they continue generally poor'. A small but reasonably thriving cotton industry existed at the same time. Salt, produced from ponds which were considered to be common property, began to be exported from around 1760.

Although this broadening of the economy led to an increase in the number of slaves, from less than 1000 in 1724 to over 2000 by 1770, the white population was less than 400 throughout this period. None of this activity did much to draw the island to the attention of anyone in the outside world except a few ship-owners, one or two merchants and, for good measure, individuals such as Malachy Postlethwayt, the author of *The Universal Dictionary of Trade and Commerce*. In an edition of this work, published in 1774, he said of Anguilla.

> They have no great quantities of sugar upon the island but
> addict themselves rather to farming, in which they had
> very good success: and this it is that enables them to live in
> the old patriarchal way, every man being a kind of
> sovereign in his own family, and no other Government
> there is in Anguilla.[11]

Other individuals who must have given Anguilla a passing thought from time to time were successive holders of the post of governor-general. All that one of these, Sir Ralph Payne, could add to Postlethwayt's comments in 1774 was that 'Very few of the Inhabitants of Anguilla can in any Degree be called opulent'.

Administration

Unlike Anguilla, St Kitts and Nevis by 1734 had each had a Council for over a hundred years, and their form of government was well established – as was their independence from each other. In 1723 John Hart, who had taken over as governor-general from Hamilton two years before, proposed a union of the two islands with a single Council and Assembly. Echoes of the reply he received from the Board of Trade and Plantations can still be heard ringing between the islands today:

> We can by no means think of advising His Majesty to do
> an act of this nature by the sole power of his Prerogative
> without the consent of the people. If the two islands are
> both of them convinced that it would be for their mutual
> convenience that such an union should be made between
> them, let their respective Councils and Assemblies address
> His Majesty for leave to make this alteration, which will
> bring this affair properly under his royal consideration,
> and in case the same should be approved of by His
> Majesty, they may then pass bills for this purpose.[12]

Hart knew better than to try to convince the legislature of either island to vote itself out of existence, and each continued to be administered by a governor (more properly a deputy- or lieutenant-governor, as he was subordinate to the captain-general or governor-in-chief of the Leeward Islands), a Council and an Assembly.

The Council, consisting of 12 'of the principal Planters and inhabitants' appointed by the Crown on the governor-general's recommendation, advised the latter in matters needing executive action and also functioned as a house of the legislature. The councillors were powerful men, as once appointed they could not be removed without very good reason, nor without first obtaining the approval of the Board of Trade and Plantations. The office of president of the Council was particularly important, as he assumed charge of the island in the absence of the governor.

The Assembly, which came into being in each island some years later than the Council, was the other house of the legislature. It was made up of two representatives from each parish, and met 'according to the custom and usage of the island'. In St Kitts an Act was passed in 1727 to enable representatives to be elected from those parts of the island which had previously been French, even though the additional parishes were not created for another six years. Retaining the names of the old French divisions, the parishes of St Paul Capisterre, St John Capisterre, St Peter Basseterre and St George Basseterre were demarcated in 1733. Representatives from these and the five original parishes were then elected by all the male residents who were white, Protestant, and in possession of ten acres of freehold land or a house and land to the value of £10 a year. Very similar conditions were attached to the franchise in Nevis.

As an elected body the Assembly was difficult for the governor to control, as he could neither nominate anyone for, nor suspend anyone from, membership. The only action he could take in the event of the Assembly passing legislation with which he disagreed, was to refuse his assent, or to prorogue the sitting. Neither course could be taken lightly, as the running of the island depended on money bills passed by the Assembly and these could be withheld in reprisal. As time went by, all the Leeward Island governors, not just those of St Kitts and Nevis, ran into problems with their Assemblies, something which in 1770 caused the Governor-General to complain that there was a 'growing Disposition in the Assemblies of these Islands to extend their privileges beyond what...[is] consistent with the nature of their Establishment and the intention of the Government'.[13] The Assembly of St Kitts, which by this time was elected by a tiny number of voters, was particularly culpable. Two years earlier, immediately after an election and in order to prevent the Council from having any say in the composition of the Assembly, its members had passed a resolution to exclude councillors from voting in elections. This was then used to disqualify the votes which had been cast by Council members, and three new representatives were ejected from the Assembly. The row which followed after seven more assemblymen had walked out in disgust showed only too clearly the sort of rancorous and narrow-minded men the island had as its legislators. The remaining representatives, who could hardly form a quorum, had the dissident members imprisoned for two weeks and then expelled. Although the same seven were later re-elected, the dispute rumbled on until 1772 when the Privy Council affirmed the right of councillors to vote. In the letter informing the Governor-General of this decision the Board of Trade and Plantations instructed him 'to keep the Assembly of St Christopher's more within the legal bounds of a Provincial Council and to hinder them from usurping authorities inconsistent with the peace and good order of the said island'.[14]

No guidance was forthcoming in how he was to do this, and nor would any have been possible given the way in which the Assembly was formed. Membership for years had been restricted to a very small group of people. In 1746 nearly half the Assembly consisted of six brothers and one of their nephews, all named Phipps. Thirty years later elections were even more farcical, so much so that in 1768 the Council noted that the ridiculously small size of the electorate had 'thrown the Elections in some parishes into the hands of two or three People so that the Assembly is in Danger of becoming a Junto, influenced by the private views of a few individuals'. The situation was made even worse by a system in which a man could vote in every parish in which he held the required minimum freehold. In the elections of 1768 and 1770, the vote of Samuel Crooke determined the election of three members. He was the only freeholder among 46 men in St Mary, Cayon, and in 1772, because he died before the election, this parish did not return a member, 'there being no Freeholder to poll'. A year later the vote of his son was responsible for the election of no less than five members of the Assembly.[15]

The composition of the legislature in both islands had been amended by this time, with the membership of the Assembly increased to 24 in St Kitts and 15 in Nevis, and the number of councillors reduced to ten and seven respectively. Regardless of these reductions to the Council it became increasingly difficult to find men suitable for nomination during the latter half of the eighteenth century. In 1773 the Governor-General, Sir Ralph Payne, complained of his inability to find men of any standing to nominate for vacancies in the Council of Nevis, 'or in prevailing with them to undertake an office of trouble, which neither produces profit, nor creates public interest or importance'.[16] Seven years later his successor, Sir William Burt, reported a similar problem with finding enough men suitable for the Council of St Kitts. The reason why there was such a dearth of public-spirited men of probity was made all too clear in a letter written by the Chief Justice of St Kitts in March 1798. This was addressed to the Secretary of State for Home Affairs, whose department had assumed responsibility for colonial matters after the Board of Trade and Plantations had been abolished in 1782. Although the letter referred only to St Kitts, its contents could equally well have applied to Nevis:

> This Island, my Lord, among the many distinguishing
> Advantages, which it possesses over her Sister Colonies,
> from her preeminent Fertility, has this singular melancholy
> Consequence to lament, 'that all the Land Proprietors are
> settled in Great Britain which has produced a Substitution
> of the most ignorant of the English, Scotch and Irish as
> their Attorneys and Managers'; Your Grace will
> consequently be at no loss to Conclude that our Branches
> of Legislature are not composed of very respectable
> Members.[17]

It was very much the same small group of men who ran the local government of each island. This was based on the parishes where vestry boards, elected by the local freeholders, were responsible for things such as poor relief, the appointment of town wardens, and the upkeep of roads and bridges. In each parish the most important men, apart from the rector who sat on the board as of right, were the churchwardens. These were elected from among the vestrymen and were responsible for the collection and management of the parish taxes. Given the small number of freeholders in most of the parishes, and the general scarcity of disinterested men, it is hardly likely that many vestrymen were without some connection to either the Council or the Assembly in both St Kitts and Nevis.

The Stamp Act Riots and other Disturbances

The sort of society from which the Council and Assembly members of St Kitts and Nevis were drawn during the second half of the eighteenth century was made all too obvious in a series of events beginning in 1765. A year previously the British Parliament had passed an Act imposing stamp duties on all the colonies, in order to cover part of the cost of their defence. This was something which would later become a major issue in the American Revolution, but at the time, especially as it imposed a high rate of duty on land transfers, it was a greater burden on the West Indian islands. Although it was unpopular and much resented in all the islands, the only resistance to its imposition occurred in St Kitts and Nevis.

At the end of October 1765, on the eve of the introduction of the duty, a large-scale riot involving about half the adult white population of St Kitts took place in Basseterre. An organized and well-planned demonstration involving a protest march and the burning of effigies soon deteriorated into violence and the destruction of property. The stamp agent for St Kitts and Nevis, William Tuckett, and the local merchant who acted as his distributor in Basseterre were assaulted and threatened with hanging, and £2000 worth of stamps were burned. Tuckett managed to rescue the remainder of his stock, and escaped with it overnight to his home island of Nevis.

News of his escape incensed the rioters, and the next day, before he could deposit the stamps with the local distributor, he found many of them had sailed across and were baying for his blood in Charlestown. In the riot which followed, several buildings were burned, together with the remaining stamps and other property, and Tuckett was fortunate to escape with his life. In early December he informed the Governor-General, 'I dare not go to St Kitts...as I have been advised by my Friends there that I shall certainly be assassinated if I attempt it'.

He was undoubtedly right to remain where he was, as feelings had continued to run high in St Kitts throughout the previous month. His effigy and that of his deputy were burnt on 5 November following another noisy procession through Basseterre, his correspondence was intercepted, and at the end of the month demonstrators prevented a new supply of stamps from being landed. That all of this met with widespread approval was shown by a total lack of response to the offer of a reward made by the Governor-General for information about those responsible for instigating the riots. Fortunately for all concerned, the Stamp Act was repealed in the following February. The news of this was received with 'great rejoicing' in St Kitts, and no doubt with great relief by Tuckett.

A similar episode, and one which illustrated that the general condition of white society and the quality of its leadership were, if anything, even worse than they had been nearly twenty years earlier, took place in St Kitts in 1784. Another riot broke out in Basseterre towards the end of the year. This time the fury of those leading it was directed on the island's customs officers, following a lengthy period of dissatisfaction about their enforcement of the new customs regulations introduced at the end of the American War of Independence (see Chapter 12). Even though considerable violence took place, and at least one officer was tarred and feathered, the Assembly refused to condemn the action or to offer a reward for information about those responsible. That the riot had met with wide approval, both inside and outside the Assembly, was made evident later after those responsible for instigating it had been identified. A bill of indictment prepared by the Attorney-General was dismissed by a Grand Jury, and it was found impossible to bring the ringleaders to justice.[18]

11

Maintaining Plantation Societies

By the third quarter of the eighteenth century St Kitts was the richest colony in the British Empire. Raw sugar, which had sold in Britain for less than £20 a ton in the 1730s, now averaged over £50 a ton. It had long been obvious that it was more profitable to grow sugar on a large scale, and the wealthiest planters were those whose estates had been increased by buying out their smaller and less successful neighbours. By 1775 the best land sold for £100 an acre, and there were no more than about 120 proprietors, with a total worth of £4,000,000 (the equivalent of £300,000,000 in the year 2002). Although many of them did not stay on the island once they had made a fortune, those that did made sure they lived in style. A Scotswoman, Janet Schaw, who visited the island in 1774, has left a description of the house at Olivees plantation near Basseterre, owned by her host and hostess:

> The elegance in which they live is not to be described.... This hall and every thing in it is superbly fine; the roof lofty, and ornamented in a high degree. It is between fifty and sixty feet long, has eight windows and three doors all glazed; it is finished in Mahogany very well wrought, and the panels finished in with mirrors.... The drawing room and bed-chambers are entirely fitted up and furnished in the English taste...[It] is esteemed the finest house on any of the Islands....[1]

It was very much the same in Nevis, although climatic conditions and land formation made sugar production rather more difficult. The main body of planters prospered, if not all to the same degree as those on St Kitts, and gradually increased their land holdings at the expense of the less successful. This process of amalgamation continued rather longer in Nevis where, between 1770 and 1800, the number of proprietors was reduced from about 60 to less than 40.

Absenteeism

Non-resident plantation owners were not common before the middle of the century, but after that time more and more proprietors, as they made their fortunes, became absentee landlords. Their prosperity enabled them first of all to educate their children abroad, then to be able to afford properties in Britain to which, sooner or later, they could retire. In 1770 the legislature of St Kitts, in an address to the Crown, reported 'Very few of the Proprietors of Estates reside in this Island, but have retired with their Families to Europe'. It was same, if not worse, in Nevis. Successive owners of one of the largest plantations in the south-west had not lived on the island since the end of the previous century. This was the Jennings and Balls Range Estate, over 600 acres in size, owned by the descendants of the early Governor, William Stapleton.

In the absence of their owners such plantations were supervised by resident attorneys. Each of these, in return for a salary or more usually a commission on the annual yield of the plantation, assumed control over all financial and commercial activities connected with its operation. The plantations themselves were run by salaried managers with the assistance of overseers. The sort of men needed to fill these positions, if such estates were to be run profitably, were not found in great numbers in the society of either island and many had to be hired abroad. In April 1794 the Stapletons' attorney in Nevis informed the then proprietor, a Welsh clergyman:

> The estate very much wants two good overseers. They
> must be young men, brought up as Farmers, and who can
> read & write – indented for four or five years – Wages
> about twenty or twenty five pounds Sterling, being found
> in Bed, board & washing.[2]

As a result of the employment of such 'young men' as overseers, and some of their more mature fellow-countrymen as managers, not only were many plantations operated inefficiently, but the same men assumed places in the society of the islands far removed from those they would have occupied in Britain. In 1774 Janet Schaw noted that St Kitts was 'almost abandoned to overseers and managers'. Twenty-four years later the Chief Justice of St Kitts, in his diatribe to the Secretary of State for Home Affairs (p. 92), complained of the 'most ignorant' men who were being made plantation managers. As he saw it, even though they were without 'accomplishment of good Breeding, or urbanity of Manners', they 'affect Independence' and 'aspire to Importance'.

One man who possibly may have been more acceptable to the Chief Justice was William Davis who, in 1788, after many years managing plantations in both St Kitts and Nevis, had been made attorney to Lord Romney, the owner of a large estate near Old Road. Three years later, having now decided he wished to enter holy orders, Davis paid a brief visit to England. The state of the clergy in the West Indies was such that soon after his arrival, and without much if anything in the way of training, his wish was granted. The shortage of West Indian priests was so great that 'on the same day [he] was made Deacon and ordained Priest by the Bishop of London in the Chapel Royal St. James' Palace', something which has been categorized as 'unusual but not unprecedented'.[3] After his return to St Kitts he resumed his position as the Romney attorney, while assisting the beneficed clergy until being given his own parish in 1807.

The absence of so many of the proprietors not only changed the make-up of society but brought about a weakening of community feeling and a decline in public spirit. In each island, with too many mediocre men in the Assembly, the parish organization began to deteriorate and little effort was put into public works. The latter was well illustrated by the indifference shown to the undignified way in which visitors were forced to enter the islands, as described by someone arriving at St Kitts in 1774:

> We landed by a boat from one of the ships nearest the
> town, but had a third Voyage to make, which was on the
> back of Negroes, and tho' there was not a breath of wind,
> we were much wet and incommoded by the Surge.[4]

Even so, a proper landing place in the form of a pier was not to be built in either Basseterre or Charlestown before the beginning of the second half of the next century. Public buildings and the estate houses now occupied by managers were not maintained, roads and bridges fell into disrepair, and churches lost most of their congregations.

As the churches became less well attended the clergy were tempted to neglect parochial duties in favour of other pursuits. Another priest who, like Davis, considered he could serve both God and Mammon, was the Reverend Samuel Harman, rector of one of the Nevis parishes, whose father was manager of the largest Stapleton plantation. In November 1799, following the death of his father, Harman wrote an unctuous letter to the owner of the plantation, his fellow cleric the Reverend William Shipley, Dean of St Asaph. After informing the Dean that he was in 'the Profession of a Clergyman of the Church of England', and in a manner worthy of Trollope's Obadiah Slope, he came to the point:

> Upon the death of my poor Father Mr Thomson [attorney
> of the Stapleton estates in St Kitts] has been pleased to
> place my younger Brother, who is now of age, in the
> direction and management of your Property, under my
> immediate inspection and superintendence....You will, I

believe...receive some further mention of me from Mr
Thomson and should you thence be induced to honour me
with appointment as your Attorney in this Island, you
may rely that I shall be animated by the example of my late
Father, in order to procure to myself a transfer of that
approbation, which you have so repeatedly expressed of
his conduct.[5]

He had no doubt that he was suitable for the position, being 'intimately
acquainted' with the Dean's property, just as he was sure that 'while much
of my time and attention may be employed in your service, my mind will
not be too much abstracted from my necessary Parochial duties'.

It might have been expected that at this time, at the height of a period
now known as the 'Age of Enlightenment', such parochial duties could
well have included the encouragement of learning, but this was far from
the case. At the end of the eighteenth century little more thought was
given to education in either Nevis or St Kitts than had been since they
were first settled. In 1724 the rector of St Paul's in Charlestown had
informed the Bishop of London:

The Parish Clerk...has sometimes taught Reading. Writing,
& arithmetic, but he grows old and infirm, & can't do it now,
notwithstanding his numerous family. Neither has it been
worth his or any Body's while, these last twelve years to
teach school here. Several have attempted it, but they always
failed in Two or Three Months.[6]

Similar attempts to establish schools, purely of course for white children,
had taken place since in both islands, but none had lasted very long.

Slave Society

Given the size of St Kitts and Nevis, the wealth generated by their planters
during the latter half of the eighteenth century was extremely impressive,
but it was made only at the cost of untold human suffering. The operation
of a profitable sugar plantation entailed a most brutal regime for the slaves.
Working hours were from dawn to dusk every day, except for Sunday and
every other Saturday, with daily breaks of half an hour for breakfast and
two hours at midday. During harvest time work was continuous. Milling
and boiling continued around the clock, and the slaves worked in shifts
which could last for as long as 16 to 18 hours. The only holidays granted
were at Christmas, Easter and Whitsuntide.

On any plantation only about half of the slaves would be field hands, the other half being made up of artisans, servants, herdsmen, the old and frail, and very young children. The field hands were divided into three groups. The big gang, consisting of the most able-bodied, and frequently made up of more women than men, did all the hard work of clearing, hoeing, planting and harvesting. The second gang, made up of adolescent boys and girls, convalescents and pregnant women, did lighter work such as weeding. The small gang contained young children who cut grass or tended stock. None was trusted to work without close supervision. A trusted elderly female slave was usually in charge of the small gang but, as Janet Schaw noted in 1774, carefully selected male slaves were employed to keep a close eye on the other two gangs:

> The Negroes who are all in troops are sorted so as to
> match each other in size and strength. Every ten Negroes
> have a driver who walks behind them, holding in his hand
> a short whip and a long one. You will too easily guess the
> use of these weapons; a circumstance of all others the most
> horrid. They are naked, male and female, down to the
> girdle, and you constantly observe where the application
> has been made.[7]

The reason they wore only a minimum of clothing had nothing to do with heat, lack of shame, or that they or their ancestors were originally from a part of the world where not too many clothes were worn, but merely from the fact that it was all they possessed. Up until 1798 the only clothing an owner was legally obliged to provide was a jacket and trousers for each man and a wrapper and petticoat for each woman, or 'one suit of woolen, and one suit of [coarse linen] Osnaburghs, annually'. Only the more important slaves, such as artisans, got an allowance of hats and shoes.

As well as clothing his slaves, a planter also needed to provide them with somewhere to live. In order to retain as much control as possible over their lives, whether they were working or not, the slave accommodation was always in the vicinity of the sugar works and the estate house, sited where it would give the least offence to the inhabitants of the latter. This was made clear in a description of the Nevis plantations written in 1745:

> They [the slaves] live in Huts, on the Western Side of our
> Dwelling-houses, so that every Plantation resembles a
> small Town....we breath the pure Eastern Air, without
> being offended with the least nauseous smell: Our
> Kitchens and Boyling-houses are on the same side, and for
> the same reason.[8]

The huts were normally very simple affairs, 'composed of Posts in the Ground, thatched round the Sides and upon the Roof, with boarded Partitions'. There was some improvement as time went by, but probably less on Nevis than on St Kitts, where in 1790 it was stated that 'many of the better kind of Negroes...have timber houses regularly boarded and shingled'.

Plantation slaves were also provided with the basic medical care, and a small weekly ration of food, made up at the most of 9 pints of flour, corn or peas together with 8 herrings or other salted fish. This was because, in addition to producing sugar, they were expected grow most of their own food, and initially a reasonably large tract of land in the vicinity of the sugar works was set aside on each plantation for the growing of provisions. However, as time went by, these provision grounds were taken over for the growing of sugar. After the middle of the century the only locally grown foodstuffs came from gardens made by the slaves either in the ghuts or, as most ran 'from the sea into the clouds', in the upper parts of the plantations. Fewer such provisions were grown on Nevis than St Kitts, as the planters refused to use the upper parts of the plantations for anything but sugar. With the island being susceptible to drought, it was felt complete dependence could not be placed on the lower reaches of an estate to produce a worthwhile, profitable crop of cane.

Even on the lowlands of Nevis the planting of cane was difficult enough. The soil was very fertile, more so than that of St Kitts, but the work for men and women whose only tools were hoes and machetes, was made even harder by the rocks and stones which constantly had to be cleared from the land. Such obstacles were not a problem on St Kitts, but labour of the slaves was made just as onerous, if not more so, by the quality of the soil. This was loose and porous, and needed constant additions of organic matter in order to retain its fertility:

> But tho' perhaps there is no such rich land in the world as
> in this Island, they use manure in great abundance... No
> planter is above attending to this grand article, which is
> hoarded up with the utmost care....[9]

Everything from animal dung and cane trash to ashes, bones and spoilt provisions was used, and the pieces were prepared for planting by manuring at a rate of anything up to 80 tons an acre. All of this was carried and spread by the slaves, even if not always in the manner noted at Olivees plantation by Miss Schaw in 1774:

> When they are regularly Ranged, each has a little basket,
> which he carries up the hill filled with manure and returns

> with a load of canes to the Mill. They go up at a trot and
> return at a gallop, and did you not know the cruel
> necessity of this alertness, you would believe them the
> merriest people in the world.[10]

In fact manuring was probably the most hated task of all, and on many
plantations the contents of such a 'little basket', designed to be carried on
the head, often weighed 50 or 60 pounds (*c.*25 kg).

The dung which formed the bulk of the fertilizer, used in Nevis as
well as St Kitts even if not to the same extent, came from the animals,
cattle and mules that were needed for haulage and, on many plantations
throughout the century, for powering the mill.[11] These were kept in
large pens which, because it was more convenient for the estate's overseers, were invariably sited on the lower parts of the plantation. The
gathering of fodder was an additional task for the slaves, each one being
required to collect in their own time either at midday or in the evening,
a certain amount each day. This out-of-hours 'grass-picking', as it was
known, together with constant *uphill* carriage of heavy loads of manure,
were the two tasks most resented by the slaves, and illustrate only too
well the inhumanity which pervaded plantation life. For a proprietor
such as Dean William Shipley, and his attorneys in St Kitts and Nevis,
the well-being of the slaves was of little more consequence than that of
the plantation animals. 'The Negroes and Stock are all well', Shipley was
informed by his Nevis attorney in April 1794. 'Your Negroes & Stock
are healthy & in good Order', echoed his colleague in St Kitts a month
later.[12]

Not all the slaves were plantation workers by any means in either
St Kitts or Nevis. Many were owned by merchants and other towns-
people, and employed as servants, porters, coachmen or artisans. In
general, although by no means invariably, their work was easier and they
led rather better lives than the plantation slaves. Some of the artisans were
hired out by their owners, while others were allowed to find work for
themselves and pay their owners a fixed daily or weekly amount. The most
industrious of these often could then accumulate enough money to buy
their freedom.

There were not too many who managed to do this, but those that did
joined other men and women manumitted voluntarily by their owners, to
slowly increase the population of ex-slaves in each island. The achievement
of freedom did not bring with it any great improvement in status, or a possibility of moving up in society, and 'free Blacks' were subject to all sorts
of restrictions. It did mean, however, that they were no longer subject to
all the laws which had regulated their lives as slaves.

The Treatment of Slaves

Various Acts to control the slaves began to be passed in both St Kitts and Nevis during the seventeenth century, but true slave codes, designed to regulate their lives, fix their relationship with their masters and the rest of white society, and to lay down a scale of punishments for various offences, did not appear before the early decades of the next century. Comprehensive slave acts were passed in St Kitts in 1711 and 1722, and in Nevis in 1717. These were mainly concerned with the apprehension and control of runaways, but contained clauses covering the general government of all slaves. The wording of the preamble to the Nevis Slave Act, citing 'the insupportable Insolencies, Outrages, Thefts, and Robberies' committed by runaway slaves as the main reason for its passing, gives some idea of the tenor of the regulations and punishments to be found in all three pieces of legislation.

Under these Acts, as well as dealing with the treatment of runaways, provision was made for the punishment of slaves who were involved in planning a rebellion, who struck or killed a white person, who stole, or who were involved in any of the other activities which the Acts now made illegal. These included possession of arms, holding secret meetings, communicating by beating drums or blowing horns, and even leaving their plantations without written permission. The punishments, which ranged from flogging through dismemberment to death, could be awarded by a court made up of two or more justices acting without a jury. Further orders and regulations to control the slaves could be drawn up by the justices as they saw fit. As time went by such additions, in conjunction with amendments to the original acts passed by the legislature, created a legal code in each island intended to control every aspect of slave life.

In the middle of the eighteenth century the Solicitor-General of the Leeward Islands, John Baker, spent a considerable amount of time in St Kitts. The diary he kept there provides numerous insights into many aspects of island life, not the least of which are those concerning his or other peoples' slaves. The casual way in which slaves were punished, and the low value which was placed on their lives, are both very apparent throughout the diary, as a representative selection shows:

> *April 11* [1752]   Tried Mr. R.P.'s negro Will for breaking open his drawer and stealing about £60 out. Condemned and hanged.

> *September 8* [1753]   Mr. Wharton's overseer found strangled this morning in a tub.

> *September 10*   Mr. Wharton's negro man, Devonshire, tried and hanged for killing Runnells, his master's Overseer.

February 21 [1755]   A mulatto child of Samuel Mathews, the mason, left alone (about a year old) part eat and killed by the rats in the night.

August 8   Gave Othello a severe whipping for lying out, and Tycho a good smart one for concealing it.

October 2   This morning a negro child...found drowned in a tub of water, with its head down and heels up, how long they knew not; but brought to life by lighting a pipe of tobacco and sticking the small end in its fundament, and blowing it at the bowl.

November 3   Afternoon tried Mr. Gallwey's Chocolate for for theft.

November 4   Chocolate hanged and thrown in the sea.[13]

Dismemberment or mutilation as a punishment was common until it was banned towards the end of the eighteenth century. It took until 1783 for the legislature of of St Kitts to decide such practices were 'contrary to the principles of humanity and dishonourable to society', and to pass an Act 'to prevent the Cutting off or depriving any Slaves in this Island of any of their Limbs or Members or otherwise disabling them'. The penalty for anyone continuing the practice was a fine of £500 or a six-month gaol sentence. In spite of this, the perpetrators of two acts of mutilation which took place the following year got off with much smaller fines. One man, Jordan Burke, was fined £50 for cutting off the ear of a female slave, and another, Wadham Strode, £100 for removing the ear of a male slave. These lesser punishments resulted from being tried under common – as opposed to criminal – law, as each maintained the offences had taken place before the new law had been passed.

Cases such as those involving Burke and Strode drew attention to the difficulties of bringing prosecutions against owners or managers who maltreated, or even murdered, slaves. The evidence of slaves against whites was not accepted in court, and no jury was ever prepared to condemn one of their own to suffer more than a nominal punishment for injuring what, in their eyes, was no more than his own property. At the same time, this was not a state of affairs viewed with equanimity by every white person.

James Ramsay

The Reverend James Ramsay (see Plate 7) was in a tiny minority with his views, and a lone voice among the clergy of St Kitts, when in 1784 he condemned the situation in no uncertain terms:

> Our laws, indeed, as far as they respect slaves, are only
> licenced modes of exercising tyranny on them, for they are
> not parties to them though their lives and feelings be
> concluded by them. As well may directions for angling be
> said to be laws for dumb fish, as our colony regulations for
> whipping, hanging, crucifying, burning the blacks, be
> called laws made for slaves.[14]

Ramsay was born in Scotland in 1733, and had served for six years as an
assistant surgeon in the Royal Navy before being ordained in 1762. He
was sent to St Kitts by the Bishop of London in the same year, and was
given charge of two parishes, Christ Church Nicola Town and St John's
Capisterre. No sooner had he settled in than he began to take a keen interest in the spiritual welfare and general well-being of the slaves. In order to
convert them he invited them to attend his churches for instruction in the
Christian faith at certain times on Sundays, or to visit him at home on
other days. His actions did not meet with great success as most of the
slaves made it known they would have 'nothing to do with the prayers of
white people', but the mere fact of his having attempted to convert them
made him a pariah among the whites.

He remained in St Kitts, doing what he could for the slaves in the face
of 'unremitting persecution, bitter abuse, and even threats of assassination'
until 1777. After serving for three years as a naval chaplain he returned to St
Kitts, but only remained for a few months before leaving the island for ever
in August 1781. Three years later in England he published *An Essay on the
Treatment and Conversion of African Slaves in the British Sugar Colonies,* a
book which was widely praised in Britain but which, as might have been
expected, opened a campaign of vituperation and vilification against the
author in the West Indies which was to last until his death in 1789. In the
Saint Christopher Gazette of 20 November 1784 his *Essay* was alleged to be
a 'very impertinent, illiberal and unjust general reflection' on an island
where he had been 'as happily situated as imagination could well paint' and
he deserved 'punishment for such a libel on the colony'.[15] All such abuse
was groundless and in the end to little avail. Ramsay's detractors have all
long been forgotten, while his *Essay* lives on as a pioneering abolitionist
work, and he himself is remembered as a humanitarian in the mould of
Wilberforce and Clarkson.

Slave Resistance

The slaves demonstrated resistance to their condition from the beginning,
and in a variety of ways. It included suicide, as among those men who had

drowned themselves off the *Prince of Orange* in 1737, and murder, as committed by 'Mr. Wharton's negro man, Devonshire' in 1753, but was mostly confined to malingering and running away. Resistance in the form of a revolt was the method most feared by the white population, and as a result anything out of the ordinary which took place among the slaves was viewed with great suspicion. A number of incidents took place in St Kitts and Nevis during the eighteenth century which may have been plots to bring about slave uprisings, but in all likelihood were nothing but manifestations of white fear.

The first such 'plot' was detected in Nevis in 1725, at a time when many of the slaves were suffering malnutrition as a result of a prolonged drought. The main evidence came from a slave informing his owner of overhearing talk among his fellows of a rising, and of their appointment of leaders. Whether true or not, and with no further investigation, when this was reported it was immediately assumed by the authorities to be evidence of a conspiracy 'to cut off all the whites, and to take the island for themselves'. Following a round-up of the alleged conspirators, two were immediately burnt alive 'without any confessional material', and the rest put in gaol.

In March 1770 the planters of St Kitts became convinced that they were in danger from 'a grand plan, laid by the Negroes…to cut off every white man on the island'. Supposedly evolved at secret meetings, and led by a slave known as Archy, the 'plan' was to be put into effect with 'a piece of lead handed from one Negroe to the other' after they had rendezvoused on Monkey Hill. Fortunately for Archy and 15 other slaves, Governor William Woodley was not as hasty as the Governor of Nevis had been in 1725, and merely had them arrested while the matter was investigated. A week or so later he was able to inform London that the 'plan' had been

> nothing more than a Meeting every Saturday night of the
> Principle Negroes belonging to Several Estates in one
> quarter of the Island called Palmetto Point, at which they
> affected to imitate their Masters and had appointed a
> General, Lieutenant General, a Council and Assembly and
> the other Officers of Government, and after holding Council
> and Assembly they Concluded the night with a Dance.[16]

Further 'plots' in St Kitts were detected a few years later. In 1776 there was a large fire in Basseterre, causing some £200,000 worth of damage, and smaller ones on two or three plantations. Together, particularly as the town fire was widely believed to be arson, these were taken to be evidence of another uprising being planned by the slaves. The President of the

Council requested help from the navy, but no more evidence of a plot was then found than was at the next scare two years later. In the spring of 1778 St Kitts was placed under martial law for several days because of a rumour which circulated of an intention by the slaves 'to murder the Inhabitants' on Easter Sunday and afterwards 'to deliver the Island to the French, or any Persons who would make them free'.[17]

The failure of these 'plots', if indeed they were plots and not just the fearful imaginings of the whites, does not mean that the slaves, in Nevis as much as in St Kitts, were not prepared to continue to use and refine other less dramatic forms of resistance. Two methods which were employed almost universally were mockery of white people and malingering, each of which had been practised since the earliest days of slavery and developed into a fine art.

Mockery took place everywhere and whether the slaves were at work or not. It took many forms, ranging from rounds and songs in the cane fields, rendered in an African language or a thick patois, to elaborate ceremonies such as those which were enjoyed by Archy and his comrades on Saturday nights at Palmetto Point. That which took place within sight and hearing of white people was made all the sweeter by the knowledge that such observers, content to believe that singing and dressing-up merely demonstrated the child-like nature of the slaves, had no idea that they were the objects of derision.

The term 'malingering' can be used to cover all the other well-established, well-polished and widely practised methods of passive resistance. As plantation slaves had no possible economic incentive to work, their general aim was to do as little as possible. This was achieved by feigning illness or stupidity, and by walking and working as slowly as possible. If, in addition, time could be wasted and those set over them put to trouble and expense by wastefulness and subtle sabotage, so much the better. They did not always get away with such things, as Janet Schaw noticed in 1774, when she saw the backs of the half-naked slaves running up and down Olivees plantation, but we can take it that more often than not they did.

If mockery and malingering proved insufficient to make the burden of his or her condition supportable, a slave was then left with no option but to either commit suicide or run away. As Ramsay stated in his Essay:

> In plantations where slaves are ill-fed, hard worked, and severely punished, it is a circumstance common for a tenth, and even as far as a fourth part of the working slaves, to go off and skulk in the mountains, some for months together.[18]

The majority of runaways, however, were only absent for a short time before being retaken, or returning of their own accord. Both St Kitts and

Nevis were too small for large numbers of runaways to remain at large for very long before being caught – often by other more trusted slaves being used as 'hunters'. Individual runaways stood more change of escaping for longer periods, and the odd one or two managed to avoid recapture altogether. Frank, a slave from the Stapleton Estate in Nevis who was suspected of involvement in the 'plot' of 1725, ran away four years later and was never recaptured. He was later seen in Jamaica. Female slaves, understandably given the sexual molestation they had to endure on top of everything else, ran away just as often, if not more often, than males. One woman, Congo Sarah, managed to remain free in Nevis for nearly a year during 1730–31. It is more than likely that soon after she was recaptured she was put to death, this being the punishment laid down for any slave absent for over three months.

Free Coloureds

Well before the end of the eighteenth century St Kitts and Nevis each had a small population of free people of colour, made up of men and women recently manumitted from slavery and the descendants of those freed in the past. The majority of them were of mixed descent, either they or their forebears having been born as the result of liaisons between white men and slave women. Although such relations had taken place since the introduction of slavery, it was not until after the middle of the eighteenth century that they became more general. During the second half of the century concubinage was to be found among all ranks of society in both islands, but seemingly not to the same extent. By 1788 there were over 900 free coloureds among the population of St Kitts, but only 120 on Nevis. This intimacy between the whites and slaves, in addition to producing coloured offspring, also gave birth here and there to the assignment of peculiar roles to such children, as Janet Schaw observed in 1774. When she arrived at Olivees plantation house her hostess

> had standing by her a little Mulatto girl not above five
> years old, whom she retains as a pet. This brown beauty
> was dressed out like an infant Sultana, and is a fine contrast
> to the delicate complexion of her Lady.[19]

Although free, the adults were denied political rights or a proper place in society. In both islands the general feeling among the whites was that they were merely slaves who had been released from their masters, and as such they had no entitlement to participate in public life. This rejection, which did nothing for their self-esteem, served to make them bitter and anxious to distance themselves as far as possible from the slaves and the plantations. Even the poorest free coloured refused to hire himself out as a field labourer, while the better-off bought slaves themselves. Among those who could not afford to buy, as was recorded in St Kitts in 1789, 'It is their common Practice, if they have any land of their own, to hire poor Negroes at leisure Hours to cultivate it'. Apart from cultivating smallholdings in this way, free coloureds were also tradesmen, fishermen, hucksters, small shopkeepers or servants.

In the latter half of the century a few of the more go-ahead men even joined the British Army, being recruited as drummers or buglers by the regiments which by then had begun to be stationed in the Leeward Islands. John Charloe (or Charlow) from St Kitts served in the 29th Regiment of Foot from 1751 to 1780, while John Daine (or Deane) from Nevis enlisted in the same regiment in 1799, and fought throughout the Peninsular War in Spain. Another soldier in the same war was Charles Arundell, from St Kitts, who served as a bugler in the 43rd Foot. Later on, Joseph Fergus from St Kitts served with the 2nd Foot Guards from 1814 to 1833.[20] While nothing very much more is known of any of these, the same cannot be said of Thomas Ottley, who was born in Sandy Point and enlisted as a drummer in the 60th Foot in 1797. Some eighteen years later, having either deserted or been discharged from this regiment in Jamaica some years earlier, he met up with Simon Bolivar, the South American revolutionary leader, during the latter's brief exile in that island. Ottley obviously had much greater military potential than that of a drummer, as he joined the force of mercenaries Bolivar later recruited to invade Venezuela. With the rank of major he played a key part in the campaign which brought about the independence of Venezuela, but was mortally wounded at the final battle fought in June 1821 at Carabobo.[21]

12

War and the Islands

The start of the American War of Independence of 1775 brought an immediate end to all trade between the North American and West Indian colonies. For islands like St Kitts and Nevis this was a disaster, as both of them had come to depend on this trade for imports of livestock, lumber and particularly the foodstuffs such as corn, flour, rice, peas and salted fish needed to supplement the diet of their slaves. It also brought distress to Anguilla, where by this time many people were involved in producing salt from the large shallow pond behind the beach at Road Bay. As the greatest demand for this salt was in the North American colonies, the war cut off the island from its largest market.

The cessation of trade had a dire effect throughout the Leeward Islands. Towards the end of 1777 Sir William Burt, the Governor-General, informed London from Antigua that:

> At Montserrat they were reduced to such distress that not a Morsel of Bread was to be had in the Island for a Day or two; luckily a Sloop went from hence with Flower, since that they have scarcely had from hand to mouth. Many Negroes have Starved, the same has happen'd in Nevis. Here and at St Christopher's we have not been so Bad but in great Want....[1]

Conditions became even worse the following year, after France sided with America in the war against Britain. Although Burt allowed provisions to be imported from neutral islands, provided they were carried in British ships, slaves began to die of starvation in all the islands. Towards the end of 1778 he reported that three to four hundred had died in Nevis, and around the same number in St Kitts, all 'from the Want of Provisions'.

The loss of so many slaves did not prevent the legislature of St Kitts, alarmed by the possibility of a French invasion, from conscripting another thousand or so to work on Brimstone Hill. Since 1706, when it was last used in action, the fortress had been greatly enlarged and improved, leading to it being described 18 years later as

a noble fortification, which contains 42 acres of land and
has 42 large cannon amounted, with a magazine for 400
small arms and well supplied with all the necessaries for its
defence, and two large cisterns of water. This fortification
is intended as a receptacle for the women and children and
most valuable effects of the inhabitants....[2]

By 1753 more buildings, including barracks and another magazine, had
been added, and the fortress mounted 70 cannons and mortars. The
conscripted slaves in 1778 now added more magazines, new gun positions
and breastworks. By 1780 it was very much in its present configuration,
except for the citadel called Fort George on the summit of the hill, and the
outlying Prince of Wales bastion (see Plate 8).

At the same time as worries about a possible French invasion were
disturbing the legislature of St Kitts, even more concern was felt in
Nevis, where there was no proper equivalent of Brimstone Hill.
Following the abandonment of the rough and ready refuge on Nevis
Peak which had been used in 1706, a new fortification had been started
on Saddle Hill in the south of the island, about three miles from
Charlestown. Although grandiose in design, this had never progressed
much beyond earthern ramparts surmounted by a few guns. By 1778 it
was too late for the legislature to do anything other than to order the
fort to be manned constantly by the militia as a look-out.

Although the war between British and the American colonies ended
with the decisive British defeat at the Battle of Yorktown in October 1781,
that between Britain and France continued. A powerful French fleet under
the command of an outstanding admiral, the Comte de Grasse, had greatly
assisted the American victory by preventing British reinforcements from
reaching Yorktown, and this could now be used to attack the British
colonies in the Caribbean. News of the British defeat, and of the departure
of the French fleet from American waters, reached these colonies in
November. De Grasse arrived at Martinique the following month, with the
intention of launching an attack on Jamaica once his fleet had been reinforced by more ships being sent from France. In the meantime, having
embarked a large military force under the generalship of the Marquis de
Bouillé, he could turn his attention to British islands closer to hand.

On 9 January the Saddle Hill look-out on Nevis reported a fleet of two
dozen French ships, accompanied by numerous small craft, manoeuvring
to the south of the island. The alarm was raised in St Kitts the same day,
giving time for the militia and the garrison of regular troops under
Brigadier-General Thomas Fraser to withdraw into the Brimstone Hill
fortress. There they all came under the overall command of Major-General

Thomas Shirley, the Governor-General of the Leeward Islands, who happened to be visiting St Kitts. This left Basseterre undefended and on 11 January, when the French eventually launched their attack and troops entered the town, the inhabitants had no option but to capitulate. In spite of this de Bouillé could not claim capture of the island without first reducing Brimstone Hill, and to this end he landed well over 5000 troops to besiege the fortress.

The Capture of Nevis

The news of the surrender of Basseterre was carried across to Charlestown by a French officer on 12 January, with a request to the Council that the population of Nevis should capitulate in the same way. The Council had little choice but to accede, as the President, John Herbert, later explained:

> On maturely considering our situation that our whole
> force consisted in less than three hundred militia,
> indifferently armed and trained, that we had no post of any
> strength to retire to and that if we had time to throw up a
> redoubt, it must be defended by the planters and
> inhabitants, who would of course be thereby obliged to
> abandon their lives, families and estates to the mercy of a
> soldiery irritated by an ill judged resistance; that the militia
> were already nearly worn out with fatigue and watching. It
> was therefore thought that any opposition would be little
> better than madness.[3]

Two Council members immediately sailed for Basseterre, where they agreed very favourable terms with de Bouillé. Under these, the inhabitants of Nevis were to be considered as neutrals, their property was to be inviolate, their forms of government and religion were to remain unchanged, and their produce could be exported to other British colonies or to any neutral port. In return the militia was disarmed and disbanded, all the guns in Fort Charles and on Saddle Hill were removed or spiked, and a small French garrison was quartered in Charlestown.

The Siege of Brimstone Hill

Meanwhile, a few miles away on St Kitts, de Bouillé's troops had quickly occupied Charles Fort and the nearby village of Sandy Point and begun the siege of Brimstone Hill. Much of the heavy artillery needed to conduct the siege had first to be recovered from a ship which had run aground and sunk, but this set-back was more than compensated for by a discovery made by the French near Charles Fort:

> Eight brass twenty-four pounders, with 6000 shots of that weight, and two thirteen-inch brass mortars, with 1500 shells, were found by the enemy at the foot of the hill, and were used by them in the siege. They had been sent out by government for the fortress, but had not been carried up to the works....[4]

These guns and their ammunition, had the legislature of St Kitts earlier insisted on the provision by the planters of the labour necessary to carry them into the fortress, might well have saved the day for the defenders. As it was, the French began the sapping work needed to reduce the hill on 16 January and soon afterwards began putting this windfall, along with their own artillery, to good use:

> During the greater part of the last three weeks of the siege, twenty-three pieces of heavy cannon, and twenty-four mortars, were kept playing upon a spot of ground not 200 yards in diameter....[5]

The arrival of de Grasse at Martinique had not gone unnoticed by the British, particularly by Rear-Admiral Sir Thomas Hood, the naval commander in the Eastern Caribbean. When news of the subsequent departure of the French fleet from Martinique reached him in Barbados on 14 January he immediately sailed with his own fleet, consisting of some twenty ships, and headed north. A week later, by which time he had learned of the capitulation of Nevis and the ongoing siege of Brimstone Hill, Hood was ready to battle it out with de Grasse. Calling briefly at Antigua in order to embark most of the island's garrison of regular troops under Brigadier-General Robert Prescott, he made plans to attack the French fleet, then lying at anchor between Basseterre and Frigate Bay, early in the morning of 23 January. Unfortunately, as two of his ships collided during the night before the attack, it had to be called off at the last minute in order to allow time for their damage to be repaired.

The Battle of St Kitts

This delay allowed de Grasse enough time to rethink his position, and to order his ships to get under way so that they could form up in the usual and traditional line of battle out at sea. The holdup also gave Hood time to reconsider his tactics and on 25 January, after carrying out a series of manoeuvres designed to force de Grasse further offshore by giving the impression an attack was imminent, the British fleet turned away and headed for the island. There the fleet 'took possession of the anchorage, which [de Grasse] had quitted on the preceding evening, to the chagrin and astonishment of the French'. De Grasse gave chase and in the afternoon 'attacked with the greatest fury the rear of the British line'.[6] The ships under attack gave as good as they got, and towards nightfall

> The enemy finding they could not make any impression on the resolute firmness of the British commanders bore up and stood to sea.... The next morning at eight o'clock the French fleet stood in, as if determined to force the British line, which they attacked with great violence from van to rear, without making the least visible impression on it, they then wore and stood to sea.... The Comte de Grasse not yet discouraged, renewed the engagement in the afternoon directing his attack principally against the center and rear divisions; he was again repulsed, and suffered more material damage than in the previous battle.[7]

When de Grasse called off the attack in the late afternoon, what has come to be known in naval history as the Battle of St Kitts (see Plate 9) came to an end. The result was quite inconclusive. Only one ship, a British frigate, was destroyed but the casualties on both sides were considerable. The British lost 72 men killed and 244 wounded. The casualty figures for the French are not known, but as it was said afterwards that de Grasse had sent over 1000 wounded men to St Eustatius it is very likely (using the same ratio as exists between the British dead and wounded) that up to another 300 may have been killed.

Two days later, with de Grasse and his ships nowhere in sight, Hood decided that the time had come to put Brigadier-General Prescott and his troops ashore with the aim of relieving, or trying to relieve, the Brimstone Hill defenders. The General and about 1000 troops were landed in Frigate Bay under cover of the guns of four frigates, where

> After a smart skirmish with a detachment of French troops, which were beaten, and obliged with much loss to retreat into Basse Terre, the general took post upon a commanding hill. About 40 of our troops were killed and wounded in this conflict.[8]

It was just as well that the British dug in on Sir Timothy Hill, as early the next day, 29 January, the Marquis de Bouillé was seen approaching the hill at the head of some 4000 troops. It rapidly became apparent to both sides that there was little to be gained from further conflict:

> the Marquis de Bouillé...finding General Prescot's situation to be too strong to venture an attack, he retired with his troops to the siege of Brimstone-hill. As no object could be gained by General Prescot remaining on shore, he on the same evening re-embarked.[9]

The Loss of Brimstone Hill

This brief, futile invasion ended any attempt to relieve the Brimstone Hill garrison and the French were able to prosecute the siege undisturbed and 'with unabating vigour' for another two weeks. On 13 February, after the whole of one side of the fortress had been blasted into pieces, Shirley and Fraser

> having given up all hope of succour, in order to save the farther effusion of blood, which must have been the consequence of an of an assault, and the brave garrison being reduced to not more than 500 men fit for duty, they embraced the proposals of a capitulation made by the Marquis de Bouillé; who on the same day made the surrender of Brimstone-hill known to the admiral [Hood] by a flag of truce....[10]

The terms of the capitulation amounted in all to 17 articles. Under them the defenders were allowed to march out of the fortress 'with all the honours of war, with drums beating [and] colours flying'. The regular troops would then become prisoners of war and return to Britain, while the militia and any 'armed Negroes' would be allowed 'to return to their respective homes'. All the inhabitants of St Kitts would then be required to 'take oaths of fidelity to the King of France' and 'observe an exact neutrality'. True chivalry was demonstrated by de Bouillé in the final article, which stated:

> Out of Respect to the Courage and determined Conduct of Generals Shirley and Fraser, we Consent that they shall not be considered as Prisoners of War, but the former may return to this Government of Antigua, and the latter may continue in the service of his Country, being happy to testify this mark of particular Esteem for those brave Officers.[11]

Only one of the articles was considered exceptionable, but not at the time, nor by anyone in St Kitts, as we shall see later.

The loss of St Kitts in its entirety to the French now left Hood and the British fleet, still at anchor near Basseterre, in an untenable position. On the day after the surrender had taken place, de Grasse and a fleet of 34 men-of-war took up an anchorage off Nevis. As Hood afterwards reported to the Admiralty:

> Under this situation of things, I had no longer any
> business in Basse Terre road especially as the enemy were
> preparing to get guns and mortars upon a height that
> would annoy the ships in the van; and I left it that night,
> unperceived, I imagine, as not one of the enemy's ships
> was to be seen in the morning.[12]

After a quick call at Antigua, Hood sailed for Barbados and joined up with the fleet commanded by Admiral Sir George Rodney. Two months later the combined fleet, under the overall command of Rodney, defeated the French fleet under de Grasse in the Battle of the Saintes, which took place between Guadeloupe and Dominica. The largest naval battle of the eighteenth century, it brought to an end any further attempt by the French to seize British possessions in the West Indies.

Well before this battle took place, news of the loss of Brimstone Hill reached Nevis, where the terms of the capitulation were seen to include a number of references affecting the island. This caused an immediate uproar, particularly concerning the provisions of Article 8 which stated that

> The Inhabitants shall pay monthly, into the hands of the
> Treasurer of the Troops, in lieu of all taxes, the value of
> two-thirds of the Duties that the islands of St Christopher
> and Nevis paid to the King of Great Britain which shall be
> estimated according to the valuation of the Revenues made
> in the year 1781 and which shall serve as a Basis.[13]

It was insisted that the terms of the capitulation which had been negotiated by Nevis over a month earlier were far more favourable, and that these still stood. There was a general refusal to be bound by the subsequent capitulation of St Kitts, and an even stronger refusal to share any of the financial burden imposed by Article 8. Opposition, led by Herbert and the Council, continued even after the war ended in 1783 and both islands were restored to British rule. In January 1784 the Council declared, in words which have continued to re-echo ever since, that the inhabitants of Nevis were 'a People wholly independent of St Kitts', and attacked Shirley, the Governor-General, for encroaching on the independent rights of the island. Acrimony continued for well over another year, eventually ending only after Shirley received a letter from the Secretary of State in London in which he was told

> It appears to His Majesty that some of the Council of the Island of Nevis have acted in a manner unbecoming their situation and offered that sort of Treatment to you, as their Governor, which must be discountenanced; you have His majesty's permission to remove such of the Members from their seat at the Council Board of the Island of Nevis as have been most Active in this Affair.[14]

Shirley immediately got rid of two of his most voluble and objectionable opponents, one of whom, James Tobin, had been one of the men sent by Herbert to St Kitts to negotiate the capitulation of Nevis in January 1782.

The war between France and Britain ended in January 1783, with a formal peace treaty being signed nine months later at Versailles. With the end of hostilities the sugar planters of St Kitts and Nevis, as well as the few still struggling to make something out of sugar in Anguilla, must have looked forward to a return to the trading conditions which had existed prior to the beginning of the American revolution. If so they were soon disappointed, as in July they received news that an Order-in-Council had been issued which placed great restrictions on all trade with the United States by applying the terms of the Navigation Act. All goods being imported from, or exported to, an American port now had to be carried in British or colonial vessels, and no American ship was permitted to enter a West Indian port other than for non-trading purposes such as to effect repairs or to seek shelter from a hurricane. Robert Thompson, the attorney for the Stapleton estates on St Kitts, complained in a letter to the proprietor written at the end of the month that the order 'took place very unexpectedly, and at a time when there was little Lumber or Provisions in the Island'.[15] Such shortages were common to all three islands, and all had particular cause to resent the new restrictions on American trade. In addition to the distress common to all the British islands caused by the American Revolution, both St Kitts and Nevis had suffered French occupation. The poor Anguillians, having in the 1760s found a reasonably profitable product in salt, and after having established a thriving trade in it with the American colonies, now found the market closed and their salt virtually unsaleable.

Because of where Anguilla was situated and the lack of interest shown in its conditions by Britain, together with the propensity for smuggling found among many Anguillians, the consequences of enforcement of the Navigation Act left the island poorer but the general tenor of life largely undisturbed. In St Kitts and Nevis, however, it was a different matter.

Strenuous efforts were made by the authorities to enforce the Navigation Act while equally vigorous attempts were being made by the planters to continue trading with America, and mention has already been made in a previous chapter of the riots which took place in St Kitts towards the end of 1784, and which culminated in a customs officer being tarred and feathered.

The situation became so bad that at the beginning of 1785 the navy was obliged to send a frigate to patrol the waters of the two islands in order to prevent trading with American ships. The frigate chosen was HMS *Boreas*, under the command of 27-year-old Captain Horatio Nelson, a man still with a reputation to make and unafraid of any toes he had to step on to succeed. 'I, for one', he wrote home as soon as he got the job

> am determined not to suffer the Yankees to come where my Ship is.... The residents of these Islands are Americans by connexion and by interest, and are inimical to Great Britain. They are as great rebels as ever were in America, had they the power to show it.[16]

True to his word Nelson stopped, boarded and searched any American vessel he came across that seemed to be heading for St Kitts or Nevis, making himself equally unpopular in both islands. The residents, especially in Basseterre and Charlestown, went out of their way to show their disapproval of Britain, the Royal Navy and Nelson himself. On 18 March, while the *Boreas* was at anchor off Basseterre, he wrote:

> Yesterday being St Patrick's Day, the Irish Colours with thirteen stripes in them was hoisted all over the Town. I was engaged to dine with the President, but sent an excuse, as he suffered these Colours to fly. I mention it only to show the principle of these vagabonds.[17]

On this occasion he at least was able to exercise the option of going ashore or not on St Kitts; two months later he found himself in danger of being arrested if he set foot on Nevis. This situation arose after he had seized four vessels at anchor off Charlestown, following expiry of the 48 hours he had given them to hoist their proper colours and depart. All four he afterwards explained were 'carrying British Registers, although they were American-built, navigated by Americans and some of them entirely owned by Foreigners'. This had so infuriated the local inhabitants that a number of planters and merchants had clubbed together to provide the ships' masters with the means to sue Nelson for assault and imprisonment. He was then obliged to remain on board the *Boreas* to avoid arrest until the end of July when, after word had been received that the suit would be defended by the Crown, the charges were dropped.

The incident did little to bring Nelson closer to Nevisians in general, but it did much to endear him to one family. 'Don't let me forget,' he informed a naval friend afterwards,

> the President of Nevis offered, in Court, to become my
> bail for £10,000 if I chose to suffer the arrest. He told them
> I had only done my duty, and although he suffered more in
> proportion than any of them, he could not blame me.

John Herbert, the President of the Council and owner of Montpelier Estate, was the uncle of a young widow named Mrs Fanny Nisbet (see Plate 10), and she of course was the woman Nelson was to marry in Nevis nearly two years later. Their marriage took place, as no one who now visits the island can fail to become aware, at Montpelier in March 1787, a bare two months before Nelson sailed for England, with Fanny following soon afterwards in a merchant vessel. The departure of the *Boreas* did not end the navy's role in enforcing the Navigation Act, but afterwards American ships attempting to trade with the Leeward Islands undoubtedly had an increasingly easier time.

The Great Flood of St Kitts, 1792

In April 1792 St Kitts was struck by a natural disaster which caused almost as much damage and disruption to life as had the French attack ten years earlier. In the evening of Saturday 7 April, following several days of frequent heavy showers, rain began to fall 'so heavy that it appeared to come down in sheets of water' all over the island. This had a devastating effect particularly on Basseterre where, four or five hours after the downpour had begun, shortly before 10 o'clock, 'a prodigious flood came down College-Street'. This was (and remains) a long straight road running down through the town to the sea, and what followed was described by an eyewitness two days later:

> the torrent carried away all the fences, walls and steps, and
> in some places tore down the houses; some falling upon
> their inhabitants, and some being carried away with
> them…. The Parish house was broken down; the English
> church and the Methodist chapel were filled with mud and
> water. Several houses were carried into the sea with all
> their furniture, and dashed to pieces. Most of the
> merchants' cellars were filled with water, mud and sand;
> and great quantities of provisions were spoiled…. The

strongest walls were unable to withstand the vehemence of
the main current, and the oldest inhabitants cannot
remember so formidable and destructive an inundation,
whereby so many lives were lost....[18]

Floods caused just as much havoc in other parts of the island. At Old
Road some houses were washed into the sea, while to the north, in the
parish of St Paul Capisterre, several estates were ruined. On one of these
flood water 'drove before it a heap of stones not less than twenty feet
broad, and about four feet thick...carrying away every thing before it',
leaving behind 'a chasm of an hundred feet wide, and in some places seven
feet deep, in others twenty and upwards'. The town of Dieppe Bay (then
known as Deep Bay) was reported to be

> almost destroyed – all the roads...are impassable. Timbers
> of very great dimensions have been torne from the
> mountains, and are now scattered up and down on the
> cane lands. Huge rocks, that have bid defiance to
> hurricanes, earthquakes, inundations, etc for ages back,
> have been obliged to give way to this last Flood, whose
> devastation can never be repaired.

One town to escape ruin was Sandy Point, as this was in 'the only Parish
in the Island that has not been injured. The hand of Providence has been
peculiarly kind to it; – The inhabitants there have experienced nothing but
a thoro' soaking season.'

Elsewhere there was considerable loss of life among both white and
black sections of society but, as might be expected, more so among the
latter. The way in which some of these deaths were recorded, in a report of
the flood penned soon after it had happened, illustrate only too well the
gulf which, even in a disaster, separated one section from the other. 'Poor
Mrs. Tudor!' cries one newspaper report, 'who lately buried an amiable
daughter: the Mother and Son were happily taken out of the surf.... But
Miss Tudor, alas, has not been heard of since – she rests with the dead!' In
stark contrast the same report lists among the losses of property suffered
'on this truly deplorable occasion':

> Mr. Skilling – rum, furniture, and part of his house much
> rent; Captain Ford – out houses with stores... Mrs. Tudor
> – besides all the property in her house, lost a mulattoe girl;
> Mrs. Edwards – rum; Captain Slegg – a house...; The
> Editor – types, paper, books, a negro, etc...

A Mr Stanley, 'besides what he suffered in cane land & negro houses, had a
negro carried away, who was found dead near the bay, between two

stones'. The only slave who lost his life and had his name recorded was 'Dr Bridgwater's valuable negro man Cuffy' who, 'with his wife, and a child, were swept away in a small room'.[19]

Apprehensions of Danger

The doom-laden statement that the 'devastation can never be repaired' turned out to be far from the truth, and the island had more or less fully recovered from the flood within a year. This was just as well, as from February 1793 Britain and France were again at war.

The outbreak of hostilities, which followed on from the turmoil created in Europe by the French Revolution, seemed likely to bring just as much turbulence to the Caribbean, where fighting began almost immediately. Neither St Kitts nor Nevis were threatened, but this did not prevent considerable alarm being felt in the former about the island's defence and the strength of its garrison. The fortifications on Brimstone Hill had been increased substantially since 1783, with the construction of Fort George on the summit, but as far as the legislature was concerned there had never been enough regular troops stationed on the island. The size of the garrison was a long-standing issue, and all manner of reasons were used to justify an increase, including the following alarmist nonsense found in an address asking for 200 soldiers which the Assembly sent to the King in 1770:

> Apprehensions of danger even from an external Enemy are Alarming but they are considerably Encreased when we reflect upon the number of slaves, now employed and absolutely Necessary for the cultivation of our Lands and for the Manufactures of this country; this Number amount to Fifteen Thousand Men. This considerable disproportion between the white Inhabitants and the slaves, the turbulent savage disposition of the Negroes ever prone to Riots and Rebellions place the peace, security and lives of your Majesty's white subjects in a very precarious and Alarming situation.[20]

The fallaciousness of the reference to the island's slaves placing 'the peace, security and lives' of the white inhabitants at risk was demonstrated very clearly 25 years later, when the 'disproportion' between white and black was greater than ever. In April 1795 the legislature passed an Act

> That Five Hundred Slaves shall be raised for the Service and Defence of this Island of which any Number not

> exceeding Fifty shall be employed on Brimstone Hill in
> such manner in Military Service and Garrison Duty as the
> Commander-in-Chief may direct and appoint.

They were to be 'armed with pikes and Cutlasses', provided with uniforms, and paid one shilling a day. Any slave wounded 'or otherwise so maimed as to be rendered useless to his Owner' would be emancipated and allowed 'the Sum of ten Pounds Current Money per annum during his Life'; a slave only slightly wounded would receive his freedom and a yearly sum of 'Three Pounds, Six Shillings, Current Money'.

　　The Act was soon amended to allow even more slaves to be armed, and in 1797 a British general was able to record that

> in St Kitts besides the militia there are two corps of 500
> each of Negroes embodied – composed of the trustiest and
> best slaves.... These corps are only called upon
> occasionally – at other times they work upon the
> habitations. The officers are the different proprietors.[21]

　　All in all, between 1795 and 1798 nearly 1200 slaves were given training in arms, although none was ever required to use his pike or cutlass in action. St Kitts, like Nevis, remained undisturbed until the war was brought to an end by the Treaty of Amiens in March 1802. Regrettably the same could not be said of Anguilla.

The French Attack on Anguilla

Anguilla remained unaffected by the war until towards the end of 1796. So poor was the state of the island's economy and so low was the general standard of living that few of the inhabitants can have been worried by their proximity to the enemy island of St Martin, or of the possibility of being attacked. This all changed on or about 22 November when the French frigate *Le Desius,* together with the brig *La Vaillante* and several small craft, sailed over from St Martin and landed some 400 men at Rendezvous Bay on the south coast. During the next four days, in spite of determined opposition by the Anguillians under their Governor, Benjamin Gumbs, the invaders pillaged the island. Many of the defenders were killed, while women were mistreated, houses were burnt, and property was looted or destroyed. There was no military reason to invade the island, or any justification for the severity of the attack. The invaders acted like a large gang of undisciplined marauders, and it seems most unlikely that more than a few, if any, professional soldiers were involved.

Very fortunately, a day or so after the invasion began, Gumbs managed to despatch a boat to St Kitts with the news and a request for help, and if there was one thing Anguillians excelled in it was in getting the most out of a boat under sail. The passage was made in record time, and the boat (the name of which together with those of its crew are lost to history) arrived at Basseterre at more or less the same time as a British frigate anchored in the bay. The frigate's captain, Robert Barton, lost no time in responding to the news he received from the boat's crew, as he recorded in the report he sent to London on 3 December:

> I am anchored at St Kitts on 25th ultimo, when an express
> boat had been sent from the Island of Anguilla, to inform
> the Admiral, that the island was attacked by two French
> men-of-war, and several small vessels, containing four
> hundred troops. I felt it my duty (as the express boat
> returned here with the loss of her main mast), to leave the
> service I was ordered on, to endeavour to relieve the place.
> The wind being to the northwest, prevented my getting up
> there in time to stop them burning the town; but I have
> pleasure to say, after an action of nearly two hours, I
> effectually relieved the island by taking the ship and
> sinking the brig.

And so ended the invasion of Anguilla. The French who had not managed to reboard their ships (there either to be sunk with *La Vaillante* or taken prisoner in *Le Desius*) were rounded up ashore and imprisoned in the cellars of a burnt-out house. From the very scanty details available it seems that many of these were later put to death by Anguillians infuriated by the invaders' destruction and rapine, and buried in a mass grave.

The Treaty of Amiens in 1802 began what turned out to be merely a breathing-space in the British conflict with France. The treaty was unpopular in London and the French, under Napoleon, still hoped to dominate Europe and to acquire more possessions overseas. The hostilities between the two countries which resumed in May 1803 were to leave Anguilla completely unaffected, and impinge directly on St Kitts and Nevis only for a day or so in 1805.

One of Napoleon's plans of that year envisaged sending two large fleets to the Caribbean, where they would combine in order to seize control of the sea and capture British islands and shipping. Because of the British blockade of French ports, only one fleet, under Rear-Admiral Edouard Missiessy, was able to leave on time, and this arrived at Martinique in February. Once there, however, and without the presence of the second, larger fleet, Missiessy had insufficient force to attempt more than raids on some of the British islands. After trying, and failing, to capture Dominica he then extracted a ransom of £7500 from the inhabitants of Roseau in order to avoid destruction of the town. As this seemed an easy way of acquiring prize money without bloodshed, he then headed north for Nevis.

The French fleet arrived off Charlestown on 5 March, and after seizing several merchant ships which were at anchor, Missiessy sent ashore a demand for 500,000 *livres* with a threat to take twice as much by force if this was refused. While the demand was being considered by the Nevis Council he sailed with half the fleet across to Basseterre and issued a demand for even more money there. If Charlestown and Basseterre were then to be saved from destruction, neither Council had any option but to pay up. In the end Nevis got off much lighter, parting with only just over £4000, compared with more than £15,000 turned over by St Kitts, sums which at the beginning of the twenty-first century were the equivalent of around £160,000 and £600,000. Missiessy departed with the cash, called at Montserrat to threaten Plymouth to the tune of £7500, and then sailed via Hispaniola for France and out of West Indian history.

13

Administration, Law and Religion

Throughout the eighteenth century the British government did not pursue a very active role in colonial affairs, and intervened as infrequently as possible in the way colonies such as that of the Leeward Islands were administered. In part this was due to the distance which separated Britain from the Caribbean, and the length of time communications took to cross the Atlantic by sailing ship. At the same time the absence of a single authority with a proper bureaucracy to handle colonial affairs meant there was a general lack of commitment by the government to interfere except when absolutely necessary. Ministerial responsibility for colonial affairs remained ill-defined until 1782 when it was assigned to the home secretary. In 1801, as the demands of military operations overseas had thrust an increasing amount of colonial business on the secretary of state for war, the holder of this office was formally gazetted as the secretary of state for war *and colonies*. An embryonic Colonial Office was then established, but this only began to be effective after 1812, following the appointment of Henry Bathurst, the third Earl Bathurst, as secretary of state. The first specifically designated colonial secretary was not appointed until 1854.

British reluctance to make any change in the way the colonies were administered before Bathurst was appointed was demonstrated in the Leeward Islands in 1810, a year after an experienced diplomat, Hugh Elliot, had taken up the post of governor-general. In November he wrote to the then Secretary of State, Lord Liverpool, arguing for reform in the way the islands were governed:

> The fact is, the governments of the smaller islands were
> formed in times when many of the proprietors lived upon
> their estates, and the white population was, in some
> instances, perhaps ten times as numerous as it is now. Of
> the few white inhabitants who remain, managers,
> overseers, self-created lawyers, self-educated physicians,
> and adventurous merchants, with little real capital and
> scanty credit, compose the greatest part. The acquirement
> of education, among many of this description of persons,

are very unequal to the task of taking a share in the governments.... To collect from such a state of society men men fit to be legislators, judges or jurymen, is perfectly impracticable....[1]

His complaints were ignored, and it was not until after his term of office ended in 1814 and he had been able to discuss reform with Liverpool's successor, Bathurst, in London that any change took place. As nothing could be done about increasing the number of white inhabitants, or to improve their fitness to govern, it was decided to split the colony into two and appoint an individual 'Captain-General and Commander-in Chief' for each half. The change took place in 1816, when St Kitts, Nevis, Anguilla and the Virgin Islands were placed under a man named Thomas Probyn, with his headquarters in Basseterre. Antigua, Montserrat and Barbuda then formed an entirely separate colony under Major-General George Ramsay based in St John's. This division may well have been considered by the Colonial Office as a move in the right direction towards imposing greater control over the way the islands were governed. If so, this was not how it was viewed by the white inhabitants of St Kitts, who merely saw it as the long-overdue recognition by London of the island's equality with its main rival, Antigua. In any case, nothing very much was achieved by the split and the experiment was abandoned in 1833.

The Administration of Justice

Elliot's scathing references to 'self-created lawyers' and the impracticability of collecting 'men fit to be legislators, judges or jurymen' from among the island societies may have been harsh but contained a great deal of truth. The common law of England had been in force in the Leeward Islands since the early days, with the courts modelled on the English system. Unfortunately, as qualified lawyers had always been in short supply, the justice these courts dispensed was often of an arbitrary, biased or unorthodox nature.

Before the Leeward Islands were divided in 1816 the governor-general, as well as being the commander-in-chief and vice-admiral, was also the senior legal official, the chancellor, of the colony. Although in islands such as St Kitts and Nevis there was a system of courts – Chancery and King's Bench to deal with civil and criminal cases, and Vice-Admiralty to adjudicate in cases involving the sea and shipping – for most of the eighteenth century none of the judges had any legal training whatsoever. It was also not unknown for one man, untrained as a lawyer, to hold more than one position. In the 1780s in St Kitts a Council member, Archibald Esdaile, was not only master in chancery and an associate justice in the Court of King's Bench and Common Pleas, but also a judge of the Court of Vice-Admiralty. Only a slight improvement took place by the end of the century. In 1794 it was recorded that in St Kitts 'the jurisdiction of both the King's Bench and Common Pleas, centers in one superior court, wherein justice is administered by a chief justice and four puisne judges. The chief is appointed by the crown, the others by the governor in the King's name'. Those so appointed by the governor, as was almost invariably the case, would have been drawn from among the Council members. In Nevis at this time all the judges, including the chief justice, were nominated members of the Council. Some check on the Courts of Chancery and King's Bench was provided by allowing appeals to be made to the governor-general in his capacity as chancellor. Appeals were also allowed against decisions reached by the Vice-Admiralty courts, but these had to be sent to England.

The appointment of Council members as judges was far from popular, particularly by plaintiffs in the Chancery courts, which were much used by debtors to secure injunctions against proceedings by their creditors. The reason for this unpopularity was explained very succinctly in a letter sent to London in 1774, in which the then Governor-General stated that 'Courts of Chancery if constituted of the Council, will almost invariably be composed of the People who most probably have occasion to appeal to it for Redress'.[2] It may have been the custom at that time for the Council of Nevis to carry out the work of the Court of Chancery, but this was not the case in St Kitts, where in 1794 it was reported:

> The Governor[-General] is chancellor by his office, and in
> St Christopher's sits alone. Attempts have been made to
> join some of the council with him...but hitherto without
> success, the inhabitants choosing rather to submit to the
> expence and delay of following the chancellor to Antigua,
> than to suffer the inconveniency of having on the chancery
> bench judges, some of whom it is probable, from their
> situation and connections, may be interested in the event
> of any suit that may come before them.[3]

But, regardless of the quality of their judges and the precise constitution of their courts, and ignoring the fact that access to the law was confined almost entirely to their white inhabitants, St Kitts and Nevis both possessed a system of justice, however imperfect it may have been. This is more than can be said of Anguilla, which appears to have existed without very much in the way of the law or any of its appendages and practitioners well into the nineteenth century. Before 1825 justice of a sort was handed out by the men who formed the Council, but what form this took is now beyond recall. That crime and punishment may not have played too big a part in the life of the Anguillians, or possibly that natural justice prevailed, is suggested by the Council's decision of February 1822 to cease functioning as a court of judicature as there was no gaol on the island.

Such was the state of the administration of justice throughout the Leeward Islands in the early years of the nineteenth century that eventually it called for an investigation by a commission of inquiry. The commission began work in 1826 and produced a damning report the following year. As well as finding a general absence of any fixed principles of jurisprudence, it also discovered scant knowledge of the extent to which English common and statute law was in force among the islands. The Chancery Court in every island, whether constituted by the chancellor together with the Council, or by the chancellor alone, was considered to be 'uncertain and undignified'. In addition to this the Commission found the administration of common law everywhere suffered from the lack of trained lawyers.

As all this had been so for the past 200 years it was too much to hope that any quick reform would take place. There was no improvement until after 1836, when a Superior Court was established for the Leeward Islands under a chief justice, assisted by a senior puisne judge who went on circuit. Both were required to be members of the English, Scottish or Irish Bar. A resident, appropriately qualified, puisne judge was appointed in each of the main islands at the same time.

The Established Church

As well as the government and the administration of justice, a third pillar of the Establishment came under scrutiny during the first decades of the nineteenth century. Up until 1824 the clergy of the Established Church, the Church of England, throughout the West Indies served under the ecclesiastical jurisdiction of the bishop of London. Successive holders of this office, who licensed such ministers but exercised no authority over their work, showed little interest in any aspect of West Indian life until the end of the eighteenth century. It was only after sectarian and non-conformist missionaries had already begun to work among the slaves, and an evangelically minded prelate, Beilby Porteus, had been appointed to the See of London, that this attitude began to change. Following the consecration of Porteus in 1787 the Anglican Church at last began to take an interest in the spiritual welfare of the slaves.

Before this the Church, as an integral part of the Establishment, had merely been going along with the views of the rest of white society. These had been well summed up in the early years of the century by the Reverend Francis Le Jau, the man in charge of the windward parishes on St Kitts. In 1705 he had informed the Bishop of London that although he had about 2000 slaves in his parishes who were 'sensible and well disposed to learn', the planters objected to any attempt he made to convert them by arguing 'that baptism makes negroes free'. This of course was nonsense, as they knew only too well. The real reason for their objection, as Le Jau pointed out, was that, if he was allowed to convert the slaves, their owners would then be 'obliged to look upon them as Christian brethren and use 'em with humanity'.[4] Other clergymen, such as Robertson and Pope on Nevis a couple of decades later, took an easier way out by treating the conversion of slaves to Christianity as 'a work the difficulty whereof can hardly be credited by any one who has not seen these Negroes'. Given such attitudes among the clergy and planters alike, it is hardly surprising that in the 1760s and 1770s James Ramsay found his desire to assist the slaves largely thwarted by their refusal to have anything to do with 'the prayers of white people'. It took until 1792 for the Church to accept that in each island it had no less a duty towards the many thousands of slaves than it had towards the (in comparison) handful of slave-owners. In that year Bishop Porteus established 'The Society for the Conversion and Religious Instruction and Education of the Negro Slaves in the West Indian Islands', to oversee the sending out of both clerical and lay missionaries to assist the regular clergy in converting the slaves. In spite of its prelatic sponsorship, ponderous title and good intentions, the formation of the Society was not widely welcomed in the West Indies by either the planters or the clergy. And in any case it came into existence far too late, as by this time in many islands, including St Kitts and Nevis, sectarian missionaries had already taken on the task.

The 'Conversion Society', as it soon came to be called, made very little headway in either St Kitts or Nevis for the first twenty years of its existence, and even less in Anguilla where the one and only church, built only twenty or so years earlier, had been burnt down during the French invasion of 1796. In 1811 Daniel Davis, a son of the Reverend William Davis (the sometime attorney for the Romney estates in St Kitts and now rector of St Peter Basseterre), complained in a letter to a friend:

> It ought indeed to be considered disgraceful to the policy
> of any Society, that the space of nearly three centuries
> should have expired since one people or other, professing
> civilization and Christianity, have made but feeble efforts,
> or rather no efforts for the extension of their blessings
> among the laborious and ignorant.[5]

Davis wrote from England where he had gone, like his father, to be ordained. A year later he returned to the West Indies and became the rector of St Paul Charlestown. There, as in all the other parishes in Nevis and all but one in St Kitts, the stipend was still being paid in sugar. The amount of 16,000 lb (7250 kg) had no fixed monetary value, as this depended on the price at which the sugar was sold in Britain. It took Davis some time to find his feet in his parish but in 1814, in order to receive some backing in his intention to convert plantation slaves, he applied to become a missionary of the Conversion Society. When he began this work at the end of 1815 he found it almost as hard going as Ramsay had in St Kitts fifty years earlier. Just how hard was made very evident about 18 months later.

In April 1817 the Secretary of State for War and the Colonies, Lord Bathurst, sent a circular despatch to all the West Indian colonies, asking for information about the Anglican Church, its clergy and its efforts to convert and baptize the slaves. Probyn forwarded a copy to each minister in the islands under his jurisdiction (other than Anguilla which was then without a minister), asking each to supply the required information, and four months later, expressing his belief 'that these reverend gentlemen discharge the sacred duties of their office with propriety and talent', sent their replies to London. It is impossible to tell whether his tongue was in his cheek at the time, but the individual responses from five clergymen in St Kitts and four in Nevis, with regard to the attention they paid to the spiritual welfare of the slaves, would suggest that, if it were not, it really ought to have been.

William Davis, then in charge of St Peter Basseterre and St John Capisterre, began by stressing that

> My churches have ever been open to the Black population,
> and in the course of my long ministry, I have been
> invariably solicitous to instruct them in the principles and
> doctrine of the Christian religion, and to impress on their
> minds their moral duties as connected with their happiness
> here and hereafter.

He then went into a great deal of detail about how he was, or felt he ought to be, paid for 'the baptism of Negroes', before admitting that he could provide no figure for the number of slaves he had so far baptized. In addition he also found it 'impossible, at present, to say what is the exact number of the negroes in my parishes who are members of the Established Church'. His fellow priest in St Paul Capisterre was more reserved, but able to state that he had baptized 413 slaves in the previous five years. The rector of the united parishes of St Thomas Middle Island and Trinity

Palmetto Point was equally brief, but able to say that he had carried out 924 such baptisms during a six-year period. The Reverend Joseph Barnes, who also was in charge of two parishes, St Mary Cayon and Christ Church Nicola Town, could provide no baptismal figures but left little doubt about how he viewed both the conversion of slaves and Methodist missionaries:

> In each of [my] parishes there are about three hundred
> Christian slaves, some of whom attend Divine service very
> regularly, others are induced to follow the Methodists,
> whose doctrine and form of worship have, as I have been
> informed, many allurements for the illiterate and
> uninformed, for those who will not be at the trouble of
> thinking, and those who cannot.

The rector of St George Basseterre, the only incumbent who received a stipend in cash, estimated the number of slaves he had baptized at 'between three and four hundred, infants and adults included' in five years, but he also did not take kindly to the presence of missionaries as

> what proportion even of those are now members of the
> Established Church, can scarcely be ascertained, as many, on
> their application to me to be made Christians, were probably
> adherents to the persuasion of the Moravian and Methodist
> missionaries, and others may have since become so.

The comments from Nevis about slave conversion, and the figures for baptisms, were even worse. Only Daniel Davis replied with any feeling, stating that since he had been inducted to his living in Charlestown

> my church has not only been open to the Black
> population, but I have used every means in my power to
> induce them to frequent it: that I have not succeeded as
> well as I could wish, I must both confess and lament.

In three years he had managed to baptize 48 slaves only. The incumbents of country parishes had done rather better. The rector of St Thomas Lowland and St James Windward, in three years, had managed 165 baptisms. The Reverend Joseph Pemberton at St John Figtree could give no figure for the number of slaves who had become members of the Church of England 'as they frequently go to the Methodist chapels after the church service is over'. He had, however, baptized a total of 98 slaves in three years.

The fourth Nevis minister, John Walways, was in charge of St George Gingerland. In the two years he had had the living he had baptized 37 slaves but, as he made very evident, none with any good grace. He was unable to state 'the number of slaves in my parish who may be accounted members of the Established Church, from the circumstance of many of them attending at one time the service of the church, and at another the dissenters' chapel'. Additionally, in his view 'the clergy of these Islands cannot fail to regret the insuperable obstacles that exist (under the present system) to any beneficial result from their labours for the advancement of religion among the slaves'. This reference to 'insuperable obstacles' brought a swift response from Probyn who, before forwarding Walways's comments to London, felt it politic to ask for 'an elucidation of the same'. This provided Walways with the opportunity to voice opinions which there can be no doubt were widespread among the Anglican clergy, not only in Nevis and St Kitts, but throughout the West Indies. He minced no words in his reply to the Governor:

> 'The insuperable obstacles' to the advancement of religion
> among the negroes…exist in the gross state of ignorance in
> which the far greater part of them are living, together with
> the total want of any system of instruction, or any means by
> which that ignorance may be dispelled, and their minds
> prepared for the reception of religious truth. Need I add, that
> so long as these impediments to the growth of Christianity
> among the slaves subsist, they are in a perfectly unfit state to
> derive any benefit from the labours of the clergy.

He then felt free to contradict those parts of Bathurst's despatch in which he had stated that he believed improvements in the lot of the slaves would come through the exertions of the clergy and 'a more active discharge of their duty'. As far as Walways was hypocritically concerned no such improvement was possible: the slaves existed in ignorance and the clergy, 'however zealous in the cause, know to their heart-felt regret (awfully responsible as is the office of a Minister of the Gospel) that their endeavours will be unavailing'.[6]

A genuine effort by the Anglican Church to introduce the slaves to Christianity, and to counteract the baleful opinions of men like Walways, had to wait until after the creation of the two West Indian dioceses of Jamaica and Barbados in 1824. The Leeward Islands, as part of the latter, were toured by the first bishop, William Coleridge (a nephew of the poet Samuel Taylor Coleridge) the following year. He visited Nevis and St Kitts at the end of May, and Anguilla at the beginning of June. His tour was carried out in the company of a cousin, Henry Coleridge (another of the poet's nephews), who acted as his secretary and later recorded his impressions of the islands in the well-known book *Six Months in the West Indies*.

At Nevis, where he found there were then 'five parish churches and two large private chapels', Henry Coleridge observed that in spite of this 'there are only two clergymen at present on the island, and so the parishes are merely served in turn'. This situation he believed was because

> the salary which the legislature gives to each parish
> minister is wholly inadequate to a decent maintenance and
> what makes bad worse is, that the planters pay it in sugar.
> Now this practice not only makes the clergy to a certain
> extent traders, but they, poor souls, are fain to take their
> miserable stipend in worse sugar than the king himself,
> which all the world knows is in the other islands the very
> vilest that can be found.[7]

Two days later on St Kitts he had more to say about work of the Methodist and Moravian missionaries than the Anglican clergy. In Basseterre, after complaining that St George's Church was very 'irregularly built, and cannot contain one third of the inhabitants', he noted with tongue firmly in cheek that

> the Methodists have kindly stepped in and offered their
> assistance, and, in order to demonstrate their affection to
> the church, have erected their conventicle so close to it, that
> the voice of the clergyman is often drowned in the hearty
> chorus which proceeds from the open doors and windows
> of the great house over the way. This is something
> inconvenient, and I would humbly suggest it might be
> avoided, or turned to a good account by a previous
> agreement between the two parties to sing in concert....[8]

He mentioned only one Anglican clergyman, 'The present rector of Basseterre, Mr. Davis, a native of the island', whom he praised as 'one of the most powerful preachers in the West Indies'. This was Daniel Davis, newly transferred from his living at Charlestown, where over the years he had devoted much of his time to work among the slaves. His devotion now stood him in good stead, as the Bishop immediately appointed him one of his chaplains and earmarked him for preferment. In 1838 he was inducted as Archdeacon of Antigua, and four years later became the first bishop of the newly created Diocese of Antigua.

The visit to Anguilla which followed introduced both the Bishop and his secretary to the harsh realities of life on a small, backward and neglected West Indian island for the first time. 'There are 365 whites, 327 free-coloured, and 2,388 slaves in Anguilla', noted Henry Coleridge, and

> One small methodist chapel is the only place of religious
> worship... the minister is a coloured man with a stipend, as

I was informed, of £200 per annum from the Society in
England, and is consequently the richest man in the island.
He has 250 admitted members, and his congregation rarely
exceeds 400 souls. There remain therefore about
2600 human beings without, or only with the name of
Christians.[9]

The Methodist Church

The Methodists who were mentioned, often in less than complimentary
terms, by the various Anglican ministers referred to above, established
themselves in the first place on St Kitts in 1787. In January of that year
Thomas Coke, an English Methodist bishop and John Wesley's
'Superintendent' in America, accompanied by three other men, William
Hammett, John Clarke and John Baxter, visited the island in order to
establish a mission. They received a very cool reception, except from men
and women of the free coloured community, people generally ostracized
by the Anglican Church and who, when attending a service, could only
sit 'in certain pews at the extreme ends'. Coke and the others were made
particularly welcome by Samuel Cable, the founder and editor of the *St
Christopher Advertiser and Weekly Intelligencer,* and a Mrs Molly
Seaton, both of whom, according to Coke, 'had not only a relish for the
excellencies of religion, but had in an eminent manner the fear of God
before their eyes'.[10]

After a stay of only a few days Coke departed with Clarke and
Baxter for Nevis, leaving Hammett behind to begin his missionary
activities. Within two years, preaching at first to free coloureds but
quickly beginning to work among the slaves, he had some 700 'hearers'.
By 1794 a wooden chapel with a schoolroom attached had been built at
Old Road, and 13 white people were numbered among the total of 1423
acknowledged Methodists on the island. The first chapel in Basseterre, a
wooden building, was erected in 1817, by which time out of around
3000 registered members about 50 were white. The present stone-built
Methodist church in Basseterre, which was begun in 1822 to replace the
wooden chapel, opened in 1825, shortly before Henry Coleridge visited
the adjacent Anglican church and heard the clash of hymn-singing. By
then Methodism had spread throughout the island, there were well over
5000 'hearers', and the majority of the preachers in the country chapels
were drawn from among the free coloureds. In 1830 actual membership
consisted of 3104 slaves, 713 coloureds and 75 whites.

Methodism took rather longer to get established in Nevis. When Coke arrived there from St Kitts in 1787 he found 'every door was shut against the exercise of his Ministry. No Mission had been established previously by any other body of Christians, and yet all access to the slaves was forbidden.'[11] He left after three futile days and the first missionary, Thomas Owens, did not reach the island for another two years. The first simple wooden chapel was built in Charlestown in 1790 and Owens was able to report a congregation of 400 'hearers' three years later (see Plate 11).

Although the open aim of the Methodists was to introduce the gospel to the slaves in such a way as to promote acceptance of their present condition in return for a better after-life, both Owens and his successor, John Brownell, suffered 'much persecution'. After an incident in May 1797 the latter complained to his superiors in London that

> The enemy raged violently, several great men being
> ringleaders. They frequently attended the preaching, and
> disturbed us by swearing, brandishing their bludgeons,
> swords, etc, and forced us often to break up our meetings.
> I applied to a Magistrate for redress, but could obtain none.

As members of the Council may well have been among the 'great men' who disturbed the meetings, and all councillors were magistrates, it is hardly surprising that he got nowhere with his complaint. It may well have exacerbated the situation, as six months later a mob attempted to burn down the chapel. As this failed, the arsonists were then 'restrained from doing any thing further, except venting their rage on some coloured people, who were obliged to flee from the Island, in order to preserve their lives'.[12] A few days later, after Brownell had been waylaid and beaten up, he finally managed to find someone in authority with a conscience and the power to act, and the attacks on him and his chapel were brought to a halt.

Six years later he was still in Nevis and able to report to London 'we have built a commodious chapel, but the increase of hearers has already made it too small. Not only the coloured people and blacks join us, but the whites also, which is a kind of miracle in these regions'.[13] A year later he was able to report the number of members (as opposed to 'hearers') in the island had risen to 1200, of whom four were white. By 1844, when the old 'commodious chapel' in Charlestown was finally replaced by a bigger one built of stone, the Methodist Church in Nevis had over 4000 members.

Given the lack of interest shown by anyone outside the island in the welfare of Anguilla, spiritual or otherwise, it is hardly surprising that it took until well into the nineteenth century for Methodism to arrive there. It was introduced by John Hodge, a free coloured native of the island, who began preaching there in 1813. As the small chapel he built was for many years the only place of worship, as Henry Coleridge noted in 1825, he soon acquired a congregation of two to three hundred 'hearers'. By the time of Coleridge's visit Hodge had been properly ordained and was responsible for '250 admitted members'. Three other Methodist ministers served in turn between 1827 and 1832, but otherwise Hodge was alone until his retirement in 1840. By then there were two chapels on the island, at Road Bay and The Valley, with about 700 members between them.

The Moravian Church

When the Methodist minister William Hammett began preaching in St Kitts in 1787 missionaries belonging to another Protestant Church had already been at work on the island for the previous ten years. These belonged to the Moravian Church, or United Brethren, an evangelical Christian communion which, having been founded in Germany in 1727 had begun work in the West Indies five years later. Their mission to St Kitts began in the middle of 1777, when John Gottwalt, a German, and James Birkby, an Englishman, arrived on the island at the express invitation of John Gardiner, a lawyer and the owner of a plantation at Palmetto Point. Gardiner had been so impressed by what he heard of the Moravian activities in Antigua, where a mission had been in existence since 1756, that on a visit to the Church's offices in London in 1774 he had asked for a similar mission to be established on St Kitts. Gottwalt and Birkby, having first spent six weeks in Antigua acquainting themselves with work among slaves, arrived at Basseterre on 14 June 1777.

As might have been expected, their arrival, together with their stated intention of working to convert slaves to Christianity, was not widely welcomed. Fortunately for Gardiner, the Governor-General of the Leeward Islands, Sir William Burt, had been born in St Kitts and spent most of his time there. As Burt was prepared to welcome the missionaries and offer his support, no serious opposition to their work arose. Even indifference to their activities soon faded, as the planters became aware that the Moravians were solely interested in saving the souls of their slaves, with much emphasis placed on 'industry, frugality, attention to the interests of their masters and the support of their families, together with all their other moral duties'.[14]

At first meetings were held only in a rented house in Basseterre and on Gardiner's estate, but gradually the two missionaries began visiting other plantations. As they had very strict views about suitability for baptism and admission to Holy Communion, the first converts, two female slaves known as Catto and Present, were not baptized until November 1779. Their work proceeded very slowly and in 1786, although there was already a chapel on the site of the present church in Basseterre, there were still less than 100 communicants. The rate of conversion began to pick up after the aged Gottwalt retired in 1788. He was replaced as head of the mission by another German, George Schneller, who was to remain on the island for the next 22 years. During that period the Moravians, working on an ever-increasing number of estates, baptized nearly 3000 adults and well over 1000 children, the chapel in Basseterre was replaced by a larger building and other wooden chapels were built near Cayon and Sandy Point.

Fifteen years later, when Bishop Coleridge visited the island, the Church had about 4500 members. Of these less than 200 were free coloureds, and not one was white. 'The Moravians are numerous and have many establishments in the island', recorded the Bishop's secretary, 'They labor in stillness, as they say of themselves, and are, I really believe, a good and innoxious class of people'.[15] Such innocuousness at this time would have been welcome to the Established Church and to the planters of St Kitts, and to both it must have appeared that the missionaries had done their work very well. Gottwalt, Birkby, Schneller and their assistants had also worked to an undeviating remit, and no attempt was ever made to establish a Moravian presence in either Nevis or Anguilla.

14

Amelioration and the Approach to Emancipation

In the same month in 1792 that many slaves in St Kitts were swept to their deaths in the Great Flood, the British Parliament approved a motion 'that the slave trade ought to be gradually abolished'. This caused outrage among the West Indian planters, nowhere more so than among those of Nevis and St Kitts, as is shown in a letter sent from the latter island in July, addressed to William Shipley, the Dean of St Asaph (see p.96) by his attorney Robert Thomson:

> I am very sorry to observe the Event of the Question on the Slave Trade in the House of Commons, for were they to succeed in putting a Stop to all importation from the Coast of Africa, I very much fear the Sugar Colonies would gradually dwindle & at last be wholly lost....

Thomson, who was also President of the Council, was very much aware of the effect such news had on all the islands' slaves, and of how it would lead to the institution of slavery itself coming under increased scrutiny:

> There is not a word said in Parliament on the Subject but what is conveyed to the Ears of the Slaves, either by those among them who can read & write or by the free Coloured People; and it is not in our power to prevent it.
>   You may then easily conceive the Impressions that some Speeches which have been made there must make on their Minds...they are led to consider their Masters as cruel Tyrants, that their State of Bondage is in sufferable & that the Abolition of the Slave Trade is quickly to lead to the Abolition of Slavery itself. Certain is that they have got the Idea that a general Emancipation is soon to take place, & any Attempts of ours to undeceive them are fruitless & vain.[1]

In the event his forebodings were premature. The outbreak of war between Britain and France in February 1793 combined with the effects of the slave rebellion in Saint-Domingue served to delay abolition of the slave trade for another 14 years. This gave the West Indian planters plenty of time in which to see how Parliament and public opinion in Britain responded to the growing demand for the abolition of slavery, and to mount a counter-campaign.

The Amelioration Act, 1798

The success of this was shown in April 1797 when the House of Commons passed a resolution asking for the King to recommend to the colonial legislatures that they

> adopt such Measures as shall appear to them best calculated
> to obviate the causes which have hitherto impeded the Slave
> Trade, and ultimately to lead to its complete termination;
> *and particularly to the same effect* [author's italics], to enjoy
> such means as may conduce to the Moral and Religious
> improvement of the Negroes, and secure to them
> throughout all the British West India Islands, the certain,
> immediate, and active protection of the Law.[2]

A month later a circular letter from the Secretary of State ordered the various legislatures to act on the resolution. The copy sent to the Leeward Islands was received in St Kitts where, in the middle of a period of over four years in which the colony was without a resident governor-general, Robert Thomson as the senior of all the council presidents was acting in this capacity. In order to come up with changes which would satisfy the Secretary of State without causing dissension among the various islands it was found expedient to revive the General Council – a body consisting of representatives from each island which had been set up by Stapleton in the 1670s but which had not been convened for over 70 years.

A joint legislature, made up of a General Council formed by two councillors from each of the island councils of Antigua, St Kitts, Nevis, Montserrat and the Virgin Islands, together with a General Assembly of five elected representatives from each island, met in Basseterre on 1 March 1798. Thomson insisted they concentrate on four issues: the removal of 'every kind of impediment' against the natural increase of the slave population, improvements in the moral and religious lives of the slaves, a replacement of the existing 'harsh and oppressive' slavery laws with 'an entire new code', and the introduction of new standards for feeding and clothing slaves. An Amelioration Act covering these subjects was produced at the end of eight weeks in session. It was accompanied by two other Acts: one to free white Roman Catholics from civil disabilities, and the other to restrict further payment of the $4\frac{1}{2}$ per cent duty which had been payable on all sugar leaving the island since 1663. All three were immediately sent to London for approval.

Thomson lost no time in informing Shipley of the extra expense which would be incurred in the running of his estates in St Kitts and Nevis once the Amelioration Act had been approved. Writing on 9 May he reported that the 'general Council and Assembly of the Leeward Islands' had passed 'Laws for meliorating the Condition of the Slaves; and by a Law they have passed, their food has been encreased about one third, & their Clothing doubled'. He gave no details of the many other clauses, but instead restricted himself to explaining why the Act had been called for in the first place:

> The Intention of the Resolution of the House of
> Commons, was, by rendering the Condition of the Slaves
> more comfortable to them, to try whether it would have
> the effect of encreasing the Species, and thereby render the
> Importation of Negroes from Africa unnecessary. This
> certainly is a better mode than an abrupt & forced
> abolition of the Slave Trade, & I wish it may have the
> effect, but I have my doubts about it. It would appear that
> this measure was suggested by some West-India
> Proprietors in Parliament, with view of getting rid of the
> agitation of the question of abolition so often in
> Parliament which they conceived might be sooner or later
> productive of much mischief in the Colonies.[3]

The Amelioration Act was approved by Order-in-Council on 20 May 1799. It set minimum standards for the more humane treatment of slaves, by specifying increased scales of clothing and provisions, making the provision of regular medical attendance and sick quarters obligatory, and by replacing the old 'harsh and oppressive' slavery laws with 'an entire new code'. Under this code an inquest had to be held on any slave over the age of six who died suddenly without having been seen by a doctor in the previous two days, and all deaths had to be reported within six hours and before any burial had taken place. In addition, on the first day of every year, each owner had to provide the legislature with 'a just and true Account' of all the births and deaths which had taken place among his or her slaves during the previous twelve months. With regard to punishments, slaves were no longer to be imprisoned or flogged without good reason, and the use of 'unnecessary severities' such as iron collars, chains and weights could make an owner liable to a fine. When it came to the employment of slaves, none was to work for more than 14 hours a day (with meal breaks of two and a half hours) 'unless in crop time, or from evident necessity'. Women more than five months pregnant, and those who had six or more children, were to be given only light work.

Although the Secretary of State had indicated that marriage among the slaves was to be encouraged, his views were ignored by those drawing up the Act, which stated contemptuously that it was 'unnecessary and even improper to enforce the Celebration of any religious Rites among the Slaves...less the Violation of sacred Vows be too often added to the Crime of Infidelity.' However, it was taken that an improvement in morals would result from the recording of any unions, from the encouragement of couples to remain together, and from the rewarding of faithful women who gave birth with cash payments. Finally, it was found necessary to insert a clause which made the sexual molestation of such a 'married' female slave by a white man a criminal offence worthy of a £100 fine.

The Amelioration Act came into effect in all the Leeward Islands at the end of June. The other two Acts which had been sent to London were both disallowed. The 'Act to admit upon Conditions, White Persons professing the Catholic Religion in the Leeward Islands to all the Rights and Privileges enjoyed by Protestant Subjects within the same' stood no chance of being approved. As 'Catholic Relief' laws introduced in Britain some years early had precipitated riots, it was hardly likely the government would extend rights abroad which were still denied at home. It was equally unthinkable that the $4\frac{1}{2}$ per cent sugar duty would be abolished. This paid the salaries and pensions of governors and other officials and would continue to do so for another 39 years.

The provisions of the Amelioration Act were intended mainly to increase the slave population by natural means, and to delay as long as possible the abolition of the slave trade – then seen by men like Thomson as being eventually inevitable. The passing of the Act was also seen as a means of taking the initiative away from the abolitionist movement, by demonstrating that the planters themselves could legislate to improve the life and well-being of their slaves. This had the desired effect. Although the slave trade was banned from the beginning of 1808, much earlier than the planters would have wished, a concerted effort to abolish slavery altogether was not mounted until after 1823, when the London Society for the Gradual Mitigation and Abolition of Slavery was founded. In the interim, although now perhaps better clothed and fed, life for the slaves in St Kitts, Nevis and Anguilla continued very much as it always had.

The Huggins Affair in Nevis, 1810

One man who probably resented the ending of the slave trade more than most was Edward Huggins of Nevis who, having been born on the island and started out life as an overseer, was by 1810 the owner of several estates and over 200 slaves. Some of the latter, who had been sold together with an estate he had bought in 1808 and then placed under the supervision of one of his sons, proved particularly troublesome, either by running away in small groups or feigning illness. As a result, by the beginning of 1810 the son, Peter Huggins, had to all intents and purposes lost control of the estate.

This so infuriated his father that on 23 January he ordered Peter to take the worst-behaved slaves, ten men and ten women, under two trusted slave-drivers, to the market-place in Charlestown. Once there the drivers were set to work flogging each slave in turn, a process which took a very long time and was witnessed by a large crowd. Among the onlookers were three magistrates (one being another of Huggins's sons, also named Edward) and the Deputy Secretary of the island, John Burke. Edward Huggins senior seems to have had no set punishment in mind, possessed nothing in the way of humanity, and had no intention of observing the law which prohibited cruel punishments. No two slaves received the same number of lashes, the women suffered just as much as the men, and the length of the floggings varied enormously.

The first to suffer was a man who was whipped non-stop for about 15 minutes. After that Burke took it upon himself to count the number of lashes given to each of the other 19, in the end finding these ranged between 47 and 242 for the men, and from 49 to 291 for the women.[4]

A week later the Nevis Assembly passed a resolution stating that Huggins had been 'guilty of barbarity altogether unprecedented in this island', and at the beginning of May he was brought to trial, accused of administering excessive floggings. As he was prosecuted in a half-hearted fashion by a lawyer named James Weekes, before a jury packed with men beholden to the defendant in one way or another, his eventual acquittal came as very little surprise to anyone on the island. The President of the Council, Thomas Cottle, who was Huggins's son-in-law and whose estate attorney had been a juror, showed his approbation by recommending Weekes for the post of chief justice. Outside the island it was a different matter. The Governor-General, Hugh Elliot, was so incensed by the verdict that later in the year, as we have seen, he told Lord Liverpool the island courts could no longer be trusted to provide justice as there were not enough decent white men around to provide them with proper judges and juries. Liverpool responded by ordering the dismissal of the magistrates who had stood by during the episode in Charlestown. Another man who had cause to regret the episode lived in Basseterre. He was the printer of the *St Christopher Gazette,* whom Huggins successfully sued for libel for having precipitously published the condemnation contained in the resolution passed by the Nevis Assembly.

Edward Huggins seems to have been nothing more than an uncultivated bully with a sharp nose for business, and none of his sons was much better. One evening in October 1812 the younger Edward Huggins shot and killed a young slave in the street, alleging that his victim had been about to commit a theft. Following his arrest he was granted bail by James Weekes, then the Chief Justice, to await the findings of the Grand Jury convened to decide what sort of case he had to answer. As this jury threw out a murder charge he was eventually tried for manslaughter, found guilty and fined £250. In Antigua Elliot found this verdict nearly as upsetting as he had that of the elder Huggins over two years earlier, but could do little but question the wisdom of the accused being allowed bail. This caused Weekes to resign as Chief Justice, complaining that the Governor-General's comment infringed on the constitutional independence of judges.

The Davis Episode in St Kitts, 1813

It was not only in Nevis that slaves suffered from villainous punishments or died unnatural deaths. In St Kitts towards the end of 1812 a female slave named Eliza on one of the Romney estates died under suspicious circumstances. The attorney for the estate was the Reverend William Davis, and it was soon being voiced around the island that Eliza had succumbed from a flogging he had ordered or even administered. One of his principal accusers was John Julius, President of the Council and the man Davis had replaced as the estate's attorney. In March 1813, mostly as a result of Julius's accusations, it was decided that Davis with three of his sons and a son-in-law should all stand trial for murder.

Even though all were acquitted at the trial which took place a few months later, the case – involving an Anglican minister charged with the murder of a female slave – caused a sensation in London, greatly perturbing both the Secretary of State (now Earl Bathurst) and the Bishop of London. Soon after the acquittal Elliot sent details of the case to Bathurst. 'The Reverend William Davis has been acquitted by the verdict of the jury of the heinous crime of murder', he reported, 'and this therefore must be deemed a proof of his innocence in that respect.' But, as far as Elliot was concerned, that was not the end of the matter. 'It behoves me, however, to remark', he continued:

> that his conduct towards his slaves has been very
> unbecoming to the sacred character of a clergyman, such as
> striking them occasionally with his hand or with the whip.
> If the nature of such punishment should be administered in
> however slight a degree by the Attorney or Manager of an
> estate personally, or even by his directions, I conceive this
> alone to be a sufficient reason why a clergyman holding a
> living in any of the islands ought not to permitted to act in
> the capacity of an Attorney or Manager of an estate.[5]

The whole affair was not only a great embarrassment to the Bishop of London, who subsequently ordered William Davis to withdraw from the management of any estate, but also to the rector of St Paul's church in Charlestown who, of course, was William's son Daniel.

Around this time in Nevis the Reverend Daniel Davis was having problems enough of his own in connection with slaves. His attempts to convert them or even interest them in the rudiments of Christianity were not only meeting with little success, but were upsetting many of his white parishioners. An incident in 1816 caused even wider ructions, following his informing the Bishop of London that he had 'recently met with a serious obstruction in the discharge of a duty' arising when

> I lately attempted to marry by Banns an enlightened slave
> in my parish after having obtained both a verbal and
> written consent of his Master.... My attempt was no
> sooner known publicly than the marriage of slaves became
> a subject of warm legislative discussion and marked
> reprobation; and I was accordingly instructed by the
> President of His Majesty's Council...to suspend the
> marriage until the Governor's opinion was taken on the
> subject.

Needless to say, as marriage among the slaves had been ruled out of the Amelioration Act 18 years earlier, Davis was soon informed that Governor Probyn in St Kitts, having consulted with the Attorney-General, 'found that such marriage would be merely nugatory, and therefore highly improper'.[6]

As the Bishop of London believed marriage would help to improve the slaves' morals he took up the matter with Bathurst. Referring to the letter from Davis, he urged action to prevent the West Indian legislatures from continuing 'to act in such direct opposition to the laws of God and nature', while acknowledging that 'we are not to judge the West Indies in general by the spirit which prevails in the small island of Nevis'.[7] There was not much Bathurst could do except to seek the opinion of the Law Officers, who 'found that the ecclesiastical law has always held that slaves are competent to marry without any reference to the master's consent'. This opinion was common knowledge in both islands by early in 1818. Although no change was made in the law and records are few, it seems very probable that slave marriages in Anglican churches began to take place early in the 1820s, at first in St Kitts and somewhat later in Nevis.

The Huggins Case in Nevis, 1817

In the spring of 1817, while Daniel Davis was struggling to sow the seeds of Christianity among the slaves in his Charlestown parish, Edward Huggins was once again making free with the whip and inflicting suffering on other slaves in the north of the island. This took place on 28 March at the Round Hill Estate, owned by Huggins's son-in-law Thomas Cottle who was then in England. While visiting the estate in his capacity as Cottle's attorney, Huggins was told by the estate manager Francis Newton that one of the slaves, William Nolan:

> had broken into and robbed the house of another slave
> residing in the town, of three pairs of stockings and eight
> yards of calico; that the receivers of the stolen goods
> would not restore the property, and requested that
> Mr. Huggins would interfere.[8]

Huggins needed no second request to take action. The first of the three miscreants to be punished was Richard, who was found in possession of one pair of stolen stockings. Having been forced to lie down he was then flogged by the driver with a cart whip. 'I reckoned 90 lashes whilst I was there,' Newton stated later,

> I then left the place, and went upstairs, where I live.
> During that time the flogging continued; and after I had
> gone up stairs (which are a considerable flight of steps) and
> gone to a window, three lashes were given. To the best of
> my knowledge, he received altogether 100 lashes.[9]

The next to suffer was a slave named David, who had also obtained a pair of stockings. He too was made to lie down and Newton observed from his upstairs window that 'he received 80 lashes with the cart whip, from the same driver'. Nolan, who had already been flogged for the theft by Newton, 'was then laid down, and received from 25 to 30 lashes'. All of this took place in front of the rest of the estate's slaves, among whom were two young women named Thisbe and Cressy. As the former was Richard's sister and the latter David's half-sister it is hardly surprising that long before the flogging was over both were sobbing loudly. Their tears so annoyed Huggins that as soon as the flogging of Nolan had ended he had both girls pulled out of the crowd, laid down and each given at least 20 lashes.

Six days later, after news of what had transpired had become common knowledge, two magistrates conducted an examination of a charge of cruelty against Huggins. This led to a bill of indictment being drawn up by a Grand Jury and on 20 May, to Huggins standing trial, accused of cruelty under the Amelioration Act. James Weekes once again acted as the prosecutor, and once again only in a half-hearted manner. So much so, that the defending counsel had little difficulty in refuting the charge. As 'the crime for which Richard and David were thus punished was one which in England might have subjected the person guilty of it to fourteen years transportation,' he told the jury, 'it could not therefore with any propriety be pretended, that in their case [Huggins] had exceeded the limits of that authority which the law had vested in him'. As for the two girls Thisbe and Cressy,

> it was not within the bounds of credibility, that they
> should have been punished merely for crying, unless there
> was something of a clamour or disturbance in their cries,
> though perhaps not absolutely amounting to what [a]
> witness calls riot....[10]

Not surprisingly, in the face of such specious arguments, Huggins was acquitted once again. The verdict was probably no more than the majority of the white population of both Nevis and St Kitts would have expected, but it was not so in England. When details of the case were discussed in the House of Commons a year later they made a distinct impression on the abolitionist members. 'What must be the state of the population of those islands if they [are] to be whipped at pleasure for giving way to feelings of nature at the distress of their friends?' queried the distinguished law reformer Sir Samuel Romilly,

> Poor unprotected female slaves were to be whipped with
> the greatest severity – and for what? for nothing more than
> their being possessed of those feelings of humanity,
> tenderness, and compassion, which were an ornament to
> the highest class of their sex in any country & feelings
> which did honour to society.[11]

The Rawlins Case in St Kitts, 1817

In St Kitts in early September 1817 it was reported 'to a gentleman of the island, by a slave belonging to Hutchinson's estate', that a fellow slave called Congo Jack had recently been punished so severely that he had died and then been buried without any inquest taking place. This news was passed on to a judge and, after the Attorney-General had been consulted, an exhumation of the body was ordered. '[T]he 'magistrates went down to the estate', Governor Probyn reported to Bathurst a few days later, where they 'had the body taken up, examined by two surgeons; when several marks of violence appeared on him, an inquest sat, and, to the astonishment of every person, they gave it in, "Died by the visitation of God."' Understandably this caused Probyn 'great uneasiness' and he ordered a fuller investigation. The examination of several of the estate's slaves, including one called Tom Titley, led to a driver named Creole Jack being charged with murder.

During the trial, which took place on 27 September, it was discovered that Congo Jack had been a recaptured runaway who was flogged on two successive days for refusing to work after his recapture. Several slave witnesses were called but all except one were obviously too frightened to say anything which might land them in trouble. The exception was Tom Titley, who had run away with Congo Jack and been recaptured at the same time. After their return they had been chained together day and night. His testimony, as transcribed in the court, provided a graphic account of Congo Jack's final hours:

> the negroes were carrying dung, when [Creole] Jack ran
> them all down; he began to lick Congo Jack…licked him
> with a cart-whip, did not count the licks; licked him with a
> cart-whip all the time he was carrying dung; deceased cried
> out that he could not go any more, he was sick: he called
> for water; he lay down in the field, and could not do any
> thing; lived until the negroes went for cow meat; was
> chained with witness when he died; prisoner beat deceased
> with a stick which drivers walk with; he had his whip
> round his neck; beat deceased with a stick on his head, on
> his shoulders, on his side, on his back….

Even though it was obvious to all that Congo Jack's death had been brought about by the severity of the driver's flogging and beating, the trial ended with his acquittal. Creole Jack was a slave himself, and as such he had had no option but to carry out the orders he had been given by the estate manager, the recently ordained Reverend William Rawlins.

A few days later a Grand Jury was convened, and on 16 October Rawlins was brought to trial for murder. It lasted only one day. In spite of testimony to the effect that on his orders Congo Jack had been flogged not only by Creole Jack but by a second driver called Big Stephen, the jury found itself unable to find Rawlins guilty. Instead, showing what little value they placed on the life of a recalcitrant slave, and in order to protect one of their own kind as much as possible, the jury found him guilty of manslaughter; a verdict which earned him a three-month gaol sentence and a fine of £200. When details of the case were forwarded by Probyn to the Secretary of State in London, Bathurst was incensed. In a letter sent in early January 1818 he criticized Probyn for appearing 'not to consider the transaction in so very serious a light'. In his opinion it was a most serious matter:

> the body of the unfortunate victim was buried without any
> coroner's inquest, in direct violation of the law of the
> Island, in cases (as this was) where a slave dies without
> having been attended, previous to his death, by a medical
> person...[also] it is stated to have been proved, that the
> most horrid cruelties had been inflicted on this
> unfortunate individual.... If this statement be true, or in
> any way approaching to truth, Mr. Rawlins could not have
> been guilty of manslaughter; it must have been murder, or
> an Acquittal.[12]

There was nothing Probyn or anyone else could do about this particular case or the verdict, but there was something that could be done to try to prevent a repetition. In May the 1798 Amelioration Act was amended 'in order to prevent any person from mutilating, dismembering, or cruelly beating or confining any slave or slaves'. From now on, any 'master, mistress, owner, possessor or other person whatsoever' who mutilated or dismembered a slave, or who 'wantonly or cruelly' whipped, maltreated, beat, bruised, wounded, or imprisoned a slave without sufficient support would suffer fine or imprisonment, or both. Also, 'in atrocious cases', the maltreated slave could be given his or her freedom 'and discharged from all manner of servitude to all intents and purposes whatsoever'. Another clause specified that 'in order to restrain arbitrary punishment' from now on no slave was to receive more than ten lashes at any one time and for a single offence, unless 'the owner, attorney, guardian or manager' of the estate was present. Even then the maximum punishment which could be given was limited to 39 lashes at any one time.

The Betto Douglas Case in St Kitts, 1825

The amended Amelioration Act followed on from an Act of 1816, which gave slaves the right to trial by jury, and another in 1817, which required their annual registration with a strict account of births and deaths. Taken together they provided the slaves with some protection from gross oppression, but did nothing to make life less unpleasant or more bearable. Nor did they prevent particularly cruel methods from being used to coerce slaves considered to be intransigent or over-argumentative, something made all too clear in St Kitts in 1825.

In April of that year a 52-year-old female slave named Elizabeth Douglas, who belonged to the absentee proprietor Earl Romney, petitioned the Governor-General (by this time Colonel Charles Maxwell) to be granted her freedom. Betto, as she was more usually known, had for the previous three years been allowed to find work for herself in return for a set monthly fee. She based her claim on a firm belief that her manumission had been agreed to by Romney many years earlier, but that successive attorneys for his estate, because of her value, had refused to take the necessary action. Maxwell had the matter investigated but as her claim was not supported by the current attorney, Richard Cardin, or any of the previous attorneys who were questioned, her petition was rejected and she returned to the estate as a slave. Soon afterwards, because Betto now refused to continue paying the estate part of the wages she earned, Cardin had her put in the stocks, where she stayed for 20 hours each day 'from about the beginning of May to the 2d day of December'.

When this came to light, although it seemed to Maxwell to be 'strong evidence of the illegal treatment of the old woman', he had to confess that 'this sort of confinement being a common usage, it is from custom considered justifiable and proper'. But, because 'this opinion is strongly reprobated by the Attorney General and some humane thinking gentlemen in the island', the matter did not end there. In the following March Cardin appeared before a Grand Jury, charged with reference to 'a certain mulatto slave called Betto Douglas', that he 'did, with force and arms assault and cruelly maltreat and confine and keep in confinement, by enclosing and locking up the leg of the said mulatto slave in certain wooden stocks'. Regrettably, as far as poor Betto was concerned, none of the 'humane thinking gentlemen in the island' sat on the jury:

> In returning this Bill of Indictment ignored unanimously,
> the Grand Jury feel themselves called upon respectfully to
> state to the Court their regret that a prosecution should
> have been founded upon so frivolous a complaint, and

supported only by the slender evidence adduced before
them, whereby the feelings of an honourable, humane and
respectable man have been considerably wounded
unnecessarily....

In June Maxwell forwarded details to London, where once again
Bathurst must have been infuriated by what he read. 'It is far from my wish
to use any expressions which could be painful to the feelings or injuries to
the reputation of any gentleman in the Colony', he replied through gritted
teeth at the beginning of August.

> but I cannot withhold the expression of my deepest regret,
> that such proceedings...should have occurred.
> I have not particularly adverted to the offence with
> which Betto Douglas was charged by Mr. Cardin, because it
> is not very easy, nor perhaps very material, to discover the
> precise nature of it. But it would appear from the language
> of Mr. Cardin himself, that she was kept in confinement 'in
> consequence of her refusal to continue the payment of the
> hire she had been in the habit of giving her master'.
> If this were really the offence, it would be superfluous
> to observe how utterly the punishment was dispropor-
> tionate to such an offence.[13]

The Annexation of Anguilla, 1825

There are no known cases of extreme cruelty to slaves recorded in
Anguilla, such as took place in St Kitts and Nevis. This is not to say that
events such as severe floggings did not take place, but on the whole, the
islanders, white or black, and in the case of the latter free or slave, lived too
close to the soil or the sea for such events to be other than very infrequent.
'The colony is very poor', observed Henry Coleridge in 1825, before
adding,

> I fear the slaves suffer a good deal from want of certain and
> adequate provision, and the mode of meeting the scarcity
> by giving them one, two or three days liberty to seek it any
> where is decidedly an aggravation of the evil. This time,
> which is almost always devoted by them to idleness or
> stealing, should be employed even compulsorily, if
> necessary, in the planting of provision grounds of which
> any quantity may be taken in, and of any quality.[14]

At this time Anguilla was described by another writer as 'scarcely more than a third cultivated', with less than a dozen sugar plantations employing under half of the island's slaves.

Three years earlier Maxwell had been asked by the Secretary of State to suggest that that the legislature of St Kitts assume responsibility for the administration of Anguilla. This had produced such an outcry in both islands that Maxwell reported it could not be done, but Bathurst was not deterred. He persisted with the idea, writing to Maxwell in May 1824: 'I have to observe that the moral condition of the [Anguillian] community, which is itself the evil to be met, renders the community an unfit instrument of counter action.' In his view, the state of Anguillian society was such that he would not 'hesitate in rejecting the expedient of convoking any portion of such a society with the view of entrusting to it the charge of a corrective legislation'.[15] Maxwell was ordered to make every effort to get the legislature of St Kitts to accept responsibility for the enforcement of order and the administration of justice in Anguilla.

In Basseterre the Assembly submitted to the demand, but only on condition that a commission of enquiry should first determine the state of the island and make recommendations concerning its future administration. This was arranged and in February 1825, after the commission had reported, an Act was passed to bring about the annexation of Anguilla, but specifying that this should entail no financial commitment by St Kitts. The post of lieutenant-governor was abolished and the island's chief official became a stipendiary magistrate, who would also function, in the absence of a resident doctor, as the dispenser of medicines. The Anguilla Council was dissolved and replaced by a Vestry consisting of the magistrate, the rector of the Anglican church, and 12 members elected by those male inhabitants who paid rates and taxes. Administration of justice passed to the chief justice of St Kitts, and the island was permitted to send one representative to the House of Assembly there. These changes did not meet with the whole-hearted approval of the Anguillians, who in March protested to Maxwell that the abolition of the Council was not in their best interest. Their protest was of no avail, coming as it did from an island which was then being cited in the House of Commons as being

> in a most wretched condition both as relates to its internal
> Government and the resources of the inhabitants. As to
> the first of these, nothing could be worse; there is not a
> semblance of law or justice, and consequently acts of the
> greatest outrage are committed with impunity.... With
> regard to the resources of the island, they are poor
> indeed...the minute subdivision of property, and the

> dispersion of properties in this island...the general
> poverty of its resources, insomuch, that though its
> inhabitants are more than three thousand, it contains no
> town, and its circulating medium is stated to be under five
> hundred pounds.[16]

The Vestry Act passed in 1827 divided the island into three electoral districts, called Spring, Valley and Road, each electing four vestrymen. At around the same time Jacob Hardtman was elected as the island's first representative to be sent to the St Kitts Assembly.

Free Coloured Society

The life of all those making up the free coloured population (here, a term also taken to include free blacks) of St Kitts and Nevis during the first three decades of the nineteenth century was confined not only by discriminatory laws and regulations, but also by the intolerance and prejudice of the whites. At the beginning of the century free coloureds enjoyed none of the political privileges available to whites. It was not until 1824 that males with the necessary property qualifications were given the vote, and then another nine years passed before they became eligible for election to the Assembly. Even then discrimination continued, as was made evident in St Kitts, where the legislature immediately increased the property qualifications for candidates, arguing that to leave them unchanged would 'give the ascendancy in the Legislative and Executive Branches to the free people of colour, and free Blacks, over the Whites'.

Free coloureds were treated with equal contempt by the Established Church, being made to sit only in 'certain pews at the extreme ends' when alive, and buried in a part of the churchyard quite separate from the whites when dead. They were debarred from the legal profession: an Act passed in St Kitts in 1820 openly specified that only white men would be admitted to the Bar...of the Court' and allowed 'to plead as counsel there'. Discrimination also extended into education: for example, in Basseterre up until 1830, a school which was supported in part by the charitable offerings of free coloureds denied entry to any of their children. As a result it was such children who probably got the most benefit from the early schools established by the Methodist and Moravian missionaries, and which are discussed in Chapter 19. Not a great deal is known about the free coloureds of Anguilla but their lives, in comparison with those of their fellows in St Kitts or Nevis, and because of the poverty of the island and the effect this had had on the way society developed, were undoubtedly both much simpler and considerably less restricted.

Some of the better-off among the free coloureds, of St Kitts in particular, became slave-owners. Most owned only one or two, but of the total of 169 owned by 23 free coloureds in that island in 1829, a third belonged to one man, Jedekiah Edmeade. Others deprecated slave ownership. Ralph Cleghorn, who was born in St Kitts in 1805 and educated in England, inherited a thriving business from his white father in 1825. He later became very active in the struggle to obtain civil rights for free coloureds and, on a visit to England in connection with this in 1829, became a friend of a leading abolitionist, Zachary Macaulay. His views about slavery were stated in a letter sent to Macaulay in June 1833:

> I freed my own Slaves (never desiring to own one – but I had acquired some by marriage and some by bequest in all 14 or 15). I induced my wife's only sister to manumit hers 4 or 5 in number. I undertook the Cause of the Coloured people, I became the avowed enemy of Slavery, and as a consequence a victim to the displeasure of the Planters and others of the White Population.

He had provided details of the form taken by this 'displeasure' earlier in the letter. 'It may seem strange to your mind', he told Macaulay,

> that in consequence of my having espoused the negro cause positive combinations have been formed against my *pecuniary prospects*. Clerks of the white population, (*Planters*) *who are of course the only buyers* have been desired not to purchase a single article at my Establishment, and so pertinaciously adhered to has this system been, that I am now *endeavouring* to make arrangements with a person who is to assume my concerns.[17]

Cleghorn, to his credit, was also involved, in a way which it is now impossible to determine, with the events which transpired as a result of the Betto Douglas case of 1825. At some time after her release from the stocks she ran away from the Romney Estate and, aided and supported by men like Cleghorn, provided with a safe refuge. In his letter to Macaulay, in order to stress his sincerity as 'an avowed enemy of Slavery' he drew attention 'to the great risk that I have ventured to run in poor Beta Douglass's Case'. This was something

> which if the fact of her being enabled by pecuniary assistance to evade the grasp of her persecutor could be traced and *fixed on me*, I should incur *under an act of this island* a liability to pay her owners an amount which in her case would be most enormous she having been in

concealment about 8 years…. The Act to which I allude
provides that persons who shall be in any [way]
instrumental in keeping slaves from their owners shall be
liable to pay such owners not less than 12s. currency per
day for *every* day of such absence of said slave. Up to this
date I have fortunately avoided this penalty, although
general suspicion attaches to me the blame in many cases
of which I am innocent…[18]

Betto, who remained in hiding until after 1834, was not the only slave
in St Kitts to seize her own freedom during the last years of slavery. A
male slave named Marcus ran away from the Cunningham's Estate near
Cayon in 1831, and took to the mountains. During the next three or four
years 'Marcus of the Woods', as he soon was known, organized other runaways, who came and went, into raiding parties which harassed estates on
the leeward side of the island for food and supplies. Nothing much else is
known about him other than that, like Betto, he was never caught and
remained at large until after slavery had ended.

Although, as Cleghorn made clear, a free coloured man's business
could be ruined by 'displeased' planters, none of the discrimination foisted
on the free coloureds by the whites did anything to stem a rapid increase
in numbers of the former or to prevent a decline from taking place in the
numbers of the latter in both St Kitts and Nevis. Between the opening of
the nineteenth century and the emancipation year of 1834 the free
coloured population of St Kitts more than doubled to around 3000, and
that of Nevis increased threefold to well over 1500, while their white pop-
ulations fell to about 1600 and 1000 respectively. In Anguilla in 1834 there
were very nearly the same number, about 350, of whites and free
coloureds.

15

Emancipation and the Aftermath

Towards the end of 1832 Lieutenant-Colonel Robert Nickle took over from Colonel Charles Maxwell as governor-general of the Colony of St Kitts, Nevis, Anguilla and the Virgin Islands. He was to hold the post for only a matter of months, as in the following year the British government decided to resuscitate the Leeward Islands colony, and put these islands, together with Antigua, Barbuda and Montserrat, under a governor-general based in Antigua. When Sir Evan MacGregor assumed this post in 1833 Nickle became the lieutenant-governor of St Kitts and Anguilla, with a president in charge of the administration of Nevis.

No sooner had these changes taken place than in London on 28 August the royal assent was given to a bill to abolish slavery throughout the British colonies on the first day of August one year later. This had only been achieved through the efforts of the Anti-Slavery Society which, following its formation in 1823, had orchestrated a campaign both in and out of Parliament. Two major problems had had to be resolved by the government before the bill was passed. These were to decide on the way in which the slave-owners were to be compensated for the loss of their property, and

> to devise some mode of inducing them [the slaves], when
> relieved from the fear of the Driver and his whip, to
> undergo the regular continuous labour which is
> indispensable in carrying on the production of sugar.[1]

The first had been solved by voting the sum of £20,000,000 to be distributed among the slaves' owners, and the second by introducing the concept of 'apprenticeship', and making the granting of freedom a two-stage process.

The Emancipation Act laid down that the only slaves who would become free on 1 August 1834 were children under six years of age. All the rest would be apprenticed: field slaves for six years and the remainder for four years. During the apprenticeship period all would have to work for $40\frac{1}{2}$ hours a week for their former owners, who in turn would be responsible for all food, clothing, housing and medical care. Apprentices wishing to work outside the set hours were free to offer their services to anyone and demand wages. Apprentices could not be sold, other than together with the estates on which they worked, and neither could they be summarily punished, all disputes between owners and apprentices having to be dealt with by specially appointed magistrates.

Emancipation and Apprenticeship

Details of the apprenticeship system reached the Leeward Islands long before emancipation day and produced a lot of discontent, particularly among the slaves of St Kitts. Early in 1834, much to the distress of the other planters, Earl Romney manumitted all of his 300 or so slaves. This act must have been especially pleasing to Betto Douglas, who could now come out of hiding, but it served to fuel the dissatisfaction felt by the rest of the island's slaves. Early in July the Lieutenant-Governor (by this time Lieutenant-Colonel John Nixon) held meetings on a number of estates around the island in order to spell out the reasons why a period of apprenticeship was thought necessary, and to counteract the effect of Romney's action. '[If] any master chooses to say he will not have apprentices, you must not think that will release you from labour', he informed the assembled slaves on one estate, 'there are other laws that will compel you to work'.

Whatever good he may have achieved by this was immediately negated by the receipt of news from Antigua that the legislature there had voted to dispense with the apprenticeship period altogether. As a result, as Friday 1 August approached, many of the slaves in St Kitts made it known that they had no intention of returning to work as apprentices on the Monday which followed emancipation day.

This caused great alarm and, together with the general resentment felt by all the slaves about apprenticeship, went a long way towards curbing any planned celebration of freedom. Nixon was particularly worried about the threat of a general strike, and how it might be dealt with. The small detachment of regular troops which had been stationed on Brimstone Hill since early in 1833 was hardly big enough to cope with incidents which could occur anywhere around the island, and in his view the militia was 'worse than can be expressed for want of arms and accoutrements'. As a result he sent word to the Governor-General in Antigua, asking for more troops. MacGregor responded by sending a request to army headquarters in Barbados, and then crossing over to St Kitts to take charge of the situation himself.

On Monday 4 August on over a dozen estates the labourers, as they had now become, refused to turn out to do any field work. Once this became known in Basseterre, MacGregor convened a Privy Council meeting, at which it was decided to offer rewards for information about 'the person or persons who have originally and secretly instigated the labouring classes to oppose or resist the operation of the Act for Abolition of Slavery, by misleading them as to its true intent and meaning or otherwise', and those who were 'engaged in inducing the labouring classes to continue their opposition to the Laws'. Later in the day copies of a proclamation, stating that martial law would be declared if the labourers did not go back to work, were posted around the island. They had no effect as within 'an hour or two after they had been posted up, not one copy could be seen'. This gave MacGregor and Nixon cause to believe 'that the domestic apprentices, and perhaps the lower class of free people, were in council with the general mass of the disaffected'.

As a result of this, and the fact that no one came forward with information which might earn a reward, another Council meeting was held on 6 August. Reassured by the arrival of two warships from Barbados, and because 'the labouring classes are still in a state of insubordination and open resistance', the Council had little hesitation in resolving 'that His Excellency the Governor be advised to proclaim Martial Law'. No sooner had this been done, and marines had landed from the two ships to reinforce the local garrison and the militia, than action began to be taken against the striking labourers, many of whom by now had taken to the hills. As little civilian control was exercised over the troops, and all the labourers they apprehended were given a summary flogging, within three days the situation showed every sign of getting out of hand.

On Saturday 9 August MacGregor decided an amnesty was needed. He issued an instruction that word was to be sent 'to the runaways...informing them that should they be at work on Monday morning no notice will be taken of their conduct during the present week'. At the same time he called for 'a return from every estate...on Monday of the persons absent from work that morning', and ordered 'no farther punishments be inflicted'. This attempt to restore order to the island was only partially successful, and Monday morning came and went without a general return to work. A possible reason why this did not take place, and many labourers still remained in the hills, is given in the return sent in from one of the estates where work did resume. The manager of Cunningham's Estate reported

> that all the people on this estate are at work except James
> alias Baller who was so desperate a character, that I felt it

my duty to lodge him in gaol…previous to 1st August
1834. And a man named Markus an African a most daring
and dangerous character, who has been absent three years
and has always been a runaway, goes by the title King of
the Woods, has been condemned for murder, has now a
charge of felony…hanging over his head and as I am
credibly informed…has a gang of 30 and upward under his
command in the mountains…. No order may be expected
in the Country, unless he is taken….

The hunt for the striking labourers continued, but as the days went by
MacGregor and Nixon came under increasing pressure from the planters
to force the pace, and bring the situation to an end. This led to an all-out
effort being launched on Friday 15 August, with troops sent to comb the
mountain slopes where it was believed most of the runaways had gone to
ground. This was so successful that 'they took prisoners and drove off
from the woods negroes who had never before been seen by their present
proprietors, and others who had been absent from the estates three, four,
five and six years'. At the same time, other troops began to destroy the
huts and provision grounds of missing labourers, particularly those from
some of the estates on the leeward side of the island. All this had the
desired effect and before the weekend was over the rest of the runaway
labourers, with the exception of one who had been killed and the elusive
Marcus, had capitulated. Martial law was lifted on Monday 18 August.

During the 12 days the island was under martial law, as well as handing
out summary punishments in the field, the military authorities arrested
over 100 labourers and convened 16 courts martial. Fourteen men and two
women were tried for crimes ranging from neglect of duty and disobedi-
ence to mutiny and sedition, and all but two of them were convicted. Nine
of the guilty were punished by flogging or imprisonment or both. The
rest, four men named John Dickenson, Cook, Henry and Teague, and a
woman called Bronte, were sentenced to be banished for life. These five
were sent to Bermuda where, considering the difference in affluence which
now exists between that island and St Kitts, no doubt more than one
family has good cause to bless the court that handed down this particular
punishment to an ancestor.

The remainder of the labourers who had been taken into custody were
released under a general amnesty proclaimed by MacGregor before he
returned to Antigua. His relief at the restoration of order is made very
apparent in a letter he sent to the Council before leaving. 'All Circumstances
considered', he wrote,

> it will appear to you, I earnestly hope, that the
> insubordination in this Island, so fraught with Peril, at this

> crisis, to the surrounding Colonies, has been checked with
> as little asperity as could have been well anticipated...several
> of the apprenticed labourers personally assured me of their
> contrition and between 80 and 90, whom my concluding
> Proclamation released from the Jail of Basseterre, requested
> the Reverend Mr. [Daniel] Davies to Convey to me the
> expression of their thanks and gratitude.[2]

Had the same labourers then known what the planters were soon to receive in exchange for the freedom they, the labourers, were to get after another four or six years of a tightly controlled, wageless existence, they might not have been quite so contrite and grateful.

Out of the £20 million voted by the British Parliament to be given as compensation to slave-owners, a total of well over £1 million was paid to owners in the Leeward Islands. Some £329,393 (the equivalent of about £17,500,000 at the beginning of the twenty-first century) was received by 1202 owners for 19,780 slaves in St Kitts, and £151,007 (or the equivalent of more than £9,000,000) by 399 owners for 8815 slaves in Nevis. The slaves in Anguilla, numbering about 2300, were included with those of St Kitts; and as they formed about 12 per cent of the total it would follow that their owners (perhaps 150 or more in number) received 12 per cent of the compensation paid to St Kitts, or about £39,200 (the equivalent of £2,300,000).

Nothing similar to the actions of the labourers in St Kitts took place in either Nevis or Anguilla. Equal resentment about apprenticeship was felt by the labourers of Nevis, but the imposition of martial law in St Kitts soon made it obvious that any resistance would be pointless. In Anguilla, where the majority of the labourers had, as slaves, not been fully employed or kept under the constant control of their owners, apprenticeship meant very little anyway. But in each island the granting of something less than complete freedom to the majority of its population only served to embitter and antagonize black and white society alike. In a report concerning St Kitts, but equally relevant to Nevis, which was sent to London in October 1834 Nixon remarked:

> At present there exists a jealousy between some of the
> managers or overseers on estates and the work-people, the
> former not recollecting that slavery no longer exists, and
> the latter forgetting themselves, and behaving in a very
> insolent and provoking manner towards their superiors.[3]

As such attitudes showed no signs of disappearing as long as apprenticeship lasted, a bill was passed in Charlestown in March 1838 to allow it to be terminated. A few weeks later a similar bill was passed in Basseterre, and on Wednesday 1 August the apprenticeship system was abolished in St Kitts and Anguilla, and in Nevis. After five days of rejoicing and thanksgiving, the islands' labour forces returned to work on Monday 6 August.

The Contract Acts

The labourers resumed work on the estates of St Kitts and Nevis under similar contract Acts, committing them to work a set number of hours a week for a set period, in exchange for a set wage, continued occupation of estate accommodation, and continued use of a plot of estate land on which to grow food. Both Acts were passed in advance of a model Contract Act approved in London in September, and so each ignored a key requirement of the latter. This was that no agreement between a labourer and his employer was to be for more than one month, unless it was in writing and signed before a magistrate who had to ensure the labourer entered the agreement voluntarily and fully understood its terms. Because of this omission, the Acts of St Kitts and Nevis were disallowed later in the year. This resulted in the labourers being left with no statutory regulations governing their terms of employment, and no legal foundation to their tenancy arrangements. They were free to set their own value on their labour, to choose whom they would work for, and to decide on the kind of work they would undertake. But at the same time, if they were living in estate housing and growing provisions on estate land, they could be summarily evicted if they refused to work on the estate. In the absence of any Crown Land on which they could settle, these then had great difficulty in finding work and housing except on some other estate.

By 1840 the threat of eviction was in common use as a means of subduing an estate's labour force, with immediate eviction as a punishment for anyone who offended in some way. Some employers adopted a different method of coercion, by threatening to sue any labourers who failed to turn up for work for a week or two for the value of the houses they occupied and the provision grounds they planted. Other, more enlightened, estate owners and managers saw that a better way of ensuring a more settled and reliable work-force would come from paying higher wages, and from renting labourers their houses and provision grounds. By 1845 the majority of the labourers in St Kitts and Nevis were renting their accommodation, with the right to work where they pleased, while some had leased land on which they had built their own easily removed wooden houses. Four years later a new Contract Act was passed. The Masters and Servants Act which came into law in April 1849, and which defined and enforced 'the relative rights and duties of masters and servants, with a view to the fostering of a system of continuous agricultural labour', was to govern labour relations in the islands for the next three-quarters of a century.

Free Villages

In both St Kitts and Nevis by this time a few labourers were living away from any estate. From about 1840 in St Kitts some occupied a few houses in what was soon to become the first of the island's free villages, called Challengers. Situated about halfway between Basseterre and Old Road this was named after a coloured customs officer named John Challenger who, in 1840, was reported to have

> a tract of land, which he is selling and renting in small lots, forming what they call an independent village…. He remarked that he had been censured for this course by the proprietors of estates in his neighbourhood. The fear of drawing from under their control the laborers who locate in them, appears to be the ground of their opposition.[4]

Although there was opposition among the proprietors, it was not universal. Among those who saw the advantages of having such 'independent' villages were the owners of estates which had either been abandoned or had become increasingly unprofitable. The renting of 200 acres of idle land on Sadler's Estate in small lots led to the founding of Sadlers Village in the north of the island. Other villages such as St Paul's and Tabernacle were founded in the same way.

Free villages also began to be established at much the same time on unproductive estate lands in Nevis, where their foundation met less opposition than in St Kitts. As wages in the island by the late 1840s were anything up to one-third lower than in St Kitts, the estates had already begun to employ labour on a crop-sharing basis (something which was to continue until well past the middle of the next century) and it hardly mattered to the proprietors where the labourers lived. 'The labouring classes submit cheerfully to the decreased wages', the President of Nevis informed the Colonial Office loftily in 1849, 'and do not feel to an equal extent the depression experienced by the planters. The metayer system, now generally adopted, provides an ample remuneration for their labour.'[5]

Distress in Anguilla

By the time apprenticeship ended in 1838 Anguilla's few remaining sugar estates had all but gone out of business. Many of the owners then packed up and left the island. Some, before leaving and glad to make any sort of profit, sold off some of their land in small lots to those who used to work it. As not too many of the now out-of-work labourers could afford to buy, far more of them squatted on estates which had been abandoned. Within a few years a very large part of the population of Anguilla consisted of subsistence peasants, black and white, all living legally or otherwise anywhere where the land was fertile. 'We were sorry to learn that Anguilla is not in so prosperous a condition as many of the neighbouring British islands', a visitor to St Kitts recorded in 1840.

> How it fares with the laborers, I know not; but as it is a
> poor island, it is probable that many of them have been
> induced to quit it, under the temptation of higher wages in
> other colonies. With regard to the white inhabitants, we
> were told that they had expended their compensation
> money somewhat too easily, and were reduced to a state of
> no small poverty and distress.[6]

Two years later the standard of living had fallen so low that the Methodists, who formed a large proportion of the population, found they could no longer raise their minister's stipend and he was withdrawn. Some idea of what life was like at this time is contained in a report by the Lieutenant-Governor of St Kitts, Charles Cunningham, who visited the island in 1843:

> I found a good many people...reaping large crops of
> provisions...one black man with nearly twenty acres of
> very good productive land on which he planted corn and
> cotton. In one small settlement...there were 5 women
> whose united families consisted of 37 children, the eldest
> of which was 16 years of age. The husbands of two of these
> had been drowned, two had died in Demerara and one was
> missing. These women and their families were cultivating
> 12 to 15 acres of land....[7]

Emigration

The two Anguillian husbands reported to Cunningham as having 'died in Demerara' were among the 1000 or more men and women – about one-third of the population – who left the island between 1837 and 1845 for other, larger colonies. They formed part of a migration which took place from all of the Leeward Islands during the first dozen years or so after emancipation. British Guiana, which had been created in 1831 by uniting the old colonies of Demerara, Essequibo and Berbice in South America, was the most attractive. With an acute shortage of labour it offered higher wages and much better prospects than any of the others. In 1836 alone over 350 labourers from St Kitts and more than 200 from Nevis sailed for the capital, Georgetown. Trinidad was the next most popular destination for migrant workers, as it too was very short of labour. Both colonies were prepared to pay bounties to employers who brought in workers, and by 1838 each had recruiting agents travelling around the islands of the Eastern Caribbean.

In July of that year Sir Henry Macleod, Nixon's successor as lieutenant-governor of St Kitts, alarmed by the number of labourers who were leaving the island, tried to halt the flow by issuing a statement suggesting that some of those who had already left had been 'sold as slaves into strange countries', and calling upon the Assembly to erect legal barriers to make emigration as difficult as possible. Under the regulations which were then quickly passed into law, the master of any ship from Trinidad and British Guiana had to post a substantial bond on arrival, and recruiting agents were prohibited from taking up residence on the island. In addition, every prospective migrant worker had to obtain a licence to leave, having first informed a justice of the peace of his intention and after having proved that he was not leaving behind any 'aged or infirm Father or Mother, Wife, or Infant child' dependent on him for support.

These restrictions, which were also applied in Nevis, had only a limited effect. Ways to circumvent or ignore regulations were soon found, and many more labourers left both islands than were ever accounted for in the official statistics. The main reason why so many were so keen to go was given in a letter sent to the Council of St Kitts in 1840 by Charles Cunningham, shortly after he had taken over from Macleod as lieutenant-governor:

> I am sorry to believe that the peasantry are emigrating
> from this Island in considerable numbers...[but] having
> made personal enquiries from many of the most intelligent
> of the Emigrants, as to the reasons for leaving their homes
> all assign the same cause – the uncertainty of the tenure by
> which they hold their houses and grounds.[8]

Within another two years, by which time Trinidad had become the more popular emigrant destination, there were at least four ships carrying labourers to that island from St Kitts and Nevis on a regular basis. The numbers who went between 1839 and 1845 are grossly underestimated in the official figures of 2441 from Nevis and 876 from St Kitts. It is very probable that at least half as many again left illegally.

Even though not all of the labourers who went stayed away, very few of those who returned were prepared to go back to work on the estates. 'Yes, there are labourers, but there is not labour enough', one planter complained in 1842 when asked by a Parliamentary Committee in London if there were enough workers in St Kitts, adding that 'Emigration is our greatest evil'. It was another three or four years before the labour migration began to tail off, and it had ended by 1849. In his report on St Kitts for that year the Lieutenant-Governor – now Robert Mackintosh – informed the Colonial Office that 'No immigration or emigration to any great extent can be said to have taken place during the last year, and the population may therefore be said to have remained stationary': a comment which was equally applicable to Nevis.

The emigration which took place during the post-emancipation period produced labour shortages in St Kitts and Nevis which were more imagined than real. The sugar estates, mostly belonging to absentee proprietors, were badly run and only capable of producing a profit using labour which could be worked as hard and for as long as possible in return for the lowest possible wage. These conditions were unacceptable to men and women who had spent their years as slaves in trying to ease the burden of such work, and all who could tried to find employment away from the estates. The majority though had no option but to stay, and these were no more inclined than the people who had left to put up with conditions worse than those they had endured before August 1834. The only reason there was 'not labour enough' in 1842 and later was because the conditions under which the labourers were employed were no incentive for them to work harder, or for longer, or to do anything more than they were told to do. Men and women struggling to make ends meet were not prepared to do anything more than the minimum they could get away with.

The Cholera Epidemic, 1853–55

In the autumn of 1853 Nevis 'received a sudden shock by the outbreak of Asiatic cholera', a deadly infectious disease which had been unknown in the Americas before the 1830s. Following an outbreak in Cartagena in 1849 it had spread to Cuba and Jamaica, and from these two islands carried to the Eastern Caribbean. As a disease which is transmitted by means of contaminated water and food, and to which people in crowded living conditions are particularly vulnerable, once it had broken out in Nevis it soon reached epidemic proportions. In March 1854 it was reported that 'deaths from cholera have been most appalling, and almost entirely confined to the labouring classes. The numbers are 406 males and 485 females'. A year later, after the epidemic had ended, the President, Frederick Seymour, reported to the Colonial Office that the island's Treasury had been

drained to meet the expenditure caused by the endeavours
to mitigate the ravages of the disease, and by the necessity
of burying at the public charge those who fell its
victims.... But the dearrangement of the finances was not
the greatest evil which the cholera inflicted on the island.
Nearly one tenth of the population...were carried off, and
the colony appeared to be threatened with a disastrous
change in its industrial condition.[9]

Despite the best efforts of the authorities in St Kitts, in ordering the
towns and villages to be kept clean by public scavengers, and in distributing supplies of 'medicines, with printed instructions for their use...among
the ministers of religion, the members of the Board of Health, and others',
cholera broke out in Basseterre on 1 November 1854. Amongst the poor
labourers of St Kitts, crowded together in estate housing or in the bur-
geoning free villages, it was even more virulent than it had been amongst
their counterparts in Nevis. The number of deaths rose steadily, passing
100 a day on 19 November, and reaching a peak of 181 six days later. After
that the numbers fell steadily until the last death was reported on
31 January 1855. The rate of mortality increased with age, and one quarter
of the population over the age of 60 was killed. Out of the total of 3920
people who died, representing one-sixth of the population, only five were
white.

Labour Conditions in St Kitts

The cholera epidemic transformed the labour situation in St Kitts and, a
year after it had ended, the Lieutenant-Governor, Hercules Robinson,
reported that 'the employer here is striving by a desperate offer of wages,
frequently higher than the ruling price of produce will admit of, to obtain
a sufficiency of labour'. As a result, wages for unskilled workers rose to 8d
(eight pence) a day, a rate judged to be at 'the very extreme of what the
market price of the produce will justify, often indeed far beyond it'.[10] This
led to the passing of two Acts in 1855: one in April for 'the encouragement
of the immigration of agricultural "labourers", by means of bounties to be
raised by a tax upon exports', and another in December imposing 'a small
tax upon provision grounds' in an 'attempt to stimulate the actual resident
population to greater industry'. Neither did anything to improve the situation. The importation of outside labour was something which had already
been tried without much success (as will be seen in the next chapter), and
any tax imposed on people who were already desperately poor was hardly

likely to stimulate anything but resentment. In April 1857, Robinson was forced to admit 'The want of continuous labour still constitutes the chief impediment to the further development of the productive resources of this island', and give his opinion 'that no permanent remedy for the evil can be found short of the advancement in civilization of the labouring classes'.[11] Regrettably, as education for the children of the labourers was then being actively opposed by the planters (see Chapter 19) very little improvement in the 'advancement of civilization', or in the provision of 'continuous labour', was to take place until long after Robinson's term of office had ended in 1859.

Sir Benjamin Pine, who took over from him in 1860, had qualified as a barrister before joining the colonial service and then had many years of experience as a governor of colonies in South and West Africa. He was to remain in St Kitts for ten years, and undoubtedly was the best administrator the island had during the nineteenth century. In the long and very detailed report he sent to the Colonial Office at the end of his first year in office he noted that 'relations between the planter and his labourer are scarcely satisfactory; and the blame of it must, I think, be pretty equally shared between them'. He found the wages being paid to labourers averaged 11d a day for men and 8d a day for women (the equivalent of about £2.00 and £1.50 in the year 2002),

> But a wretched system of underhand competition goes
> on for labour between the planters, which consists in
> offering the labourer 'privileges' as they are called; that is
> to pasture his cattle on the estates, to take sugar, wood,
> and other productions, and sometimes to squat. There is
> seldom any specific agreement on this point, so that the
> line between the fair use of the 'privileges' and theft and
> encroachment is continually passed by the labourer, and
> his moral perceptions with regard to the right of
> property are obscured and blunted. No system could be
> better devised than this to make thieves of the labouring
> population....

A survey he conducted into the amount of stock on the island found that on 76 of the estates some 600 horses, 1000 cattle, 1200 sheep, 2400 goats and 2900 pigs belonged to labourers. He was unable to find figures for another 57 estates, but reported some of these were 'out of cultivation, and overrun with labourers' stock'. As many more animals were owned by people who lived in the towns and villages, this produced a total which Pine found 'very large when it is considered that the whole of the labourers scarcely own an acre of pasture land'. He condemned the system of 'privileges', and argued that the labourers would be better served by paying them higher wages and having 'thefts and trespasses...stringently repressed by law'. At the same time he made it clear that

> In speaking of the error of the lower classes, I have not forgotten that scarcely a generation has passed away since they were freed from slavery, and that these errors, to a great extent, owe their origin to that accursed institution.... [Their] progress would have been more rapid had legislative and other measures been adopted calculated to lead the people safely out of slavery into the full enjoyment of freedom.[12]

Labour Conditions in Nevis

The way that many of the labourers in Nevis were employed by the middle of the nineteenth century was observed by a visitor to the island in 1852. 'A portion of the labour here is done on a very singular system, called "shares"', Charles Day observed, noting that the planter who gave 'a negro ground for the canes' received in exchange 'half the produce'. This system worked 'tolerably well' he believed,

> as from a variety of causes the produce is greater than by ordinary estate labour. First, the negro takes good care that the canes are not stolen, the common source of loss to the planter. Then again, he can employ his wife and children in weeding, and as the patch does not average more than an acre or an acre and a half, it can be kept very clean. Thirdly, the man, instead of drumming and dancing, can employ himself in catching the rats, which do so much mischief by gnawing the canes half through....[13]

At the time a labourer living and working on an estate earned eight pence a day, and had to pay sixpence a week as rent for his house. As the President, Frederick Seymour, was to record in his report to the Colonial Office in 1855, their employers had continued, 'under a system where there is no compulsory labour, all the peculiarities they could retain of one based entirely upon compulsion'. No contract law had been passed and in its absence a labourer had no means of recovering unpaid wages other than through a court action 'at an immediate cost to him of between sixteen and twenty shillings'. Not surprisingly, as this represented between three and four months' earnings, it was 'a proceeding which has never yet been resorted to'. According to Seymour, a magistrate could do nothing if a labourer was cheated, but then neither could 'he assist the master if his workmen walk away from the mill or the boiling-house when most wanted'. And this is exactly what many labourers did, rejecting the option of becoming share-croppers and choosing instead to eke out an existence as squatters on abandoned estate land.

> The dwellings of the negroes who, giving up the
> cultivation of sugar cane, have retired to abandoned
> portions of estates, and exist upon the proceeds of the
> increase of their stock, are often, I regret to say, miserable
> to a degree which I have rarely seen in any of the other
> West Indian Islands

Seymour had reported to the Colonial Office in 1854. 'No articles of domestic comfort are to be found therein, and the neat furniture of the Antigua negro houses is here exclusively confined to the habitations of the more industrious.' A year later he returned to the subject in a more intemperate fashion, recording in his report that

> the encroachments of the bush on the cane lands, the
> increase of cattle, and the erection of kennels, scarcely fit
> for human habitation, on the skirt of the forest which
> covers the central mountain, show that there is a tendency
> on the part of the negroes to escape from the cultivation of
> the sugar cane towards the wilder districts, where,
> unconscious of any duties to be performed for the rest of
> the community, they lead a vagabond life, and allow their
> children to grow up without clothing and without
> education.[14]

It is difficult to see how such people were to avoid having children who were unclothed and unschooled. On the island at the time, in Seymour's own words, there was 'no shop in which a couple of peasantry, desirous of furnishing a small house...would get what they require', and 'no public money [was] given in aid of the new schools'.

In 1856, in his final report as President, Seymour regretted the 'downwardly progressive course' and current state of an island which formerly had been 'one of the most flourishing in the West Indies'. He laid the blame on 'the legislature and proprietors of Nevis', who at the time of emancipation he believed had 'regarded the liberation of their slaves as an arbitrary interference on the part of the Home Government, which, though they could not prevent, they would continue to protest against and resist'. As a result, by 'clinging to any remnants which still existed of a bygone institution' they had 'succeeded in retaining but too many reminiscences of slavery time'.[15] Such reminders provided a powerful incentive to men and women to have nothing more to do with estate work, and the number of share-croppers, subsistence peasants and squatters continued to increase. There were 800 freeholders on the island by 1863, and well over 2000 (of whom only a handful owned more than two acres of land) by 1876. In that year the wages being paid to those who still worked on the estates were 1s (shilling) a day for men, 10d for women, and 6d to 7d for children.

The Noahite Movement

Given the prevailing attitude of most of the white inhabitants of Nevis, and the effect this had on the development of black society, it is not surprising that in 1855 Seymour reported that 'a strange form of worship [had] sprung up amongst the negroes'. This in fact had been started many years earlier by a man named Brown who, as a self-proclaimed prophet and 'comforter', preferred to be known as Noah. His followers, known as 'Noahites', numbered between 600 and 700 by the time Seymour became aware of their existence. 'The sect professes a belief in Christianity', he noted, 'and its members are considered steady workers', but

> Their rites offend more by folly and the deplorable
> admixture of African superstition than by actual
> immorality; but the general tone of feeling of the sect is
> bad; and I regret to hear that a special service is held to
> rejoice over the departure of any white family, and the
> preacher then points out how few of that colour remain.[16]

This sort of behaviour was more than enough to damn the Noahites in the eyes of the authorities, even though 'In their discipline they insist on frequent ablutions, abstinence from intoxicating liquors, and from the use of tobacco; concubinage is forbidden, and monogamy is inculcated.' None of this was good enough for the Anglican and Methodist Churches which, because the sect's adherents also claimed 'prophetic inspiration, and pretend to a familiar intercourse with the world of spirits', considered them a threat to respectability. Pressure was brought to bear on the movement, especially by the Methodists, and by the early 1870s it no longer existed.

16

Islands in Decline

The profitability of the sugar estates of St Kitts and Nevis was in decline long before emancipation added to their proprietors' woes; a situation brought about by the abolition of the slave trade and the opening up of new sugar-producing territories such as Mauritius, Trinidad and British Guiana. Sugar which had sold for £3 a ton at the end of the eighteenth century fetched only a third of this price by 1831. Abolition of the hated $4\frac{1}{2}$ per cent duty in 1838 did little to improve matters, as eight years later a Sugar Duties Act was passed decreasing the duty on foreign sugar entering Britain. 'You ask me how we have got over the difficulties of the act of 1846', an estate owner in St Kitts wrote to a friend in 1853,

> We certainly have not got over them, though we seem to exist in defiance of them.... As a whole, the island has, unquestionably, been cultivated at a loss ever since.... Those that did not owe, now do, and those that did, owe more.... In several instances, small properties have been taken over into larger ones, and more engines (steam engines) have been erected. The price of labour too is reduced, so that variously, the cost of production has been lessened, but the value of the product has fallen from year to year in greater proportion, so that the premium of profit has never been realized.[1]

At this time there were over 40 steam engines in use for crushing cane in St Kitts, but only half a dozen in Nevis.

The Sugar Estates of St Kitts

In 1834 the 156 estates (ranging in size from 37 to 1200 acres (15 to 486 hectares (ha)) into which St Kitts was then divided had a total of 89 owners, of whom less than a third actually lived on the island. The value of all the estates had dropped considerably during the previous thirty or forty years, and would continue to do so. Two estates which had been valued at £45,000 in 1817 had been sold for less than half this amount five years later. Olivees Estate, consisting of the house which Janet Schaw had found so grand in 1774 and some 280 acres (113 ha), was sold in 1847 for £3000, less than half the original cost of the house alone. In 1850 Wingfield Estate, which in the late eighteenth century had attracted a rent of £1200 a year, was being rented for not much more than a tenth of this amount, while an adjoining estate of 120 acres (49 ha), with a house and sugar works, was for sale for as little as £600. Such buying, selling and leasing produced a constantly fluctuating number of estates, owners and lessees, with equally varied annual amounts of sugar being produced.

In 1847 the largest estate, Salt Pond on the south-eastern peninsula, produced very little sugar from its 2300 acres (931 ha), although about 200 labourers lived on it. According to a visitor of that year, as the labourers had 'the privilege of collecting wood to sell in the town', something which occupied them 'three or four days in the week', very few wanted to work on the land planted with sugar-cane for the then going rate of 8d a day. Other labourers found it more profitable to harvest salt from the large pond, as they were paid half of the price for which it was sold. 'In some years immense quantities have been obtained, and a labourer has made as much as twelve dollars a week. The salt is sold chiefly to the Americans'.[2]

This estate, like so many others, was under the supervision of a manager; in this case one who lived near the salt pond 'in a roomy rude wooden house adjoining'. That so many of the estates were being run by people other than their proprietors became of increasing concern to the administration as the century progressed. In his official report for 1849 the Lieutenant-Governor, Robert Mackintosh, informed the Colonial Secretary that the 'absentee system…has been allowed to develop itself in this island to an excess which has produced its usual concomitant evils', before going on to add:

> there are many estates in this island which are the property
> of opulent individuals residing in England (some of whom
> have never seen their properties), who, apparently, utterly
> forgetful of the peculiar responsibilities which can never be
> separated from the ownership of land, are content that
> their estates shall be cultivated through the agency of
> mercantile houses at home…. The effect of this disastrous
> practice has been that a body of men have grown up in
> consequence, who, though calling themselves merchants,
> derive all their profits by simply reducing absentee
> landlordism to a profession.[3]

The sugar industry remained depressed, as estates continued to be sold, with the overall number being slowly reduced and more passing into the hands of local residents. By April 1856 there were only 137 estates, of which 128 were growing sugar-cane, and nine were in pasture or growing ground provisions. 'Of the 137 estates in the island', Lieutenant-Governor Robinson reported that year, 'fifty-eight belong to resident proprietors, [and] twenty-two are worked by resident lessees, who supplying the necessary capital for their cultivation have at least an equal interest in their success with the proprietors themselves'. The remaining 57, he observed, 'belong to absentee proprietors, most of whom are, however, wealthy mercantile firms at home, who are represented here by some of the most respectable and influential gentlemen of the community'.[4]

A degree of prosperity returned to the sugar industry in the 1870s, but by then the island's dependence on one product had begun to concern the administration just as much as the proportion of the industry which was in the control of absentee proprietors. 'I think it is a subject for regret that more of the lands on the heights is not utilized in the cultivation of cocoa and tobacco', wrote President Alexander Moir to the Colonial Secretary in 1873 (the title of president having replaced that of lieutenant-governor two years earlier),

> but it is difficult to move men to venture from the beaten track to which they have been for long accustomed, especially when the great majority of estates...are the property of absentees, or so mortgaged as, to a great extent, to tie the hands and cramp the energies of – the great desideratum – an independent body of local proprietors.[5]

Some of the estates then in the hands of absentee proprietors were those recently acquired under an Act passed by the Assembly a few years earlier. This was a local version of the British Parliament's West Indian Encumbered Estates Act of 1854, intended to provide an easy and cheap method of disposing of estates which were heavily in debt. Using the local court or the Encumbered Estates Court in London, application for sale of such an estate could be made by either the owner or one of his creditors. Following advertisement, sale and the equitable distribution of the proceeds among all the creditors, the purchaser then received a new and unassailable title to the estate. Four or five estates in St Kitts had already been sold in this way, and these would form part of the total of 15 dealt with under the Act before it was repealed in 1892.

By the beginning of the 1880s much of the island's sugar was being shipped to the United States, where it was sold for a higher price than could be obtained in Britain. The period of relative prosperity in the industry which followed came to an abrupt end in 1895, when the USA gave preferential sugar duties to Brazil, Cuba, the Dominican Republic and Puerto Rico. Three years later, when Puerto Rico became an American territory, following the Spanish–American War, the market in the United States was closed to British West Indian sugar altogether. Cultivation was immediately reduced in St Kitts, and, following a public meeting held by the planters, the rate for cutting a ton of cane was reduced from 8d to 6d. The overall effect of this on the labouring population was devastating, as the writer of a letter to a local newspaper recorded in September 1898:

> the mass of the people here are in a deplorable state of
> starvation, which I regret to say is daily increasing.
> Generally speaking it's no exaggeration to remark that hale
> strong men and women are now daily seen begging their
> bread, most willing to work but unable to procure same.[6]

The century ended with the sugar industry in deep depression, under 60 estates being cultivated, the crop reduced to less that 7,500 tons from an annual average of 12,000, and a work-force worse off than at any time since the end of apprenticeship.

The Sugar Estates of Nevis

Although Nevis had a smaller number of estates than St Kitts, by the 1840s a higher proportion of them belonged to absentee proprietors who, as most of them were already in debt, were unable or unwilling to raise further capital for investment. There were only four steam engines in use on the island by 1847, compared with 33 in St Kitts, and in the following year it was recorded that, other than on one estate, 'neither the Plough nor any modern implements of husbandry have yet been introduced'. The total amount of sugar produced in 1848 was just over 1300 tons, compared with the average of 3000 which had been produced each year before emancipation. This threatened the island with ruin, as the President, Willoughby Shortland, made clear in his report on the island for that year, sent to the Governor-General of the Leeward Islands. 'Your Excellency', he wrote, 'will scarcely expect from me on this occasion any other than an unfavourable statement of the condition and prospects of this colony'. A year later, with sugar production down to less than 900 tons, he reported the estates were continuing to have 'difficulty in obtaining the necessary capital to ensure efficient cultivation...and a spirit of extreme despondency is very general'.[7]

The despondency continued, and in 1855 Frederick Seymour, in his second annual report as president, having categorized the population of Nevis as living in a 'state of freedom beset with difficulties', wrote that this had

> reduced most of the proprietors to poverty, and driven the greater part of them into emigration. Where formerly a numerous and efficient white militia was kept up, the present adult male population of European extraction does not amount to 60 individuals. To those who still make the colony their home the state of existence is not very satisfactory…. So that, upon the whole, though nature has done as much for Nevis as for most places, the general aspect of things is sufficiently gloomy.[8]

Not all the proprietors could afford to pack up and leave, as was made clear the following year when the President's annual report recorded that the island's five parish churches were 'under the ministration of three clergymen' who were 'all holders of sugar estates'. This called for a loud sniff of disapproval because, 'as their stipends are not regularly paid from the Treasury, much of the time which should be directed to the spiritual oversight of their cures is necessarily given to the management of their private properties'.[9]

The general abandonment of the Nevis estates could not go unnoticed in other parts of the Caribbean, and in 1859 a number of them were bought by a wealthy planter from Barbados named Thomas Graham Briggs. Within four years, by introducing labour-saving implements and by employing managers from Barbados, he was reported as having 'imparted new energy to the agriculture of the island; not only has the cultivation of the cane been immensely extended and improved, but Indian corn, yams, and other provisions have been largely grown'.[10] Unfortunately for Briggs, the conditions for sugar production in Nevis bore little relation to those in Barbados, and after six or seven years most of his estates were returned to pasture. Despite this set-back he was still wealthy enough to acquire more property, and by 1871 he owned no less than 14 of the island's 91 estates. An attempt to switch to another crop, which took place on one or two estates in 1864, lasted an even shorter time than Briggs's sugar renascence. 'A decided extension in agriculture has taken place,' trumpeted the annual report for 1865, 'The article cotton, for half a century abandoned, now promises to become a staple in the true sense.' This was a hollow promise as the demand for cotton had arisen only as a result of the outbreak of the American Civil War, and was hardly likely to continue once the war ended. By 1867 cotton in Nevis had been 'thrown out of cultivation, as being unremunerative'.

Less than ten years later Nevis was in a very poor way. 'By far the greater acreage of the Island is not cultivated' the President wrote in his report for 1876, adding 'There can be no doubt that this arises chiefly from the want of capital, and in some measure from a scarcity of labour.' Of the 8000 acres which were being cultivated only just over half were planted with sugar-cane, while provisions were growing on the remainder. Conditions began to improve as the island entered the next decade, when it was found that there was a ready market for sugar in the United States and that it could be sold there for 'an advance of £2 or £3 per hogshead on the price obtained in England'. The opening up of the American market had an immediate effect, and the President was able to report in 1881 that a few 'long neglected estates have been again reclaimed and put under cultivation, and there is an increasing disposition apparent amongst the more wealthy planters of St Kitts to invest capital in this Island'. This was largely wishful thinking, in view of the fact that the majority of the estates were being worked on the métayer system, and over a quarter of the island's sugar mills were still wind-powered, but a partial recovery did take place. It lasted until the late 1890s, when it was brought to an abrupt end by the closure of the United States market to sugar from the British West Indies. The century ended with the sugar industry of Nevis in an even worse condition than that of St Kitts.

The State of Anguilla

The first genuine official interest in Anguilla to be shown in the nineteenth century by the administration of St Kitts did not take place until 1861, a year after Sir Benjamin Pine had taken over as lieutenant-governor. His views on 'the state and prospects' of Anguilla, compiled in June shortly after he had visited the island, were forwarded to the Colonial Office in October as part of the long and very comprehensive document he prepared as his first annual report. 'In former times the island was productive and prosperous', he stated, 'but of late years it has sunk into nearly total ruin, and a large part of its population has at times been reduced almost to starvation.' The number of people then on the island was about 2500, of whom only 100 or so were white. 'The black and coloured people', he considered,

> are among the most intelligent of their class in the West
> Indies. This fact has been attributed to the circumstances
> that these people, owing to their straightened condition at
> home, are constantly roaming about the other islands
> seeking employment or carrying on petty trade....

Those who were not 'roaming' or trading depended for the most part on subsistence farming. This was something Pine found to be 'in a very backward state', as there was 'neither a plough nor a cart of any kind on the island, and the only implement of husbandry is the hoe'.

The produce of the island at this time consisted of no more than salt and cotton. One small sugar estate still existed, but this was so badly run, with a mill still worked by cattle, that it did not even 'yield sugar enough for home consumption'. The salt ponds were worked by a public company which had been established in 1855. In spite of poor management, the company gave 'employment to a large number of people and in 1860 produced 100,000 barrels of fine quality salt'. With regard to cotton, although there were over 60 acres (24 ha) under cultivation, the crop 'would be cultivated much more extensively were it not for the extreme poverty of the people, who have not the means of buying gins and other things required for its preparation'. In order to help, Pine

> proposed to the vestry that they should vote a small sum
> of public money for the purpose of purchasing two or
> three gins, which should be set up in central places, and of
> which every grower might have the use upon payment of a
> small sum to Government towards defraying the
> expenses.[11]

The Vestry accepted his suggestion and within two years 500 acres (202 ha) of cotton were being grown. By 1865, because of the high prices it could be sold for as a result of the American Civil War, cotton was being cultivated on between 800 and 1000 acres (320 and 400 ha). It was all too good to last, and the market collapsed as it had in Nevis, with the end of the war.

By this time, very fortuitously, a new source of employment had opened up. This was on Sombrero, a small island 34 miles (55 km) to the north-west of Anguilla, which at the time was part of the Colony of the Virgin Islands. After 1865, when the island was leased for 21 years to the American-owned Sombrero Phosphate Company, nearly all the workers needed to mine its large guano deposits were drawn from Anguilla. Shipping began soon after accommodation and a rock-crushing plant had been built, and a light railway laid down, and 3000 tons a year were being exported to Baton Rouge in Louisiana by 1870. The amount increased steadily until 1881, when 20,000 tons were shipped, but fell off rapidly after that as mining operations, involving much blasting and underwater work, became increasingly expensive. The last shipment, consisting of about 7000 tons of very low-quality material, took place in 1888, two years before the company abandoned the island. The only residents after that year were four Anguillians employed as keepers of a lighthouse which had been built on the island in 1867. (As a result of the continued employment of Anguillians in this role, ownership of Sombrero was eventually transferred from the Virgin Islands to Anguilla in 1956.)

After Pine's 1861 report on Anguilla, the next one of any substance was written 17 years later by Alexander Moir, who was then styled the President of St Kitts. 'Anguilla is partitioned into three divisions, viz. the road, the valley, and the spring', he stated in 1878,

> and the only buildings of any importance are the court-
> house, Episcopalian church, and parsonage. A school-house
> and teacher's house in the first of these divisions, and two
> Wesleyan chapels, one in the road and the other in the valley,
> with a mission house and school-house. The great majority
> of the people's dwellings are formed of wattles thatched with
> the branches of the dwarf palm.

Even with such accommodation, and in spite of the fact that 'not more than 800 acres are cultivated, if the return for the land tax can be relied on', he categorized the inhabitants as being 'comfortably off, being proprietors of spots of land, owners of boats, raisers of small stock, and fishermen', who were 'generally peaceable and law abiding'. He found that salt was being exported in much the same quantities as in Pine's day, at an average of 98,000 bushels a year, while in addition,

> the produce of the Island consists of corn, yams, cassava,
> pease, beans, and sweet potato, while many of the people
> raise ponies, cattle, mules, pigs, goats, sheep, and poultry,
> for which is found a ready sale in St. Thomas and the
> nearer Islands.[12]

This view of Anguilla was much too sanguine. The great majority of the 'peaceable and law abiding' Anguillians lived on the very edge of poverty, with their crops regularly afflicted by the severe droughts to which the island was prone, their basic needs largely ignored by both Britain and St Kitts, and their existence virtually unknown to the rest of the world. A letter written in 1887 by the chaplain of a visiting British warship provides a rather more realistic glimpse of life on the island:

> Here is a population of 3200 (only about 100 of them
> white) and yet they have not a single Doctor.... Here no
> Court of Chancery.... Here they have a worthy Presiding
> Magistrate...but they have no Barrister.... Certainly there
> is no local paper, printing press, ice house, club, hotel or
> drinking saloon....[13]

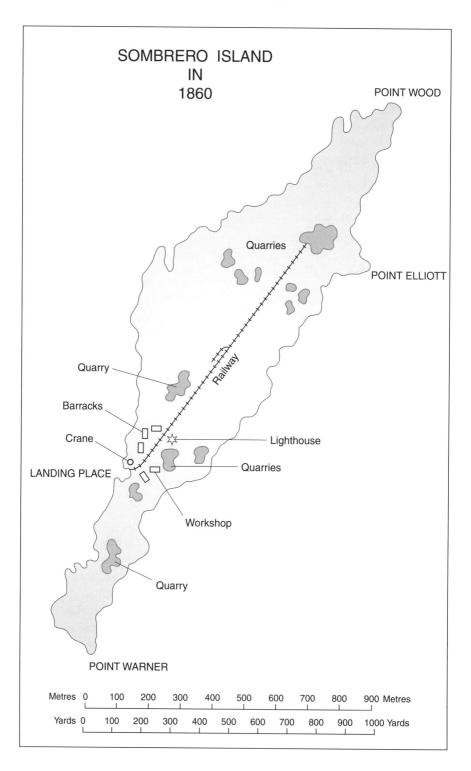

SOMBRERO ISLAND
IN
1860

POINT WOOD

POINT ELLIOTT

Quarries

Quarry

Railway

Barracks

Crane

Lighthouse

LANDING PLACE

Quarries

Workshop

Quarry

POINT WARNER

| Metres | 0 | 100 | 200 | 300 | 400 | 500 | 600 | 700 | 800 | 900 Metres |
| Yards | 0 | 100 | 200 | 300 | 400 | 500 | 600 | 700 | 800 | 900 | 1000 Yards |

Three years later, after work on Sombrero had ceased, and a prolonged drought had ruined crops and killed livestock, many people were starving, with three-quarters of the entire population needing government assistance in order to survive. But even then it proved impossible to let the Anguillians have something for nothing. Each man on relief received a ticket worth 6d, and each woman one for 4d, which could be exchanged for food at a canteen set up in one of the island's three divisions, but only after they had put in a full day's work on some government project. Their children meanwhile were expected to survive on whatever was doled out to them from school-house kitchens.

By 1898, when yet another detailed report on Anguilla was compiled, the state of the island was only marginally better than it had been 100 years earlier. Only about a third of the island was cultivable, and this was divided into some 500 holdings, of which only 50 were more than 10 acres (4 ha) in size. 'The people subsist chiefly on sweet potatoes, to which are added by a few either fresh fish or salted fish from America', the author of the report stated bleakly before adding, 'Their diet, generally speaking, may be considered a vegetable one.' Very few people lived in anything but 'thatched and unfloored huts with mud walls', and nowhere were they collected in villages. 'Were the land constantly productive', the report concluded,

> the conditions under which they live would be very
> favourable for the development of the people; but,
> unfortunately, in consequence of the rapidity with which
> rain-water sinks through the thin layer of soil and the
> subjacent coral, and the irregular and small rainfall, the
> crops wither very soon after the rain ceases. Frequent
> droughts and gales reduce the people periodically to a state
> of destitution, in which they are kept from being starved
> to death by relief works and supplies of food provided by
> the Government. When, again, on the other hand, they
> have reaped an abundant harvest, they find, on going to
> the neighbouring islands, that the market in these places is
> already over-stocked and that there is no sale for their
> produce. As a result of this hand to mouth existence, the
> whole population lives in a state of chronic poverty and in
> frequent danger of starvation.[14]

Immigrant Labour

The exodus of labourers from St Kitts and Nevis, which took place in the decade after emancipation, initiated a demand from the planters of both islands for replacement workers from other parts of the world. In February 1841 the Nevis Assembly passed a resolution to import 'liberated Africans'. These were people found on slave ships bound for Cuba or Brazil which had been intercepted by the Royal Navy in the Atlantic, and who, as 'recaptives', were not returned to Africa but landed at selected ports in the West Indies. Unfortunately for the planters of Nevis, Charlestown was not one of these ports and so no recaptives ever came their way.

The Assembly of St Kitts took a different approach and voted £1000 to cover the cost of importing a large group of men and youths from England. These arrived in 1845, after having signed agreements before they left under which 'they bound themselves to a service of three years for wages at the rate of 10s 6d a week', together with 'house, garden, and medical attention'. If the planters, who bid for their services in some form of lottery, expected that poor whites would perform any better as labourers in 1845 than they had in Thomas Warner's day, they were quickly disabused of the notion. 'Of the whole number imported...', a contemporary visitor recorded, 'many were ill-selected, ill-conducted, ignorant, infirm, totally unworthy of the name of skilled labourers.'[15] One at least was literate, as on 20 August a petition prepared by William Reynolds (a prototype migrant English whinger if ever there was one) on behalf of all the rest was sent to the Colonial Secretary, asking for repatriation because

> ever since we placed our feet on these shores, we are
> continually ailing, – a complication of diseases or distempers,
> some with headache, others debility, complaint in the
> bowels, a rash all over their bodies, which makes them very
> uncomfortable, accompanied with uneasiness of mind, etc.
>   We humbly beg to observe to your lordship that the
> climate is so miserably close and warm altogether that we
> can scarcely withstand it, perspiration to such an extreme,
> and then dreadful cold ensues....[16]

The petition elicited no response and by March of the following year the President of the Council informed Charles Cunningham, the Lieutenant-Governor, that there were then 'from 70 to 100 Europeans dispersed over the island, and actually employed in agricultural duties',. and in his view doing so well that, 'by their example and skill in the application of implemental husbandry, they are likely to elicit native talent, and excite emulation in native industry'. Cunningham found this hard to accept and, after pointing out that 'from some cause or other nearly one-fourth of the male adult immigrants are no longer at work', he expressed his

> entire belief, that no benefit which may accrue to the
> community from their greater skill in the use of

agricultural implements, can compensate for the misery
which too often befalls themselves, and for the sad
example as to habits and conduct which they present to the
negro population.[17]

Little more was ever heard of the English labourers, and presumably by 1848 all who had not succumbed to the climate or one of Reynolds's ailments had been repatriated.

Their place was taken by workers drawn from the Atlantic islands of Madeira and St Helena, from India and, incredibly, from West Africa, all of whom arrived at various times between 1846 and 1870. By far the largest number, arriving in groups almost annually during this period, came from the Portuguese island of Madeira. 'The Madeira peasant', Cunningham's successor, Mackintosh, reported in March 1850,

> continues to be of great service in submitting to the call for
> regular and sustained labour, which the creole negro finds
> so irksome. But with him the tendency to withdraw from
> predial labour for the purpose of establishing small retail
> shops is still on the increase. Many Portuguese, moreover,
> have of late left the island altogether. The desire of
> bettering their condition, so remarkable in their character,
> renders them restless....[18]

The demand for immigrant labour increased after the cholera epidemic of 1854, and early the following year the legislature of St Kitts passed an Act for 'the encouragement of the immigration of agricultural "labourers", by means of bounties to be raised by a tax upon exports'. This, it was felt, might 'stimulate to increased energy and activity the resident labouring population of the island'. It certainly reactivated recruitment in Madeira, and over 600 more Portuguese arrived during the next five years. This was not wholly welcome by the administration. 'Immigration...must always be considered of secondary importance compared to any attempt to stimulate the actual resident population to greater industry', wrote Lieutenant-Governor Robinson in April 1856. In his view 'all real improvement' in the island would come from 'the civilization and elevation in the social scale of the people themselves, and in the implantation and growth of right principles in their hearts'. In the opinion of his successor, Benjamin Pine, four years later, when apprenticeship ended

> had the negroes... been submitted to a legislation suited to
> a people just emerging out of slavery into freedom, instead
> of being placed at once under a legislation, the growth of a
> thousand years of freedom and progressive civilization...

> I feel assured that the island, with a teeming population,
> would not have been under the necessity of seeking for
> labour in distant lands.[19]

On completion of the three-year indenture period, the Portuguese were
free to stay, to return to Madeira, or to move to another island. In 1868,
when from among over 800 on the island less than 100 were still under
indenture, it was recorded that 'Nine-tenths of our respectable and
well-to-do shopkeepers are immigrants who have served out their
indentures here.'

In the same year there also were 50 Africans and 10 Indians under
indenture on St Kitts. The former were the only ones still indentured out
of over 450 who had come to the island since 1846. The early arrivals had
'given general satisfaction to their employers, both in rendering compara-
tively steady continuous labour and in deporting themselves peaceably',
but by May 1851 it was found that many of the newer immigrants were
'very young persons; and many of them in weak health, and incompetent
to render an immediate return, on this account, of sufficient labour'.[20] This
produced a demand among the planters for their indenture periods to be
extended, but virtually all when questioned about 'their readiness to enter
afresh into agreements for the further period of twelve months' rejected
the proposal.

> The prevailing feeling appeared to be a dread that by
> 'putting a hand to paper' they would be sacrificing their
> liberty, and that it was intended by the proposed
> instrument to keep them in a state of servitude to which
> the native labourers were not liable.[21]

Many of the last group to arrive in August 1863 initially had difficulty in
finding work as field labourers, and were taken on as domestic servants.
This did not work out too well, as these

> for the most part proved during the period of their indenture
> stubborn and willfully disobedient to their employers, with
> the avowed object of getting themselves transferred to work
> on the estates as agricultural labourers....[22]

The reason for the handful of Indians under indenture in 1868 was
given in the report on the island for that year compiled by the Chief
Secretary. 'Only one batch of 337 coolie immigrants has been imported
here', he wrote, employing a term in common use at the time,

> When their term of indenture expired, and they saw that
> there was no probability of further cargoes of their fellow-

people being imported, a great exodus took place to Demerara and Trinidad, whither they went to obtain, as their own importers, the liberal bounty given by those Colonies on an indenture. Of these coolies some have found their way back, and ten signed a second indenture for three years, on the payment to them of £6 5s. each. Others are working on the estates here as free labourers, on the same terms and with the same privileges as the native labourers.[23]

The demand for immigrant labour in Nevis quickly faded away after the resolution passed in 1841 failed to produce any. From then on the general state of the sugar industry, together with the widespread use of the métayage system, made it unnecessary to seek labourers from overseas. Some of the Portuguese in St Kitts were induced to cross over in 1847, when labour was still in short supply, but the majority of them 'fell victims to the climate' and soon died. By March 1849, 'almost all of those who remained alive [had] quitted the island in search of higher wages on more prosperous shores'.[24] Over twenty years passed after that before the subject of immigrant labour was raised again. The author of the 1870 report on the state of the island, the Colonial (that is, Chief) Secretary, took it upon himself to grouse about both the island's labour force and the terrain. 'The apathy of the labourer is the planter's bane', he bleated,

> the prospect of reward fails to stimulate him to exertion; offers of continuous service produce no attraction; erratic habits, love of change and pleasure, disregard for the morrow, inexpensiveness of living, either as to food or clothing, together with the salubrity of climate, all combine to produce in the native labourer an indisposition for steady employment.

Matters were made worse by the island's 'peculiar geological features' and numerous rock outcrops, which made ploughing and the use of 'implemental husbandry' virtually impossible and manual labour essential. 'The only remedy for this state of things is immigration', the report continued,

> and this is only required to a limited extent; 200 or 300 indentured Coolies or Portuguese would be sufficient, on the one hand, to stimulate the native labourer to industrious habits; and on the other, to place the agriculturist...with the aid of the better disposed and more domesticated natives, in an independent position of extraneous assistance.[25]

No Portuguese could be induced to the island, so an Immigration Act was passed in 1872 for the supply of Indian labourers. A ship carrying a total of 315 arrived two years later. Expiry of their indentures in 1879 was followed by 'a general refusal on their part to re-engage themselves for a further term', and they began to leave the island. Less than 200 remained two years later, working as free labourers, but all had left by 1885.

The 'Portuguese Riot', 1896

The loss of the American market for sugar in 1895 presaged financial ruin for the estate owners of St Kitts, but the swingeing cut in wages which they immediately imposed on their workers, most of whom were already living on the poverty line, threatened life itself. As the start of the 1896 harvest approached, and having little to lose, some of the labourers on Needsmust, an estate near to Basseterre, announced their intention of refusing to cut the cane unless wages were increased. This had no effect on the owner, Joaquin Farara, a merchant and store-owner in Basseterre who over 40 years earlier had been among the first immigrant labourers to reach the island from Madeira. His refusal to consider any rise in wages, combined with considerable unpopularity 'on account of his miserly disposition', was enough to spark the series of events which led to what afterwards came to be known very misleadingly as the 'Portuguese Riot'.

These began with the Needsmust cane fields being set on fire. Such incendiarism, considered at first as 'simply an act of isolated revenge', soon spread to many other estates where, by the beginning of 1896, their owners were having to face demands for higher wages and threats of strike action. By early February, with gangs of labourers roaming the island, nearly every estate was affected. The authorities, led by a man named Thomas Griffith with the title of Administrator, remained undisturbed until the situation began to get out of hand late on Sunday 16 February, when violence broke out on Stone Fort Estate outside Challengers Village. Grossly exaggerated tales of 'men being killed and the plantation house in a state of siege' reached Basseterre the next morning at much the same time as 'a gang of field labourers, men and women' began 'parading the streets with drums and tambourines'. They were soon joined by others and in the afternoon 'affairs began to assume a more serious aspect'. The harbour boatmen decided to go on strike unless the fares they were allowed to charge for landing passengers from ships were doubled, and hauled up their boats before joining the labourers. After that, because by the 'most culpable negligence on the part of the authorities the rum shops had been allowed to remain open...the mob grew more savage and noisy every hour'.[26]

As night approached, and the mob, by breaking street lamps and throwing stones, showed every sign of instigating a full-scale riot, it became increasingly difficult for the residents of Basseterre to understand why the supine Griffith still refused to take any action. One member of the administration, James Burns, the Treasurer, was particularly incensed, as his son recorded many years later:

> While the mob took possession of the town the authorities, I regret to say, did very little. The police were badly led and were practically useless, while few of the white population were armed. Fortunately, however, HMS *Cordelia* had arrived, but again the Administrator refused to take my father's advice to ask for marines to be landed. When circumstances later compelled him to ask for their assistance he refused to allow the marines to fire on the mob, even after houses in the town had been set alight and the rioters were trying to cut the hoses of the fire brigade. Later that night, as the situation grew worse. one of the officers of the *Cordelia*...took upon himself the responsibility of giving the order to fire; two men were killed and the riot immediately collapsed.[27]

The officers and men of the corvette HMS *Cordelia* (which just happened to be in harbour at the time) undoubtedly saved the island from further distress, particularly as the previous day a detachment of sailors had managed to quell the disturbance at Stone Fort Estate without the use of force. The marines who opened fire in Basseterre, and who killed not two but three of the rioters, only did so as a last resort and when their own lives were in danger. 'But for the chance arrival of the HMS *Cordelia* the town would certainly have been burnt to the ground even if we had escaped with our lives', the somewhat prejudiced and intemperate James Burns wrote to a friend later, 'I have a full knowledge of the nigger and I know that full of rum and excited by plunder the quasi-civilisation of the last fifty years falls from him and leaves him in a greater savage than his African ancestors.'[28] A letter scribbled on Tuesday 18 February by Samuel Shelford, the manager of an estate well removed from Basseterre, would seem to indicate that, had the riot not been put down so quickly, there might well have been more serious trouble in rural areas:

> Terrible riot about higher wages. Marines landed from gunboat – fired on mob – killed 3, wounded several. Cane fires everywhere – nothing to speak of at Estridge's. Have

granted demands for higher wages. Men came at me with
cutlasses – rural police joined mob – Basseterre and island
in hands of mob – only about $\frac{1}{2}$ a dozen working in yard.[29]

Shelford's employer, Henry Estridge, was in a minority in allowing an
increase in wages. Most owners either granted one, and then withdrew it
once any danger had passed, or refused to contemplate it under any circumstances. One absentee owner went so far as to suggest that they should
organize themselves, not only for mutual protection, but to resist what he
considered to be, at a time when virtually the entire work-force was in distress, 'unjust demands on the part of the labourers'.[30]

17

Government, Justice and Defence

The second half of the nineteenth century, as well as seeing the three islands sink into economic depression, also saw some important changes take place in the way they were governed. Reform was long overdue. In both St Kitts and Nevis all the Council members were appointed for life, the majority of Assembly members were elected by a mere handful of voters, and a small white population exercised authority and control over nearly every aspect of communal and economic life. It was a situation which was not without its critics. In St Kitts in 1850 a group of coloured men, including several who were in the Assembly, complained to a visiting Methodist that they were 'excluded...systematically, from nearly all offices of honor of emolument in the disposal of the Executive government'. As an example of this discrimination, he was told that of the nine men who had been 'appointed to the magistracy' during the previous year there was 'not one colored individual among them, although some of the white men so appointed, are totally unfit for office, or unworthy of it, and there are several colored gentlemen well qualified to fill it'.[1] In Nevis seven years later the President, Sir Arthur Rumbold, forwarded a report to the Colonial Office in which the island's senior magistrate, Isidore Dyett, decried the applicability 'of the forms of the British constitution to the small West Indian dependencies', where

> without a sufficient number of men qualified for the duties
> of the smallest English vestry, the legislation...is distributed
> among three distinct branches – typical of King, Lords and
> Commons. As might be expected, narrowness of view and
> selfishness of object come commonly to play, and progress is
> retarded rather than furthered by the measures and influence
> of such a Legislature....

In Dyett's opinion, if the island was to advance and be able 'to support all the institutions necessary to a civilized community', a change was needed 'in its constitutional forms, and the substitution of a more compact body for the present cumbrous machinery of legislation'.[2]

Dyett's views were echoed by both the Lieutenant-Governor of St Kitts and the Governor-General in Antigua. 'A reform in the system under which the public affairs of this island are administered is much required,' urged Hercules Robinson in April 1857 from an island where he found

> The House of Assembly by gradual encroachments have
> practically acquired the control of financial affairs, and
> assumed many other purely administrative functions,
> which by the theory of the constitution belong, not to a
> legislative body, but to the executive Government.

A week or two later, in forwarding Robinson's views to London, Governor-General Ker Hamilton agreed that 'a better system of Government' was needed, adding

> It cannot be expected that persons residing in these
> colonies, and engaged in pursuits requiring great attention
> to realize subsistence, competency, or wealth, can devote
> themselves to the administration of public affairs,
> requiring consecutive attention; and a general feeling is
> beginning to prevail that certain responsible persons
> should be selected, and charged with the duty of
> performing these subordinate offices of Government
> essential to the due organization of modern society.[3]

The Government of St Kitts

The first reform carried out in St Kitts was the abolition of the parish vestries in 1850. Up until this time each of the island's nine parishes had been responsible for the upkeep of its church, payment of the rector and other church officials, care of the poor, sick and indigent, and a few other civic matters, using revenue raised from taxes on land and property and the issuing of liquor and other licences. Their responsibilities and powers of taxation were now transferred to a committee of the legislature.

At this time the Council consisted of ten members, and the Assembly of 24 members elected from the nine parishes (four from St George Basseterre and two or three from each of the others) together with one member from Anguilla. These were elected by a tiny number of voters. In 1855, out of a population in St Kitts of nearly 21,000, only 166 men were eligible to vote. As 87 of these lived in Basseterre, and 26 in one of the other parishes, a mere 53 were left in the other seven parishes to return a total of 17 members. Nowhere near all of those with the vote ever used it. In the election held in 1856 a mere 47 voters returned 22 members, with one parish being unable to return the two representatives it was allowed, as its solitary voter was then on leave in Europe. 'Some reform in this particular is surely needed', wrote Robinson in his report for that year: 'Indeed to designate a House of Assembly of 22 members, elected by 47 voters, out of a population of 21,000, as the "representatives of the people", and the "popular branch of the legislature", is simply ridiculous.'[4]

It was judged impolitic to try to extend the franchise by lowering the voting qualifications, but reformation of the legislature began at the end of the following year, when the Assembly was eventually persuaded to pass an Act which Robinson hoped would 'establish an effective and responsible administrative system'. The Act provided for the formation of an Executive Council made up of half the members of both the Council and the Assembly, and for the appointment of a paid committee of three members (one from the Council and two from the Assembly) to liaise between the governor and the legislature, and to have 'under the supervision of the Executive...responsible superintendence of the finances'. The members of the Executive Council were to hold their positions by political tenure, and in debates the minority was expected to yield to the majority or to retire from office. The three members nominated by the Executive Council to form the Administration Committee were also expected to resign if they lost the confidence of the legislature.

Any further reform had to wait until after Robinson had been relieved by Sir Benjamin Pine who, in his monumental first annual report, made his intentions quite clear. With regard to the change introduced under his predecessor:

> To say that it is an improvement upon the system which
> preceded it, is small praise; for it is hard to conceive what
> change could have been made in that utterly vicious
> Constitution without bettering it. Still the new measure
> has some intrinsic merits; and it further, perhaps, deserves
> the credit of containing as much good as the local
> Legislature would have sanctioned.

While acknowledging that the legislature had not been deprived 'of its exclusive and irresponsible control over the finances', he saw that the new system left 'intact in the Constitution other defects which not only mar the efficiency of the Government, but which may hereafter impair the value of the advantage it has conferred'. In his opinion a complete reform of the constitution was needed, including the combination 'of the two Houses of Legislature into one, composed of a certain number of nominees of the Crown, and a larger number of representatives of the people', but with the total number being 'far less than the aggregate number of the two existing houses'. In addition he felt it important to separate the political and administrative functions of government by having the latter firmly under the control of the governor, assisted by 'three paid and permanent chief officers'.[5]

It took six years for his suggestions to be accepted by the legislature, but in the interim Pine made sure the amended constitution he had inherited worked as well as possible. In 1864 he 'assigned to each member of the Administrative Committee a department of the Administration – one having charge of public works, another of finance, and the third of other business'. Other small improvements were made but, as he was keen to remind the Colonial Secretary in August 1865, the administration was 'still far from altogether satisfactory', and the amended constitution was 'capable, if properly directed, of working out the other reforms which are required'.

In April 1866 Pine sent to London two Acts which had been passed unanimously by the legislature. The first of these abolished the Council and Assembly, and substituted a single chamber to be composed of three officers of the Crown, sitting *ex officio*, seven nominated members, and ten members elected from the existing constituencies. The second Act replaced the Administrative Committee with the three paid officials he considered necessary to assist the governor: a secretary to government, an auditor-general and the attorney-general. There was no objection to these changes from the Colonial Office, where there was already a strong body of opinion in favour not only of making St Kitts and the rest of the Leeward Islands into Crown Colonies, but of uniting them in a single colony. Pine was the obvious man to carry this through and early in 1867, after being relieved as lieutenant-governor of St Kitts, he was selected to take over as the governor-general in Antigua. In April he was told that the end he was to 'keep steadily in view is to form these islands into one Colony, with one Governor, one Council, one Superior Court, one Corps of Police'.[6]

The Colonial Office's intentions soon became known in St Kitts and created great consternation in the legislature and among those occupying the higher reaches of society. 'The part of the scheme...to which their antagonism is chiefly directed', Pine wrote to the Colonial Secretary in September, 'is that which proposes to establish one Treasury for all those islands. "What!" they say, "shall the rich and prosperous island of St Kitts share its overflowing treasury with the bankrupt island of Antigua"'. But in his view this was not all there was to their opposition:

> One of the real objections to the scheme is the removal of
> a Lieutenant-Governor from the island.... Few persons
> contend that for administrative purposes a Lieutenant
> Governor is at all necessary. During the whole period of

> my administration I was strongly of the opinion that I was
> unnecessary. The mere ordinary work of the Government
> did not occupy me, on average, for more than half an hour
> a day – scarcely so much. Had I not had some hobbies,
> such as studying languages and making codes of law, I
> should not have known what to do with myself....[7]

Such a frank confession of the *longueurs* of life in Government House,
very unusual for the day and unheard of from an inhabitant of such an
establishment since, did Pine no harm. He spent four years as governor-
general of the Leeward Islands after taking over in 1869, and another two
as governor of Natal, before retiring at the age of 65 in 1875.

He got down to work on creating a unified colony as soon as he was
established in Antigua. 'I shall try to work these mixed Constitutions
fairly and in the sense in which they were founded', he informed the
Colonial Secretary in September 1869, but warned that he would 'not hesitate to exercise the power given me' or to replace 'nominated Members
decidedly hostile to my policy, by others who will support it.' As it was,
because earlier while acting as governor-general for a short period he had
been instrumental in getting Nevis, Antigua and Montserrat to adopt
single-chamber legislatures, he found it a matter of

> regret that I did not make all the Islands Crown Colonies
> when I had the power to do so. That form would have
> been intelligible to any one, and more easily worked. The
> representation of the people in these Islands is a mere
> sham.[8]

The truth of this last statement in the case of St Kitts was borne out in the
following February, when a petition signed by 47 of the island's leading
inhabitants, or about one-sixth of all the registered voters, was sent to the
Colonial Secretary. This expressed their 'dismay that it is the intention of
the Imperial Government to require the local Legislature to pass an Act
for the purpose of uniting this island with Antigua, Dominica, Montserrat,
Nevis, and Tortola, under one Federation'. This was a measure which the
signatories, who of course were all white, representing nothing but their
own narrow interests, considered 'most repugnant to the wishes of all
classes of the inhabitants of this island', and the Colonial Secretary was
implored to act to prevent the legislature from being 'pressed into joining a
Federation which can in no way benefit this colony, and which is considered so objectionable throughout the length and breadth of the community'.[9] Their self-serving pleas fooled no one, and they were fobbed off
with an anodyne reply which concentrated on how a federation would

bring about 'a better and more economical administration' and a 'reduction of the present taxation'.

The Leeward Island Act which was passed in 1871 set up a federal colony, in which St Kitts and Anguilla formed one of six presidencies, the others being Antigua and Barbuda, Dominica, Nevis, Montserrat and the Virgin Islands. After the new colony had been inaugurated on 30 March 1872, each of the six presidencies retained its own single-chamber legislature, but 'controlling power of legislating on certain important subjects' now rested with the General Legislative Council established in Antigua. This was composed of the governor-general as president, the colonial secretary (not to be confused with the secretary of state for the colonies), the attorney-general and the auditor-general, with one nominated member for each presidency, and ten members elected by the representative portion of the local Councils. Six years later the elected members of the Council of St Kitts moved a resolution to amend the constitution to that of a Crown Colony, a proposal which was adopted by a majority eleven to six members of the Council, with one elected and two nominated members being absent. The Act was passed and in November 1878 the Legislative Council was reduced to five official and five unofficial members.

The Government of Nevis

Sir Arthur Rumbold, who became president of Nevis in 1857, soon came to view the island's legislature in much the same light as his contemporary, Robinson, saw that of St Kitts. He discovered he had little power, few opportunities to propose or advise measures of reform, or to affect the way financial affairs were handled. Other than 'to veto the legalizing of any essentially mischievous enactment' he found himself 'powerless to effect good'. In his opinion there were not enough suitable men to form a Council and Assembly: 'The material for two houses does not indeed exist', he wrote in his first annual report, but if they

> could be consolidated into one, so as to form a Legislative
> Council, a portion to be nominated by the Crown, the
> other portion to be annually or triennially elected, the said
> Council to hold a short but continuous session in each year,
> I conceive that great benefit would result to the colony.

No change took place for another two years, and then it was only the example set by the legislature of St Kitts in passing an Act to establish an Executive Council and Administrative Committee that caused the legislature of Nevis to follow suit.

Further reform had to wait until 1866, and once again in the wake of events in St Kitts. In July the Administrative Committee was replaced by an Executive Council of officials, and the two houses of the legislature united in a single chamber made up of the colonial secretary and the solicitor general with three nominated and five elected members. The new chamber also took over local government, which up until then had been run by parish vestries. Parochial taxation, which was categorized as 'arbitrary, unfair, and in practice founded upon no principle of uniformity' had by then 'literally ceased to exist'. Taxes had been levied in each parish 'according to the will of each respective churchwarden', men criticized in the annual report for 1866 as 'officers [who] acknowledged no superior' and who did not account 'for receipts and expenditure but at pleasure'.[10] As a result, and because there was no tax on land,

> when any financial pressure is felt, resort is still had to the clumsy, inconsiderate, and, indeed, inhuman expedient of taxing the industry of the Colony, and the food of the people, in the shape of a twenty-five per cent enhanced duty upon imports and exports.[11]

By 1870 it had become obvious that Nevis, like St Kitts, was going to be incorporated into a federal colony of the Leeward Islands. 'The measure was unpopular', noted the Colonial Secretary, Charles Eldridge, in compiling the official report for that year, 'partially from fear that the overwhelming influences of the larger Colonies would create offices and cause increased expenditure and taxation; and in a great measure from personal hostility to the talented Governor who inaugurated the scheme.' Pine, the 'talented Governor' in question and the man to whom the Nevis report was sent, was the last person to be worried about such hostility, particularly from an island where out of a population of nearly 12,000 the five elected members of the Legislative Assembly had been returned by only 49 votes. 'This limited use of the franchise', he was informed by Eldridge, 'does not evince much interest in the political affairs of the Colony'.[12] Nevis duly became a presidency of the Leeward Islands Colony in March 1872. Six years later the island's Legislative Assembly passed an Act to produce a new procedure for the registration of voters, and another to abolish the property qualification needed to become a member of the Assembly. It was too little, too late, as President Arthur Havelock recorded in March 1878, because they immediately

> became of no effect in consequence of a complete change in the Constitution. The Government was somewhat unexpectedly moved by a resolution emanating from the

elective side of the Assembly, to introduce a Bill to change the form of the Legislative Constitution to that existing in Crown Colonies. This important measure, which was the last of the session, was carried by a large majority.[13]

The Union of St Kitts and Nevis, 1883

The chief town of Nevis, Charlestown, is exactly eleven miles from Basseterre, and the latter is just about the same distance from Sandy Point, the other town in St Kitt's. Basseterre is therefore fairly situated for being a centre and capital for both islands; and the fact that two small islands, so situated, should each have its separate machinery of government, does strike the mind of a stranger as something very unnecessary, and unnecessarily expensive, if not absurd.[14]

So wrote Robert Baird in 1850, undoubtedly echoing an opinion which must have been voiced by many other strangers who had visited the islands before him. His view of the absurdity of the situation began to receive some official recognition five years later when the Governor-General in Antigua, Mackintosh, complained to the Colonial Office that 'the enormously disproportionate establishment' of Nevis was 'crushing the resources of this little community'. He argued that 'The proper remedy for this evil would evidently be an incorporate union of Nevis with her more important neighbour St Kitts', but was forced to add that 'proposals to such effect have never met with any favour in the Legislature of the smaller dependency'.[15] This was reaffirmed by Mackintosh's successor, Hamilton, in October 1852 when he informed London that

Antigua, St Kitts, Montserrat, and Nevis are all within view of each other: I frequently see the whole of them at one view. They are minute Monarchies with separate Legislatures, different tariffs, distinct provincialisms, and with antipathies strong in the ratio of approximation. A gentleman of Nevis says it is a duty he has inherited to abhor everything belonging to St Kitts, which, he adds, is the faith of all true Nevisians. This isolation and the consequent difference might be surmounted by the consolidation of the civil Establishments of the Islands.[16]

Such a consolidation began to appear inevitable once Nevis and St Kitts had been subsumed into the Leeward Islands Federation in 1871, and even more so seven years later when they had adopted Crown Colony Constitutions. Neither the abhorrence of St Kitts which was the 'faith of all true Nevisians', nor any antipathy the Kittitians may have felt towards Nevis, could impede a union which by 1878 the Colonial Office considered long overdue. In May of that year bills were introduced in the legislatures of both islands to sanction such a union. In St Kitts it was passed with some reluctance but no opposition, but in Nevis the non-official members not only opposed the bill but boycotted any further meetings of the Council. The protest was of no avail, as the bill was passed by the official members alone, at an extraordinary meeting of the Council convened at the end of the year. The union of the two islands took place three days later on 1 January 1883. It was followed by an enlargement of the Legislative Council of St Kitts and abolition of that in Nevis. At the end of April, Charles Eldridge, who had left Nevis to become the first president of the united islands, stated that the union, in addition to being 'a measure of vast importance, the results of which will be watched with marked interest', was also something which, because of the nearness of the islands to each other, had been contemplated by 'nature herself'.[17]

The Administration of Anguilla

Until 1867 Anguilla was administered by a Vestry of 13 members, consisting of the stipendiary magistrate, the rector of the Anglican church, and eleven men elected by all the male inhabitants in possession of the necessary property qualifications. Under an Act passed in 1846 the Vestry was authorized to raise money for local purposes from taxes on houses, land and imports, from the issuing of licences to sell liquor and other goods, and from a royalty on salt exports of $2\frac{1}{2}$ pence a barrel. The Vestry was also responsible for public works, but had no power to enact any by-laws. Although the magistrate combined his legal duties with those of the president of the Vestry and the dispenser of medicines, he was rarely overworked. A long-serving holder of this office, named Pickwood, had to be recalled to St Kitts in 1853, in order to avoid being driven insane by the solitude.

In 1861, as might have been expected of the man who had just taken over as lieutenant-governor of St Kitts, Sir Benjamin Pine carried out a thorough familiarization tour of the island and examined every aspect of the life of the inhabitants. He found that the way they were governed by the Vestry was in several respects 'defective', and proposed a major change. In his view Anguilla needed to be separated from St Kitts, and given its own independent executive authority in the form of a legislature made up of six to eight members, half of them being elected and the other half nominated. His proposal went off to London, but was immediately rejected by the Colonial Office. 'I should fear', a senior official commented, 'that the interest which very few Anguilla negroes would exhibit might be much more lively than enlightened.' Unflattering views of this sort were not confined to officials in London. In 1862 when Isidore Dyett was appointed as the stipendiary magistrate he lamented he fact that, after more than 30 years of public service, he was not thought worthy of 'some better fate, some happier lot, than that of a hopeless immolation at a place like Anguilla'.[18] In 1867 the Vestry was reconstituted to consist of the magistrate with three nominated and three elected members. This change caused Mackenzie, Pine's successor in St Kitts, to remark the following year that 'the vestry has been reduced from 13 to 7 members. The former number was much in excess of that which so small a community could hope to furnish respectably.'[19]

Five years later, after St Kitts and Anguilla had become one presidency of the Leeward Islands Federation, there were more than enough 'respectable', not to mention very literate, inhabitants of the latter island to sign a petition sent to the Colonial Office, requesting they be given their own independent administration. 'The interests of Anguilla, its resources and capabilities of development', the petition stated,

> are not understood by the legislative body of St
> Christopher, who are strangers to us, ignorant of the
> community, careless of our wants, and therefore unequal
> to discharge…the important duties of legislation for
> us…this legislative dependence on St Kitts can in no sense
> be called a legislative union. It has operated and continues
> to operate most injuriously against us, and is mutually
> disliked.[20]

The contents of the document were a cry in the dark, and after the petition had been forwarded, via St Kitts and Antigua, to London in August 1873 nothing more was heard of it. After 1878, when the constitution of St Kitts was converted into that of Crown Colony, the position of the Anguillian representative in the Legislative Council was filled by a man nominated by the president of St Kitts, presumably after consultation with the stipendiary magistrate.

Such a nominee sat on the Council for only five years. When the union of St Kitts and Nevis took place in 1883 the right of Anguillians to send a representative to the Council was repealed. The Vestry was abolished at the same time, and from then on the administration of Anguilla was solely in the hands of the magistrate. In time it was realized that as this official spent less time in dispensing justice than in dispensing medicines it might be better to appoint a medical officer in his place, and this had become the regular practice by the end of the century. But regardless of who administered the island, his work was far from arduous, as the 23-year-old Clerk to the Magistrates in St Kitts discovered in 1910. In that year, as he recalled nearly 40 years later, the medical officer had been invalided off the island and as 'there was no other doctor available to take his place, it was decided to send me'. After taking two days to cross over:

> When I arrived at Anguilla I found there was little to do....
> I tried such trifling cases as there were, kept the treasury
> books, supervised the repairs of the roads, kept an eye on
> the Customs officers, and directed the energies of the two
> or three short-term prisoners who remained, almost
> willingly, in prison.[21]

Law and Order

By the middle of the nineteenth century, although access to the law was now available to all, the standard of law enforcement and the quality of justice were hardly any better than they had been 100 years earlier. The first Police Acts, passed in St Kitts and Nevis in advance of emancipation, had both proved to be deficient. In April 1858 it was reported that in St Kitts there was 'no militia or local corps of any description, and the police are numerically insufficient to cope with any popular disturbance'. An Act 'to establish an efficient police force' was eventually passed in 1863. It was much the same in Nevis, as Sir Arthur Rumbold discovered when he took over as president. 'I found a hybrid police in existence on sufferance', he reported in March 1858, 'the law embodying it had expired, and the absence of legislative authority, or means to pay the men, compelled me to disband them'. At the same time he was able to record his

> unqualified gratification at the general peaceable and
> orderly behaviour of the inhabitants of Nevis; for, despite
> the freer scope thus afforded to outrage and lawlessness,
> crime has not been increased, nor have acts of violence
> multiplied; and, with the exception of perhaps some
> occasional disorder in the town, the want of a paid police
> has in no other way been evidenced.[22]

It was just as well that the Nevisians were law-abiding, as the island's gaol, a former barracks built in 1820, had been burnt down in August

1856, and prisoners were then confined in the 'cells formed within the archway of the stone gallery, which ran along the western entrance' of the ruins. Those occupying these cells, which were 'not adapted to the purpose', endured 'a degree of punishment not contemplated by law, and not, indeed, to be tolerated in a civilized community'. Prisoners were only locked up at night, having, 'from the intense heat of the cells under exposure to the sun, [to] be released during the day'.[23] A new Police Act was passed in 1858, but a new gaol was not completed until two years later.

As might have been expected of a man whose hobby was 'making codes of law', Sir Benjamin Pine devoted a sizeable portion of his all-embracing 1860 report to the way in which justice was administered in St Kitts. The island then had, in addition to the Court of Queen's Bench and Common Pleas and the Court of Chancery, a Court of Ordinary dealing with wills and powers of administration, a Divorce Court, a Vice-Admiralty Court, a Small Debts Court dealing with cases in which the amount in dispute did not exceed 24 dollars, and Courts of Magistrates in Petty Sessions. Pine had very little good to say about any of them. In his view the proceedings in the Court of Queen's Bench and Common Pleas were 'so cumbrous, complicated, and expensive as to amount to a denial of justice to poorer suitors', while those in the Court of Chancery were 'even more complicated and expensive, so that for years past no suitor had been bold enough to seek "relief" at its hands'. He believed a breakdown of all the cases which had come before the civil courts during the year showed quite clearly

> to what extent the expense and complication of the
> proceedings in the higher Civil Courts debar the people
> from resorting to them. While eight hundred cases came
> before the Small Debts Court, only twenty-six came before
> the Common Pleas, and none whatever before the
> Chancery. It is evident that this vast difference cannot be
> wholly explained by the assumption, that it represents the
> difference between the cases arising, in which the amount in
> dispute is under, and those in which it is above, twenty-four
> dollars.

He was also highly critical of the petty sessions, each held before two unpaid justices of the peace, finding there was great discrepancy between the punishments awarded by the court in Basseterre and those in rural districts. '[T]he administration of justice in all these courts' he considered, 'never will command the full confidence of the mass of the people while planters and others having local interests take part in the proceedings'.[24]

Pine was not a man to find fault without attempting rectification, and improvements soon followed. An Act passed in 1862, appointing a paid police magistrate for the rural districts to sit with the unpaid justices of the peace (JPs), was followed two years later by one to provide a similar police magistrate in Basseterre. As both of these magistrates could sit without the assistance of the unpaid JPs, cases were then dealt with much more speedily. More important legislation was contained in an Act passed in 1863 'to simplify and amend the administration of justice'. This was all Pine's own work, and something of which he was rightly proud. For two years much of the spare time he had had at his disposal after his daily half-hour of 'mere ordinary work of the Government' had been spent in drawing up

> a very elaborate and comprehensive measure, compiled
> with great care from various sources, such as the Imperial
> Common Law Procedure Acts of 1852 and 1854, and the
> Irish Common Law Procedure Act of 1853. Resort has
> also been had to the laws of New Zealand, to the Danish
> law as existing in the islands of Santa Cruz and St. Thomas,
> and to the New York Code of Procedure.[25]

This was quickly approved in London, and in October 1864 Pine was able to report that the new code, which had been in operation for some months, 'worked very easily' and had 'been attended with complete success'. To illustrate this he quoted similar cases tried under the old and new codes, which resulted in taxed costs under the former of about £100, compared with only £15 under the latter.

The changes introduced in St Kitts were not Pine's only contribution to improving the administration of justice in the Leeward Islands. He was equally critical of the way justice was dispensed in Anguilla where, in 1860, he found only a Magistrate's Court which dealt with all criminal cases of minor importance, and a Small Debt Court handling cases involving £10 or less. 'There are also supposed to be Courts of Queen's Bench and Common Pleas and Chancery in the island', he noted 'and the Chief Justice of Saint Kitts visits it once a year to hear cases, criminal or civil'. But, as he had found in St Kitts, proceedings in these higher courts were 'so expensive as to prevent suitors from applying to them, and so complicated as to render it quite a matter of chance whether the true issues are presented to the judge on his flying visits'. Because of this, titles to land in Anguilla were 'in many cases very insecure, owing to claims hanging over them which can never be settled without the intervention of Chancery'. Four years later the Small Debt Court was abolished, and a single court established combining its jurisdiction with that of the superior Courts of Law and Equity. The magistrate was constituted a deputy judge, and given

cide most cases when the amount in dispute did not exceed £25
e consent of both parties, to try a case outside his jurisdiction
,ury before sending the evidence to the chief justice in St Kitts
for his decision.

Another contribution was made by Pine in 1866 when he was asked by the Secretary of State to give his opinion of the Leeward Islands Court of Appeal, which had been established in 1853, and of the possibility of setting up a combined court for the Leeward and Windward Islands. He was uncompromising in his reply, stating that the court failed to give satisfaction in any of the islands, and that it was particularly disliked in St Kitts. 'An appeal to this Court is attended with great expense to Suitors, almost as great as an Appeal to Privy council', he wrote, and

> its decisions do not command confidence, partly certainly
> because the judge from whom the appeal is made, sits in
> the Appeal Court (one of the three who constitute it) and
> is supposed to act more as an advocate of his own decision,
> than as an impartial reviewer of it.

In his view 'the Appeal Court as now constituted should be abolished'.[26]

Following a trend which became more marked as the century progressed, improvements in the way justice was administered in Nevis lagged behind those instituted in St Kitts. In May 1857 the stipendiary magistrate Isidore Dyett complained that

> The laws of Nevis are not printed, and can only be known
> to judges and magistrates by reference to the manuscript
> copies in the secretaries [sic] office. They are not indexed,
> and it is a matter of some difficulty to find out whether a
> particular Act, or a particular provision of some
> enactment, has or has not been repealed…. [T]he criminal
> law of Nevis calls loudly for revision and consolidation. At
> present it is merely a collection of indescribably confused
> materials.[27]

Possibly because of this legal ragbag, by this time the island shared the services of the chief justice of St Kitts, who crossed over 'at stated periods for the purpose of holding the courts, of which he is the sole judge, having jurisdiction in common law and equity, as well as in ecclesiastical…and criminal cases, and by a recent statute in insolvent cases also'. This state of affairs could hardly fail to annoy the leaders of Nevisian society, and in 1864 the legislature 'passed a bill granting a salary of £600 to a Chief Justice who shall reside in the Colony, and give his services exclusively to the Colony'.[28] The following year, using the code drawn up by Pine for St Kitts, another Act was passed 'to simplify and expedite the Administration of Justice'.

The Laws of Nevis finally achieved printed form in 1862, which was just as well as, following the union with St Kitts in 1883, 'there were no less than four different sets of laws in force'. These consisted of:

> (*a*) those of the federal Colony of the Leeward Islands, dating from 1872; (*b*) the laws of St Kitts, passed between 1723 and 1882, which applied only to that island and its dependence Anguilla; (*c*) the laws of Nevis, passed between 1681 and 1882, which applied only to Nevis; and (*d*) the laws of the united Presidency of St Kitts-Nevis, which date from 1882.[29]

A guide to this 'legal labyrinth' was not available until after 1911 when, in St Kitts, the Registrar of the Supreme Court and the Clerk to the Magistrates (soon after returning from his spell as the Magistrate in Anguilla) were given the job of compiling an *Index to the Titles of the Laws of the Leeward Islands and its Presidencies*.

Defence

British interest in the defence of St Kitts and Nevis (none had ever been shown in Anguilla), which had waned very quickly after the end of the Napoleonic War, was negligible after the early 1860s. In St Kitts, when the garrison of regular troops was withdrawn from Brimstone Hill in 1852, it consisted of no more than two companies of infantry, a few artillerymen, engineers and commissariat staff: perhaps 250 men in all. None of them could have had any regrets at leaving a fort in which the barracks were described by an army surgeon of the day as 'a striking example of defective construction in a sanitary point of view: the worst of them have undrained and unventilated ground floors, the flooring of boards, pervious to exhalations from beneath and to all liquid impurities from above'.[30] Three years later all the fortifications on the island were transferred to the control of the local legislature.

Many of the structures on Brimstone Hill were 'at once dismantled, and all the building material worth removing either used for public purposes or sold to private parties'. Charles Fort at the foot of the hill was abandoned, but some effort was made to keep others, at either end of Basseterre Bay, in a reasonable state of repair. Neither of these ever amounted to very much, any more than did a third fort built in 1861 (of which the only remainder today is the name Fort Street in Basseterre), and all three were soon abandoned. By about 1870 all the fortifications in St Kitts were in ruins, and slowly rotting away in the sun just as those in Nevis – Fort Charles to the south of Charlestown and the unfinished refuge on Saddle Hill – had already been doing for the previous 60 years or more.

In 1862 an effort was made in both islands to create a useful militia. An Act passed in St Kitts in August of that year called for the formation of two troops of cavalry and an artillery corps which could also function in the infantry role. As the unwritten primary purpose of the militia was to quell any serious disturbance which might be caused by the working class, black Kittitians were effectively debarred from service by the qualifications for enrollment. The cavalry troopers were to be supplied by the sugar estates in proportion to their size and output, with none being required to provide more than two men and two horses. Only men in possession of 5 acres (2 ha) of freehold land or a house and land worth £15 a year, or who leased 10 acres (4 ha) or a house and land worth £20 a year, or who had an income of over £35 a year, were able to join the artillery. Within a year the cavalry consisted of 80 officers and men, divided into the Windward and Leeward troops, and there were 70 men being trained for the artillery corps. In Nevis by this time an Act passed in 1862 had brought about the formation of a 'Volunteer Protective Force', with 60 men in the Charlestown area and another 30 drawn from the north of the island around Newcastle.

The enthusiasm of the volunteers in Nevis did not last, and they were disbanded after three years. From then on the island was without a military establishment of any kind. Things were rather different in St Kitts, where many an otherwise undistinguished estate owner, manager or overseer felt he cut quite a dash in a military uniform on a horse. By 1865 the militia, with the lieutenant-governor as its honorary colonel, consisted of 18 officers, 14 non-commissioned officers, 48 artillerymen and 58 troopers These were probably the highest figures ever reached, as total membership (but not the ratio of officers to men) gradually decreased as the century wore on. Regardless of its strength, the militia was never employed on anything other than ceremonial duties. By the time a well-trained and properly disciplined military force would have been of some use, that is in 1897 when the 'Portuguese Riot' took place, it was no longer in existence. Following the riot, a Volunteer Defence Force was raised, drawn almost exclusively from among the higher reaches of society. In 1900 this consisted of just over 100 officers and men divided into three companies: one intended for use in Basseterre, another in the country districts of St Kitts, and the third in Nevis.

21 The Bath House, Charlestown, Nevis

22 Market Place, Sandy Point, St Kitts, c.1900

23 The Bridge, Cayon, St Kitts, c. 1900

24 Brighton Estate, St Kitts

25 Anguilla salt pans in 1939

26 Salt workers, Anguilla, c.1930

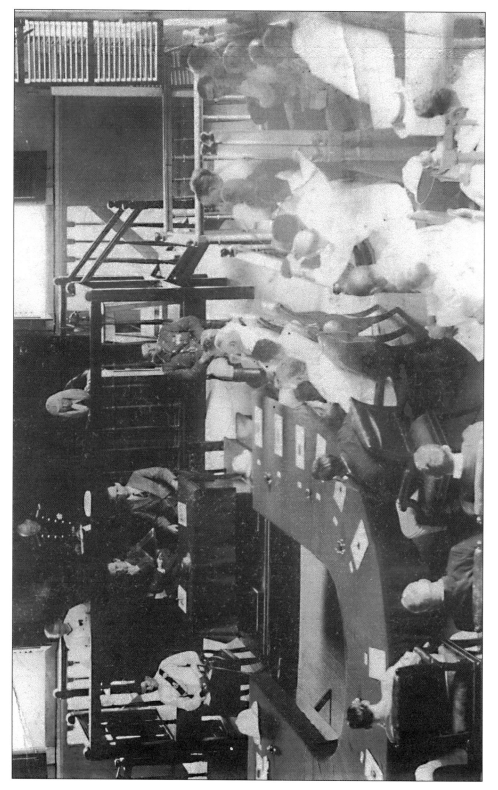

27 Leeward Islands Federal Council, 1939

28 Golden Rock airstrip and the sugar factory, c.1950

29 Nevis airstrip, c.1957

30 Aerial view of Basseterre Bay, St Kitts, with Nevis in the distance, 1959

The St. Kitts (Basseterre) Sugar Factory. South view.

31 Sugar factory, Basseterre, 1912

32 Derelict sugar mill, Nevis, in 1939

33 Robert Llewellyn Bradshaw (1916–1978)

34 Paul Southwell (1913–1979)

35 The Government leaders of Antigua and St. Kitts and Barbuda/St. Kitts-Nevis-Anguilla, 1961

36 The Administrator with the Bradshaw Government after the 1966 elections

37 Kennedy Simmonds meeting President Reagan

38 Ronald Webster, backed by a crowd of supporters, meets Lord Caradon, Britain's representative at the United Nations, on his arrival in Anguilla in March 1969

39 Government House, Anguilla, in 1965

40 The so-called 'Anguilla invasion', 1969: 'No opposition has been reported', an official announcement said.

18

Towards a Modern Society

During the second half of the nineteenth century, while radical and long overdue changes were made in the way the islands were administered, equally belated improvements to the conditions under which the great majority of their inhabitants lived were all instituted at a far slower pace. 'Ottley's village –', a visitor to St Kitts scoffed in 1852, 'a few negro houses, with a store, where bread, salt fish, ale, porter and new rum, with the other luxuries of negro life, were vended on the usual terms.'[1] Life did not improve much for the inhabitants there, or in any other village, during the next 50 years. In 1860 Sir Benjamin Pine estimated there was a total of about 5500 houses on the island. As the population at the time was 24,300 this gave an average occupancy of four and a half people to a house, something he considered 'a large number, considering the size of the generality of the houses'. Most of the houses inhabited by 'the lower classes', he observed, were

> Generally speaking wooden erections, about 14 feet square, consisting of one or at the utmost two rooms. A European lady lately compared them to bathing machines with the wheels off; a comparison scarcely complimentary to the latter.[2]

Nothing had changed nearly 40 years later, when another visitor to the island found a village near to Basseterre to be nothing more than 'rows of negro huts of the flimsiest construction, whose inhabitants live mostly in open air, and from whose yards rises the smoke of the cooking fires'.[3] Housing was almost as bad in Nevis and even worse in Anguilla where, as late as 1911, the majority of Anguillians were described as living 'in thatched and unfloored huts with mud walls' and 'nowhere collected in villages'. A lucky few owned stone cisterns to collect rainwater, 'but the water used by the people generally for drinking and other purposes is that of the wells, which is brackish on account of the admixture of sea-water'.[4]

Only slow improvement to the general standard of housing in all three islands took place until after a Central Housing and Planning Authority was set up in January 1949. The Administrator's annual report for the previous year described a situation which had hardly changed in a century:

> The poorer sections of the community in both urban and
> rural areas live in semi-detached houses of one or two
> rooms. In the main these houses are constructed of timber
> and have roofs covered with galvanized iron, 'Wallaba'
> shingles, genasco felt shingles and a few with local grass.
> There exist in rural areas houses built entirely of local grass
> with wooden floors and shutters. Cooking facilities in
> both areas are still very primitive, and sanitary
> accommodation almost non-existent.[5]

Government interest in the quality of housing made a big difference, particularly to St Kitts where the worst conditions existed. Seven years later, after the villages of Sadlers, Molyneux and Lodge had all been greatly enlarged through new housing schemes, it was reported that

> As a result of the prefabrication of timber buildings by the
> Central Housing and Planning Authority, the number
> 'Trash Houses' (mountain lumber covered with cane
> leaves) has been greatly reduced: it is envisaged that this
> form of assistance will continue.[6]

Other housing schemes followed, but the last 'trash houses' probably did not disappear until sometime in the 1960s, and sub-standard housing could still be found all around the island for many years after that.

During much of the nineteenth century the poor people of Nevis, as well as having to put up with primitive housing conditions, were also forced to save what little money they had, and conduct their business affairs, in money which had no legal value. In 1855 President Seymour reported that for the previous 50 years or more 'all local exchanges' had been conducted using 'the *peceta provincial,* a Spanish coin of base silver, which purports on its issue from the mint to be worth the fifth part of a dollar, twenty cents, or their recognized equivalent, tenpence sterling'. Because these had been allowed to circulate in Nevis 'at a fraction under elevenpence' for so long, all legalized coins had been 'driven away'. Seymour tried twice to get the legislature to impose a value of tenpence (10d) on the 'peceta', but failed on both occasions to get the Assembly to agree. 'The anomaly therefore continues', he wrote in April 1856, 'of the whole revenue being collected in a coin which is not a legal tender.'[7] Nearly 20 years later a 'proclamation decrying them' was issued, but as no provision was made 'for their redemption at the nominal value', this achieved nothing. It was not until 1879 that these Spanish coins, by then known as 'sheedies', were finally taken out of circulation, the loss 'attendant on their withdrawal [being] borne by the public revenue'.[8]

The Growth of Basseterre

By mid-century Basseterre had a population of around 5000. The town had expanded well inland of St George's Church, and also to the west along the bay front, where an insalubrious area known as 'Irish Town' had been created. Expansion to the east was prevented by a large area of salt marsh – a feature which was to present health and housing problems until the end of the century. 'The only eye-sore is a swamp, generating miasma and mosquitoes, a little east of the town', an irascible visitor named Charles Day recorded in 1852, while the town itself he found to be a dusty and dilapidated place 'composed of groups of half a dozen negro houses, and then a decent structure, with struggling, withered cocoanut palms, here and there.... Its streets and lanes are covered with volcanic sand-lava, triturated by the tread of centuries.' Day found very little to his liking. 'Basseterre has not even a stationer's shop', he fulminated,

> but every store peddles in the commonest sort of stationery at an exorbitant price. There is not a hair-cutter or cutler's shop in the town...nor is there a tailor's shop, though there are several botchers of clothes, living in wretched negro-houses.... So great is the general mismanagement out here that even the newspapers are not published for two or three days after they are due.... Only one or two of the streets are named, and those have not their names written up, nor are there any names over the stores.[9]

An effort to provide the town with proper management took place in 1860 when a municipal corporation, consisting of a mayor and five councillors elected by the freeholders, was established by Lieutenant-Governor Pine. The corporation failed to live up to Pine's expectations, causing him to complain after five years that it 'had not done the good it was designed to accomplish'. Although Basseterre had been provided with street lighting, in the form of kerosene oil lamps, no local rates had been imposed and the corporation appeared 'determined not to tax for any purpose whatever'.[10] In December 1865 any further town elections were suspended and Pine appointed a new mayor and council together with a town clerk. This also failed to achieve very much, and two years later Basseterre was put under the supervision of the surveyor of roads and superintendent of public buildings, who was made responsible for public order and cleanliness.

In May 1854, well over 200 years after the town was founded, a 200-foot (61 m) 'wharf [more correctly a pier] for the landing and shipment of goods, produce, and passengers, a luxury hitherto unknown in St Kitts, was commenced' in the centre of the bay front. After its completion in the following year, a 'commodious barrack, 116 feet long by 42 broad' was brought down from Brimstone Hill and re-erected at the head of the pier for use as 'a treasury and a police barrack'. A second, longer jetty, which came to be known as the East Pier, was constructed in 1859 alongside what by then was known as the Treasury Pier, and work on the more imposing Treasury Building which exists today began in 1891 (see Plate 19). The Treasury Pier (see Plate 18) was completely reconstructed in 1954, at the same time as a third jetty was being built between it and the East Pier. The Customs Pier was nearly 450 feet (137 m) long, but as it still did not extend into water more than about 20 feet (96 m) deep it remained, like the other two, of use only to inter-island shipping. No provision was made for the alongside berthing of ocean-going vessels until 1980, following the construction of a deep-water port at the eastern end of Basseterre Bay.

Basseterre was provided with piped water in 1857. Before this the majority of the inhabitants, those not living in houses with roof areas large enough to collect rainwater in cisterns, had been forced to rely on well-water 'frequently laden with salts and other matter, rendering it neither palatable nor wholesome'. In times of drought, when the wells ran dry, water had been carted in and sold, 'so far as the poor [were] concerned, at a ruinous and prohibitory price'.[11] When a constant supply of water finally became available in the town, carried from the mountains through pipes laid by convict labour, it was hailed an 'an improvement talked of for upwards of a century'. The supply was considerably increased in the early 1870s when a new waterworks, involving five miles of pipe and a reservoir, was constructed. Efforts to fill in the swamp to the east of the town began in 1852, when several acres were reclaimed, also with the use of convict labour. This resulted in an extension of Basseterre called New Town, and some additional fields for sugar-cane. An epidemic of yellow fever which broke out in New Town in 1879 prompted the reclamation of most of the remaining marshland, leading to the creation of Pond Pasture, but the final swampy pools were not filled in until the early years of the twentieth century.

The Basseterre Fire, 1867

Even though a constant supply of running water was available in Basseterre by the middle of 1867, it proved to be totally inadequate in dealing with a conflagration which took place there in July of that year. The fire broke out early on 3 July, in a bakery near Pall Mall Square, and spread very rapidly through the town destroying, 'with some few exceptions, every building, and thereby rendered homeless several thousand of its inhabitants'. The immediate relief provided 'for the suffering poor' by means of a grant from the legislature was later supplemented by 'liberal contributions from England and the neighbouring islands', and rebuilding eventually took place. The fire had a number of beneficial results: some of the roads were widened, a 'fire company, composed of eight men as a permanent staff' with 42 'supernumaries', was established, and a new and better waterworks was authorized. In addition the town was extended to the north by purchase of part of an adjoining estate. The fire also drove the final nail into the coffin of the municipal corporation, which was abolished after its 'utter confusion and disorganization' was seen to have 'signally failed in the time of need'.[12]

Among the many larger buildings ruined by the fire was St George's Church, which was rendered totally unusable. The damage was so bad that the legislature had to pass a bill authorizing a loan of £8000 to be raised in England for its restoration. The legislature must have found the necessity for this particularly galling, as the church was then less than ten years old. It had been built, amid much controversy and at a cost of over £10,000, 'nearly treble the original estimate', between 1855 and 1858 in order to replace a smaller church which had been badly damaged in an earthquake in 1843. St George's was fully restored in 1869, a year after an Act had been passed in England to disestablish the Anglican Church in the West Indies but, unfortunately for the legislature and Treasury of St Kitts, five years before they got round to passing their own disestablishment Act. In 1882, in advance of the union of St Kitts and Nevis, St George's rectory, a large building some distance to the west of the church called Springfield House, was taken over by the government for use as the official residence of the island's administrator. Government House, a grander building to the north of St Georges' which had been occupied in the past by the administrator of St Kitts, had, since 1871, been reserved for the use of the governor of the Leeward Islands.

The Great Flood of Basseterre, 1880

Government House, standing between College Street and Victoria Road, was situated in the path of a catastrophic flood, far worse than that of 1792, which swept through Basseterre on the night of 11 and 12 January 1880. This followed an evening during which the 'atmosphere was close and oppressive, lurid clouds hanging over the east-north-east of the Island, one or two showers of rain falling before nightfall, and eye-witnesses declaring that water-spouts were seen hovering in the same direction'. Steady rain fell from about 10 o'clock until midnight, and then torrentially for the next three hours before gradually moderating. The effect of this on Basseterre was revealed at dawn when, in the words of a report compiled later, 'the eyes of those on the neighbouring hills' were presented with 'a scene of desolation which it is impossible for a non-beholder adequately to imagine'. Great portions of the surrounding cane fields had been

> scooped out into hideous gullies of 100 feet wide and 30 feet deep, the water bearing earth, boulders, and sand down upon the low lands, and into the devoted town of Basseterre.
>
> The canes which were not bodily washed away into the town and sea were buried under the accumulated debris, and the former courses followed by the water, when heavy rains occasionally occurred, were either altogether changed from their previous direction or transfigured from mere surface drains into deep and wide gorges.

This, however, was nothing compared with 'the scene of utter confusion and ruin which was presented in Basseterre'. Flood water, 'discharging principally from Greenland Gut, the Market Gut, College Street, and Victoria Road', had uprooted houses and shops and deposited a colossal amount of earth, sand and stones, in places up to twelve feet deep, throughout the town. 'Government House was little injured', but the water had rushed through the Methodist Church immediately to the south, and covered St George's churchyard 'many feet deep in sand'. An anonymous eye-witness in the vicinity reported seeing the water flowing past his house in three great waves

> the result, most probably, of the successive ruptures of the gorges bordering Monkey Hill, discharging therefrom the temporarily pent up rain falling around. He saw houses lifted from their foundations and broken to pieces, or borne away on the bosom of the swelling flood, and his fellow creatures, sometimes singly, sometimes in whole families, swept past in the relentless stream, without the possibility of his rendering assistance.

A total of 42 people were buried later in the day, followed by another 61 over the next five days 'as they were recovered or dug out from the sand or the cellars where they had perished'. These, together with the bodies of seven other people found weeks later, accounted for less than half of all who died. Fifteen bodies were eventually washed up on St Eustatius and buried there, but another 115 swept out to sea were never recovered. All the dead, whether their bodies were found or not, were black. The only white person mentioned in the report of the disaster prepared by the Relief Committee appointed by the President, was a girl who, having been washed out to sea during the night from Irish Town, was rescued by a boat after daybreak. She was one of half a dozen people who had particularly fortunate escapes from death. Among these were two women 'picked up next morning between St Kitts and St Eustatius, one of whom was safely delivered next morning of a child', and a boy 'floating on a plank, with a duck as his companion', hauled out of the sea near Old Road.

The Relief Committee, formed in the afternoon of 12 January, began its work by arranging the provision of some emergency accommodation, the issuing of 'relief tickets to destitute sufferers...especially to those in the immediate want of food', and the employment of a cook 'to prepare daily a good and substantial meal, equal to that issued to the prisoners in gaol'. The work needed to clear the town of the flood deposits began a little later and was still in progress at the end of March. The committee subsequently stated, from observations made of boats and an iron tank which had filled up with rainwater, 'that they cannot be far wrong in estimating the rainfall, during the night of 11th and morning of the 12th January, at not less than between 30 and 40 inches, the great bulk of which was precipitated within three hours'.[13] The value of the houses and private property destroyed or damaged was at least £9000 (the equivalent of nearly £500,000 at the beginning of the twenty-first century), and by the end of the year well over £6000 had been spent on repairs to public buildings, roads, walls, bridges and wharves. Soon after this work had been completed the size of Basseterre was increased by the purchase of a large area to the west of Irish Town, the 'Town Extension Lands', for the erection of various public buildings and some private housing.

The Spread of Basseterre

At the close of the nineteenth century, in spite of the provision of running water, reclamation of swamp land, and other efforts made to improve Basseterre, the town was no more appealing to visitors than it had been 50 years earlier; even less so, if the observations made by a female passenger on an American yacht are anything to go by. 'Seen from the water the town is handsome, with its white houses and public buildings. We tell ourselves that here we see the evidence of English thrift and cleanliness', Susan de Forest Day recorded in 1899. But:

> As we go ashore, the nearer we come to those white houses the more dilapidated do they look. The plaster is peeling off in patches, and the best of them have a forlorn expression which even the pretty gardens cannot brighten.
> But when we turn into the negro quarter, we are sickened. The huts – one cannot dignify them by the name of houses – are huddled close together pell-mell, on the streets where the mud is ankle deep. They are dirty, one-roomed wooden cabins, in every stage of decay, with often only the muddy ground for a floor....[14]

Very little change to the extent and general appearance of Basseterre took place until the second quarter of the twentieth century. Reginald St Johnston, who was the Administrator from 1925 to 1929, took some pride in acquiring 16 acres (6 ha) of land to the north of the town for the sum of £1600 ('which seemed high, but I suppose was reasonable in view of its proximity to the town,')[15] and converting this in 1926 into Warner Park. Two years later he took even more pride in obtaining part of La Guerite Estate to the west of the town, where he introduced a model housing scheme, which provided new fire- and hurricane-proof concrete houses for rent 'at half a crown a week each, a price well within the means of the artisan class for whom they were intended'.[16] Building lots for more substantial, middle-class houses began to be sold at Fortlands, the 'Government Reserve' between La Guerite and Fort Thomas, at the same time.

More substantial development did not begin to take place until after the Second World War. As a result of a housing survey carried out in 1946, which found New Town to be a grossly overcrowded slum, 10 acres (4 ha) of the Pond Estate were bought for a re-housing scheme, something which took until 1954 to complete. While this was under way, land to the west of St George's Church was bought and sold off in lots to create the Greenlands housing estate. During the 1960s private speculators extended Basseterre even further, creating housing estates such as Shadwell, to the north of Greenlands, and New Pond Site, to the north-east of Warner Park. At much the same time, efforts being made to diversify the economy brought an industrial estate into being well to the east of the town on Pond Pasture. By the late 1970s, when seen from seaward, the town extended virtually the entire length of Basseterre Bay.

Growth of Charlestown

Although ever since their foundation neither Basseterre nor Charlestown had ever amounted to very much, by the middle of the nineteenth century the latter was, using words favoured by the testy Charles Day, even more scrambling, dusty and dilapidated than the former. Charlestown's 'well-built houses, on the shores of one of the best roadsteads in the West Indies, have been gradually falling into decay', wrote the President, Frederick Seymour, in 1856.

> The few shop windows present little to catch the eye, and the price of such articles as are exhibited is exorbitantly high, for the shopkeeper must protect himself by high charges against loss in accepting at its artificial value the coin of impure silver to which the people have secured for the last 40 years a favoured currency.[17]

The town had always lagged behind its counterpart in St Kitts in size, population, amenities and the way it was run, and it was all set to fall further behind still as the years went by.

Possibly the largest building in Charlestown in the 1850s was 'a curious-looking edifice' known as the Bath House (see Plate 21), which had been erected in 1778 and which was described 75 years later as having been

> built of granite, at a vast expense, by the late Mr John Huggins for himself and married sons, so that each family, though under the same roof, might have a distinct house, offices, etc.... This arrangement turned out to be a failure, and after many vicissitudes ruinous to its occupants, part of it (the centre) became an hotel. Its arrangements are *bizarre*, but comfortable.[18]

Whatever comfort the building then provided had disappeared altogether by 1870, and it remained closed and falling into dereliction for the next 40 years.

Seymour's successor as president, Sir Arthur Rumbold, was particularly put out on his arrival to discover there was no Government House in Charlestown, and that he was required to live in unfurnished rented accommodation. 'On my arrival', he grumbled to the Colonial Office in May 1857, 'I had, at great cost and inconvenience, to purchase every article of furniture; this, probably, is the only colony which does not provide to some extent for the comfort of its chief local officer.'[19] The construction of 'Queen's House', a building 'intended as a residence for the officer administering the government' began in March 1860. It was built on the site of the old barracks cum gaol which had been burnt down four years earlier, this site having become available when the inmates were removed to a new purpose-built prison. Queen's House, the first proper Government House on Nevis, was completed in December 1862. It remained the official residence of whoever was in charge of the administration until 1911, when it was replaced by a large building erected to the east of what was then the Bath Hotel.

Charlestown was also provided with its first pier and its first public well in 1862. The well was dug near the root of the pier, where it was intended to 'furnish the shipping and many of the poorer inhabitants (these latter often deprived of this necessary of life) with the essential requisite of water, for which they mainly depended on the kindness of the proprietors of a few cisterns'.[20] Together with one or two others which were soon sunk, this only partially alleviated the problem of supplying the town with enough fresh water. In 1877 it was reported that

> a limited water rate would willingly be paid by the
> inhabitants to obtain what is so necessary and essential to
> health, viz., a good and unfailing supply of wholesome
> water; at present a few wells and rain water gathered in
> small cisterns from the roofs of houses afford the only
> supply for the inhabitants of the town.[21]

A year later the Colonial Office was told that the town's water supply was 'insufficient and precarious', something which, because it made the drainage and sanitary condition...not satisfactory', called for 'early and serious attention'.[22] Such attention, particularly after the union of Nevis with St Kitts in 1883, was not forthcoming. Some improvements were made, but Charlestown remained without a full, unfailing supply of piped water until the late 1940s.

The pier, which was opened in March 1863, was longer and more substantial than the one built at Basseterre. Over half of its 266-foot (81 m) length was built of masonry, the rest being of wood. It was completed with a tramway carrying a mobile crane, and its outer end was in about 12 feet (4 m) of water. The pier served its purpose very well, with the outer timber section not requiring to be replaced until 1911. After that, even though it had become essential to all the island's shipping activity, no further attention to its maintenance was paid for over 50 years. By 1966

> the main jetty was in a dreadful state. At one spot on the
> concrete walk of the rapidly disintegrating structure,
> whenever the sea-water under the jetty reached that spot, as

the tide ebbed and flowed, the water would spurt into the air and drench anyone who happened to pass in the vicinity.[23]

Only an imminent visit by the Queen and Duke of Edinburgh prevented the pier being rendered totally unusable. As was ever the case under colonial rule, the prospect of a royal visit unlocked previously unavailable finance, and as soon as this was announced funds were found to effect the much-needed repairs.

In 1883, in order perhaps to offer the inhabitants of Charlestown some small compensation for the lack of running water, street lighting similar to that which the citizens of Basseterre had been enjoying for the previous 20 years was provided. This made little difference to the overall appearance of the town which, at the end of the century, still appeared to a visitor as no more than 'a small hamlet', consisting of

> hardly more than a single street, stretching along the open beach. On the sea front there is a single line of cocoa palms lifting their heads high in the air, and beneath them are the huts of the negro fishermen, with their boats hauled up on the beach and their nets drying in the sun. The town is made of quaint old houses of the ancient period of West Indian architecture, with mossy stone walls and tiled roofs. There are no signs of any business except a few shops of general merchandise, and an air of gentle decay broods over the whole place.[24]

The development of Charlestown during the next century bore no comparison with that of Basseterre. To all intents and purposes, and as far as most visitors to Nevis were concerned, the town merely stagnated. 'Charlestown', wrote one such visitor in the early 1960s, 'is a sweet little place with the Supreme Court House and public library overlooking a miniature square containing a cenotaph'.[25] His single sentence description, followed by equally brief references to 'the ruined battlements and ancient cannon of Fort Charles, swarming with goats' and the 'imposing three-storey building, although empty for years' which was the abandoned Bath House, added up to as much as anyone had been able to say about the town since the beginning of the century. Nor would much be able to be added for at least another decade.

Water Supply

Throughout their history all three islands suffered from prolonged periods of drought, with Nevis suffering more than St Kitts, and Anguilla suffering most of all. As a result, that most basic of human needs, fresh water, was always at a premium, and its provision in reliable and adequate quantities remained a source of concern until well into the twentieth century.

In St Kitts, as would be expected in the most mountainous of the islands, there were fewer problems involved in obtaining than in distributing water. Although a scheme for providing Sandy Point with a supply similar to that in Basseterre (p.204 above) was drawn up in 1860, nothing very much came of it and that town, along with the rest of the island, had to wait many more years before piped water became available. The distress caused by the lack of a proper water supply was made very obvious to the Governor of the Leeward Islands, Sir John Glover, in 1881 when, on an official visit, he drove around the island with his wife. '[D]rinking-water in some parts was much needed', Lady Glover wrote later,

> and the Governor visited different places where he was
> anxious to make reservoirs to collect supplies. Here the
> natives came in crowds pressing round the carriage, yelling
> and shouting, 'water!', holding up their children to pray,
> implore, and beseech 'water' to be given them. The
> pressure became so great that it was difficult to get the
> horses to move on without injuring the people, who threw
> themselves on their knees in front of the carriage.

Glover, who was in poor health and by no means the most dynamic of administrators, although as much moved as his wife at the time, did little after he returned to Antigua but wring his hands. 'When, for want of money', Lady Glover continued through crocodile tears, 'or from the difficulty of getting the home authorities to realize how much such improvements are needed, a Governor is obliged to sit quiet, and look on at the sufferings of the people, it is hard indeed to feel inaction is enforced where action is so much needed.'[26] By August 1883, although 'supplying the towns of Sandy Point and Dieppe Bay, and the surrounding country, with water' was now considered to be 'of the utmost importance', it was still only being 'contemplated'. It was to be another decade or more before all the villages were provided with a piped supply of fresh water.

In Nevis, although Charlestown had been provided with a piped water supply of a sort before the end of the nineteenth century, it was well into the second half of the next century before every village on the island had access to running water. After 1911 the villages on the southern side of Nevis Peak began to be supplied from a reservoir constructed at Rawlins, high up on the south-eastern flank of the mountain, but elsewhere on the island it was a different story. In 1931 the colony's Public Health Officer, in reporting that Charlestown 'enjoys a piped water-supply, and most of the villages are also provided with stand-pipes', failed to comment on the quality of the town's supply, or say just how many villages remained without running water. The supply to Charlestown, drawn from the Rawlins reservoir, was not improved until the late 1940s, when a new, larger diameter pipeline was laid down, and a few villages remained without stand-pipes for long after that. In 1958 water was 'promised' to the village of Jessups to the north of Charlestown, while pipes were still being laid to supply other villages in the area.

In Anguilla, where access to fresh water had been a problem since the earliest days, conditions were much worse than in either St Kitts or Nevis. In 1922 a government geologist, Kenneth Earle, stated that the provision of an adequate water supply was 'a matter of considerable difficulty…accentuated by the fact that nearly all the wells of the island have to be excavated below sea level before reaching a permanent water supply of water'. Because of this 'they all become contaminated, and, if not actually brackish, are what is known locally as "heavy"'. In some parts of the island, such as Road Village and West End, Earle considered that to provide water fit for human consumption from any underground supply was 'a practically impossible proposition'. He failed to understand why the collection of rainwater from roofs was not more widely practised. 'Either obstinacy, or failure to realize this, prevents the inhabitants adopting this procedure to any great extent', he expostulated without, perhaps, appreciating that not too many Anguillian houses then had roofs suitable for this. 'When the inhabitants of West End Village are content to walk three miles each way for water', he continued with all the colonial official's insensitivity he could muster,

> and the inhabitants of Crocus Bay prefer to climb a steep
> hill 120 feet high and down the other side to the Valley
> well – a total distance of nearly two miles there and back –
> rather than catch water off their own roofs, just because it
> has been the custom from time immemorial to do so, we
> are faced with the question as to whether it is worth while
> to provide a water supply for a population who apparently
> do not need it.[27]

While it is impossible to say whether such comments were responsible or not, nothing very much was done to improve the Anguillian water situation for the next 30 years. A pump supplying a maximum of 50 gallons a minute was fitted at The Valley well in 1932, which was of some help to the 1600 or so people who depended on the well, some of whom lived a mile and a half from it. In 1938 the Senior Medical Officer of St Kitts reported that the water level in the well was often so low that it became

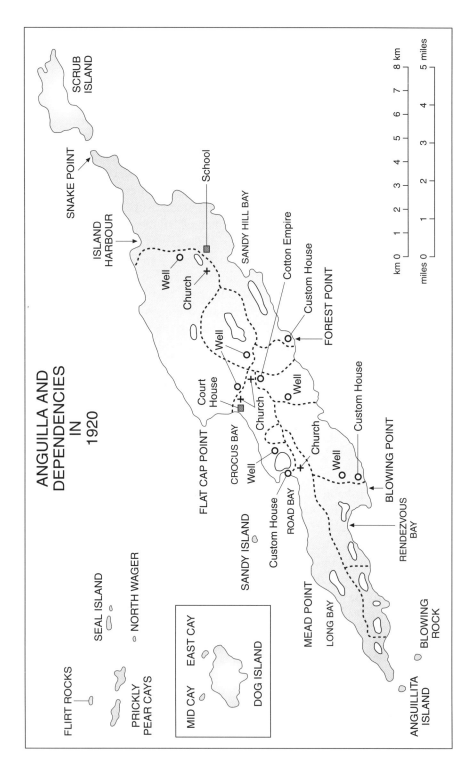

ANGUILLA AND
DEPENDENCIES
IN
1920

necessary to wait before any could be drawn. For some of the users, obtaining a pail of water then involved not only a three-mile walk but a wait of anything from one to three hours. This situation was improved in the 1940s by the erection of a storage tank, and the lives of people in Sandy Ground were made a little easier after 1952, when another storage tank was erected on Crocus Hill and a pipeline laid as far as South Hill. Thereafter very little was done to improve the water situation for the next 20 years or more.

Electricity Supply

Providing each of the three islands with an electricity supply followed an almost identical timetable. Basseterre became the first place to enjoy its benefits when a small generator was installed in 1928, but the rest of St Kitts was not supplied until after a proper power station was built in 1952. In Nevis, only Government House and the hospital in Charlestown had electricity (each being supplied by its own generator) between 1932 and 1954, when the island was given the old power plant from St Kitts. This could only supply Charlestown and that part of the island between Cotton Ground to the north-west and Gingerland in the south-east. Two new generators were supplied to Nevis by the British government in 1961, after which power was gradually extended to the whole island with 'six street lamps in each village'. Anguilla remained without electricity until the beginning of the 1970s, when a small generator was installed in The Valley. A power station just about capable of supplying the entire island was not built until 1977.

Communications

The way in which, during the second half of the nineteenth century, St Kitts drew ahead of Nevis while more or less abandoning the wardship of Anguilla is illustrated by the difference in the time taken to provide each island with the new means of communicating with the outside world that developed during this period. When a post office was established in Anguilla in 1904, a similar facility had been available in St Kitts since 1860, and in Nevis since 1866. After 1870 most of the West Indian islands, including St Kitts, were provided with telegraphic communication with America and Europe by undersea cable, but both Nevis and Anguilla were bypassed. To leave out the latter was perhaps understandable but, as Thomas Berkeley, a prominent citizen of St Kitts, wrote later, it was

difficult to see why Nevis was 'excluded from the benefits of the tele-
graph', when the cable between St Kitts and Antigua passed 'within
gunshot distance of the land'.[28] A telephone system which was installed in
St Kitts in 1890 had exchanges in Basseterrre, Sandy Point and Cayon with
nearly 200 island-wide subscribers by 1921. Nevis was not provided with a
telephone service until 1915, and Anguilla, unbelievably, not until 1971.

St Kitts was also favoured in physical communication with the outside
world carried out, of course, by sea. From some time in the early 1840s the
island was included in the itinerary of the ships of the Royal Mail Steam
Packet Company which provided a regular service linking the West Indies
with Britain and North America. 'The mail steamers do not call at Nevis,
though they pass within two miles of the town,' Berkeley complained in
1881, 'it is a disadvantage which would probably be removed if…it had
some persons in this country sufficiently interested and influential to
remonstrate against the hardship.' It is not known whether any such
remonstration was ever made but even if it was it got nowhere. It made
little economic sense for any ocean-going ship to call at Charlestown when
the island's export trade was virtually at an end and the port of Basseterre
was only ten miles away.

Travel between St Kitts and Nevis was much improved after 1863, following the construction of a pier at Charlestown to match that which had
been built nine years earlier at Basseterre, but it depended solely on sail
until well into the twentieth century. 'The commencement of the fast
motor boat service between St. Kitts and Nevis has been deferred owing to
difficulties which have arisen', the Administrator recorded in his official
report for 1911,

> but it is expected that it will be inaugurated before long.
> Meantime, there is daily communication between the
> Islands by means of large sailing boats of 10 to 12 tons, one
> of which carries the mails and provides passenger
> accommodation under contract with the Government.[29]

The change from sail to power had still not taken place 18 years later.
'Communication between St. Kitts and Nevis is by sailing boat daily',
Administrator Reginald St-Johnston stated in 1929 before adding, 'The
Government is inaugurating an efficient motor boat service (mail and
Passenger) between the two islands and a double trip will be made by this
boat.'[30]

The new service may well have deserved to be called 'efficient' when it
was finally started, some time in the 1930s, but it did not remain so for
very long. In 1947, a teacher transferred from St Kitts to teach at a school
in Nevis discovered

it was not always easy to get passage across. One steam launch only plied daily between the islands, and that took passengers alone. The other boats, called locally 'Nevis boats', were fair-sized, one-masted, open sailing boats ... built to take both passengers and cargo.[31]

The first reasonably efficient and reliable service using a motor vessel was not inaugurated until 1959, when the brand-new, purpose built ferry *Christena,* capable of carrying five tons of cargo and 150 passengers, began operating.

At the beginning of the twentieth century, communication between St Kitts and Anguilla was maintained, as it almost always had been, by Anguillian-owned schooners, one of which was given a government subsidy to operate a fortnightly mail service. This had become a weekly service by the 1920s, but hardly improved after that, despite the Executive Council's decision in 1931 to begin 'a regular weekly motor-schooner' service. The means and speed of the administration's communications with Anguilla matched the amount of interest shown in the island. When the Governor of the Leeward Islands flew to Anguilla for the first time in 1956 he later recorded that: 'up until then my annual visits were by sailing schooner or by fishing boat – a twelve to sixteen hour journey each way'.[32]

The first aircraft ever seen anywhere near St Kitts and Nevis were four American seaplanes which flew past the islands in April 1927. The first to actually visit St Kitts was a seaplane piloted by Charles Lindbergh, which landed in Basseterre Bay two years later. Before leaving again on his good-will tour to inaugurate the Pan-American seaplane service between North and South America, the famous aviator had time for a brief appearance at a public reception in the Treasury Building. There was never any question of Basseterre being included as a port of call on the Pan-Am route and St Kitts, like the rest of the Leeward Islands, remained without any contact with other parts of the world by air until well after the start of the Second World War. In September 1940 the British government signed an agreement to allow the United States to lease large parts of various Caribbean territories for the construction of military bases. One such base, built in Antigua for use by the US Army Air Force, received its first squadron of aircraft in October 1941. In the same year, in order to give these planes the ability to make emergency landing, airstrips were created on many of the surrounding islands, including St Kitts and Anguilla.

The landing strip on St Kitts was constructed on the Golden Rock estate to the north of Basseterre (see Plate 28), and when completed was completely surrounded by cane fields. Its use during the war is unrecorded, but afterwards it was found to be a little too short for use by anything but the smallest commercial aircraft, as a DC3 belonging to the Dutch KLM airline found to its cost when it ended up amidst the sugar-cane. Steps were taken to extend and improve the landing strip, and by 1946 both KLM (which had been operating in the Caribbean since 1938) and British West Indian Airways (BWIA, which had been formed in 1940) were making 'regular calls at the St Kitts airport', between them connecting the island with Antigua, St Martin and Curaçao. After an Antigua-based airline, Leeward Islands Air Transport (LIAT), began operations with much smaller aircraft in 1956 St Kitts was provided with a service to Puerto Rico and to each of the surrounding islands that had an airport. The runway was extended to 6000 feet in 1958, and the whole airfield extended and considerably improved eight years later.

The 1000-foot grass airstrip on the Wallblake Estate, close to The Valley in Anguilla, did not come into commercial use until 1956, when LIAT started operations. It was paved in 1968, extended to 3600 feet twelve years later, but not made capable of handling night flights until 1983. The connection of Anguilla with St Kitts by air in 1956 inspired the construction of an airstrip on Nevis (see Plate 29). In the same year work began on a level piece of ground on the north coast close to the village of Newcastle, and a small airport with a 1500-foot grass runway and bearing the name of the village was opened in June 1958.

19

Progress in Health and Education

Health

It was not until well into the second half of the twentieth century that health services for the three islands were provided in anything but an inequitable manner. Up until emancipation medical attention for the great mass of the people in each island was provided by doctors paid by individual slave-owners. The owners themselves, along with rest of the population – white, free coloureds and free blacks – were treated by the same doctors as long as they were able to pay for whatever treatment they received. As such treatment was not cheap, this meant that after the abolition of slavery the largest and poorest section of society in all three islands was, by and large, left without access to any health care whatsoever. This took a long time to change but, once improvements did start, they came more quickly in St Kitts than in Nevis, and in both of these islands much faster than in Anguilla.

Health Services in St Kitts

For many years after emancipation the general inability of the poor to pay for medical attention was lost on those in authority in St Kitts. 'In addition to the carelessness as to infant disease and life which distinguishes the negro', wrote the island's somewhat unfeeling Administrator in 1848,

> I regret to have to report a further cause of this fact, so
> anomalous in a country so favourable to the increase of his
> race, in the increasing disinclination to resort to fitting
> medical advice for patients in cases of extremity on the
> part of their relations.[1]

The institution to which the term 'hospital' was attached which opened that year in Basseterre was far from being one where such 'fitting medical advice' could be obtained. The 'Saint Christopher Poor House and Cunningham Hospital', named after the island's Lieutenant-General who had been responsible for its foundation, was nothing more than a work-house, designed as 'a refuge for the destitute and friendless, labouring under the visitations of poverty and disease'. Each inmate required a ticket issued by a member of a parish vestry in order to gain admission. To give the place even more of a Dickensian appearance a lunatic asylum was added the next year.

Despite the absence of a genuine hospital, some improvements in general medical care began to take place after 1850. A Board of Health was appointed that year in order 'to establish sanitary regulation' and three years later an Act was passed to provide free 'medical attendance of the infant population of the labouring population'. The latter was considered necessary because 'Neglect of proper medical attention to their infant off-spring has been often noticed as a prevailing characteristic of the class alluded to.' To overcome this, five doctors, provided five could be found who were willing to do the work, were each to receive £100 a year to treat children under nine years of age. It seems unlikely that five were found, as in February 1855 Dr Thomas Cooper, the Medical Inspector General from Barbados, who had been called in at the start of the cholera epidemic (see p.162 above) was appalled by the lack of doctors on the island. 'Unless some steps be taken to induce medical men to settle or remain in the island', he wrote in his report on the epidemic, 'their absence will be most seriously felt.' In spite of his medical knowledge and organizing ability, both of which were well displayed during the crisis, Cooper was another colonial official unable to appreciate the true extent of the poverty which existed among the great majority of the labourers. 'In the time of slavery, the owners of slaves on every estate paid the medical men of the dis-trict...for medicines and attendance', he wrote before adding:

> Upon the abolition of slavery this payment by the
> proprietors was given up, and the labourers left to find
> their own medical attendant. The result has been, that
> either from the habit of having had this found them
> gratuitously, or from a natural dishonesty of character, or
> from a want of forethought, the black and coloured people
> seldom think of paying a medical bill.[2]

His suggestion for dealing with this, that doctors be paid for treating labourers out of a general medical fund created by compulsory deductions from wages, was both ahead of its time and, given the state of the labour market and the wages being paid, unworkable.

The Board of Health was remodelled in 1857, its predecessor having proved to be 'a striking example of the hopelessness of expecting from unpaid and virtually irresponsible persons...that systematic application which in a matter of this kind can alone effect any permanent reform'.[3] An Act to 'establish Registration of Births and Deaths', hitherto something which had never been required, was passed in the same year. Further improvements followed, and by 1860 each of the five districts into which the island was divided had a paid medical officer 'whose duties are to attend women in childbirth, and children under nine years of age, belonging to the labouring classes'.

In 1865 a major change took place at what by this time, even though it was still nothing but a workhouse, was generally known as the Cunningham Hospital, when the Board of Guardians was abolished and replaced by a medical superintendent. The institution at the time was so full that it was found 'very difficult to treat satisfactorily the cases of mental derangement', and 'impossible to prevent casualties occurring by the escape of lunatics, or by their quarrelling with and assaulting the other inmates of the establishment'.[4] The new superintendent certainly had his work cut out, as not only was a separate lunatic asylum required, but there was an equally pressing need for an isolation home for those among the population suffering from leprosy. '[F]or some years past every leper in the Island has received a weekly allowance from the hospital', stated the Administrator in his annual report to the Colonial Office, before adding:

> The superintendent, however, complains, and not, I think,
> without some reason, of the inconvenience, nuisance, and
> danger of a weekly assemblage of these unfortunate
> persons at the entrance of the public hospital, and
> recommends, on that and other grounds, the establishment
> of a lazaretto.[5]

Regardless of the obvious need to separate the crazed and the incurably diseased from the old and infirm, the hospital was to remain the setting for such Dionysian scenes for many more years. The mentally ill were separated from the sane reasonably quickly and shipped to an asylum established for the whole of the Leeward Islands in Antigua, but no home for those with leprosy was found until 1890 when they were provided with accommodation, of a sort, in Charles Fort near Sandy Point.

Another improvement in the provision of health care took place in 1868, when the island was divided into seven districts, each with a doctor obliged to give medical attention not only to all children under nine years of age, but to others 'requiring the same', to 'any sick, poor or destitute person desirous of admission into the hospital', and 'in cases of sudden illness to attend without in any case demanding pre-payment'. In 1872, by which time medicine and surgery had begun to take precedence over workhouse practices in the Cunningham Hospital, a supplementary establishment, called Pogson Hospital after its benefactor, was opened at Sandy Point. This increased the total number of beds available for treating the sick, but it became increasingly difficult for the staff of the larger hospital to put up with the continued presence of so many indigent men and women. 'The want of a poor house as a separate institution is one of the subjects to which I have called attention very often, but in vain', wrote the Chief Medical Officer in 1885, stressing that during the year

> a greater proportion even than usual of the inmates of the
> Cunninghame [*sic*] Hospital were sufferers from incurable
> chronic disease in its last stage, or from old age. The mixed
> character of the institution, which is both a poor house
> and a hospital, necessarily causes its death rate to be higher
> than it would be were it a hospital only. This is especially
> noticeable in a year like the last when there was such a
> large influx of patients of whose recovery their friends had
> long since abandoned all hope, but whose funeral expenses
> they were anxious to avoid.[6]

It was a cry in the dark. Although the hospital was enlarged in 1893, and further enlarged and modernized in 1926, no separate institution for the aged and chronically ill was opened until 1927. The hospital itself was eventually replaced in 1967, and nearly 125 years after it was built, by the Joseph N. France General Hospital. Erected on a new site on the western outskirts of Basseterre, this was named after the man who, as Minister of Social Services, had been responsible for getting it built.

The Public Health Department which was formed in 1918 proved, for many years, to be little more effective in improving the overall standard of health than the Board it replaced. A suspected outbreak of bubonic plague was reported in 1929, after nearly 100 cases and a dozen deaths had been recorded. A bacteriologist summoned from Trinidad determined that it was in fact a severe form of infective septicaemia connected with filiariasis (elephantiasis), which may have had some connection with a deadly epidemic which had broken out among pigs around the same time. The epidemic among the population was later recalled as having 'lasted a considerable time, with many deaths'.[7] The more prevalent diseases found among the children of St Kitts around this time included gastro-enteritis and yaws, while among the adult population enteric fever, dysentery, filariasis and syphilis were all far from uncommon. All of these dreadful conditions, with the possible exception of the last, and like the cholera which had wrought such a death toll in the 1850s, afflicted and were quickly transmitted among people forced to live in crowded and insanitary conditions with poor nutrition and without access to a sufficient supply of clean water. Another chronic disease was spread under the same conditions. 'High authority now connects the incidence of leprosy with poor diet', the historian W.M. Macmillan wrote in 1936, 'and it may be more than an accident that cases are still particularly numerous in St Kitts, which has wretched living conditions, and whose working population are among the poorest in the islands'.[8] By the beginning of the 1940s there were at least 100 people diagnosed with this disease incarcerated in Charles Fort.

Just why the majority of the people who were exposed to such conditions could not afford the medical care which would have alleviated, or even have helped to prevent, such diseases was made very clear in December 1938 to a Commission investigating social and economic conditions in the British West Indies by a man named Thomas Manchester (of whom more will be heard later):

> A labourer who earns 10d or 1/- a day and living five or six
> miles away from the doctor has to pay six or seven
> shillings, and then there is medicine which comes to about
> two or three shillings, and that is ten shillings for his first
> visit. The doctor's diagnosis may be wrong and he has to
> be recalled, so that it costs the patient another ten shillings
> and that makes twenty shillings. How often could a
> labourer call a doctor? He calls him at the first or else
> when he sees death coming in order to get a death
> certificate. They find it extremely hard.[9]

Although some improvement was brought about after the opening of district health centres in the mid-1940s the overall standard of health right up until independence was well below that achieved in other West Indian islands. One sure indication of this lay in the infant mortality rate (the number of deaths in the first year of life in proportion to every 1000 registered live births in that year), long accepted as one of the most important criteria for assessing the health of a community and the standard of the social conditions of a country. The rate for St Kitts, which gradually decreased from about 350 to just over 200 during the nineteenth century, had actually increased to over 400 by 1920 and did not fall below 200 again until well into the 1940s. Although it continued to decrease thereafter, the average figure of 43, reached between 1975 and 1983, was then the highest in the English-speaking Caribbean. Comparative figures for Britain were 150 in 1865, 90 in 1920, 23 in 1960 and 11 in 1983.

A social security scheme, providing sickness, maternity, funeral, age and invalidity benefits in return for compulsory contributions, was introduced in February 1978, one hundred and twenty-three years after something similar had been proposed by Dr Thomas Cooper, following the mid-nineteenth century cholera epidemic.

Health Services in Nevis

At the time when cholera was raging in Nevis, there was but one doctor on the island. An almshouse in Charlestown, providing indoor relief for some of the island's infirm and destitute, was similar to but smaller than the one in Basseterre, being maintained 'at a charge of only £150 a year'. Although the almshouse was supposed, in part, to be a hospital, it had no nursing staff and the doctor was only called in for special emergencies. It also lacked proper control or supervision. 'The neglect of this institution', the magistrate Isidore Dyett informed President Rumbold in 1856, 'illustrates the somnolency of colonial legislators, and their apathetic indifference to some of the most important duties and obligations devolving upon them'.[10] In the face of such indifference on the part of the legislature Rumbold could do little to improve the situation with regard to the almshouse or the labouring class in general. 'I regret to say that, in consequence of the great financial depression which has existed up to the present moment', he wrote to the Governor-General in March 1858, 'I have not been able to ask for any grants in aid of education, or medical attendance for the poor, more particularly required for the preservation of human life in infancy.' In 1869, a few years after the legislature had finally been persuaded to raise the annual grant to £250 a year, the almshouse was described as

> a wretched building, without regular medical supervision, or indeed regular supervision of any kind. Its present character is that of a lazar house; the public keep aloof, no private charity flows in its direction, and none but the homeless and incurable will resort to it for what alone it professes to give – the poorest food and merest shelter.[11]

A year later an Infirmary Act provided 'for the transfer of [this] old, but it is to be feared much-neglected establishment to the Government care': a move it was hoped would 'conduce more to the comfort of the sick and needy'.[12] After this had taken place the 'wretched' almshouse, slightly enlarged, remained the island's only hospital until the Queen's House was converted, and renamed the Alexandra Hospital in 1911. A new institution to house the aged and chronically invalided was not built until 1928.

The registration of births and deaths became legal requirements in August 1860, but nothing was done to improve the provision of health care for another ten years. The latter was a cause of concern for Rumbold's successor. 'As regards the mass of the people', he complained in April 1861,

> medical aid may be said to be out of the question, for there is but one professional man in the island; and even where the matter of expense does not prevent his services being sought, distance and bad roads in these few instances often render his aid tardy and unavailing. It appears to be admitted that many deaths take place which might have been averted by timely medical assistance.[13]

Nothing changed until 1870, when the Medical Aid Act was passed to provide for the appointment of three district medical officers, who were to give free medical and surgical aid to all children aged under ten and to all adults over 60 years of age 'of the labouring population'. The Act also provided for the same aid to be made available to any other members of the same population at a fixed, 'moderate scale of charges'.

Throughout the colonial period, no more concern about public health was shown by the authorities in Charlestown than by their counterparts in Basseterre and, although the infant mortality rate figures for Nevis were always rather better than those for St Kitts, they were still alarmingly high when compared with those in Britain and other parts of the world. 'The rate of mortality among infants is always disproportionately high', the President of Nevis wrote in 1878, 'and…is to be attributed, in addition to other causes, to the extreme poverty, if not actual want, that prevails among the labouring population'. Under such conditions, very few men and women could have afforded to visit a doctor, regardless of how moderate the fixed scale of fees might have been. By 1930 there were only two district medical officers, and another 20 or more years were to elapse before district health centres were introduced. The Alexandra Hospital, converted from the old Queen's House in 1911, was completely reconstructed and given a new lease of life in 1954.

Health Services in Anguilla

Other than whatever services were provided by the occasional doctor who found his way to the island from time to time, and the pills and potions dished out by the magistrate in his secondary role as a dispenser, the Anguillians were without health care until the closing decade of the nineteenth century. At the end of 1871 the Vestry pleaded with the President of St Kitts to provide medical attendance 'for the poor and destitute of the labouring population of this island', arguing that 'undue mortality is ascribed to want of such'. The absence of such aid, if small-pox or any 'other fatal and epidemic malady' broke out, 'would render the ravages and consequences awful to contemplate'. This plea may have touched the President's heart but, as no doctor could be found who was willing to become the district medical officer of Anguilla, it went un-answered for 20 years. The registration of births and deaths was made a legal requirement in 1883, and a doctor was finally appointed as the island's magistrate in 1891.

Nearly another 30 years passed before any thought was given in St Kitts to providing Anguilla with a hospital. The Executive Council finally gave approval for a small eight-bed cottage hospital to be built in May 1919. Construction then began but was stopped three years later through lack of funds, and the hospital was not completed until 1927. As the total cost was around £700 (£25,000 at the beginning of the twenty-first century), the length of time taken to complete the project gives some idea of the importance which must have been attached to it by the authorities in St Kitts. After it was opened it remained the island's only hospital until 1993.

Regardless of the lack of medical attention and proper facilities, the people of Anguilla were generally always more healthy than those in St Kitts or Nevis. Despite frequent droughts which caused deaths from star-vation, and outbreaks of malaria of a severity not experienced in the two larger islands, the Anguillians benefited from not living cheek by jowl in insanitary villages. In 1898, according to a detailed study made of the vital statistics of the island, the death-rate was 16 per 1000 of the population. This was not only much better than either St Kitts (23.37) or Nevis (19.78), but also England and Wales (about 19). The infant mortality rate of 138 was considerably better than St Kitts (207), Nevis (196) or London (155). By the 1930s the infant mortality rate for Anguilla was less than half of that for either St Kitts or Nevis, a ratio which still applied when the politi-cal links between them were eventually severed 40 years later.

Education

There was very little in the way of education for black or coloured chil-dren before emancipation, and not a great deal of any worth for many years afterwards. The Negro Education Grant, which formed part of the Emancipation Act, allocated an annual sum each year between 1835 and 1846 'for the purpose of promoting Christian education in those British colonies in which slavery has hitherto existed'. For this reason, and because any existing schools were run by the various missionary societies, the money was paid to the religious bodies concerned. The initial grants for St Kitts and Nevis, allocated in proportion to the number of ex-slaves in each island, amounted to £800 and £350 respectively. In St Kitts the contribution made by the Moravians was ignored and the grant divided between the Church of England's Society for the Propagation of the Gospel and the Methodist Society. In Nevis it all went to the Methodist Society. These grants were intended merely to guide the black population through the transition out of slavery. By the time they ended in 1846 it was the British government's hope that the local legislatures would not only have taken on the continued funding of schools, but also have made education compulsory.

Schooling in St Kitts

In March 1846 the President of the Council reported that the legislature had 'pledged themselves to the consideration...of the interesting question of general education', and that he had 'every hope that it will be entered upon and matured with that spirit of liberality which its importance, in regard to the temporal and spiritual welfare of the community, so imperatively demands'. Such highfaluting sentiments were all very well, but the 'spirit of liberality' certainly did not extend to improving on the British grant, nor to making the education of black children compulsory. Two years later Mackintosh, the Lieutenant-Governor, informed the Colonial Office that a 'liberal grant for the year of £600 had been made, but only 'on the principle...of enforcing a regular proportional payment by each scholar'.[14]

In 1849, following an island-wide general reduction in the rate of wages and just at the time when school fees could be least afforded, 'the legislative grant to the schools of £600 yearly was withdrawn, and they were committed to their own unaided resources'. As a result three schools closed down, and a fall in attendance took place at all the others, with those attached to the Anglican Church suffering most. Five years later only about two-thirds of the less than 2000 children left on the registers attended school regularly. In May 1854, Mackintosh's successor was forced to report that no change had taken place and that, because many of the Assembly members were not in favour of any education for the labourers' children, an 'attempt to reconcile the differences of opinion on the subject of a public system of instruction failed...during the past session of the Legislature'.[15] At this time there were ten Anglican, nine Methodist and four Moravian schools, all 'supported entirely by school fees and voluntary contributions'. None of them provided anything other than the most rudimentary education, largely because

> the class of persons employed as teachers, both male and
> female, is anything but satisfactory; the salaries paid are so
> small, sometimes not exceeding £5 per annum, and the
> payment even of these so precarious and irregular that
> persons of intelligence, and sufficiently educated for the
> purpose, can hardly be found to undertake the office.[16]

The impasse between those members of the community who were in favour of a national system of secular education, those in favour of education with 'a small amount of religious instruction as might be acceptable to all without offending the prejudices of any denomination', and those 'opposed to education in any shape', was finally broken at the beginning of 1856. On 1 January every school in the island was placed under the control of a Board of Education, and an 'Act for raising a fund for educational purposes by means of a tax upon provision grounds came into operation'. From then on schools were given public aid in proportion to the number of regular attendants. The tax on provision grounds, which fell on the proprietors and not on the labourers who used the land, was replaced in 1860 by an annual grant of £500 to aid 'the education of the labouring class'. By this year, although the number of schools had increased to 29, the average total attendance was only just over 1600. Sir Benjamin Pine was lieutenant-governor by this time, and it was largely at his instigation that not only was the annual education grant restored, but a grammar school was brought into existence. This school opened in April 1862 with 16 pupils, under a headmaster who was also 'ex officio Inspector of schools for the labouring classes'. It was not a great success, and at no time was attended by more than one or two dozen boys. In 1870, when there were only 12 pupils registered, the headmaster reported

> I have throughout [the island] seen a fair number of boys
> whose age and position should make them eligible for the
> Grammar School, but I also know thoroughly well that
> their parents are unable to meet the expense, low though
> the scale of fees may appear, of sending them, anxious as,
> I also of my own knowledge can affirm, some of them are
> that they should have the benefits of an education which
> they have no chance of elsewhere obtaining.[17]

As there were still only a dozen pupils by 1892 it was then closed down.

Pine was also largely responsible for persuading the legislature in 1864 to raise the educational grant from £500 to £1100 a year, an increase by then long overdue. It was also something the island could well afford, seeing that in the same year the legislature set aside £1250 'for the entertainment of Prince Alfred', Queen Victoria's second son who was then swanning around the Caribbean as a naval officer, and another £500 as 'a present to our late able Attorney-General, now Chief Justice Burt'. The increase did little to expand the number of schools or improve the number of children who attended regularly. By the beginning of 1891, when compulsory education was finally introduced, there were still only 30 schools on the island, and out of the 4800 pupils on their registers less than half attended regularly. A privately run High School for girls which was opened in 1892 remained, except for a brief period, the only secondary school until 1901 when the boys' Grammar School was reopened. A Convent High School established by the Roman Catholic Church in 1896 closed within a year due to the sudden death of the Mother Superior, and was not reopened until 1912.

In the late nineteenth century those children who did attend their primary schools conscientiously only received a very basic, perfunctory education, but even this was enough to cause resentment among those in the higher reaches of society. 'As to the general question of educating indiscriminately the negro classes', Administrator Thomas Risely Griffith wrote in 1897,

> a preponloring percentage of the negro classes are absolutely spoilt by the smattering of reading and writing which the present system of education involves. The negro child, if a boy, the moment he knows how to read and write is imbued with the opinion that field work is beneath him and that such labour is undignified. He desires to become anything else but a manual agriculturalist. If a female, it grows into the belief...that field work is utterly beneath them and that even domestic service is humiliating and they attain a position which is untenable from their own view and end in becoming worthless.[18]

This sort of attitude, as well as the general standard of education, remained unchanged long after the government assumed responsibility for the running of all the primary schools in 1917. 'I do not believe in over-educating the working class,' stated Sir Eustace Fiennes, the Governor of the Leeward Islands, in 1928. 'It simply fills their minds with inflated ideas.' There can have been little danger at the time of many children in St Kitts having their minds so inflated. Most schools were no more than large one-room buildings, each with a platform at one end, and the subjects taught consisted of reading, writing, arithmetic, religious knowledge, hygiene, and a little geography and history, with needlework for the girls. It is hardly surprising that at the end of the Second World War, well over 50 years after the introduction of compulsory education, nearly a third of all the children enrolled in the 18 primary schools were not attending regularly.

There was also very slow progress in broadening access to secondary education. The Girls' High School which had opened in 1892 closed with the retirement of the headmistress in 1925, and was not replaced for another four years. Provided with a government subsidy, a new High School with an initial enrolment of nine girls opened on the Bay Road in Irish Town in October 1929. In 1946 the school was transferred to what until then had been Government House on Victoria Road, and 12 years later the boys' Grammar School moved to a site on the opposite side of the same road. The two schools were merged into the Basseterre High School in 1967, the year in which a second comprehensive High School was opened at Sandy Point. The sixth-form tuition needed by those boys and girls aspiring to a university education did not become available until 1950, and then, for many years, only at the Grammar School.

Schooling in Nevis

The Methodists had established several schools in Nevis by 1834, and were providing education, or a sort, to about 600 children. As schools, they were rudimentary in the extreme, teaching their pupils, most of whom attended irregularly, very little other than how to read, spell and sing. But, as even this was more than the Anglican Church was prepared to do for slave children, there can have been no argument after emancipation about which denomination was to receive the Nevis share of the Negro Education Grant. When the annual grants ended in 1846 President Willoughby Shortland reported to the Governor-General in Antigua that the education of the labourers' children was 'making satisfactory progress under the vigilant superintendence of the Wesleyans', but that

> your Excellency will be sorry to observe by a reference to the Returns furnished by the Ministers of the Established Church, that no progress has been made towards increased efficiency in the Church schools; in fact, in most instances, they have little more than a nominal existence; even Sunday schools, it would appear, are disregarded.... Many private schools are springing up, and in justice to the negroes, I am bound to state, that no unwillingness to obtain instruction for their children, prevails on their part.[19]

A contemporary visitor recorded his impressions of an infant school run by the Methodists in Charlestown, where about 70 children were being 'taught their letters and prepared for the other, the juvenile school' which was 'kept in the chapel itself'. The boys and girls attending the latter, aged between ten and fourteen, 'were taught either reading, writing or arithmetic, and the girls the use of the needle'. The payment made by their parents, which 'differed according to what was taught', ranged from two and a half to seven and a half pence a month.[20]

Teaching continued along not very dissimilar lines for the next 40 or 50 years. Some 20 years after the first instalment of the Negro Education Grant had been received, the state of education in general was hardly any better or more extensive than it had been prior to emancipation. 'On the whole', President Frederick Seymour recorded in his official report for 1855, 'the state of things connected with education may be considered as tolerably satisfactory, making allowances for the circumstances that no public money is given in aid of the schools.' There were then only 708 children attending the day schools.[21] Two years later both the President, Sir Arthur Rumbold, and the senior magistrate Isidore Dyett, found reason to criticize the schools and the legislature's refusal to provide money for education. 'Nevis is not, indeed, altogether without schools', wrote Dyett in May 1857, 'there being day and Sunday schools unaided by any public grant...but these schools are not adapted to the wants of a West Indian community, limiting, as they do, the instruction they afford merely to the elementary branches of a literary education.' At the same time the schools were

> unaided by any legislative grant or other provision from
> any public fund; they are under no legal or administrative
> control. The education afforded by them is not directed by
> any Government or official supervision, nor is it directed,
> so far as I can learn, into any immediately practical
> channel.

Rumbold, in forwarding Dyett's comments, added his own condemnation of the legislature's parsimony, stating that 'far from education being "pushed through every avenue we can find for it", every public avenue in Nevis is pertinaciously closed against it'.[22]

The first grant of public money for educational purposes was made by the legislature in 1861, fifteen years after receipt of the last of the funds provided by the Negro Education Grant. The amount voted was £30. This figure, a fraction of the amount of money wasted on entertaining a royal visitor the following year, makes it quite clear what importance was attached to education. In 1862, 'A debt of £286 in excess of the original grant of £250 made for the reception of His Royal Highness Prince Alfred, had to be liquidated.'[23] The amount voted for education thereafter varied dramatically from one year to the next. It increased from £50 in 1864 to £150 the following year, but in 1866 'not a shilling of the public revenue' was 'appropriated for this essential purpose'. In that year, although there were now eight schools on the island, the number of pupils 'under tuition is less than that of 10 years ago'.[24] By 1870 the legislature was providing only £100 a year, and the average attendance was still well under a thousand. More regular, but still 'absurdly small', grants followed the establishment of the Federation of the Leeward Islands in 1871, but this made little difference to the overall number of children who attended school on a regular basis. Twelve years later, on the eve of the Union of Nevis and St Kitts, there were ten schools, some 'utterly destitute of all the modern necessaries of school keeping', with a total average attendance of 705 – three less than in 1855.

Although attendance figures had improved during the interim there were still only ten primary schools on the island after the end of the Second World War. Many were badly maintained and some were hardly any different from when they had been built in the previous century. James Sutton, who became headmaster of the school in the village of Whitehall in 1947, arrived to find 300 children crowded in a building which 'was old and dilapidated, with a leaky roof and shingles falling off'. The school, situated in what was then the poorest and most remote part of the island, had no running water on the premises, only a stand-pipe in the school yard. 'But for the two years I worked at the school', Sutton recalled many years later, 'I saw water come from it only once...a trickle that lasted a few minutes.'[25] Although a limited amount of secondary education seems to have been available in one or two small private schools during the previous 20 years or so, the first government secondary school was not opened until 1949. The Charlestown Secondary School was then the only such institution in Nevis for the next 24 years. Another secondary school was opened at Gingerland in 1973, and a sixth-form college was established next door to the Charlestown Secondary School ten years later.

Schooling in Anguilla

The paucity of the education available to the children of Anguilla for approaching 150 years after the abolition of slavery was even worse than that afforded the children of Nevis. In 1837, when a small school run by the Anglican minister in The Valley was the only one on the island, an official sent from England to report on the status of negro education in the

West Indies visited the island. Asked to give an opinion on whether another school was needed he reported 'such was the diminished and scattered state of the population, it is difficult to say how and where to place a school house'. In spite of his negativism six more schools were in existence by 1845, and a total of about 500 children were being taught. All of these schools did not last, and for most of the nineteenth century primary education, for what it was worth, was provided by two Anglican and three Methodist schools. Responsibility for their running was assumed by the Government of the Leeward Islands in 1915, and the first government-owned school was erected at East End two years later. Some 246 children were enrolled in the new school, but less than half this number attended the opening in January 1918. Such a rate of attendance in this poverty-stricken island was not unusual for any of the schools. In 1938 five teachers informed the education authorities in St Kitts that, following a series of droughts in Anguilla, the condition of many of the parents had become 'acute as regards their ability to provide food to send to their children to school'. As a result, only about 600 out of nearly 1000 children on the school registers were attending, and among these many arrived without having eaten before they left home and carrying nothing to eat at mid-day. The gradual improvement in living conditions which took place after the Second World War also improved the school attendance figures, but there were still only five primary schools in 1953 when the first secondary school was opened in The Valley.

20

The Development of Organized Labour

The Sugar Industry

The Presidency of St Kitts-Nevis (the name Anguilla was not added to the title until 1952) entered the twentieth century with the mainstay of the economy – the sugar industry – in decline. The amount of sugar produced each year, which had averaged 16,000 tons from 1881 until 1894, had fallen rapidly after the produce of Brazil, Cuba and the Dominican Republic had been given preference in the American market (p.171 above), and was only 7451 tons in 1900. The situation in Antigua was just as bad, and in the official report on the colony for that year, prepared by the Colonial Secretary for the Leeward Islands, it was stated that 'the sole hope of restoring the sugar industry' in each island lay in the erection of a central factory. 'The antiquated machinery and obsolete methods now employed in the manufacture of sugar in these islands should years ago have been replaced by modern factories', complained the Colonial Secretary, 'but year after year no improvement takes place, the crops become shorter, and hundreds of acres of what were formerly valuable cane lands are now thrown out of cultivation.'[1] Five years later, the colony's Superintendent of Agriculture reported on the reluctance of the planters to introduce modern sugar-making machinery in St Kitts, where he found that except on one estate 'the muscovado process is followed throughout'. If the industry was to be revived

> the attention of the owners of sugar estates should be
> centred on the question of the advisability and and
> possibility of introducing modern methods of sugar
> manufacture. Along this line appears to lie the course of
> development in the immediate future.[2]

In 1905 it would have been difficult to find a group of people more set in their ways, and more opposed to change – in business practices as much as in social life – than the estate owners of St Kitts and Nevis. As a result another five years passed before an agreement was signed between an English firm and 'several of the owners of sugar estates in St Kitts, for the

234

establishment of a central sugar factory in the rich and fertile Basseterre Valley'.[3] This brought about the creation of the St Kitts (Basseterre) Sugar Factory Ltd, a public stock company registered in London, with the equity held by two British sugar companies and individual estate owners. The erection of the factory, about one mile north-east of the Treasury Building, began soon afterwards and was completed in 1912 (see Plate 31). Its construction, together with that of the housing needed for the senior staff, involved the destruction of the thriving village of Kit Stoddarts and the transfer of its residents to the Town Extension Lands (p.207 above). The narrow gauge railway needed to ensure the efficient running of the factory, by providing a constant flow of freshly cut cane throughout each year's harvest, was begun at the same time. When completed in 1926 the railway, with a branch line to the factory, encircled the island, passing through or close to most of its 61 sugar estates, and a bulk storage facility for the refined sugar was built at the eastern end of Basseterre Bay.

It took until the mid-1920s to get production back up to the level of the early 1890s, but the consolidation of the industry which took place soon provided the impetus for a steady increase. Production passed 20,000 tons in 1932, 30,000 tons in 1937, and 40,000 tons in 1945. In 1956, by which time production exceeded 50,000 tons a year, cane was being grown on only 49 estates. Four estates were owned by the government by this time. One of them, Frigate Bay, was being used to try and establish a dairy farm, while the other three had been leased out in small lots to peasant farmers. More than half of the sugar estates were owned by companies either in Britain or, like J.W. Thurston & Co. and S.L. Horsford & Co., in Basseterre.

The profits which Thurstons, Horsfords and the other estate owners of St Kitts had enjoyed since the factory was opened were not shared by their counterparts in Nevis where, of course, the establishment of a similar facility was never contemplated. After 1912 most of the island's sugar-cane, now only grown on a few estates in the north and west, was shipped across to St Kitts for processing. As it went in sailing barges, this was a slow and, because of the rate at which cut cane lost its sucrose content, uneconomical procedure. However, not all the cane was allowed to leave the island to be used in the production of refined sugar. Several estate owners, as if to demonstrate that they were even more reactionary than their fellows in St Kitts, decided to persevere in the production of muscovado and its by-product molasses. As a market for the latter lasted little longer than a decade, the last plant, at Cane Garden, was forced out of business in 1925. The production of muscovado sugar then continued fitfully until the last mill closed in 1958. The island's last shipment of cane was sent across to St Kitts, still by means of a sailing barge, eleven years later.

Over the years, as the sugar industry of Nevis gradually disappeared, more and more estates began to be sold. Some were bought by speculators who then sold off house plots or leased out larger areas to peasant farmers. By 1931 there were over 270 peasant proprietors, who between them owned about 330 acres (134 ha) and leased another 1500 acres (600 ha). Three years later there were over 360 proprietors, each with a land holding of up to 10 acres (4 ha). In St Kitts at this time there were only 11 such holdings. Estates also began to be bought by the government for use in a land resettlement programme, with 3750 acres (1518 ha) being acquired between 1933 and 1954. Various attempts were made to utilize some of the estates in other ways. By mid-1950s several were being used for the raising of livestock, and three had been planted with around 1000 acres (400 ha) of coconut trees, allowing some 200 tons of dried coconut to be exported each year to Barbados. In 1960 a vegetable-oil processing plant was established which it was hoped, very optimistically, would provide enough oil from processed copra to supply local needs. In fact the plant turned out to be very uneconomical to operate and had to be closed down in 1962.

To many people at this time, with the sugar industry very much on its way out, the economic future of Nevis must have looked extremely bleak. In fact, although there were still some dismal years ahead, the loss of sugar was in time going to be the making of the island. This was hinted at by an academic who visited the island in the mid-1960s, gathering material for a political and economic study of the region. 'Nevis presents a sad picture', Professor Sir Harold Mitchell wrote afterwards;

> Ruined Great houses and sugar-mills testify to by-gone
> prosperity. Yet the beauty of the island and the courtesy of
> its inhabitants suggest that it may yet find recovery in
> attracting overseas visitors, just as it did in the eighteenth
> century when its mineral springs were famous.[4]

It is not known where Mitchell stayed during his visit, but well before his prophetic statement was published three of the island's unruined Great Houses had been converted into hotels, and the foundations of a tourist industry had been laid.

Sea Island Cotton

In 1896 the future for the sugar produced not only in the Leeward Islands, but throughout the English-speaking Caribbean, had looked so uncertain that a Royal Commission headed by a former Governor of Jamaica, Sir Henry Norman, was appointed 'to enquire into the conditions and prospects of the Sugar-Growing West India Colonies'. The Commission reported the following year that the colonies had little option but to continue with the sugar industry, as there was nothing else which could replace it completely. However, there were ways in which the situation could be improved, such as in the establishment of central factories, the setting up of a Department of Agriculture for the West Indies, and the encouragement of small farmers to produce alternative crops for export.

Another ten years passed before the Presidency of St Kitts-Nevis got round to serious consideration of a single, modern sugar factory, but the prospects offered by an alternative export crop produced quicker results. Trial areas of Sea Island cotton were planted in St Kitts and Nevis in 1901, and in Anguilla in 1902. Although the results obtained were described as 'somewhat variable', they were judged promising enough to permit 'a considerable expansion of the industry', and by 1904 cotton was being grown on 1000 acres (400 ha) in St Kitts, 1050 acres (425 ha) in Nevis and 300 acres (120 ha) in Anguilla. There were then three ginneries in St Kitts, two in Nevis and one in Anguilla. By 1909 it was reported that 'the cultivation of cotton has proved an immense blessing to the Presidency, especially to the island of Anguilla, which it has rescued from the most abject poverty'.[5]

Cotton did not have quite the same effect on the other two islands, but it soon became of more importance to Nevis, where there were many peasant farmers prepared to clear bush in order to grow it, than to St Kitts, where it was grown as a 'catch' crop on cane fields which were lying fallow or on land which was unsuitable for cane. There were 2000 acres (800 ha) under cotton in Nevis by 1912, with 1650 acres (668 ha) in St Kitts and 1000 (400 ha) in Anguilla. 'The increased area planted in cotton in Anguilla has justified the opening of three new roads to facilitate transport', crowed the annual report on the presidency for that year. 'The generally improved condition of that island is principally due to the introduction of the cotton industry and it is desirable to do all that is practicable to encourage it.'[6]

Between them the islands exported a total of nearly 783,000 lb of cotton lint in 1912, twice as much as in the previous year. The annual export figure fell off after this, but increased again during the First World War, particularly after 1917 when the British government prohibited the sale of West Indian cotton anywhere other than to the United Kingdom for the duration of the war. By 1918 cotton was being grown on over 1000 acres (400 ha) in Anguilla, around 2000 (800 ha) acres in St Kitts, and over 3000 (1200 ha) in Nevis, where it had become the main cash crop. The end of the war brought an end to the boom, and thereafter cotton exports slowly declined. In 1931, with cotton being grown on 1200 acres (486 ha) in St Kitts, 1500 acres (600 ha) in Nevis, and only 400 (160 ha) in Anguilla, the total amount exported was a little over 321,000 lb. The industry further declined in the 1940s mainly due to the outbreaks of pink bollworm disease, and by the mid-1950s it was only of any importance to Nevis, where it was still being grown on 2600 acres (1050 ha). Cotton remained the principal cash crop of Nevis for another twenty years or more, and in 1976 about 500 growers, nearly two-thirds of them women, all working small plots, produced 117,662 lb of lint. Cotton was still being grown on 150 acres (60 ha) of Nevis in 1983, long after the crop had ceased to be of any relevance in either St Kitts or Anguilla.

Emigration

During the last decade of the nineteenth century an increasing number of labourers escaped from the appalling economic, working and social conditions under which they were forced to live in all three islands by seeking work in other parts of the world. Some left for ever, or with the hope of never having to return, but the majority, with families to support and lacking the wherewithal to emigrate *en bloc*, had no option but to travel to and fro each year. For such migrants by the mid-1890s the premier destination was the Dominican Republic, where an enormous amount of labour was needed every year to harvest the crop on the vast, American-owned sugar plantations.

By the beginning of the twentieth century about 10 per cent of the population of St Kitts and Nevis, and perhaps 20 per cent of that of Anguilla, were travelling to the Dominican Republic and back each year. Nearly all were men, employed on the estates as cane cutters, reaping a harvest which lasted from January to July. The few women who were able or prepared to go were employed as cooks or servants for the white estate officials, and sometimes in the workers' barracks. Until the 1920s when steam ships began to take over, they travelled in schooners, many of which were Anguillian-owned and more often than not grossly overcrowded. These conditions, along with those they had to put up with while living and working on the estates, were made acceptable by the rate of pay they received. At between 80 and 120 US dollars a month, wages were five or six times higher than those that any of them could earn at home.

Temporary labouring jobs of a different kind became available in 1901 in Bermuda, when approval was given for the construction of an extension to the naval dockyard at the same time as work began on modernization of the colony's defences. Over the next three years about 2000 people from St Kitts and Nevis managed to find their way there, travelling mostly as deck passengers on the steamers which since 1899 had been operating a scheduled service between Canada and the Eastern Caribbean via Bermuda. On arrival the men were mostly employed on unskilled or semi-skilled harbour construction work, while the few hundred women who accompanied them found jobs as cooks or maids. After all naval and military construction had come to an end in 1906, about 1000 men and women stayed on, forming a link between Bermuda and St Kitts-Nevis which survives to this day.

The steamship service which had carried people from the presidency to Bermuda in the first place also gave others, once they had the money to pay for the passage, the chance to emigrate to North America. This was viewed with mixed feelings by the Administrator, Thomas Roxburgh, as he made clear in the annual report for 1911:

> It is often regretted that so many persons leave the Islands
> for work in the United States of America, Canada, and
> other places. It is a fact, however, that a very considerable
> sum of money is remitted each year by such emigrants to
> their relatives here, all of which goes into circulation, to
> the great advantage of the community.[7]

However, it seems there could be no gain without pain. 'The emigration of persons of the servant class to the United States and Canada continues', moaned Roxburgh a year later, 'and is causing much inconvenience here.'[8] Whether inconvenient or not, neither he nor his successor, Major John Burdon, could do anything to prevent people of any class from seeking a better life elsewhere. Legal emigration to the United States, a destination far more popular than Canada, continued until July 1924, when an immigrant quota law came into effect. By then it is likely that between eight and nine thousand people from the presidency had gone to North America, with by far the largest number being from St Kitts.

In 1929 stringent immigration rules were introduced in the Dominican Republic, specifically designed to bring an end to the seasonal migration of cane cutters from the English-speaking islands, and over the next few years many of the men from St Kitts and Nevis who had taken up residence were deported. Although the new rules were not totally effective, and some labourers still managed to find work there for a few more years, to all intents and purposes the economic benefits offered by employment in the Dominican Republic ended in 1930.

The Stirrings of Organized Labour

For the men and women of the presidency who did not emigrate or take part in the seasonal migration of workers during the early decades of the twentieth century, life improved very slowly or not at all. This was particularly so in St Kitts, where the sugar industry continued to dominate, and where the bulk of the labour force, in the absence of any land to buy, had to live in squalid, crowded villages huddled in the ghuts, on infertile bits of land between estates, or immediately alongside the road which encircled the island. As a result, and because similar conditions were not found to the same extent in Nevis or at all in Anguilla, the impetus to bring about change was largely confined to St Kitts. Nine years after the so-called 'Portuguese Riot' of 1896 another attempt was made to call a general strike, this time in response to a swingeing cut in wages imposed by the planters. Some cane fires were started and the waterfront workers joined in the strike, but no labourer was in a position to survive for very long on no wages. A threat issued by the magistracy to imprison anyone brought up for breach of contract prevented any rioting, and the strike soon petered out.

Nothing had changed by the time the First World War started in August 1914, an event which for no very good reason caused martial law to be declared throughout the colony. This may well have been seen by the labourers as a move directed more towards making sure they remembered their place than anything else: Germany was, after all, some 4000 miles away. Whether this was so or not, they cannot have been reassured by the decision to increase the size of the all-white Volunteer Defence Force which followed, as this led to 'some attempts to create disaffection among the lower classes'.[9] Nor could people living under the sort of conditions described in a previous chapter have been too thrilled to learn, a month after the war began, that the legislature had voted £5000 to be sent to the National Relief Fund in Britain (a sum followed in February 1918 by another £2000 'to provide an aeroplane bearing the name of St Christopher'). Although there was no shortage of volunteers for the army, navy and, after its formation, the Royal Flying Corps among the white and coloured members of society, the prosecution of the war was on the whole, and understandably, of little consequence to the majority of the black population.

The gulf between the black labouring class and the rest of society was made even wider by the war. A dramatic rise in sugar prices and in the cost of food was not accompanied by any increase in wages, and well before the end of 1915 many workers were in distress and feeling extremely resentful. Nothing was done until shortly before reaping of the 1916 crop was about to start, when a shopkeeper named Joseph Nathan organized a petition to the Executive Council. This described the plight of the workers and called not only for an increase in their wages but also for the administration to impose regulations about their working hours and conditions. Presumably shamed into action, and not unaffected by a number of cane fires which followed soon after the petition had been received, the Council lost no time in consulting with the planters and a wage increase was negotiated. Nathan, together with the handful of other men who had assisted in drawing up the petition, were so pleased with the result that in November they announced they were forming a trade union. This was greeted by the administration and the planters with dismay: a man with a petition was one thing but a trade union, even though such organizations had had legal recognition in Britain since 1871, was something else altogether. Two weeks after Nathan had made his announcement the legislature passed the Trade and Labour Unions (Prohibition) Ordinance, threatening anyone involved in the formation of a trade union with a six-month prison sentence or a fine of £50, and imposing a prohibition on the publication of any literature about such a union.

The new law was a set-back for Nathan and his associates – Frederick Solomon, an undertaker, George Wilkes, a barber, William Seaton, a clerk, and a merchant named St Clair Podd – but they were not entirely thwarted. Determined to do something for the working class, early the following year they registered the St Kitts-Nevis Universal Benevolent Association (UBA) under the Friendly Societies Act of the Leeward Islands, with Nathan as president, Solomon as secretary and Wilkes as treasurer. The true purpose of the Association was made clear at a public meeting in February, when Solomon informed his audience that the only difference between it and the trade union which had been intended was that 'with the Labour Union we could fix the price of labour for you, but under the heading of this Society, we cannot fix the price but you ought to know how much to ask for your labour and see that you get it'.[10]

Whether prompted by the UBA or not, fresh demands for a wage increase began to be made towards the end of the year and as the next crop time approached. The need for such an increase was again recognized by the administration and, after the Administrator, Burdon, had personally intervened, the planters agreed to raise the average rate to 2s a day for men and 1s a day for women (the equivalent at the beginning of the twenty-first century of £3 and £1.50). This was accepted by all but the workers on two adjoining estates near the village of St Paul's in the north, who in October began a strike. Nineteen of them were immediately prosecuted for breach of contract, under the Masters and Servants Act (p.158 above), and each sentenced to a fine of 8s or ten days in gaol. As none could or would pay the fine, after their release from prison they became known locally as the 'St Paul's Martyrs'.

Their 'martyrdom' inspired the UBA to begin a public campaign for the repeal of the Masters and Servants Act, something which became much more effective after the appearance of the first edition of the Association's newspaper, the *Union Messenger,* in 1921. This was founded and edited by J. Matthew Sebastian, the man who earlier in the year after the death of Solomon had become the UBA's secretary. The paper, after starting life as a monthly, became a weekly in July 1922 and then a daily in 1929. By providing the workers for the first time with a public medium of expression it became hugely successful. Its pages carried not only news of immediate interest about sugar prices and workers' rights, together with articles reprinted from other papers such as Marcus Garvey's *Negro World*, but also editorials criticizing the administration and attacking the 'oligarchy' exercised by the estate owners.

Understandably the *Union Messenger* was read with little pleasure by anyone outside the villages or the less salubrious parts of Basseterre, and elsewhere was probably more disliked than the UBA itself. Possibly because of this, neither the Association nor its mouthpiece achieved very much by their campaign to get rid of the Masters and Servants Act. When this was eventually repealed in 1922, nearly three-quarters of a century after it had been enacted, it was replaced by an Ordinance intended as a means of securing 'the continuous labour' believed to be essential to the sugar industry while maintaining order and industrial discipline. Under its provisions any worker who began work and then stopped after entering into a contract, whether oral or written, became guilty of a criminal offence which could lead to a large fine or one month in gaol. The passing of the new Act (which was not repealed until 1938), together with other repressive measures and general government intimidation during an era when emigration was at its height, led to the gradual demise of the UBA. Membership steadily declined during the 1920s, and its influence among the workers had largely disappeared by the beginning of the next decade. By this time, however, and in spite of its failure to organize the labour force, the UBA had succeeded in adding a political dimension to the workers' demands, broadened the scope of the workers' protests, and provided them with new ideas about how their objectives might be achieved. It was unfortunate for Nathan and his colleagues that, such was the state of the economy by the early 1930s, there were very few working-class men or women able to give much thought to anything other than where their next meal was coming from.

The decline in the UBA's membership which had taken place was just another symptom of the deterioration in the general condition of the working class which had taken place during this period. There was acute distress in the island by the beginning of 1932, with over 16 per cent of all estate workers unemployed and wage rates for those still at work reduced to a pre-1900 level; while the numbers of destitute people had risen sharply, as a result of a fall in the remittances from North America and the forced repatriation of labourers from the Dominican Republic. Hopelessness prevailed, with the working class in no position to help itself, the UBA no longer capable of offering much in the way of leadership, and the administration seemingly apathetic. Fortunately the island was not totally bereft of individuals with decency and common humanity, and in March a new workers' organization came into being. The Workers' League was founded as a limited company by a group of middle-class coloured men, led by an estate owner named Thomas Manchester, who became its president. Three men from the UBA, Joseph Nathan, William Seaton and J. Matthew Sebastian, were among the founding members. Two other men, Edgar Challenger and Joseph France, both of whom were to play an important part in future events, became associated with the running of the Workers' League a year or so later. Challenger, who had lived in the USA for many years, returned in 1933 in order to assist Manchester, who was his cousin. France became involved through his role as printer of the *Union Messenger,* the paper which was to remain the sole news-sheet of the labour movement until he founded the *Workers' Weekly* in 1942.

Manchester and his colleagues, although altruistic and very aware of the need for social change, were equally well aware of the constraints under which, as the formation of a trade union remained illegal, the Workers' League had to operate. In addition, as they were, for the most part, successful members of the middle class with professional or business interests, they were hardly radical firebrands ready to risk ostracism and the possibility of gaol in order to bring about the wholesale changes needed to improve the lives of working-class people. This was made apparent in an article by Manchester, published in the *Union Messenger* in November 1932. The main purpose of the Workers' League, he wrote, was 'to criticize constructively and fight constitutionally for the removal of the many evils that exist in the various branches of West Indian life'. With regard to the alleviation of some of the more immediate evils, the League wanted to see the establishment of a 'Charity Day', during which funds could be collected for 'assisting with the relief of the needy', the provision of a 'Motor Ambulance for conveying maternity and emergency cases from outlying districts to the Hospitals', and the 'introduction of a Workmen's Compensation Ordinance...in order that any unfortunate disabled workers may have some means provided for existence'.[11]

This was hardly the stuff of revolution and, regardless of the League's good intentions, the lot of the working class in general, and the estate workers in particular, continued to deteriorate. Whether Manchester or anyone else connected with the League recognized that such a state of affairs could not go on indefinitely without some form of protest taking place is not known, but by 1934 to a few other people around the island this had become a very real possibility. In October of that year, after all the labourers on an estate near Sandy Point had been laid off following the intestate death of the owner, the rector of the local church felt the need to send a warning to Douglas Steward, the Administrator. 'As a result of so many people being thrown out of employment a very great deal of distress is bound to occur', he wrote, adding that this could well 'result in much unrest amongst the labouring people'. A month later the senior district magistrate, in informing Stewart that 'year after year, the number of poor and destitute in Basseterre have increased, and most markedly so this present year', left unsaid his obvious apprehension of similar unrest.

The Riot of 1935

No one, minister, magistrate or administrator, had to wait very long for their fears to be realized, as the first signs of trouble were seen in early January 1935, after the estate owners made it known that they were unwilling to increase wages, or to guarantee a bonus payment at the end of the harvest which was about to begin, similar to the one which had been paid at the end of the previous year's crop. This was particularly hard on the cane cutters, whose rate had been cut by a third, from 1s to 8d a ton, in 1932, and calls for a general strike began to be heard. Although by no means every estate worker responded to such a call, and the Workers' League made a half-hearted attempt at a public meeting to oppose such action, a strike duly began on 28 January, the day reaping should have started. It seems very likely that it was instigated by a group of unem-ployed men in Basseterre, who turned up at Shadwell Estate on the out-skirts of the town just as work was about to begin and persuaded the cutters to join them in a march around the island. Such an event was bound to attract attention very quickly, and once the marchers set off along the road to Cayon they were soon joined by labourers from every estate they passed. 'A gang like this marching along a road, especially if a man at the head of them beats a drum as was done in this case', the Governor, Sir Reginald St-Johnston, wrote later, 'will in the West Indies quickly attract hundreds of followers, who can easily be stirred up to any excesses. It is significant that they started out on their march with big stout cudgels, not usually carried in quantities by bodies of labourers'.[12]

A couple of hours after the march began 'the Inspector of Police, Major Duke, the Magistrate, Mr. Bell, and several non-commissioned officers of police went up to the crowd and urged them to disperse', but their efforts 'proved fruitless' and were brushed aside with the demands for higher wages. Some of the 'cudgels' which were carried came into play at mid-day when the marchers, having passed through Cayon and into the Brighton Estate yard, were confronted by the irate manager.

> He ordered them out, telling them that they were on private property. The crowd, still armed with sticks, and numbering by estimation, between 300 and 400, surrounded the manager...in a threatening manner by raising their sticks over his head. He again spoke to them. No personal violence was done to him. His estate labourers were ordered to stop work. Mules and cattle, which were harnessed in their carts, were taken out and the working gear cut up in order to prevent any immediate use being made of the carts.... The manager and his employees were put in fear by the action of the crowd. His principal 'cutter' was forcibly ordered to join the crowd and a stick was placed in his hands.[13]

Inevitably, the longer such an undisciplined and leaderless march continued, the worse the ever-increasing numbers taking part began to behave. At Lodge Estate, next door to Brighton, the owner was attacked by four men with their sticks after he had brandished a shotgun, and stones were thrown to drive him and his domestic servants out of the estate yard. Incidents involving threats of violence, together with 'unharnessing all cattle carts and damaging the working gear', took place on other estates throughout the afternoon until finally, at about 5 o'clock, the mob reached Estridge Estate near the village of Tabernacle. By this time, perhaps alarmed by the lawlessness being incited by a handful of those taking part, the number of marchers had decreased to between two and three hundred. Also at this time, a good seven or eight hours after their first confrontation, the police inspector, Major Duke, and the mob met up again. As he was accompanied by only eight armed constables there was not much Duke could do except to arrest those he considered to be the ringleaders and to issue an order for the rest of the mob to disperse. With such a tiny force at his command, and with five men in custody, he could do nothing when this order was ignored. 'The crowd moved onward, but were not followed by the police, who were then 12 to 13 miles from headquarters and with hostile villages in their rear'.[14]

The hours of darkness passed quietly, but attempts to bring about an island-wide general strike resumed at dawn the next day. Labourers on the estates not affected during the previous day's march were soon being intimidated into joining the strike, and one man in Sadlers Village who refused received a severe blow on the head from a piece of iron pipe. Disturbances took place later in the day at Buckleys and West Farm Estates, to the west of Basseterre. At the latter a confrontation between estate workers and strikers led to stone-throwing which only ended after the police had been called in and the Riot Act had been read. While all this was going on Sir Reginald St-Johnston, the Governor of the Leeward Islands who 'happened to be in St Kitts at the time, on one of my routine visits of inspection', was driving around the island on the pretext of a school inspection, 'but principally to see for myself whether the labourers had been intimidated into striking or not'. He had got no farther than the Estridge Estate when he received a message from the Administrator requesting his immediate return to Basseterre in order to preside over an emergency meeting of the Executive Council.

He returned to find the Administrator, Steward, and the members of the Council in a state of considerable alarm about the deteriorating situation, and was immediately plunged into a discussion about the action needed to quell a possible wholesale riot. After hearing a report from Major Duke of the events which had taken place at West Farm and Buckleys Estates, St-Johnston

> decided to send off two telegrams at once, one to the Admiral at Bermuda warning him that it might be necessary to ask for a warship, and the other to Colonel Bell [the colony's senior police officer] at Antigua instructing him to proceed to St Kitts at once with reinforcements of police.[15]

Even before the wording of these telegrams had been agreed, Duke was called out of the meeting to deal with a new situation at Buckleys Estate, on the outskirts of Basseterre, where a large mob was reported to be 'making a hostile demonstration against the manager, Mr. Dobridge'. Duke arrived at the estate at about 3.45 p.m., together with the magistrate, Bell, and eleven armed policemen, to find the manager and his overseer besieged in the estate house by a mob of infuriated labourers, three of whom were bleeding from superficial shotgun wounds inflicted by Dobridge. A little over an hour later, having failed to pacify the mob by asking the wounded and witnesses of the shooting to accompany him to the police station to make statements, Duke sent a message to St-Johnston stating 'that in his opinion the time had arrived to call out the Defence Force and the Defence Reserve'.[16]

At some time after 5 o'clock Duke and Bell were joined by four other men – a popular Moravian minister, a well-known Basseterre merchant, a lawyer named Clement Malone, and the President of the Workers' League,

Thomas Manchester – all of whom it was hoped 'might speak to the people and get them to disperse'. The pleas of the first three, presumably concentrating on the spiritual, commercial and legal consequences of 'attempting to use force for the purpose of getting increased wages', were ignored. Only Manchester struck the right note, and when he left the estate after speaking to the crowd 'a large number left with him'.

Their departure still left something like '400 to 500 men, women and children' milling around in front of the estate house when the 11 policemen were joined by perhaps two dozen armed members of the Defence Force shortly before 6 o'clock. The arrival of the latter, most of whom were estate owners or managers, only exacerbated an already volatile situation, and shortly afterwards Duke, who was now in overall command, felt obliged to ask Bell to read the Riot Act. This had no effect whatsoever and so, after an interval which was later stated to be from four to fifteen or twenty minutes, it was read again. Stones began to be thrown as Duke ordered the police to move the crowd away from the estate house, and very soon both they and the Defence Force in support at the rear were 'being subjected to a continuous fusillade of stones of dangerous sizes'. In the midst of this bombardment, which had the effect of driving Duke and his men off the estate in the rapidly failing light, the order was given 'to the Forces to fire on persistent stone-throwers on the flanks'.[17]

In the utter confusion which followed during the next half hour or so the total of 55 rounds which were fired resulted in the killing of three men – John Allen, James Archibald and Joseph Samuel – and the wounding of eight other people. Details of how and where these shootings took place, and even of whether it was the police or members of the Defence Force who carried them out, are far from clear. According to one modern historian, Samuel was mistaken by whoever killed him for Sebastian, the editor of the *Union Messenger*, and shot deliberately.[18] The official report on the whole affair, written over three months later by James Rae, the Chief Justice, provided only sketchy details and was far more concerned with making the case that the shootings had been in response to 'a serious civil disturbance which threatened the lives and property of law-abiding citizens of the Crown as well as the peace and good order of the Colony'.[19] That the threat may not have been quite as grave as Rae made out is surely borne out by the fact that, at the time Bell was reading the Riot Act at Buckleys, in Government House only a mile away the Governor and Lady St-Johnston were hosting a garden party. In his covering letter to Rae's report, St-Johnston wrote that it was not until after 6 o'clock on that day that he felt 'the affair was assuming more seriousness', and that 'the Garden Party had better be concluded while there was still daylight for the people to get to their homes'.[20]

During the night following the shootings six more policemen arrived from Antigua, and on 31 January a party of marines was landed from the cruiser HMS *Leander*. The shootings brought a swift end to the call for a general strike, and although a few cane fires were started neither the extra police nor the marines were needed for more than a few days. From among the men arrested two, John Palmer and Simeon Prince, were found guilty of leading the riot and were each given five years' hard labour. No formal investigation of the episode was ever carried out, as the Secretary of State for the Colonies considered 'no useful purpose would be served by such an enquiry'.

Even so, the three deaths and the travails of the general body of labourers were not in vain. The riot was one of a series of such disturbances which took place throughout the British West Indies between 1934 and 1938, which in the latter year forced the British government to appoint a Royal Commission, headed by Lord Moyne, 'to investigate social and economic conditions in all the West Indian territories, and to make recommendations'. Recognition of the particular need for reform in labour conditions was shown in the appointment to the Commission of Sir Walter Citrine, the General Secretary of the British Trades Union Congress. Within a year of the Commission's visit to the Caribbean, which lasted from October 1938 to April of the following year, an Act legalizing the formation of trade unions had been passed in every territory where such a provision was needed.

The St Kitts-Nevis Trades and Labour Union

The Leeward Islands Act containing the regulations concerning the registration and operation of trade unions, which also gave them protection from actions for tort and the right to carry out peaceful picketing, was passed at the end of December 1939. Three months later in St Kitts, before the officials of the Workers' League had got round to taking advantage of the new Act, a strike began at the sugar factory. This was called in an attempt to secure a pay increase commensurate with the estimated 15 per cent rise in the cost of living which had taken place since the outbreak of the Second World War. As the factory management made it clear that no increase would be given until inflation reached 20 per cent, and the strikers were without the support of either a union or the vast majority of the field workers, the strike collapsed after seven weeks. Some 75 factory workers were then sacked.

The distress caused by the stoppage, not only to the factory's labour force, but also amongst the estate workers who, willy-nilly, found themselves unemployed as a result, served to concentrate the minds of the leadership of the Workers' League and, a few days before the strike collapsed, the St Kitts-Nevis Trades and Labour Union was registered. Thomas Manchester, who was to die less than three years later, took no official position. Edgar Challenger became the president, with Joseph France as the general secretary and John Harney as the treasurer. At the end of May a young man who had been one of the factory workers fired at the end of the strike was hired to assist in the running of the union's office. This was Robert Bradshaw, a 24-year-old man from the wretched village of St Paul's in the north of the island: a man who had never known his father and received nothing but a primary school education, but who was soon to begin to show that such a start in life was of no consequence to a man born with intelligence and the will to succeed. Although no one could have foreseen it in 1940, for the last 25 years of his life his name was to be virtually synonymous with that of the island where he was born.

In January 1941, at the request of the Governor in Antigua, each of the colony's trade unions passed a resolution to abstain from strike action for the duration of the war. That passed by the St Kitts-Nevis Trades and Labour Union remained in force for only two and a half years. At the start of the 1943 sugar crop, the union entered into wage negotiations with the Sugar Producers' Association (SPA) (an organization which had been set up soon after the union had been formed) with the payment of an end-of-crop bonus as a key issue. These were short-lived and ended in a settlement which caused Challenger to be criticized by France and others in the union for a too-hasty acceptance of the offer made by the SPA. This caused Challenger to resign in disgust and to be replaced by J. Matthew Sebastian, with Bradshaw as the union's vice-president.[21] General dissatisfaction with the deal which had been agreed with the SPA then brought about rescission of the no-strike resolution in July. Sebastian remained in office for less than a year, his sudden death in February 1944 allowing the vice-president to step into his shoes. Bradshaw was then to remain president of the union until his own death 34 years later.

His early years as president saw the union involved in a number of acrimonious disputes, but also in establishing itself through proper organization and education as an institution capable of bringing about social change. His refusal to enter into an agreement to outlaw a closed shop at the sugar factory which had been demanded by the management led to a go-slow and a strike which lasted for two weeks in 1946. Another short strike involving workers at the sugar factory took place the following year, but the severest test of Bradshaw's leadership came in 1948. Negotiations with the SPA about pay and bonuses for the new season's crop began in January, as had become routine by this time, but were soon broken off. An offer of a general increase of 15 per cent was rejected by the union, and the SPA refused to consider the union's request to change the system of paying the cane cutters from 'by the ton' to that used in Antigua of 'by the line'. Seeing no possibility of reaching a settlement through further talks, on 16 January Bradshaw issued a call for a general strike. This began the following day and lasted until 19 April. It involved the sugar industry's entire labour force of about 10,000 people, and the loss of over 6,300,000 man-hours of work.[22] Acute suffering occurred among the strikers, and over the weeks a huge acreage of sugar was set ablaze by the more trenchant. In the end, of course, just as it appeared that mass starvation was about to set in and the entire sugar crop was going to be ruined, a compromise was reached and the strike ended. Such a long stoppage may not have achieved everything the workers wanted, but it left them aware of the power that could be wielded by organized labour, and of Bradshaw's value as an inspirational and committed leader. It also left the SPA conscious of the need for proper labour relations and, more importantly, the administration in no doubt about the need for social and political reform.

21

Constitutional Reform and Responsible Government

During the long strike of 1948 the acceptance by the striking workers of Bradshaw's leadership and authority stemmed not only from his position as president of the Trades and Labour Union, but also from his status as an elected member of the legislature. The latter was something he had enjoyed for less than 18 months by the time the strike began, although the constitution had been amended to allow the return of an elected element to the legislature in 1936. This was the year in which the British government finally began to accede to the demands of the various representative government associations which had been formed around the region since the end of the First World War.

The constitutional reform of 1936 replaced the five unofficial nominees to the St Kitts-Nevis Council with five elected members – three from St Kitts and one each from Nevis and Anguilla. The franchise remained very restricted. Only people with an income of £30 a year, or owning property valued at £100 or with a rental value of £12 a year, or paying at least 15 shillings a year in taxes, were allowed to vote. When the first triennial elections were held in June 1937 there were 1168 registered voters in St Kitts, with 328 in Nevis and a mere 133 in Anguilla. Extremely few of these in any island were black and, as the qualifications for a candidate were even higher than those for a voter, the election was very much one confined to the white and brown sections of society. The latter, being in a majority everywhere, swept the board. Thomas Manchester, Edgar Challenger and Clement Malone won in St Kitts, while a merchant named Henville was elected in Nevis, and a planter named Owen was returned unopposed in Anguilla.

The return of elected members to the Legislative Council, after a gap of 60 years, was a significant step forward but, as they remained in a minority, their scope for bringing about any of the social changes that Manchester and Challenger, at least, believed were necessary was severely limited. Nothing very much had changed for the better in any of the islands by the time the next elections took place in September 1940. Nor did very much change in the election results, except that J. Matthew

Sebastian took the place of Malone, who had been appointed a judge, and in Anguilla, where the number of voters had increased by one, Owen had had to face an opponent. A complete change in the elected membership, but not in the amount of good they were able to achieve, followed the 1943 election, which took place after the death of Manchester and Challenger's retreat into his library, and less than a year before Sebastian died. The only member of any significance left among the five after that was Sebastian's replacement, a lawyer named Maurice Davis.

It was not until after July 1946, when Bradshaw and the general secretary of the Trades and Labour Union, Joseph France, were elected, and Davis was re-elected, to represent St Kitts, that the elected section of the Legislative Council began to exert some real influence on the administration. All three represented the Workers' League, and every opportunity was taken to draw attention to the conditions under which most of the population of the islands were still living after more than 300 years of colonial rule, and to demand social and political reform. One such demand, which had no chance of being met but which Bradshaw saw would appeal to his supporters, was that the islands' elected representatives should have some say in the selection of future administrators and governors. The arrival of a new Administrator, Leslie Greening, in 1947, without any such reference having taken place, provided the perfect excuse for a protest demonstration. The new resident of Springfield House can hardly have felt he had been rewarded by the Colonial Office with the most enjoyable posting within its gift, when on 16 October he heard the marchers in a torch-lit procession through Basseterre endlessly chanting 'Go, Greening, go! Papa Bradshaw say that Greening must go!' Whether this was in any way responsible or not Greening left after just two years, unlike both his predecessor and his successor who each spent seven years in the job. The appointment of Hugh Burrowes, who relieved Greening in 1949, was also made without reference to anyone outside the Colonial Office, but by then Bradshaw was occupied with more important matters.

In 1949 the British government, recognizing that constitutional reform in the Leeward Islands was long overdue, agreed to the setting up of a committee made up of the elected and nominated members of the various legislative councils to determine the changes needed. Bradshaw could see no reason why the nominated members should have any say in the matter, and at his instigation all five elected members for the St Kitts-Nevis Council refused to serve on the committee. It seems very likely that their absence made a difference, as the committee ended up recommending the introduction of adult franchise subject to a simple literacy test, an increase in the number of elected members with the abolition of property qualifications for candidates, and the trial of a committee system of government. Given Bradshaw's determination to bring the swiftest possible end to colonial rule, it is difficult to believe he would have accepted a test of any sort for voters, or the retention of nominated members, or any suggestion of a 'trial' form of government. However, he was left in no doubt that Britain was now committed to introducing major constitutional reform, and all he could do was wait and see when this would take place. Those in St Kitts who resented his union and political activities, and feared the power he might attain once full adult suffrage was introduced, had already taken steps to try to safeguard their position. The St Kitts Democratic Party was formed early in 1949 with the tacit support of the Sugar Producers' Association, and with its own weekly newspaper, the *Democrat,* to act as a mouthpiece for its 'planter class sympathizers'.[1]

Universal Adult Suffrage and Moves Towards Ministerial Government

Nothing was done to change the constitution until after a Colonial Service high flier, Kenneth Blackburne, had been appointed governor of the Leeward Islands in 1950. He had arrived in Antigua in September to take over, as he had been informed loftily by a London newspaper shortly before he left England, 'half-a-dozen scattered, backward, and poverty-stricken islands where the greatest need is capable, practical administration of the kind required to manage a not too prosperous country estate'.[2] Fortunately for all concerned, in the face of such outdated metropolitan moralizing, Blackburne also took up his post knowing that he was to introduce universal adult suffrage, and that '[i]t had already been agreed before my arrival that the number of elected members in the Legislatures of Antigua, St. Kitts and Montserrat should be increased to give them a majority over nominated and official members'. Such a constitutional reform, he believed,

> presented no problem in peaceful Montserrat, but there were obvious difficulties in Antigua and St. Kitts with their labour leaders thirsting for political power. In both places the labour members would dominate the legislatures and could bring government work to a grinding halt unless they were also made to accept responsibility for their votes and actions.[3]

The new Governor was given a foretaste of the 'obvious difficulties' he was going to experience with one of these labour leaders when he paid his first official visit to St Kitts in October. Bradshaw, he discovered, 'had conceived the idea of assembling every worker on the island to line the route from the airfield [p.217] to Government House', in order to boo and 'make loud noises' while beating pots and pans. Such an unprecedented demonstration drew a lot of unfavourable comment from other parts of the region, but none that caused either Bradshaw or Blackburne to worry very much. The latter accepted the former's explanation that it was not intended as a personal affront, but rather that it was organized in support of Bradshaw's views that

> the people of the colony should have been consulted, and, in future, must be consulted (through their representatives, of course) about the appointment of the new Governor, in order that they might seize the chance of declaring what type of Governor, and with what outlook and what policy, they desire to hold the reins of the Government of the Colony.[4]

Bradshaw would have appreciated just as much as Blackburne that there was no chance of the Colonial Office acceding to this, any more than there was to his other demand that in future consideration had to 'be given to the appointment of a West Indian as Governor', but that was not the main purpose of what came to be known as 'Operation Blackburne'. The successful organization of the demonstration, along with the festooning of Basseterre with 'Blackburne and Burrowes must go' posters, can have had little real purpose other than to raise even higher Bradshaw's stature in the eyes of his downtrodden followers.

Bradshaw also found reason to object to the terms of the new constitution, when these were outlined by Blackburne to a meeting of the General Legislative Council in Antigua in December, and instituted a policy of non-cooperation with the administration. This caused some consternation and delay, but did not prevent the Governor, using his reserve powers, from pushing through the long-awaited constitutional reforms in the following year. These included the introduction of universal adult suffrage (with no test of any kind), the creation of electoral constituencies with the interval between elections extended to five years, and a complete overhaul and democratization of the legislative council in each presidency. In St Kitts-Nevis the new Legislative Council was to consist of the administrator (as president with a casting vote only), the financial secretary, the attorney-general, three nominated unofficial members, and eight elected members (five from St Kitts, two from Nevis, and one from Anguilla). The elected members would then choose three of their number to join one of the nominated members on the Executive Council.

A general election, following a year-by-year postponement since 1949, took place on 6 October 1952. Representatives of the Workers' League stood in all eight constituencies, and all eight were returned. Independent candidates in Nevis and Anguilla received only 15 per cent of the total votes cast, while the Democratic Party which had opposed the Workers' League in St Kitts ended up with less than 4 per cent. Those elected in St Kitts, besides Bradshaw, Francis and Davis, were the vice-president of the Trades and Labour Union, Caleb Azariah Paul Southwell, and its treasurer, Frederick Williams. Southwell, who had been born in Dominica and understandably preferred to be known only by the third of his forenames, had served for six years as a policeman before obtaining a job as a clerk at the sugar factory in 1944. He had been vice-president of the union since 1947, the year in which he had lost his job at the factory for trying to obtain a pay rise. All five were joined by Robert Gordon and James Liburd from Nevis, and David Lloyd from Anguilla. For the first time, and what was to turn out to be the only time in their history, all three islands were represented by one organization (the Workers' League being far from a true political party) with Bradshaw in an unassailable position as its leader. There was no dissent when he, France and Davis became members of the Executive Council.

Another part of Blackburne's remit from London was to introduce a new form of government in each presidency, once the elections following the constitutional change had taken place. '[T]he legislatures in Antigua, St. Kitts and Montserrat', Blackburne recorded later,

> would appoint three committees from among their members to watch over the three main fields of government activity – trade and production; social services; and public works and communications. The three elected members of the legislature to be appointed to the Executive Council…would be the chairmen of these committees.[5]

Although this may have been acceptable to the elected members of the Executive Councils of Antigua and Montserrat, where according to the Governor it 'worked like a charm', it was not good enough for Bradshaw. He refused to accept the committee system and insisted that he, France and Davis became, respectively, 'Members' for Trade and Production, Social Services, and Public Works. Regardless of what they were called, the three proto-ministers in each presidency performed so well that three years later Blackburne had few misgivings about the introduction of more substantial reforms. The Leeward Islands Federation was abolished at the beginning of 1956, and the four presidencies became separate colonies once again, although still under a single governor living in Antigua. This was followed in St Kitts-Nevis by a new constitution creating an elected majority on the Executive Council, and turning the three 'Members' of the Executive Council into ministers, with Bradshaw as before very much *primus inter pares*.

Soon after this the elected membership recognized that the time had come to create a genuine political party out of the Workers' League, and the St Kitts-Nevis Labour Party came into existence later the same year. The party's newspaper, the *Labour Spokesman*, was founded soon afterwards, taking the place of the *Workers' Weekly* which had been published since 1942. In spite of its name the new party made little attempt to establish itself outside St Kitts; it held little appeal for anyone in Anguilla, and membership in Nevis never amounted to more than two or three hundred. It achieved complete success at the general election of November 1957 only in St Kitts, where all five seats were won. The election in Nevis and Anguilla of men opposed to Bradshaw and the Labour Party brought an end to the appearance of unity which had been given by the results of the election held five years earlier, and from then on politics in all three islands became increasingly polarized. Following the election, the disdain with which Bradshaw treated the members for Nevis, Wilmoth Nicholls and Eugene Walwyn, and the sole member for Anguilla, Kenneth Hazell, merely served to create more disunity.

Emigration

The political developments of the 1950s took place during another period of mass emigration from all three islands, with the people involved from St Kitts being drawn almost entirely from among those who made up the natural constituency of Bradshaw, the Workers' League and the trade union. Given the social conditions of the time, as outlined in previous chapters, it must have appeared to many men and women in Nevis and Anguilla, as well as St Kitts, that their only hope of a decent life lay in some other part of the world. This view can only have been reinforced by the complacency with which their plight continued to be ignored by the British government and the colonial administration. 'One of the outstanding events of 1955', Governor Blackburne opened his report for that year to the Colonial Office,

> was the visit to St. Kitts made in February by Her Royal Highness the Princess Margaret during her Caribbean tour. Her Royal Highness spent most of one day there and in the course of it drove round the island and visited the sugar factory.[6]

It is difficult to imagine what purpose was served by this visit, and even harder to understand why it was considered worthy to be thought 'outstanding'. At this time many of the 7000 people working on the estates or in the factory were still living under conditions not too different from those which would have been found in the princess's great-great-grandmother's day. The average weekly wage for all male estate workers, working a 40- to 48-hour week, was (converting British West Indian dollars (BWI$) then in use into pounds sterling) no more than £1.60 or (converting BWI$ into today's Eastern Caribbean dollars) about EC$7.00. At the beginning of the twenty-first century this sum would have been the equivalent of £24 or EC$103. A cane cutter earned about £3.50 (£42.50 or EC$183) and a tractor driver a little more, while in the factory a skilled artisan could make around £4.60 (£70 or EC$300). The weekly wages of those outside the sugar industry were equally poor. In the cotton industry they averaged £1.50 (£22.50 or EC$97) for men, and £1.00 (£15.00 or EC$65) for women. Store clerks did little better, with men making up to £4.60 (£70 or EC$300) a week, and women £2.50 (£37.50 or EC$160). Domestic servants, who were the lowest paid, were lucky to ever earn more than one pound a week (£15 or EC$65).[7]

In 1955 the only country to which West Indians could emigrate freely and with no restrictions was Great Britain, entry into the USA under the quota system which had been in operation since 1924 (p.239 above) having been stopped after 1952 by the passing of the McCarran Act. Until July 1962 every citizen of the British West Indies, along with all those of every other Commonwealth country, had an unrestricted right to enter and live in the United Kingdom. People in St Kitts, Nevis and Anguilla were no less ready to take their chance on the opposite side of the Atlantic than those of any other Caribbean territory, and between 1955 and 1965 (when the British government introduced legislation to prevent further immigration) almost 15,000 people from the three islands moved to Britain.

Establishing the Federation of the West Indies

The abolition of the Leeward Islands Federation was brought about in 1956 in order that its four constituent presidencies could enter a new and much larger federation as separate units. Discussion about some larger grouping of the West Indian colonies had been taking place by this time for well over 30 years, both within the region and in London. In 1922 the Parliamentary Under-Secretary of State for the Colonies, Edward Wood, after touring the region the previous year, had reported that although more unity and cooperation between the West Indian colonies was very desirable there were too many political and practical obstructions to make any kind of federation a possibility. In his opinion the establishment of any political unity was 'likely to be a plant of slow and tender growth'. This remained the generally accepted view in London until the end of 1931, when the Colonial Secretary, Lord Passfield, announced his intention of appointing a commission to examine the possibility of closer union and cooperation.

Receipt of the news in the West Indies induced the Taxpayers' Reform Association of Dominica to invite representatives from other representative government associations in the Eastern Caribbean to attend a conference on the island, in order to draw up proposals which could be presented to the Commission when it arrived. The invitation was sent to the Workers' League in St Kitts, and Thomas Manchester and William Seaton joined delegates from Antigua, Grenada, Montserrat and Trinidad in Roseau at the end of October 1932. After six days of deliberation it was decided to recommend the establishment of a federation of all the islands in the Eastern Caribbean and to present the Commission with the draft of an outline federal constitution.

General Sir Charles Fergusson and Sir Charles Orr, who comprised the Commission for West Indies Closer Union, began their enquiries in November. As might have been expected they were more interested in obtaining the views of those who administered the various colonies than those of, as these two worthies probably thought, an unknown group of men who had been at some get-together or other in one of the more backward islands. Their enquiries uncovered very little of the unity which had existed among those attending the Roseau conference. According to the Commission's report, published in April 1933, each island paid 'scant attention to its neighbours', and there were 'deep-seated divisions even among islands administratively linked as one colony'. All the islands were generally in favour of federation, but only if this brought with it 'economy in administration', and did not involve any one of them being absorbed 'by some larger unit or destruction of its own individuality'. Regardless of all these caveats, the report ended up by recommending that the Leeward and Windward Islands all be united under one governor with his headquarters in St Lucia. This caused an outcry among the islands, and after most of them, including St Kitts, had reported that unification would involve them in additional administrative spending, the report was quietly shelved.

It was not until the closing months of the Second World War that the idea of a closer union was resurrected, this time with no commission or inquiry being involved. In March 1945 the Colonial Secretary merely informed the West Indian governors that it was now the firm intention of the British government to bring about a federation, and suggested a debate on the subject take place in each legislature. As a result of such debates, and following a meeting in Grenada, a conference attended by representatives from all the legislatures in the Eastern Caribbean was held in Basseterre at the beginning of February 1947. The conference, which was chaired by Clement Malone, who by this time was Chief Justice of the Windward and Leeward Islands, passed a resolution stating that 'there should be a federation of the islands of the Windward Islands and the Leeward Islands with a strong government'. This, however, was not the sort of union envisaged by the Colonial Secretary of the day, Arthur Creech Jones, who two weeks later proposed a conference in Jamaica to discuss the establishment of a federation of all the British West Indian colonies. This conference was convened at Montego Bay in September, with Maurice Davis representing St Kitts-Nevis as one of three delegates from the Leeward Islands.

The Montego Bay Conference ended with a firm commitment to a federation and the setting up of a Standing Closer Association Committee to consider the form of its constitution, judiciary, and matters such as taxes, tariffs and currency. It took this committee nearly nine years to hammer out details of the federation, during which time British Guiana, British Honduras and the British Virgin Islands all opted out of joining, and its final report was not signed until February 1956. Five months later the British Caribbean Act was passed to set up a federal union consisting of Jamaica, Trinidad and Tobago, Barbados, Grenada, St Vincent, St Lucia, Dominica, Antigua and Barbuda, Montserrat, and St Kitts-Nevis-Anguilla. The federation was given a semi-colonial constitution, with a governor-general appointed by the Crown, a nominated 19-member Senate (with two from St Kitts-Nevis-Anguilla), and an elected House of Representatives of 45 members (again with two from St Kitts-Nevis-Anguilla). The Federation of the West Indies was scheduled to come into being in early January 1958, with the first elections taking place two months later.

A meeting to discuss the formation of a federal political party to fight the election was called by Grantley Adams in Barbados in June. It was attended by Norman Manley of Jamaica, the leading politicians of Antigua, Grenada, St Lucia and Montserrat, and by Bradshaw and France from St Kitts. The West Indies Federal Labour Party, which was formed as a result, held its inaugural conference in St Lucia in September, where Manley was elected as its president with Adams and Bradshaw as the first and second vice-presidents. The time had then come, as Bradshaw recalled later,

> when one had to decide whether one would leave one's
> own bailiwick and venture into Federal politics. I chose

the latter, believing that I had a duty to make available to the nation which we had set out to form whatever little experience I had gathered in public life from 1946 until then. So I gave up my position in St Kitts....[8]

Not too many of the other island leaders felt the same way, and he, Adams, and William Bramble of Montserrat were the only ones to contest the federal elections held in March 1958. The results gave the Federal Labour Party a slight lead over the opposing Democratic Labour Party, allowing Adams to become the Federation's first and, as it was to turn out, only prime minister. Bradshaw, who had been elected along with the Anguillian David Lloyd to represent St Kitts-Nevis-Anguilla, was appointed minister of finance. His two nominees to the Senate were William Seaton (no relation of the Seaton connected with the United Benevolent Association) from St Kitts and James Liburd from Nevis. From then on, the activities of all four men were concentrated in Trinidad, which had been chosen as the site of the Federation's capital.

The vacuum in the political life of St Kitts that was left by Bradshaw's departure for the federal Parliament was rapidly filled by the burly, bearded presence of Paul Southwell. He, like Bradshaw, was a self-made and self-educated man who, overcoming his humble beginnings, had developed a considerable presence and was more than able to hold his own both in the legislature and in the waning colonial society. On 1 January 1960 colonialism suffered another blow when the constitution of St Kitts-Nevis-Anguilla was changed once again. The post of governor of the Leeward Islands was abolished and the Administrator, now Henry Howard, became the direct representative of the Crown. The Executive Council was reconstituted with the creation of the office of chief minister, the addition of a fourth minister in place of the financial secretary, and the removal of one of the two nominated unofficial members. A month later Southwell, now aged 47, became the first chief minister and minister of finance of St Kitts-Nevis-Anguilla.

In the following year, with Bradshaw now ensconced in Trinidad, struggling to make something of his ministerial post despite having the barest of funds at his disposal (the Federation's budget for 1959 was a mere 12 million BWI dollars – less than a tenth of that of Trinidad and Tobago), it was left to Southwell to lead the Labour Party in the elections held in November. He had no difficulty in retaining power, but the results of the election further increased the division between St Kitts and the other two islands. The 1960 constitution had increased the number of seats in St Kitts from four to seven, and all were won with ease by Labour. The two seats in Nevis, on the other hand, were just as easily won by Eugene Walwyn and James Brookes representing the United Nevis Movement, a party committed to secession which had been founded by the former earlier in the year. It was much the same in Anguilla where a man strongly opposed to the Labour Party's grip on government, Peter Adams, was returned. The election of these three led to their being treated by Southwell and his Government as the official opposition, a situation under which the good they could do for their respective islands was bound to suffer. This in turn more or less guaranteed increased support in both Nevis and Anguilla for secession, or at the very least, a completely revised form of government. Matters were hardly improved a year later when the Federation, for reasons which are of little relevance here, was dissolved and Bradshaw returned to St Kitts. He could hardly resume immediately the dominant position he had held until 1958, but after one of the elected Labour Party members had resigned and an election had taken place Bradshaw entered Southwell's administration, nominally as minister without portfolio but more readily identifiable as an *eminence grise*.

The Beginning of Party Politics

The 1961 elections for the seven seats in St Kitts were contested by the Labour Party and, without the remotest chance of success, by an organization called the People's Progressive Party which had been founded in the same year by Maurice Davis. Like the Democratic Party which had contested the previous two elections, this drew its support from among those, mostly white or brown middle class, people who were opposed to all that the Labour Party stood for, and all that black men like Bradshaw and Southwell, with their demagoguery, were thought to represent. Equally like its predecessor, the People's Progressive Party could offer no real challenge to the Labour Party and once the election was over it soon ceased to exist. The first real opposition party did not come into being for another four years.

The People's Action Movement (PAM) was founded on 15 January 1965 in order, as its secretary informed the Administrator a few days later, 'to oppose the present Government' and to make 'the process of Government more democratic, more efficient and of lasting benefit to the expanding population of our islands'. One of the two prime movers behind its formation was a lawyer named William Herbert, the son of a man bearing the same names who had been on the management team of the sugar factory and among the founders of the Democratic Party; the other was a medical practitioner named Kennedy Simmonds. At the inaugural meeting Herbert was elected chairman, with Simmonds as party secretary. In order to publicize its foundation as a tri-island party, public meetings were held in Basseterre on 31 January, at Sandy Point on 7 February, at three different locations in Nevis on 14 February, at Cayon on 21 February, and finally at various locations in Anguilla for two days in April. All the meetings, particularly the first in Basseterre, attracted a great deal of interest, and within a year PAM had become solidly established in St Kitts with a reasonable amount of support in the other islands. In as much as the creation of another viable political party added to the democratic process this did not happen a moment too soon. By 1966, following the failure of all attempts to replace the defunct Federation with one made up of just the smaller islands of the Eastern Caribbean, the British government was actively pursuing plans for complete West Indian decolonization.

Progress Towards Associated Statehood

One of the first indications given to the ordinary people of the colony of the approach of yet another constitutional change came at the very beginning of 1966 when Fred Phillips, a black lawyer from St Vincent who had previously served as Cabinet Secretary in the Federation of the West Indies, was appointed to the post of Administrator. Four months after he had taken up office he accompanied Southwell, together with Bradshaw, Walwyn and Adams (as representatives for Nevis and Anguilla), and the Attorney-General, to London in order to attend a conference at which a new status for the colony, as a self-governing state 'in Association with Britain', was to be discussed.

As all the details of the form which would be taken by this association had already been hammered out at similar conferences held earlier with Antigua, Dominica, St Lucia, St Vincent and Grenada, Southwell and his team were left with little to do but carry out an exercise in rubber-stamping. In any case, knowing the British government would be only too keen to reduce aid once Associated Statehood had been introduced, Southwell, with Bradshaw at his side, preferred to concentrate on discussing 'certain problems relating to the economic development of the Territory'.[9] In pressing for a continuation of financial and technical assistance most of the Chief Minister's demands served to highlight the inequality which strained relations between St Kitts and the other two islands. In St Kitts, the British were told, there was 'an urgent need' to diversify the economy by promoting the tourist industry, and future development

> entailed attracting private investment for hotels and similar amenities. This in turn required the construction or

provision by the Government of the necessary infrastructure (e.g. roads, and water and electricity services) as well as an airfield capable of receiving medium-haul jet aircraft, and a deep-water harbour.

As for Nevis and Anguilla, perhaps an examination of some existing aid schemes could be carried out, 'to see if savings could be effected which could be transferred to schemes of road improvement'.[10] Apart from this begrudging acknowledgement, the only reference made to Nevis and Anguilla as individual islands in the conference report which was published in June, was with regard to local government. The new constitution due to come into effect early the following year, it stated,

> will provide that there shall be a Council for Nevis and a Council for Anguilla; that the Council for each Island shall be the principal organ of local government for that Island; and that at least two thirds of all members of each Council shall be elected on the same franchise as Members of the House of Assembly.[11]

With the date of 27 February 1967 set for 'Statehood Day', and bearing the promise of the services of a Commonwealth Office adviser to assist in setting up the two Councils, and of some budgetary aid which 'would not exclude the consideration of special assistance following a major natural disaster', the delegates returned home at the end of May.

At the general election which followed two months later, the Labour Party was opposed for the first time by a large and well-organized opposition party. This made no difference in St Kitts, where Labour retained all seven seats but, by taking the Anguilla seat and one of the two seats in Nevis, the PAM unintentionally increased the division between each of these islands and St Kitts. One of the Nevis seats was retained by Walwyn, representing the United Nevis Movement, while the other was won for PAM by a man named Fred Parris. Peter Adams kept his seat in Anguilla after standing as a PAM candidate, an affiliation he had adopted only in order to further demonstrate his opposition to Bradshaw and his colleagues. In all, PAM collected 35 per cent of all the votes cast, compared with 44 per cent for the Labour Party.

Following the election, and presumably in accordance with some long-standing private agreement with Southwell, Bradshaw took over as chief minister. With the colony soon to become a self-governing state, his Government had plenty to do for the remainder of the year, and it was not until October that a committee, with Walwyn and Adams as members, was formed to determine the form to be taken by the Nevis and Anguilla Councils. This met infrequently and had achieved very little by the time news was received towards the end of the year of the imminent arrival of Peter Johnston, the adviser promised by the British government to assist in the Council formation.

The committee's final proposals, drawn up with Johnston's help in January, could hardly have been bettered if it had been the committee's intention to create yet more disaffection in Nevis and Anguilla. Each island was to get a Council made up of six elected and three nominated members; with no guaranteed budgetary support other than revenue from petty taxes; with power to make by-laws for only trivial matters such as street cleaning, dog licensing, impounding of stray animals and cemetery maintenance; and under constant threat of dissolution by the central government if it was considered not to be functioning properly. There were no immediate repercussions in Nevis, when Johnston went there to hold talks about the proposals towards the end of the month, but this was far from the case when it came time for him to repeat the exercise in Anguilla. He arrived on 27 January to be met at the airport by about 400 demonstrators, led by three men who the day before had announced the formation of a political party, the People's Progressive Movement, to oppose both statehood and any further association of Anguilla with St Kitts. Following the lead of Ronald Webster, Atlin Harrigan and John Rogers, the crowd not only prevented Johnston from holding any meeting to discuss the proposed Council until mid-afternoon, but then turned the meeting into a general shouting match largely concerned with secession.

This disturbance in Anguilla took Bradshaw and seemingly most other people in St Kitts by complete surprise, and it took well over a week for them to appreciate the strength of the antagonism which had been engendered amongst the Anguillians. The PAM leadership, who saw that continued support from Anguilla was essential if they ever hoped to obtain power, merely set about preparing a plan for a stronger all-elected Council, and Adams made no attempt to return to the island until 2 February. His visit did little good as he was believed, rightly, to have gone along with the rest of the committee in drawing up the proposal for the local Council which had been so soundly rejected a week earlier. The 800 or so people he addressed at an open-air meeting the next day were not prepared to hear him advocate anything which involved Anguilla remaining part of a self-governing state under Bradshaw, and once he began arguing against secession he was shouted down and forced to abandon the meeting. The Government seems not to have considered there was anything worth worrying about until 5 February, the morning after a disturbance at The Valley Secondary School intended to disrupt a 'Statehood Queen' contest had deteriorated into a riot, involving stone throwing and use of tear gas by the island's tiny police force. This finally alerted Bradshaw to the seriousness of the situation, and the Chief of Police was despatched to Anguilla with warrants for the arrest of 11 people, including Webster and Harrigan. A handful of extra police were sent two days later and the Administrator was asked, echoing appeals made in 1896 and 1935, to seek the assistance of the Royal Navy in restoring order.

Bradshaw's rejection of the alternative plan for local government in Anguilla, which had been drawn up by PAM, took place at the same time and brought further complications. Herbert and Adams immediately departed for London in order to protest to the Minister of State for Commonwealth Affairs that the events taking place in Anguilla meant the Bradshaw Government was no longer prepared to honour its obligation to provide the island with any form of local council. With statehood now only a matter of days away, the Minister had no option but to take their protest seriously, and a Commonwealth Office official was hurriedly despatched to St Kitts. He arrived on 20 February and spent the next two days in Anguilla with Phillips, the Administrator, attempting to provide the inhabitants with some kind of reassurance about their future as part of the intended Associated State. Their efforts were to no avail, and they achieved little apart from persuading nine of the wanted men to give themselves up (the other two had been apprehended earlier). Two days after they left, a large crowd at another disorderly meeting made it quite plain that no Anguillian who valued his life would be allowed to serve on the type of council which Bradshaw intended for the island.

On Saturday 25 February 1967 the Secretary of State for Overseas Development, Arthur Bottomley, arrived in St Kitts to represent the British government at the next day's statehood celebrations. He paid a four-hour, incident-free visit to Nevis later the same day, and on Sunday morning was accompanied by Southwell to Anguilla. There, having been greeted by Adams, he had a very different sort of reception, being obliged to attend a long and noisy public meeting at which he and Southwell were harangued with complaints about the lack of facilities on the island and anti-statehood protests. Eventually, once everyone had had their say and Adams was able to bring the meeting to an end.

> Bottomley was then taken on a tour of the island over roads that were almost impassable; and the upshot of a very rough ride was that the Secretary of State approved the immediate expenditure of £16,000 to 'tarmac' 2 miles of road.[12]

Back in St Kitts, at midnight the same day, Bottomley witnessed the flag-raising ceremony which marked the colony's achievement of full internal self-government, with Britain retaining responsibility for defence and external affairs only. Phillips exchanged the title of administrator for that of governor, and Bradshaw became the state's first premier. A similar flag-raising ceremony also took place in Nevis at the same time. It was different story altogether in Anguilla, where very few people other than the Government representative, the Warden, found anything to celebrate. Before dark, both 'Bradshaw' and 'Statehood' were buried in a mock funeral ceremony, and after that, because the island was without any electricity, nothing else took place until the Warden performed his own, largely private, flag-raising ritual in front of Government House at dawn the next day.

22

The Anguilla Revolution

The man who furtively raised the flag of new state in front of his official residence in The Valley on 27 February 1967 was not an Anguillian. Vincent Byron was from Nevis, and had been made Warden largely as a result of his being a firm supporter of Bradshaw and the Labour Party. Although a sinecure, there can have been little about the position, other than the prestige and emoluments which went with it, that he would have found attractive. The Anguillian population in February 1967 numbered almost 6000, scattered throughout an island which had no electricity, no island-wide piped water supply, no telephone system, and a road system which consisted almost entirely of potholed dirt tracks (as the aptly named Bottomley had discovered to the cost of his hindquarters and the British Overseas Development Fund). Anguilla had a seaport consisting of nothing more than a tiny wooden jetty and a Customs House, an airport with a short grass runway incapable of handling night flights, a small cottage hospital which was not even able to offer blood transfusions, and a single secondary school which could provide no sixth-form education. The main settlement, The Valley, was composed of nothing but a straggling agglomeration of houses, a few stores, two banks, several bars, a small commercial hotel, the secondary school, and several churches. Neither bank was more than a year old, and the hotel, Lloyd's, had only been in existence since 1959. The island's only tourist hotel, which had opened three years later, was some miles away at the end of a long and bumpy track leading to Rendezvous Bay. In the words of a guide book of the day, 'nothing approaching luxury [was] to be found' in either establishment.

Given the conditions under which the Anguillians had to live, and the way in which their concerns about statehood had been dismissed by both the British and the Bradshaw governments, it is hardly surprising that soon after the new state had come into being more extreme forms of protest began to take place. During the night of 7 March, after an attempt had been made to barricade the Warden inside, Government House was set alight and razed to the ground. Byron was fortunate to escape with his life, and two days later, having lost everything but what he stood up in and after finding someone willing to relieve him, he departed for St Kitts. The Acting

Warden, a man named Hughes, having no official residence to occupy, moved into Lloyd's Hotel. The hotel's proprietor, David Lloyd, was one of the few Anguillian members of the Labour Party and the man who had been elected with Bradshaw to the Federation Parliament (p.260 above).

Although very little investigation of the destruction of Government House was carried out by the supine and ill-led police force, none of whose members it seems were Anguillian, this did not prevent their head-quarters becoming one of the next targets for attack. At different times over the next three months, unknown marksmen fired on the police station, on Lloyd's Hotel, and on the home of another Labour Party sup-porter. The two worst attacks took place on 11 May, when 30 rounds were fired at the police station, and on 27 May, when the hotel was raked by over 50 rounds. On 28 May the Acting Warden, perhaps understandably, decided enough was enough and left the island. This left the field clear for the island's Parliamentary representative, Peter Adams, to display some much-needed initiative. At a public meeting the next day he argued for the entire police force, as the last remaining representatives of the Bradshaw Government, to be made to leave the island. This was more than enough for the demoralized police. By late the following afternoon, having made no attempt to assert any authority whatsoever, and having abandoned almost the whole of their armoury, the entire force had left the island. The day they left, 30 May, which soon came to be known as 'Anguilla Day' has been celebrated as a public holiday ever since.

The Rebellion

The shame-faced arrival of the expelled policemen in St Kitts was the signal for Bradshaw, arguably at least two months too late and when he was left with no means of enforcing his authority in Anguilla, to declare a state of emergency. At the same time he requested assistance in dealing with the situation not only from Great Britain, but also from Jamaica, Guyana, Trinidad and Tobago, and Barbados. In Anguilla on the day after the police left, a Peace-keeping Committee consisting of Adams, Webster, Harrigan and 11 others under the chairmanship of Walter Hodge (who had been Anguilla's elected representative from 1943 to 1946) was formed to manage the island's affairs. The first act of this committee was to send a four-man delegation to St Kitts in order to present the Government with a document stating

> Anguillians do not want to be part of a State of
> St Christopher-Nevis-Anguilla. The time when they might

have accepted this is past. What they now want is SEPARATION and SELF-DETERMINATION within twelve months. By the end of this time they want to be a State in association with Britain.

In the meantime, the document continued, they wanted the immediate appointment of a British Administrator to be followed by 'a general election in the island to constitute a Council'.[1] Such demands were clear enough, but, as might have been expected, they did nothing to ease the situation. All were rejected outright by Bradshaw, who responded by halting mail deliveries, stopping payment of salaries to public employees, impounding bank and post office accounts, and withholding the island's share of development funds.

The Attack on St Kitts

The immediate Anguillian response to this was peculiar to say the least, consisting as it did of an armed raid on St Kitts carried out by, at the most, a dozen men who arrived by boat at Basseterre in the early hours of 10 June. This, as recorded in an address given by Bradshaw some weeks later,

> took the form of simultaneous armed attacks upon the Police and Defence Headquarters as well as on the electricity power station…with automatic weapons, rifles, explosives, tear gas and other weapons. Shots were fired at the homes of the Director of Public Prosecution…the Attorney General, the Senior Crown Counsel and private homes.

In his view all this amounted to nothing less than 'a dastardly attempt…to overthrow the lawfully elected Government of this State by force', carried out by 'resident Kittitians and a group comprising Anguillians and three white Americans from St. Thomas who were assembled in Anguilla and brought here by sea at night'.[2]

A slightly more plausible reason for the raid, which did little damage and caused only two people to be wounded, was that those taking part came with the intention of kidnapping Bradshaw and holding him to ransom. The consequent pointless firing at places such as the police station and electricity generating plant then only took place because the raiders had no idea where the Premier was to be found. No Anguillian has ever offered a proper explanation of the episode and, as only five of the raiders were apprehended, it has never been admitted just how many Anguillians in all took part. The incident was skated over in the first detailed account of the revolution which was published in 1983, and by 1992 was only recalled on the island as 'a tactical fiasco'.[3]

Fiasco or not, it was taken seriously enough by Bradshaw for him to order the detention of 22 people he suspected of either taking part in the raid, or of assisting those who did. As he was convinced that the opposition party must have been involved, among those detained were the PAM leader, William Herbert, and several of Herbert's friends living in Nevis. Only three of the detainees, including Herbert, were ever brought to trial and, although it took many years for a final decision in their cases to be reached, all were eventually acquitted.

This raid also caused Bradshaw to make a second appeal for help from Britain, Jamaica, Guyana, Trinidad and Tobago, and Barbados. The British government refused to get involved, but the other four put together a five-man team under the Permanent Secretary of the Jamaican Ministry of Defence, which was sent to St Kitts on 28 June to try to resolve the situation. A number of meetings were held, including one attended by Bradshaw and a five-man delegation from Anguilla, but little was achieved other than an agreement from both sides to attend a multi-national conference in Barbados at the end of July at which, it was hoped, a settlement could be reached.

Two weeks before this conference was due to convene, the Peace-keeping Committee, which was all Anguilla had had in the way of an administration since 31 May, organized a referendum to determine the extent to which the population was in favour of secession from St Kitts and the establishment of an interim government. Over 1800 people voted in support, while only five – of whom we can safely assume the owner of Lloyd's Hotel was one – opposed the proposition. The Peace-keeping Committee was then dissolved and the administration placed in the hands of a seven-member Council which included Hodge, Webster and Adams. This change, which was to last only until elections could take place, was in accordance with a new constitution that, again for reasons which have become increasingly obfuscated over the years, the committee had acquired from a Harvard University professor named Roger Fisher. This acceptance of an American 'off-the-shelf' constitution was hardly commensurate with the committee's expressed desire, made only a month earlier, of 'Direct administration from Britain under an Administrator' with a view to becoming 'a State in association with Britain', and only served to reduce Anguillian credibility in the eyes of the outside world.

The Barbados Conference and its Aftermath

The conference which convened in Barbados on 25 July was attended by representatives of all the countries to which Bradshaw had appealed for help. The delegation of six from Anguilla was led by Adams, who had now assumed leadership of the nominated Council, and included another man who in time would play a leading role in the political life of the island, Emile Gumbs. Bradshaw was accompanied by Eugene Walwyn who, having switched his loyalty from the United Nevis Movement to the Labour Party shortly after the last election, had been rewarded by being made attorney-general. Over the next four days the Anguillians were persuaded to agree to a settlement which would see the appointment of a new Warden, the return of the police, and the stationing on the island of a Caribbean peace-keeping force 'during the initial stages of the re-establishment of constitutional government'. At the same time new legislation would be drawn up in St Kitts to replace the Local Councils Act, which had come into force on 27 February, in order to give Anguilla and Nevis each a Council with greater powers. To further Anguillian acceptance of the deal, and to bring a quick resolution to what for London was becoming an increasingly embarrassing situation, the British offered £50,000 in aid – to be shared between Anguilla and Nevis, and to be spent by March 1968. The conference was then adjourned until 31 July, in order to give Adams time to return and present the rest of the Anguillians with details of the agreement.

He received a very mixed reception, and on his return to Barbados he was accompanied by Webster, Harrigan and three other delegates, all of whom were strongly opposed to any further association with St Kitts. All five refused to sign the document which purported to be the agreed settlement, and after the conference had ended it soon became obvious to Bradshaw and the rest of those who had signed that the stance which had been taken by Webster and his colleagues had the approval of virtually the entire Anguillian population. Within days of their return from Barbados Adams was unceremoniously deposed from the Council and Webster became the undisputed leader in his place. The Barbados Agreement hardly lasted any longer outside Anguilla, particularly after the Governments of Jamaica and Trinidad and Tobago found reasons not to honour their commitment to provide troops for a peace-keeping force, and it was soon forgotten. On 25 October, in an attempt to restore democracy to the island and to imbue the Council with some sort of legality, Webster called a general election. He was largely unsuccessful, as only he and four other candidates offered themselves for election to five Council seats, and all were returned unopposed.

With the Anguillians rapidly assuming what one of the local clergy at the time called 'an attitude of nihilism', the Bradshaw Government lacking the necessary means of re-establishing its authority, and the leaders of other Caribbean countries unwilling to expend more than hot air on coming to the aid of either, the British government was left with no choice but to make a move towards resolving the situation. In early December a Parliamentary mission, consisting of one Conservative MP and one Labour MP, was sent out to hold talks in both St Kitts and Anguilla. After protracted negotiations the mission eventually succeeded in getting both Bradshaw and Webster to agree to invite the British government to appoint a senior civil servant to Anguilla for an 'interim period' of a year to act as an adviser to the Council. The official chosen for the job, Anthony Lee, arrived in Anguilla on 8 January 1968, with a remit from London to work towards a long-term solution to the problem.

He met with very little success, as was demonstrated in October when the Parliamentary Under-Secretary of State for Foreign and Commonwealth Affairs, William Whitlock, invited Webster and Bradshaw to London for talks about a possible settlement. These ended in total deadlock, with Bradshaw unable to agree to any devolution of power, and Webster not prepared to consider a return to any form of association with St Kitts. The impasse resulted a month later in an announcement by Webster of his intention to declare Anguilla's independence after the 'interim period' of a year had ended. As a result, as soon as the 'interim period' did come to an end with Lee's departure on 8 January 1969, Bradshaw imposed sanctions, suspending the postal service (which had been resumed a year earlier), and banning all trade and all flights between St Kitts and Anguilla.

Unilateral Declaration of Independence

Webster's response was to organize a referendum on 6 February, the results of which – purportedly 1739 for and only four against – he claimed showed overwhelming support for a unilateral declaration of independence (UDI). This produced the first real split in the Anguillian leadership, as Harrigan, Gumbs and several others were greatly opposed to the idea of independence. 'We are British subjects, and want to remain in the Commonwealth', Harrigan wrote two days later in the *Beacon*, the newspaper he had founded in 1967, '...we agreed to bring the interim period to a close, but we must keep the link with Britain and trust her to get us out of our difficulties'.[4] He and his supporters were right not to be enamoured by the prospect of an independent Anguilla. By the time of UDI Webster was no longer content with the Fisher constitution, and had replaced it with one drawn up by an American ex-policeman and self-proclaimed lawyer named Jack Holcomb. Under this 'bogus Republic Constitution', as it was termed by Harrigan, nominations for president, vice-president, secretaries of state, national representatives, and senior district representatives took place in the second half of February. In the event no elections were needed as only one candidate for each office came forward. Webster of course was the only candidate for the highest office, and on 21 February he was declared president of the two-week-old Republic of Anguilla. This may well have pleased the 1739 people who had voted for UDI, but it left a sizeable proportion of the population far from happy about all that had happened since Lee's departure from the island, and the direction in which they were now being led.

However, any discontent felt in Anguilla was nothing compared to that experienced in Basseterre and London, particularly in the latter where the government was under pressure from the larger Commonwealth Caribbean states 'to take all necessary steps in collaboration with the Government of the State to confirm the territorial integrity of St Kitts-Nevis-Anguilla'. Webster's declaration of a republic brought an immediate response from London, and on 25 February Whitlock and a large team of officials, including Lee, arrived in St Kitts to attempt to resolve the situation for once and for all.

This was easier said than done, and after long discussions with Bradshaw it was decided that the only course of action would be to buy more time, by proposing to the Anguillians that Lee return as a Commissioner, who would govern with the help of an Advisory Committee and 'remain on the island so long as the present difficult situation continues'. Whitlock dispatched Lee to Anguilla on 9 March to clear the way for a meeting with Webster and the Council, and two days later flew to the island with the rest of the British mission. He was met at the airport by Webster, who expected to be greeted as a head of state, and a crowd of about 500 people. Unfortunately, in the light of what was to transpire, Whitlock was in no position to give even the slightest acknowledgement to anyone claiming presidential status, and most of the crowd belonged to that part of the population opposed to the idea of a republic and not totally enchanted with Webster's leadership. Any rapprochement between the high-handed Whitlock and the high-horsed Webster in the face of such a gathering was doomed from the start. After distributing copies of the proposal, the entire British mission for no very good reason refused an invitation to lunch with Webster, and left the airport to eat at a house owned by Henry Howard, the Englishman who had been Phillips's predecessor as Administrator (p.260 above). Webster stalked off in high dudgeon, and in the early afternoon, with armed men in the offing, came to Howard's house and ordered the British mission off the island. A few shots in the air ended any thoughts Whitlock may have had of ignoring the demand, and the mission was back in St Kitts well before nightfall.

Resumption of British Rule

The British response to Whitlock's expulsion followed a week later. On 18 March an Order-in-Council created the post of a Commissioner for Anguilla, and the following day Lee, accompanied by about 300 paratroops and 40 London policemen, brought to the island in two frigates, returned to take up where he had left off a little over two months earlier. The Anguilla (Temporary Provisions) Order which had just been passed by Parliament gave him the power to suspend, amend or revoke any law other than the Constitution or the Court Order, and he lost no time in exerting his authority. Various undesirable aliens were taken into custody and the most undesirable of them all was ordered to be deported. This was Holcomb, whose shady activities, along with those of other foreigners such as the 'mercenaries' who had taken part in the ludicrously inept attack on St Kitts, served only to detract from the Anguillians' true cause. The invasion force was much larger than was needed to install Lee as Commissioner, but its size had undoubtedly been determined by considerations of the resistance which Anguillians under the nefarious influence of men like Holcomb might have mounted. As the troops and police had met no opposition whatsoever, the invasion was greeted in other parts of the world with condemnation, ribaldry, or a mixture of both: 'Britain's Bay of Piglets' reported *Time* magazine on 28 March.

The appointment of Lee as the Commissioner was probably a mistake, as he was quite unable or more likely unwilling to establish any sort of relationship with Webster. It was not until the end of March, and after Lord Caradon, the Minister of State at the Foreign Office, had visited the island, that Webster and his supporters were made to realize they had no alternative but to accept the reimposition of British rule. Their acceptance came with the signing of the 'Caradon Agreement', which made it quite clear that the Commissioner would work 'in full consultation and co-operation with representatives of the people of Anguilla', and that those who had formed the 1968 Council would be 'recognised as elected representatives of the people' to serve on the new Advisory Council. Soon after this agreement had been reached, Lee asked to be relieved, and on 20 April he was replaced by an ex-Administrator of the Cayman Islands named John Cumber. Webster's demands for an early election were ignored by

Cumber, but they prompted Harrigan to formalize the break in his relations with the former by founding his own political party, the Anguilla Constructive Democratic Party (ACDP), with Emile Gumbs as the general secretary. Webster responded by setting up what to begin with he called the Anguilla Independence Democratic Party, but soon re-titled the People's Progressive Party (PPP).

While Anguillian political battle lines were being drawn up in this way the British government, fully aware that there had been no practical alternative to the course of action which had been taken, looked for a means of reducing the amount of adverse publicity the restoration of British rule had attracted. It was found in the time-honoured way of announcing the setting-up of a commission of inquiry, followed by taking as long as possible to find suitable people to form the commission, and giving it ample time in which to both open the inquiry and to present its findings. The Commission, established jointly with the Bradshaw Government, was appointed on 18 December under the chairmanship of Sir Hugh Wooding (a former Chief Justice of Trinidad and Tobago), with four other distinguished West Indians (one from Jamaica, one from St Lucia, and two from Guyana). Under its terms of reference it was to look into what had caused 'the situation that has come about in Anguilla', as well as the 'best means of dispelling any misunderstandings relating to that situation', and then 'to make recommendations that may lead to a satisfactory and durable solution'.[5]

The Wooding Commission began work on 1 April 1970 and presented its report in November. Amongst its readers, probably the only one to have been gladdened by its contents, or to have believed it offered anything even approaching a 'satisfactory and durable solution' would have been Bradshaw. The Commission rejected maintenance of the status quo, reversion to Crown Colony government, administration by the Commonwealth or the United Nations, or administration by some other Caribbean country. It also ruled out any idea of Anguilla being given the status of a state 'in association' with Britain, or of the island becoming one unit in a federation made up of St Kitts, Nevis and Anguilla. The only way forward, as far as the Commission was concerned, was for Anguilla to resume its original place as part of the Associated State of St Kitts-Nevis-Anguilla, but with a wholly elected Council given wide legislative, executive and fiscal powers.

Needless to say the report met with outright rejection in Anguilla, where the Council soon after its receipt passed a resolution affirming 'its determination not to be associated in any way whatsoever with the unitary state of St Kitts-Nevis', while calling on Britain 'to consult with the Anguilla Council and in joint agreement provide for the Government of

Anguilla free and separate from St Kitts...[and] with all possible speed...put an end to the present unsatisfactory constitutional position.[6]

If indeed Bradshaw did have a smile on his face as he read the report in November, it very soon disappeared. During a visit he made to London at the beginning of December, in order to discuss implementation of the Commission's recommendation, it must soon have become very clear to him that the inquiry had been little more than a British face-saving exercise, and that the Anguillian rejection of its findings had ended any hope of reunification. Six months later, after yet another minister had been to St Kitts, Bradshaw was told that the British 'could not allow this problem to continue indefinitely', and that 'Her Majesty's Government would have to proceed unilaterally with its proposals for an interim settlement'.[7]

The Anguilla Act, 1971

This settlement took the form of an Act, taking effect from 27 July, which empowered Britain 'to make such provision as Her Majesty thinks fit for securing peace, order and good government in Anguilla'. In order to appease Bradshaw, who perhaps felt the rest of the world might still be led to believe this involved no damage to 'territorial integrity', the name of the Associated State of St-Kitts-Nevis-Anguilla remained unchanged. This was of little consequence to the Anguillians as one section of the 1971 Act provided that, in the event of the legislature in Basseterre ever introducing a bill to end the state's association with Britain and become independent, Britain could by means of an Order-in-Council 'direct that Anguilla shall not any longer form part of that state'.

The first general election under the Anguilla (Administration) Order which accompanied the 1971 Act took place a year later, after the number of Council seats to be contested had been increased to seven. As the ACDP, Harrigan's party, had already folded by this time, Webster and the PPP had a walk-over, with two of his candidates being returned unopposed. The seventh seat was taken, also unopposed, by Emile Gumbs who ran as an independent. This was an impressive victory for Webster, but one which he soon realized gave him very little more say in how the island was to be run than before the election took place. Under the terms of the Administration Order, the Council, of which he was now the undisputed leader, was purely an advisory body. Although the Commissioner was obliged to function in consultation with the Council he could, in matters which he considered 'too important to require consultation' or 'too urgent to admit of such consultation', or which might involve 'material prejudice to Her Majesty's service', ignore it completely.

This was not a situation that Webster found to his liking, and over the next four years he led the Council in a number of 'strikes' during which the Commissioner received no advice or cooperation whatsoever. These 'strikes' took place largely as a result of the coercive and autocratic style of Webster's leadership but also, as the Wooding Report had pointed out, because Anguillians suffered from 'the disability of having no political responsibility', and had 'had no opportunity to learn politics'. The final and longest period of non-cooperation began in October 1974 and ended in December of the following year only after the British government had agreed to a new constitution for the island.

The Anguilla (Constitution) Order, 1976

The new constitution, based on that of the Cayman Islands, which came into force on 10 February 1976 had been drafted in the middle of the previous year. Given the way the Council members were then behaving, and had been behaving on and off since 1972, it was not to be expected that the British government would allow them very much say in its drafting. Webster complained of course, but cannot have been too distressed by a constitution which provided for a ministerial system of government working through a six-man Executive Council drawn from a 13-strong Legislative Assembly. The Commissioner, as chairman of the Executive Council and Speaker of the Assembly, retained overall power, but was now obliged to consult with the Executive Council on all matters except, if he chose, on those to do with internal security, external affairs and the public service. To no one's surprise, when elections took place on 15 March, Webster and the PPP again took six of the seven elected seats in the Assembly. One of the six was Gumbs, who by this time had renounced his independence and joined the PPP. The seventh seat was won by Hubert Hughes, another independent candidate and a man who, like Gumbs, would have an important part to play in the future of the island. It is perhaps unfair to say that the assumption of the office of chief minister went to Webster's head, but it certainly induced him to assume an even more authoritarian manner matched by an increasing disregard for the workings of democratic government. Within less than a year, due to some shenanigans over a disputed piece of land, he suffered the indignity of losing a vote of no confidence which had been tabled by Hughes, and then of seeing Gumbs appointed by the Commissioner to take his place as chief minister.

Gumbs remained chief minister until the next elections took place in May 1980. In the interim Webster formed a new political party, the

Anguilla United Movement (AUM), and was joined in this by Hughes, piqued by not being offered a ministerial appointment by Gumbs. The Chief Minister in turn, rather than continuing to lead the breakaway PPP, formed the Anguilla National Alliance (ANA). The change in party names made no difference to the election results: six of the seven seats went to Webster and the AUM, while Gumbs retained his alone for the ANA. On 28 May Webster was once again the chief minister. He resumed office only to find Hughes, once again denied a ministerial appointment, a thorn in his flesh. Trouble between the two men did not end even after Hughes towards the end of the year replaced a minister who had been found incompetent, but grew steadily worse. Their disagreements, details of which are hardly of relevance here, continued until May 1981 when Hughes resigned and Webster asked the Commissioner to dissolve the Assembly.

The Anguilla Act, 1980

Such had been their quarrel that the passing of yet another Anguilla Act by the British government five months earlier had gone largely unnoticed. This Act, which came about through events which are dealt with in Chapter 24, led to the passing of the Anguilla (Appointed Day) Order which stated that 'the 19th December 1980 is appointed as the day on which Anguilla shall cease to form part of the territory of the associated state of St Christopher, Nevis and Anguilla'.

But by this time Anguillians had long since ceased to worry about St Kitts and getting rid of this legal hangover from the 1971 Act: Anguilla was Anguilla and local politics – together with British aid in the development of the island – were all that mattered.[8] In the election called in June 1981 Webster, having now once more renamed his party (the Anguilla People's Party), was again returned to power. Ten months later, on 1 April 1982, Anguilla received yet another constitution. This replaced the post of commissioner with that of governor, converted the Legislative Assembly into a House of Assembly, and confirmed the status of the island as that of a British Dependent Territory.

23

Moving Towards Independence

The Anguillians' long struggle to free themselves of any connection with the Associated State of St Kitts-Nevis-Anguilla had a considerable effect on St Kitts and Nevis, and did much to warp the political life of both islands. Following the Statehood Day ceremonies which took place in Basseterre and Charlestown on 27 February 1967, one can safely assume that the specially written national anthem *Unity in Trinity*, containing the line 'Great Trinity of Islands', was rarely if ever heard again. In St Kitts, the last trace of any euphoria which may have been engendered on Statehood Day was dispelled on 10 June by the asinine Anguillian attack on Basseterre. In Nevis, a new political atmosphere came into being after the Anguillian UDI of February 1969.

Bradshaw's response to the events of 10 June in which, on no very good grounds, he detected the involvement of members of the opposition party, PAM, led to a vendetta which he pursued unrelentingly until his death in 1978. The hostility this generated between the Labour Party and PAM, with their supporters divided very much along class lines, continued long after he had died, and to a large extent still continues today. In July 1969, as he was constantly having to criticize the legal advice being offered to Bradshaw by the Attorney-General, and because he 'could no longer tolerate the consistent witch-hunting and repression meted out to the Opposition Party', Governor Phillips (now Sir Fred) resigned in disgust and was replaced by a Kittitian, Milton Allen.[1] His *bête noire*, the Attorney-General, was of course Eugene Walwyn, the mediocre lawyer and turncoat who had abandoned the United Nevis Movement (UNM) for the Labour Party on Statehood Day.

That was also the day on which the Locals Councils Ordinance came into force in Nevis, and on 20 April a Council of nine members, all of them nominated, was sworn in at the Court House in Charlestown. Well before the end of the year, in the light of events then taking place in Anguilla, the Government found it politic to repeal the Ordinance and pass the Local Council Act, in order to give Nevis a Council with more power and authority, made up with a majority of elected members. The first elections, for six of the nine seats, took place on 15 December. Five were won by PAM and the sixth by the UNM. Even though the political make-up of the new Council may not have been to Bradshaw's liking, all might have been well had it not been for a tragic event which took place, literally, between St Kitts and Nevis a few months later.

The *Christena* Disaster

By 1970 the ferry which plied between Basseterre and Charlestown, the 66-foot-long motor vessel *Christena,* had been in service for 11 years (p.217 above). It was a sound and reasonably well maintained seaworthy vessel of 22 registered tons (built in Guyana and regularly dry-docked in Barbados) which had been designed to carry five tons of cargo together with a maximum of 150 passengers. It was operated by the Ministry of Communications, Works and Transport with a crew of nine. The captain and the rest of the crew were undoubtedly very familiar with all aspects of the service, completing as they did two round trips daily except on Thursdays and Sundays or during a docking period. Unfortunately, as the ministry responsible for the ferry afforded nothing in the way of supervision of how it was operated, by 1970 the *Christena* was being run by an over-complacent crew with little regard for safety measures, and seemingly none for the total number of passengers the vessel was designed to carry.

The disaster which had been waiting to happen – unavailing complaints about overcrowding on the ferry had been made to the Ministry of Communications, Works and Transport since 1959 – took place in August. On Saturday 1 August the *Christena* left Basseterre on her second run of the day with more than 300 passengers on board. This was twice the number she had been built to carry, and nearly two and a half times more than the legal maximum set by a law passed in 1961 of six passengers for each registered ton. She sailed in a top-heavy condition with her normal two-foot freeboard reduced by half, requiring only the slightest wave motion to set her rolling alarmingly. She also sailed with a deck opening left uncovered, which meant that once any rolling began she was immediately in great danger of being flooded by any water which was shipped. Disaster struck even before the ferry entered The Narrows, the passage between the two islands. A slight swell and the constant jostling of the overcrowded passengers caused the *Christena* to begin rolling just before she reached Nag's Head, the southernmost point of St Kitts, and within a matter of minutes she capsized and sank by the stern in about 60 feet (18 m) of water.

The *Christena* turned turtle about two hours before nightfall, and sank before any distress signal could be sent or any of her life-saving equipment could be used. There were a few small boats within sight of the tragedy, and in the couple of hours or so remaining before nightfall these managed to rescue over 80 people. These, together with a few hardy swimmers who managed to reach Nag's Head, were the only survivors; 91 in all. Another 239 people including the captain and one of the engineers were drowned, and out of these only a third of their bodies were ever recovered.

As the vast majority of those who died came from Nevis, the distress there was immense, affecting nearly every family on the island. This widespread grief was intensified by the way in which Bradshaw, because the *Christena* had been a government vessel operated out of Basseterre with a Kittitian crew, dealt with the disaster. There was no question of anyone in the Government admitting to anything other than the possibility that a divine hand may have had something to do with the sinking. 'In comforting the bereaved', Bradshaw broadcast on the night of the disaster, 'we can know that there is a God who knows what is best for each of us.' Some days later, having told the House of Assembly that '[t]his is no time for apportioning blame or finding culprits' he set up a commission of inquiry under J.D.B. Renwick, the resident puisne judge. Renwick was enjoined to investigate the 'circumstances surrounding the sinking' and 'to make such recommendations' as seemed to him 'meet in the special circumstances of the case'.

After holding public meetings in Charlestown and Basseterre on a total of seven days between 17 August and 5 September, he rendered his findings on 1 October. His report showed up very clearly the perfunctory nature of an inquiry which failed to discover any reason why the *Christena* sank, and carefully avoided any attempt to identify anyone who might have had some responsibility for the tragedy. 'By the terms of my appointment', Renwick wrote,

> I was enjoyed to make such recommendations as may seem
> to me meet in the special circumstances of the case. No
> evidence was given on this aspect during the inquiry and
> unfortunately in the time and with the information
> available I have not been able to produce as comprehensive
> recommendations as I would have liked. Here however are
> a few personal random thoughts.[2]

Such 'random thoughts', dealing with petty details concerning the licensing and crewing of any future ferry, together with lists of the dead, survivors and inquiry witnesses, filled over half of the report. It was accepted without question by the Government, and no further investigation into the loss was ever carried out. As a result, no minister ever resigned, no civil servant was ever dismissed or disciplined, no one ever accepted any responsibility whatsoever, and naturally no thought was ever given to providing bereaved families with any form of compensation.

Nevis Secessionism Rekindled

Not surprisingly, all of this gave a huge boost to the secessionist movement in Nevis. Within a week or so of the publication of the Renwick Report, the Nevis Reformation Party (NRP) was formed; its executive headed by two men who would each later play a key role in the political life of the island – Simeon Daniel and Ivor Stevens. This party campaigned in the general election which took place in May 1971 on the single issue of 'Secession for the Island of Nevis', and achieved success in getting Stevens elected in place of Walwyn. The other Nevis seat was retained by the PAM candidate, Frederick Parris. The pronounced change of mood in Nevis was not lost on Bradshaw, whose party as was to be expected won all seven seats in St Kitts. In November the Local Council Act was amended to give to Nevis Council the increased authority of an all-elected membership. In the elections which followed in December the NRP won six of the nine seats and Simeon Daniel became Council chairman. As there was nothing to prevent a member of the House of Assembly from standing as a candidate, Stevens also ran, won and joined Daniel on the Council.

Exercise of the new powers which the Act conferred on the Council – to raise taxes, acquire property, borrow money, and to pass by-laws – was soon found too restrictive, and in March 1974 a resolution was passed demanding that 'the Government of St Christopher...allow the people of Nevis to administer their own affairs in their own country', and 'approve their demand for secession from the present political union and association with the island of St. Christopher'. This was hardly something Bradshaw, still mortified by the Anguilla situation, was in any mood to consider. Nor was he anything but infuriated a month later when Stevens and Parris attempted to get a similar resolution debated in the House of Assembly. This met with no success in spite of, or perhaps because of, Stevens's valiant effort to stupefy the rest of the members by means of a 25-hour speech spread over three days. The only result of all the talk came the following year after Probyn Inniss, a lawyer who replaced Allen as governor in August, proposed that Bradshaw should meet with members of the Nevis Council and discuss their grievances. Two meetings eventually took place but, as nothing was achieved by either, Bradshaw decided to sidestep any further secessionist moves by the Nevis Council. On 7 November he dissolved the House of Assembly and announced his intention of holding a general election, in which full independence for what he still called the 'unitary state of St. Kitts, Nevis and Anguilla' would be made a key issue.

Stirrings of Independence

Bradshaw's announcement galvanized both PAM and the NRP, neither party seeing any future in a country with Bradshaw as prime minister. 'INDEPENDENCE. That is a luxury we cannot afford', one of the PAM candidates in St Kitts wrote in the party's paper, the *Democrat*, on 22 November,

> We only have to look around at all the other foolish
> mistakes made by the selfish leaders of these fragile
> Lilliputian kingdoms like Grenada to see that political
> independence is meaningless without economic
> independence.

On the other side of The Narrows, the NRP manifesto made it plain that the party intended to 'strive at all costs to gain secession for Nevis from St Kitts – a privilege enjoyed by the island of Nevis prior to 1882'.

The result of the election which took place on 1 December was a foregone conclusion. Labour retained all seven seats in St Kitts, and the two NRP candidates, Daniel and Stevens, carried the day in Nevis with over 80 per cent of the total number of votes cast. PAM did so badly in St Kitts, obtaining only 29 per cent of the total votes, that Herbert gave up the leadership and Simmonds took over as president of the party. On 27 December, the *Democrat*, using words which the anonymous writer was soon going to be forced to eat (and which, surely, provide a clue as to why the party was detested by so many of the working class) reiterated PAM's opposition to independence and announced the party would 'continue to insist that our tiny insular dots, massed by illiteracy and idleness, and lacking the economic basis for self-sustenance, should not attempt the adventurous step of taking our people into the uncertainties of this strange new status'.

The lack of an 'economic basis for self-sustenance' applied to both islands, but the *Democrat* was really only concerned with St Kitts where, as it had been for the previous 20 years or so, the sugar industry was in deep recession. In 1963 the island had been classified as the wealthiest of the Leeward group, but with no growth in per capita income, an increasing population, and an economy 'strongly suspected of having a tendency towards stagnation'. In fact it was worse than this. From over 50,000 tons in 1960, sugar production fell steadily to only 27,000 tons in 1970, with the acreage under cane declining by a third during the same period. The effect this had on the economy was made much worse by the price the island had had to pay for the past prosperity of the sugar industry. According to a British economist writing in 1968 this was

> the retention of an outdated social system that has done much to frustrate the development of the people. Whatever its economic benefits to sugar, there are few doubts that it has been inimical to the development of other sectors of the economy. The problems arise from the inability of people to acquire small parcels of good agricultural land in St Kitts, the concentration of ownership with the minority white group (some of whom are persistent absentees), and the lack of choice for workers of either occupations or employers.[3]

At the end of 1972, with no end to the recession in sight, Bradshaw and his Government entered into an agreement with the estate owners, represented by the St Kitts Sugar Producers' Association, to try to rehabilitate the industry by means of a three-year 'Sugar Industry Rescue Operation' (SIRO) with a budget of EC$3,600,000. At much the same time, in order to start providing workers with some alternative means of employment, some effort was put into attracting small manufacturing industries to the island by means of tax breaks and other fiscal incentives.

The Government saw no return on the money invested in SIRO, as the average annual amount of sugar produced during its three-year life was only 25,000 tons. Towards the end of 1974, after new negotiations with the Sugar Producers' Association about the future of the industry had all ended in deadlock, it was decided to nationalize the sugar estates in accordance with a plan drawn up four years earlier. Although no agreement could be reached with the SPA about the amount of compensation which was to be paid – something which was to remain in dispute for another 12 years or more – the Sugar Estate Lands Acquisition Act was passed in February 1975. Following the acquisition of the sugar factory from its British owners for £1,000,000 at the end of the following year, the people of St Kitts became the sole possessors of the industry which had dominated life on the island for the previous three centuries.

Bradshaw's nationalization of the land met with wide approval. His decision to persevere with the production of sugar, through the National Agricultural Corporation set up to manage the estates, and the Sugar Manufacturing Corporation established to operate the factory, on the other hand was not so welcome. The young, by and large, had renounced agricultural labour as a means of livelihood, the market for sugar was all set to collapse, and it was readily apparent that, as St Kitts by this time produced less than 1 per cent of the world's sugar, the industry had no long-term future. Retention of the land for the growing of sugar-cane prevented any of it from being used for other crops or sold off for other purposes. This was in complete contrast to the situation in Nevis where by this time a considerable amount of land which had been, and was still being, acquired by the government was made available to private purchasers, particularly small farmers. In Nevis in 1975 there were 118 private smallholdings of around 5 acres (2 ha), compared with only 36 in St Kitts, and 74 farms with an average of 196 acres (79 ha).

Regardless of the fragile state of the economy and the very obvious differences which existed, both in politics and in society, between the two islands, Bradshaw took the result of the 1975 election as giving him a mandate for independence. In a broadcast to mark the ninth anniversary of Associated Statehood on 27 February 1976, he claimed the islands were approaching 'the independence which we have freely and deliberately decreed for ourselves', and called for 'all as brothers and sisters [to] link hands together and say "Out Statehood, in Independence"'. He had a number of reasons for wanting to end statehood, but none was spelt out then or at any other time. One concerned the litigation which had followed the nationalization of the sugar industry, relating mainly to the amount of compensation paid to the former owners of the estates, which he believed would be easier to bring to an end in an independent country. A second concerned the larger immigration quota an independent St Kitts-Nevis would obtain in connection with the Virgin Islands of the United States, which had been the favoured destination of migrants from the state since Britain had imposed its ban in the 1960s. The third reason was a more personal one: Bradshaw by this time knew he was suffering from a severe, life-threatening form of cancer, and dearly wished before it was too late to assume the office of prime minister of a totally independent country he had done so much to create.

The talks with the British government which followed in March and April about an independent St Kitts-Nevis, besides being inconclusive, showed up only too well the huge rift that existed between the two islands. During the first round of talks Bradshaw proposed that the state should become independent six months later, on 16 September. After the second round, in which Daniel participated and made it clear that neither this nor any other date would be acceptable to the people of Nevis, Bradshaw established an Independence Celebrations Planning Committee. While this committee then set about its business in Basseterre, both PAM and the NRP got busy organizing opposition to its purpose. In St Kitts, PAM began drumming up support for a petition to the Queen, and in August in

Nevis the NRP held a referendum on the question 'do you support seces-sion for Nevis from St Kitts?' Some 3000 signatures were obtained on the petition, which called for 'Her Majesty's Government to require the St Kitts Government...to hold a Referendum' and to delay independence 'until the people of this State have given their decision as to whether or not such a Constitutional change is desirable'. In Nevis, where more people voted in the NRP referendum than had done so at the last election, 4193 of the 4220 votes cast were in favour of secession.

Other than to rule his proposed date for independence out of the ques-tion (the committee was dissolved in October) neither the petition nor the Nevis referendum had much effect on Bradshaw who, despite his failing health, attended a further round of talks in London in March 1977. These achieved no more than those of the previous year. Daniel, who again was part of the delegation, made it plain that, rather than become independent in asso-ciation with St Kitts, Nevis preferred to secede and, like Anguilla, resume colonial status. The British government in response rejected any idea of reac-quiring yet another colony, and ended the talks with a request for Bradshaw and Daniel to seek some common ground once they returned home.

This was asking more than either Bradshaw, who had still not accepted that Anguilla would never again be part of the state, or Daniel, secure in the knowledge that virtually the entire electorate of Nevis wanted nothing more than to emulate the example set by Anguilla, could ever hope to achieve. Nothing was done to find a way out of the situation and in June Bradshaw returned to England to attend the Queen's Silver Jubilee celebrations. Later in the year, after he had paid an official visit to Nigeria and before he was able to give any fresh impetus to breaking the deadlock, he became seriously ill. In January 1978 he was operated on for lung cancer in England, and after his return to St Kitts remained bedridden until his death on 23 May.

Robert Llewellyn Bradshaw

Bradshaw died at the age of 61 with a mixed reputation. To his working-class supporters in St Kitts, by whom he was known as 'Papa', he was a hero in the mould of Martin Luther King; to his political opponents he was an unbending and vindictive foe; to the people of Anguilla and Nevis he was an authoritarian figure often compared with the Haitian dictator 'Papa Doc' Duvalier; to British ministers and officials he appeared as a stiff-necked obstructionist cum rabble-rouser too big for his boots; and to many white British and American observers, because of his penchant for uni-forms and elegant tailoring, he was often viewed as no more than a figure of fun. There was more than a grain of truth in all of these perceptions, but no more than was to be expected of a natural leader determined, perhaps, to be all things to all men.

His adulation by the workers of St Kitts was well earned, as their dire condition before he assumed leadership of the Trades and Labour Union demonstrated only too well. The unforgiving nature of his attitude towards Herbert and the rest of the PAM leadership reflected ingrained class and colour differences – and all that these had meant to people like him in the past – rather than to any diversity in political views. He was hardly responsible for the centuries of neglect which had led to the impoverishment of Anguilla by 1967 when the revolution took place, and the Anguillians were wrong to then concentrate on his failings rather than those of successive British governments. The much-quoted threats to 'turn Anguilla into a desert' or 'put salt in their coffee, bones in their rice and sand in their sugar' or 'put bones in their rice and pepper in their soup' which Bradshaw is supposed to have issued after the revolution are either apocryphal or no more than the meaningless and very understandable outbursts of a frustrated man. Even more understandable, in the light of what took place in Anguilla, is the unbending position he then adopted towards any suggestion of secession for Nevis, and the implacable face he presented in all his further dealings with the British government.

Bradshaw was well aware of the style of leadership which would have the most appeal to his supporters, and this was reflected in his lifestyle, his manner of public speaking and in the way he dressed. His most well-known aphorism, 'studyation is better than education', may have been quoted since in order to belittle his learning, but in fact it was an extremely pithy way of saying that the lack of a formal education was no disadvantage to any literate person with the determination to succeed. He himself was a prime example of a self-educated man, as Sir Fred Phillips had been made aware during his time as governor. 'Robert Bradshaw's specialities lay in the fields of antiques, wines and matters of heraldry', Phillips recorded later,

> He could lecture for hours on antiques, of which he had them to the value of thousands of pounds….
>
> He was also an oenologist, and one day he was giving me a lecture on the different types of red and white wines, when I interrupted him to say I had no interest in the subject….
>
> In the matter of heraldry, he should have been one of the 'Dragons' or 'Heralds' in the College of Arms in the United Kingdom….
>
> He was also an authority on rare and antique books….[4]

While such attributes may not have been of any great interest to the man in the cane field, this was not the case when it came to the way in which

Bradshaw dressed and comported himself. As an astute modern comment-
ator on his leadership has noted, '[t]here was certainly no precedent on
how the emergent West Indian political leader was to dress and Bradshaw
unabashedly fabricated a hybrid colourful veneer that a allowed him to
play the enigmatic role of the "great little man"'.[5] With natural elegance
and an inbred sense of style, and with the dress and uniforms of a colonial
administration and its attendant white society providing the only pattern
on which he could base his own wardrobe, it is small wonder that the
public took much interest in his appearance throughout his life. His supporters enjoyed seeing him in the role of a man of substance and style, but
in the case of the people from whom he took his lead his adoption of the
trappings of authority was frequently taken as an affront.

'[T]he Member for Trade and Production could not restrain his sartor-
ial tendencies', was Sir Kenneth Blackburne's sarcastic comment on a visit
he made to St Kitts in 1953, 'and arrived to conduct me round the livestock station arrayed, like any Farmer Giles, in boots, leggings and
breeches'.[6] Such sarcasm continued for the rest of Bradshaw's life but
without denting in any way his *amour propre*. Over the next quarter of a
century, to the appreciative delight of his followers, and the chagrin of
many white observers, he demonstrated that a black West Indian could
wear and appear impressive in anything from an estate manager's outfit to
morning dress and, occasionally after 1967, an army officer's uniform.

What might have happened to the islands he led into statehood, and was
attempting to take into full independence, had he not died when he did, it is
impossible to say. His death had ramifications for both St Kitts and Nevis,
and their subsequent history might well have been quite different had he
lived longer. As it was, and because of the events which followed his death,
his memory remained unhonoured until 1995 when Golden Rock Airport
was renamed the Robert Llewellyn Bradshaw International Airport. Three
years later, under the National Honours Act he was recognized, very appropriately, as the country's first national hero. No better words can be found to
describe the man whose name was honoured in this way than those which
had been written over 300 years earlier, following the death of a much earlier
important figure in the history of St Kitts: Robert Bradshaw, like the
Chevalier Phillipe de Lonvilliers de Poincy, was

> A man of spirit, a great politician, generous on occasions,
> affecting the grand manner in his festivities and building
> projects, well disposed towards his friends and servants
> whose fortunes he sometimes made, subject to bias and
> severe to excess toward those who did not have his
> interests at heart.[7]

24

Independence

Bradshaw's death had a marked effect on the subsequent history of St Kitts and Nevis. He died in May 1978, and the country in which he had been the outstanding political figure during the 30 years leading up to his death achieved full independence in September 1983. His presence during this period was to be sorely missed and, as was to be amply demonstrated in the long run-up to independence, there was no one truly capable of filling his shoes. During this period of nearly five and a half years, while politicians in both islands found it easy to emulate his faults – carrying vindictiveness, opportunism and mendacity to new levels – none could display any of his statesmanship. Not that they should be judged alone: there was little honour and much in the way of opportunism and hypocrisy to be found among the British ministers and officials with whom they had to negotiate. In recounting the events leading up to independence it is difficult to identify anyone among the politicians taking part, in St Kitts, Nevis or Britain, who can be said to have behaved throughout in a completely honest, dignified and statesmanlike manner.

Southwell's succession to the premiership, after long years as Bradshaw's deputy, did not take place without opposition being voiced by other members of the Labour Party leadership. Even though he had already served a term as premier, and had lived in St Kitts for over 40 years, because he had not been born in either St Kitts or Nevis 'there was a sentiment within the party that...[h]e should not lead the islands into independence'.[1] The narrow-minded objectors eventually gave way, mollified by Southwell's agreement to assume an ambassadorial role within a year or so, and undoubtedly also by the knowledge that he was far from being in the best of health. He was so ill in fact that his premiership lasted barely a year. The row about his succession took place behind closed doors, but six months later the entire population of both islands was provided with a controversy which showed only too clearly the way political life was all set to develop. In January 1979 a by-election took place for the Central Basseterre seat which had been held by Bradshaw, contested for the Labour Party by Anthony Ribeiro, and for PAM by the party's leader Kennedy Simmonds. Ribeiro won, but the count was so close – a matter of

13 votes – that Simmonds immediately challenged the result by means of a High Court petition.

While this process was under way, Southwell and Daniel went to London in March to attend yet another round of talks about independence. Once again these ended in deadlock; Southwell was ill and had limited negotiating skills, while Daniel flatly refused to discuss any proposal which involved Nevis becoming independent in association with St Kitts. Two months later, while attending a meeting in St Lucia, Southwell collapsed and died. He was then 66 years of age. His body was returned to St Kitts and, after a state funeral bearing little relation in scope or organization to that which had been given to Bradshaw a year earlier, he was buried in Springfield Cemetery.[2]

The Premiership of Lee Moore

Southwell was succeeded by a 40-year-old barrister named Lee Moore, who, after being elected to the House of Assembly eight years earlier, had served as attorney-general. Although by all accounts well versed in jurisprudence, he soon proved to be petty-minded, singularly lacking in political nous, and ignorant of the meaning of parliamentary democracy. This was demonstrated soon after he had taken office when, following a recount of the Central Basseterre by-election results ordered by the High Court, the PAM candidate was found to have won by 22 votes. As soon as this was announced, in order to prevent Simmonds from being sworn in and able to take his seat, Moore suspended all further sittings of the House of Assembly. This was a move hardly likely to meet with the approval of the official Opposition, in the persons of Daniel and Stevens, as was made obvious to Moore during the visits he paid to Nevis in June and July. Made in order to try to reach some agreement with Daniel about independence in advance of a meeting scheduled to take place in August with the Minister of State in the Foreign and Commonwealth Office, the visits were totally unsuccessful.

Daniel was one of the people who accompanied Moore to the talks which were held in Antigua on 8 August. The Minister was Nicholas Ridley, a right-wing politician who had held the job since May when a Conservative Government under Margaret Thatcher had been elected in Britain. He heard nothing from either Moore or Daniel which his predecessor in the Labour Government had not heard: Moore insisting on independence for a unified state of St Kitts-Nevis, while Daniel reiterated the Nevisian demand for separation. In the end all Ridley could do was to announce 'that the British Government wished to place no obstacle in the way of the Associated State advancing to independence', and offer Daniel 'constitutional talks to find a way of safeguarding the interests of the people of Nevis if they chose to move to independence with St Kitts'. This offer meant very little. The Thatcher Government wanted to end the concept of Associated Statehood as quickly as possible; and as Grenada and Dominica were already independent and St Lucia and St Vincent were just about to become so, this left only Antigua and St Kitts-Nevis to be dealt with. Ridley could offer the Nevisians further talks, but he made it quite plain

> that the British Government's position was that they
> would not be prepared to accept Nevis as a British
> dependency and that if they were to seek independence
> separately from St Kitts they would not be eligible for
> British aid.[3]

The offer of further 'constitutional talks', and the threat to an independent Nevis of being cut off from all British support, had some effect on public opinion in the island. This was particularly so after Moore, soon after his return from Antigua, held public meetings in Charlestown and Gingerland and spelt out the consequences of secession. However, the change was not enough to prevent the NRP, campaigning mainly on this very issue, from retaining all nine seats on the Local Council when elections took place on 6 December.

One week later a new round of independence talks began in London between Ridley, a four-man delegation under Moore from St Kitts, and a seven-strong team from Nevis headed by Daniel. The numbers attending hardly mattered; Ridley presided in his best bullying manner and the talks lasted barely two days. At the end of the second day, overriding all objections from Daniel and his delegation, he announced that 'subject to the satisfactory completion of the customary consultations and constitutional processes, St. Kitts-Nevis should move to independence as a unitary state as early as possible in 1980'.

Daniel's demand that the people of Nevis should first be given the chance to vote in a referendum, on whether the island should be part of this unitary state, was counteracted by Moore's proposal that such a referendum be held three years after independence had taken place. In the end Ridley, 'after a fruitless search for any acceptable compromise', pronounced that it should 'be held within 18 months from the date of independence'. Finally, and just as importantly for the British, an agreement was reached

> between the Minister of State and the Premier that formal
> constitutional processes would be put into effect to

separate Anguilla from the Associated State of St. Kitts-
Nevis-Anguilla as early as possible in 1980 and to provide
for her status as a separate British dependency.[4]

Soon after his return home, so confident was Moore that independence
was now a foregone conclusion and that the talks had made his premiership unassailable that he revived the Independence Celebrations Planning
Committee, dissolved Parliament, and called a general election.

A Change of Government

Moore was far too sanguine, and not a sufficiently astute enough politician
to realize that such confidence was misplaced. In St Kitts, while his own
party campaigned with independence as just one of a number of issues, the
PAM campaign was based largely on opposition to the subject. Any
decision about independence, Simmonds had made clear in an article in the
Democrat the previous August, could only be made by the people, 'after
they have had an opportunity to study and understand all the issues
involved', through a referendum. In Nevis the NRP contested the election
on the single issue of continuing 'to seek secession' for the island 'at all
costs'.

The election took place on 19 February. As was to be expected the two
NRP candidates, Daniel and Stevens, had no trouble in retaining their seats
in Nevis, but a sea change took place in St Kitts. There, enough voters
were opposed to independence or had become disenchanted by Moore's
leadership – particularly by the way he had treated Simmonds after the
previous year's by-election – to reduce the number of seats won by the
Labour Party from seven to four. The other three went to Simmonds and
two of his PAM colleagues. Within hours of the results being known,
Simmonds had contacted Daniel and Stevens in Nevis, made them offers
they lost little time in accepting, and announced the formation under his
leadership of a new five-man Government. In spite of their long opposition to central government, and the fact that they had been returned by
their constituents after campaigning solely on the issue of secession,
neither of the NRP representatives had been able to resist the status and
perquisites of office as proffered by Simmonds. Daniel, who became minister of finance, lost no time in trying to justify his acceptance of the post.
'I have not abandoned the demand for secession for Nevis', he broadcast
the next day, adding

> I must make it clear that there is no affiliation between the
> Nevis Reformation Party and the People's Action

Movement. My colleague Mr Stevens and I have agreed to
work in a Coalition Government, and we reserve the right
to withdraw our support from the government at any time
when we do not get what we want. I have accepted the
position…in order to further the interests of Nevis.

The more imperious Stevens announced in the House of Assembly a
month later that the coalition was no more than a 'marriage of convenience'.
before commenting that

> Some people want to know how we could join with the
> People's Action Movement, and how long the coalition
> would last. …it was expedient for us to do so, and when
> we are ready to end it they will know. The people of Nevis
> stand firm on their demand for self-determination for
> Nevis. Our position is secession, ever, recession never.[5]

Simmonds had no option but to put up with such talk, particularly as one
of the first things he had to deal with as premier was the agreement
reached between his predecessor and the British government over separat-
ing Anguilla from the state. The sentiments expressed by the two NRP
ministers made it impossible for him to even attempt to get the House of
Assembly to pass a bill requesting Britain to carry out the separation by
Order-in-Council: if such an act was good enough to end Anguilla's relationship with the state, might not something similar also be sufficient in
the case of Nevis? The Premier's dilemma was appreciated in London,
where Ridley informed the House of Commons in April that it was 'not
easy for the representatives of either Nevis or St Kitts to request formally
through the legislature that Her Majesty's Government separate Anguilla'.
In the end all Simmonds felt able to do was to tell the House of Assembly
that the Anguillians should be free to decide their own future, and that he
was not prepared to put any obstacle in their way. The British government
responded by passing the 1980 Anguilla Act and appointing 19 December
'as the day on which Anguilla shall cease to form part of the territory of
the associated state of St Christopher, Nevis and Anguilla'.

The way in which Britain ended Anguilla's association with the state
passed without unduly disturbing either Daniel or Stevens, but the following year it provided the disconsolate Moore, one of the four Labour Party
members who formed the official Opposition, with a means of seeking
vengeance for his loss of the premiership. Early in 1981 eight bills were
passed, each with an introductory clause stating it had been enacted by the
'House of Assembly of St Christopher and Nevis'. Ignoring the fact that
as premier in 1979 he had been in wholehearted agreement with the separation of Anguilla, he now induced one of his colleagues, Esmond Payne,

to petition the High Court to declare that these bills contravened the constitution by not referring to the state as being that of 'St Christopher, Nevis and Anguilla'. Much to his delight, when the High Court hearing took place in July, Justice Horace Mitchell, lost in the realms of jurisprudence, decided that the British Act 'could not be construed as having any effect whatsoever in altering the Constitution of the State' and upheld the petition.

Simmonds was largely unperturbed, and having instructed the Attorney-General to instigate an appeal, turned his attention to a more pressing and rather less esoteric constitutional matter involving his Government's relationship with the Governor, Sir Probyn Inniss. This concerned the refusal by Inniss to give his assent to a bill passed earlier in the year before the High Court hearing, on the grounds that to do so in the light of Mitchell's decision would be to act in an unconstitutional manner. The relationship between the Governor (who it should be recalled had been appointed on Bradshaw's recommendation) and the Premier had already been strained by a refusal by Inniss to remove or discipline a wayward civil servant, a disagreement over the level of an increase in gubernatorial emoluments, and a rancorous exchange of letters. Following the Governor's refusal to give his assent to the bill, Simmonds was in no mood to temporize, and at the end of July he informed Inniss that he had 'no intention of wasting more time on this fruitless and acrimonious exchange of correspondence' and that 'I shall expect to be informed of your resignation shortly.' Such a peremptory demand was too much for the Governor's *amour propre*, but in refusing to accede to Simmonds's demand for his resignation he let himself in for a wholly unnecessary and very undignified dismissal. In November, following the Premier's request to the Queen to withdraw the Governor's commission, a Royal Navy frigate landed an officer by helicopter at Basseterre, and Inniss was served with a document revoking his appointment and given three days to vacate Government House. He was replaced by a more compliant lawyer, Clement Arrindell, who was to remain the Queen's representative for the next 14 years. Four months later, Mitchell's decision with regard to Payne's petition was overturned by the Court of Appeal, and nothing more was heard of the matter. This was just as well for Simmonds, as by the spring of 1982 a crisis in the sugar industry and pressure from the British government about independence were giving him rather more important things to worry about than pettifogging and totally immaterial legal arguments over the removal of a redundant word from the constitution.

On 13 January Simmonds had been obliged to broadcast on radio and television his concerns about 'the critical situation affecting the sugar industry', and the effect this was having on the economy. Up until a year earlier the price of sugar on the world market was £400 per ton. Prospects were so good that all the international sugar brokers operating in the United Kingdom and the United States advised us strongly against selling any sugar so early in 1981, as they were confident that the price of sugar would rise above £400.

Regrettably, the rise in world prices forecast by these brokers turned out to be just as ephemeral as that of the opinion on the constitution reached by Justice Horace Mitchell. 'Instead of rising above £400 per ton', Simmonds continued starkly, using language which none of his listeners could fail to comprehend,

the price of sugar dropped to about £160 per ton.... Sugar production now costs £200 per ton, whereas the world price is just £160. This means it now costs much more to produce a ton of sugar than we get when we sell the same ton of sugar.

An enormous amount of money has been spent in saving the crop from the ravages of smut disease. About one third of the entire acreage was diseased....

NACO, the field side of the industry, which employs some five thousand sugar workers, already carried a huge overdraft because the industry has been losing money since NACO was started in 1975. The present overdraft is about thirty-three million dollars...if nothing is done to try to limit the increasing overdraft, the sugar industry itself will soon disappear.[6]

As the industry was still the mainstay of the economy he could do little but finish his broadcast by stressing that the country could not 'afford to ignore this serious warning', and that it was 'time for every well-meaning citizen to rally to the cause of this country...put community before self [and] above personal ambitions....[and] do everything in our power to ensure that the industry survives'. There was very little else to fall back on: a few light manufacturing and assembling factories on the outskirts of Basseterre, and a nascent tourist industry smaller than that of any country other than Dominica in the whole of the Eastern Caribbean.

Progress Towards Independence

After Antigua and Barbuda became independent in November 1981, the British government became even keener to end the concept of Associated

Statehood altogether, and pressure began to be applied on Simmonds to continue from where Moore had left off at the end of 1979. This placed him in an awkward position, as in the run-up to the election which had brought his Government into power both PAM and the NRP had campaigned against independence. He temporized to begin with, informing the nation in a New Year's Day broadcast that the Government would 'not drop independence on this country like a bomb, but we are beginning the process of seeking this necessary constitutional advancement'. It would have been well if he had said nothing more, as in the light of what he was to tell the same audience about the sugar industry less than two weeks later, there was little truth in the rest of his statement:

> We do it not because others have achieved it, but because
> we have made significant progress in coming to grips with
> the very serious problem of unemployment, and made
> visible and meaningful progress in the fields of tourism,
> industrialization, agricultural diversification, housing,
> health and education.[7]

But whatever he had to say to the people of St Kitts and Nevis was of no consequence to the British government, and in May an expert in constitutional matters was despatched from London to assist in the drawing up of a White Paper which would outline a proposed constitution for an independent St Kitts-Nevis. The White Paper, *Constitutional Proposals for Saint Christopher and Nevis,* was published on 26 July with the public given less than three months in which to discuss its contents before a resolution on independence was due to be raised in the House of Assembly. It was hardly a document which lived up to its claim of having been compiled 'after lengthy negotiation and discussions', but rather betrayed all the signs of having been cobbled together in a hurry. Nor could its readers place complete faith in its probity, as it claimed that 'in the campaign prior to the last General Election...the Government and Opposition Parties in St Kitts supported the concept of Independence', and that the Government possessed 'a clear mandate from the electorate to proceed to Independence'. As the one party which had campaigned in favour of independence had ended up by losing the election, many readers must have found it difficult to accept such statements at face value, or to think highly of the White Paper as a whole.

Moore and his three colleagues in the Opposition were immediately placed in a quandary, as although the Labour Party had been pressing for independence since Bradshaw's day no one in the party had ever considered anything other than a Labour Government being in power at the time of independence. Their initial response was in the form of a Green Paper entitled *In Place of Strife,* which was published on 2 August.

Only seven pages long, this was another document written and published in a hurry. Two-thirds of it was taken up in criticizing the stance on independence previously taken by PAM and the NRP, and in trying to justify why the Labour Party was no longer quite so keen on the idea. The latter boiled down to now deciding there was a need for a general election to take place before any further steps could be taken towards independence, and to a rejection of the Government's plans for 'an arrangement between the two islands of St Kitts and Nevis'. The latter, which was intended to stifle any further demand for secession from the people of Nevis, was a proposal to allow the island not only to be represented in a national legislature, but also to be given a separate legislature with exclusive authority in matters such as health, education and welfare. Moore and the Labour Party found this 'completely unacceptable'. What was good enough for Nevis was also good enough for St Kitts, and the final third of the Green Paper contained a demand that each island should 'possess equally the right of self-determination' with each having 'its own separate Constitution, legislature, government and political system' under 'a Treaty of Friendship and Co-operation'.

The Labour Party's choice of title for the Green Paper was perhaps unfortunate, considering the number of demonstrations which followed publication of *In Place of Strife*, and the incidents of violence that took place at one or two of the public meetings organized by the party to protest about the contents of the White Paper. One member of the party's executive, Fidel O'Flaherty, was arrested and charged with six criminal offences at a meeting held on 23 August, and the party's chairman, Fitzroy Bryant, was charged with incitement at another meeting six days later. In September, protest rallies, involving considerable numbers of people, took place in Basseterre and in a number of villages in the north of the island. Moore later estimated that possibly 9000 people took part in the last of these, held on 18 September in Basseterre. 'In any event', he was to recall three months later, 'the general view was that no one could remember a bigger march having ever taken place before in St. Kitts'. The Government's response, other than to take action against O'Flaherty and Bryant, was limited to drumming up support for the White Paper amongst PAM supporters at a convention held at the party's headquarters. On 5 October when the House of Assembly was convened in order to approve the White Paper, the Labour Party organized a final public protest outside the building, and the four members of the Opposition made their own form of protest by walking out before the resolution was put to the vote. In view of the White Paper's proposals for Nevis, the two NRP members of the Government had no such qualms and the following day a formal request for independence was made to the British government.

This was what the Foreign and Commonwealth Office had been waiting for, and two weeks later the Minister of State – now Cranley Onslow – paid a flying visit to St Kitts. Arriving on 20 October and departing the next day gave him just enough time to fix a date for a constitutional conference with Simmonds, have quick look around St Kitts, pay a perfunctory visit to Nevis, and to receive a petition from the Leader of the Opposition protesting against the contents of the Government's White Paper. It is not known what Onslow did with the petition but, as according to Moore it had been signed by some 10,000 people, it is difficult to see how a few weeks later he could assert 'My visits in October to Saint Christopher and to Nevis, brief though they were strengthened my belief that independence is the wish of the people in both islands'.[8]

An Independent Federation

Onslow made this somewhat disingenuous statement in his opening address to the Constitutional Conference which began in London on 7 December. The conference lasted for nine days, and was attended by Simmonds at the head of a 17-strong delegation which included Daniel, Stevens and Herbert, and a much smaller Opposition delegation led by Moore. It resulted in the drawing up of an Independence Constitution for 'a sovereign democratic federal state which should be described as the Federation of Saint Christopher and Nevis', with Nevis being given both autonomy within the federation and the means to secede.

Under the new constitution the House of Assembly would become a National Assembly which, after the next general election, would have a total of 14 seats. These would be filled by eight elected members from St Kitts, three elected members from Nevis, and three nominated members to be styled senators. The governor would become the governor-general, with a deputy governor-general in Nevis, which was to have its own Assembly of five elected and three nominated members under a premier. The provisions made for Nevis to secede from the federation required

> the introduction and the passage of a bill in the Nevis
> Assembly supported by a two-thirds majority of the elected
> members...subsequently need[ing] to be approved by a
> referendum in Nevis by not less than two-thirds of the votes
> cast by persons registered on the Parliamentary electoral roll.[9]

The date set for independence was the following September. Moore and his team, who had demonstrated their opposition to 'provisions which allowed for the unilateral secession of Nevis, or for the Ministers of an administration in Nevis to be Ministers in the federal administration' by walking out of the conference from time to time, showed their objection to this by refusing to attend the closing session or to sign the conference report.

However, with the date for independence set, once everyone had returned home the stance previously adopted by Moore and the Labour Party could no longer be maintained. At the end of a three-day debate in the House of Assembly in March, the Opposition, after merely pressing for a few minor amendments, joined the Government in passing a resolution asking Britain for termination of Associated Statehood and a new constitution. Although the granting of this request was a foregone conclusion, the approval of the necessary Order by the British government was not obtained without at least one voice querying its propriety. During a debate in the House of Commons on 5 May the Opposition spokesman, George Robertson, said with regard to independence for St Kitts and Nevis that 'no clear evidence, apart from the legislative assembly's majority, had been produced to show the will of the people on this issue'. Although he and the Opposition felt the islands deserved 'a more stable and more popularly based constitution to justify the Order' they were not prepared to vote against the granting of independence. 'But', he ended 'we have a right to point out that a wholly unnecessary burden has been placed on the country at its birth'. It is unlikely that Onslow or anyone else in the British government was at all disconcerted by Robertson's remarks. Following an even shorter debate in the House of Lords on 9 May the new constitution was approved, and the way was clear for it to come into force four months later.

St Kitts and Nevis became independent at midnight on 18 September, with the joy and rejoicing the world had come to expect on such an occasion being much subdued by the sour faces, contumelious language and disruptive activities of the leaders and ardent supporters of the Labour Party. Princess Margaret, representing the Queen, made a short unmemorable speech of the sort she had already made while performing the same role in Jamaica in 1962, Dominica in 1978, and Antigua in 1981. Simmonds, now the country's first prime minister, responded with a long, turgid discourse, expressing views which his local audience must have found hard to relate to the reality of life in St Kitts or Nevis, and which probably caused some of the more worldly among the numerous visiting dignitaries to shake their heads in disbelief.

He began with a neo-Nehruan reference to 'the Universe', across which 'the sun is setting on colonialism and in the soft amber glow of dawn's first light there is born to the world a new nation', but soon moved on to

> the task of developing from our slender resources a
> heritage to be enjoyed by the present generations and by

generations yet unborn. We must commit ourselves to
work harder and be more productive. We must make our
hills and valleys produce the food we need for our own use
and for the needs of industry and tourism. The sea around
us must be made to give of its bounty, whether it be
animal, plant or mineral.

But self-sufficiency alone was not enough for a new nation with an area no
larger than that of Martha's Vineyard, with a population of 43,000 people. The
Prime Minister also felt St Kitts and Nevis had a role to play in world affairs:

I will say to my international brothers and sisters that we
join your ranks fully respecting the sovereignty of every
nation, and insisting upon the same respect in return…we
can settle our disputes without resort to the needless
violence of war. We are prepared to be friends of all, and we
seek no ideological converts, and the converse holds true.

We will work for the establishment of a world where in
our time implements of war can be turned into instruments
of production, and where all men recognize that the
world's bounty should be shared by the world's people.[10]

And so, on 19 September 1983, St Kitts and Nevis ended a connection
with Britain which had lasted for over 350 years. The new state became the
eighth smallest country in the world, taking its place slightly ahead of
Liechtenstein between the Marshall Islands and the Seychelles; with a
population the same as that of the New York town of Poughkeepsie or the
English town of Banbury; and with a minute Exclusion Zone (the
surrounding sea which had to 'be made to give of its bounty') confined by
the Economic Exclusion Zones of Britain (Montserrat), France
(St Bartholomew), Holland (St Eustatius), Venezuela (Aves Island) and
Antigua and Barbuda. The prospects for such a state were hardly rosy, as
was made plain in a book published in Basseterre before the end of the
year. 'Basically, the future depends on the outcome of two issues', wrote
the former Governor, Sir Probyn Inniss,

One is, on how long the so-called Federation of St Kitts
and Nevis lasts. The islands have previously been involved
in two Federations, both of which have failed. The omens
are not favourable because in addition the arrangements
are based entirely on personal and political expediency.
The other factor on which the future depends would be
how soon the Politics of Vengeance which grips St Kitts
will end.[11]

Afterword

Neither of the two issues on which in 1983 Inniss considered the future of the state depended had been resolved by the time this book was nearing completion 20 years later. The first signs of an end to the coalition formed by PAM and the NRP became apparent four years after independence when a new party, the Concerned Citizens' Movement (CCM), was formed in Nevis under a man named Vance Amory. In 1992 the CCM defeated the NRP in the Nevis Island Assembly elections and Amory took over as the island's premier, a change which then had an effect on the elections for the federal government a year later. The election results – with PAM losing four of the seats in St Kitts to the Labour Party, and the NRP losing two of the three Nevis seats to the CCM – reflected a growing disenchantment with the PAM/NRP coalition, which had easily won the elections of 1984 and 1989 but was by now tainted with scandal.

Simmonds was only able to hang on to power because the two CCM representatives refused to associate themselves with either PAM or the Labour Party. The protest which followed, instigated by the Labour Party under a new leader named Denzil Douglas, eventually became so violent that a state of emergency had to be imposed for two weeks, with troops brought in from other islands to restore order. The Simmonds Government managed to survive the crisis but only until another election was forced in 1995 when, after 15 years in Opposition, the Labour Party was once again swept into office with Douglas as the new prime minister.

This change did nothing to improve the relationship between Nevis and St Kitts, particularly after July 1998 when Douglas announced the setting of a Constitutional Review Commission to review the 1983 Independence Constitution. A month later the Premier of Nevis, Amory, exercised his constitutional right to call for the secession of Nevis by means of a referendum. Fortunately for the Federation and Douglas, the NRP still retained some support among the people of Nevis, and although 62 per cent of the electorate voted in favour of secession this was still less than the required two-thirds. Perhaps equally fortunately, as far as Amory was concerned, the Constitutional Review Commission, headed by Sir Fred Phillips (p.262 above), completed only the first stages of its work before being halted in 1999 under circumstances which remain far from clear. In February 2003 both parties in Nevis decided to take no further part in federal elections and, as the twentieth anniversary of independence approached, Amory once again announced his intention to hold a referendum on secession.

Notes

Detail of books and articles given here in abbreviated form will be found in the Bibliography.

Foreword

1. The phrase appears in, of all things, 'Kanhai: A Study in Confidence', an article about the Guyanese cricketer Rohan Kanhai in the issue of *New World* published to commemorate Guyanese independence in 1966.

Chapter 2: The Early Inhabitants

1. Branch, p.330.
2. Ibid. p.331.
3. Douglas, p.3.

Chapter 3: The European Discovery

1. Cameron, p.9.
2. Ibid. p.96.
3. Merrill, p.14.
4. K.R. Andrews, p.237.
5. Harlow (1925), p.1.

Chapter 4: The Settlement of St Christopher

1. Burns (1954), p.188.
2. Harlow (1925), p.2.
3. The chronology of the early history of St Christopher, although it has been thoroughly investigated by several notable historians, remains imprecise. The early records are limited and largely unhelpful as many events were only recorded long after they had taken place. As such accounts rarely give an exact date for any happening, no entirely definitive chronology can be drawn up, and nothing more than 'a best guess' is possible. With regard to the arrival of d'Esnambuc in 1625, while it is quite possible that this could have taken place before Warner left for England, my own view (equally as valid as any other) is that it did not.
4. Sheridan (1994), p.85.
5. Lanaghan (1844), vol. 2, p.305.
6. E. Williams (1963), p.254.
7. Emmer and Carrera Damas, p.123.
8. Harlow (1925), p.2.

9. Ibid. p.2.
10. For example, see James Ferguson, *A Traveller's History of the Caribbean*, Moreton-in-Marsh, 1998, p.66, or Hubbard (2002), p.18.
11. Harlow (1925), p.93.

Chapter 5: Establishing Proprietary Government

1. E. Williams (1963), p.279.
2. Mims, p.20.
3. Harlow (1925), p.5.
4. Williamson, p.68.
5. Harlow (1925), p.10.
6. Ibid. p.10.
7. Ibid. p.87.
8. Mims, p.22.
9. Harlow (1925), p.14.

Chapter 6: Proprietary Rule and its Demise

1. Firth, p.30.
2. E. Williams (1963), p.283.
3. Mims, p.41.
4. Bennett, p.376.
5. Ibid.
6. Lindeström, p.78.
7. Mims, p.48.

Chapter 7: The Beginnings of a Plantation Society

1. Sheridan (1994), p.162.
2. Lindeström, p.75.
3. Burns (1954), p.269.
4. Jeaffreson, p.188.
5. Richard Pares, 'Merchants and Planters', *Economic History Review*, 4 (Supp.) 1960, p.23.
6. Higham, p.189.
7. On one night in January 2001 the author and his wife were forced to vacate their holiday accommodation at Brighton Estate for several hours because of the malicious burning of cane fields taking place in the immediate vicinity. They drew little comfort from being told by the more blasé local inhabitants that such incendiarism took place most years and was now more or less part of life.
8. Jeaffreson, p.207.
9. Ibid. p.257.
10. Higham, p.153.
11. Bennett, p.362.
12. Burns (1954), p.288.

Chapter 8: The Loss and Recovery of St Christopher

1. Harlow (1925), p.222.
2. Burns (1954), p.338.
3. Higham, p.73.
4 Ibid. p.79.

5. Ibid. p.80.
6. Sheridan (1994), p.152.
7. Jeaffreson, p.194.
8. Ibid. p.199.

Chapter 9: The French Wars and the End of S. Christophe

1. Higham, p.101.
2. Ibid. p.103.
3. Ibid. p.103.
4. Jeaffreson, p.211.
5. Harlow (1928), p.18.
6. Oldmixon, vol. p.282.
7. Sheridan (1994), p.155.
8. Harlow (1928), p.130.
9. Ibid. p.128.
10. Bourne, p.205.
11. Ibid. p.207.
12. Merrill, p.67.
13. Quoted by D. Mitchell, but without reference to source.
14. Ibid.
15. Harlow (1928), p.113.
16. David Carty, 'Address to Anguilla Archaeological and Historical Society', 31 May 1985, p.3, but without reference to source.

Chapter 10: Constructing a Plantation Society

1. Following the Act of Union in 1707, which converted the English Parliament into a British Parliament by eliminating the separate Scottish Parliament.
2. Niddrie, p.7.
3. Ibid. p.8.
4. Pitman, p.99.
5. W. Smith, p.23.
6. Walker, p.61.
7. Pope-Hennessy, p.105.
8. Oliver, vol. 3, p.322.
9. Gaspar, p.133.
10. Burns (1954), p.480.
11. Pitman, p.107.
12. Burns (1954), p.458.
13. O'Shaughnessy, p.122.
14. Burns (1954), p.509.
15. O'Shaughnessy, p.133.
16. Pares (1950), p.95.
17. Goveia, p.89.
18. A Grand Jury, made up of anything between 12 and 23 men, was formed to inquire into an indictment and to decide whether the evidence against the accused justified a trial. They were abolished in 1933.

Chapter 11: Maintaining Plantation Societies

1. E.W. Andrews, p.107.
2. Letter of 28 April 1794 in Bodrhyddan MSS in National Library of Wales, Aberystwyth.

3. Walker, p.6.
4. E.W. Andrews, p.121.
5. Letter of 23 November 1799 in Bodrhyddan MSS.
6. Oliver, vol. 3, p.323.
7. E.W. Andrews, p.127.
8. A.M. Williams, p.126.
9. E.W. Andrews, p.127.
10. Ibid. p.127.
11. Other animals were not unknown. In 1778 a proprietor in Nevis imported four camels, which were followed by several more a few years later. They were not a great success and all had died by 1801. More success was achieved with water buffaloes, imported into St Kitts from Trinidad, which were used on at least one estate from the mid-1920s until the early 1950s.
12. Letter of 28 April 1794 in Bodrhyddan MSS.
13. Yorke, p.66 *et seq.*
14. Ramsay, p.281.
15. Shyllon, p.44.
16. Gaspar, p.212.
17. O'Shaughnessy, p.173.
18. Ramsay, p.97.
19. E.W. Andrews, p.123.
20. Ellis, p.200 *et seq.*
21. Cabrera, vol. 3, p.127 *et seq.*

Chapter 12: War and the Islands

1. Ragatz (1928), p.150.
2. Buisseret, p.46.
3. Pares (1950), p.97.
4. Southey, vol. 2, p.514.
5. Ibid. p.515.
6. Ibid. p.514.
7. Schomberg, vol. 2, p.90.
8. Ibid. p.91.
9. Ibid.
10. Ibid.
11. Burns (1954), p.757.
12. Southey, vol. 2, p.521.
13. Burns (1954), p.755.
14. Goveia, p.69.
15. O'Shaughnessy, p.239.
16. Rawson, p.79.
17. Burns (1954), p.545.
18. Coke, vol. 3, p.52.
19. *Supplement to the Royal Danish American Gazette*, 5 May 1792.
20. O'Shaughnessy, p.51.
21. Buckley, p.40.

Chapter 13: Administration, Law and Religion

1. Harlow and Madden, p.100.
2. Goveia, p.61.
3. Edwards, vol. 1, p.430.
4. Dayfoot, p.89.

5. Walker, p.17.
6. *Parliamentary Papers* 1817, 'Papers relating to the Treatment of Slaves in the Colonies'.
7. Coleridge, p.197.
8. Ibid. p.270.
9. Ibid. p.277.
10. Coke, vol. 3, p.57.
11. Horsford, p.294.
12. Ibid. p.296.
13. Ibid. p.299.
14. Cox, p.112.
15. Coleridge, p.214.

Chapter 14: Amelioration and the Approach to Emancipation

1. Letter of 20 July 1792 in Bodrhyddan MSS.
2. Paquette and Engerman, p.242.
3. Letter of 9 May 1798 in Bodrhyddan MSS.
4. Pares (1950), p.155.
5. Walker, p.25.
6. Ibid. p.31.
7. Ibid. p.32.
8. Anon., *Case in Nevis, 1817*, p.4.
9. *Parliamentary Papers*, 1817, 'Papers relating to the Treatment of Slaves in the Colonies'.
10. Ibid.
11. E. Williams (1954), p.91.
12. *Parliamentary Papers*, 1818, 'Papers relating to the Treatment of Slaves in the Colonies, St Christopher'.
13. House of Commons Paper, 1 May 1827, *Slaves: Communications from St Kitt's, Respecting Prosecution for Ill Treatment of a Female Slave*.
14. Coleridge, p.230.
15. Murray, p.140.
16. House of Commons Paper, 1825, *State of the Community of Anguilla*.
17. Oliver, vol. 6, p.141.
18. Ibid. p.142.

Chapter 15: Emancipation and the Aftermath

1. Turner, p.275.
2. *Parliamentary Papers*, 1835, vol. L, p.621 *et seq*.
3. Frucht, p.386.
4. Truman *et al.*, p.47.
5. Colonial Report, Nevis, 1849, Foreign and Commonwealth Office Library (FCOL), p.64.
6. Gurney, p.41.
7. Colonial Report, St Kitts, 1843, FCOL, p.102.
8. Richardson (1983), p.85.
9. Colonial Report, Nevis, 1854, FCOL, p.169.
10. Colonial Report, St Kitts, 1855, FCOL, p.194.
11. Colonial Report, St Kitts, 1856, FCOL, p.116.
12. Colonial Report, St Kitts, 1860, FCOL, p.92.
13. Day, vol. 2, p.206. This author seems to have been the first visitor ever to record the peculiarity of Kittitian speech which is still noticeable today, 'where the v's

and w's become perverted: "vel", "vy", "vot", "wessels", "witcuals", etc. roll out...in true cockney style. How this originated it is impossible now to tell.' (p.213).

14. Colonial Report, Nevis, 1855, FCOL, p.202.
15. Ibid. p.201.
16. Ibid. p.203.

Chapter 16: Islands in Decline

1. Davy, p.458.
2. Ibid. p.472.
3. Colonial Report, St Kitts, 1849, FCOL, p.47.
4. Colonial Report, St Kitts, 1855, FCOL, p.198.
5. Colonial Report, St Kitts, 1873, FCOL, p.90.
6. Richardson (1983), p.106.
7. Colonial Report, Nevis, 1849, FCOL, p.63.
8. Colonial Report, Nevis, 1855, FCOL, p.203.
9. Colonial Report, Nevis, 1856, FCOL, p.125.
10. Colonial Report, Nevis, 1862, FCOL, p.92.
11. Colonial Report, St Kitts, 1860, FCOL, p.94.
12. Colonial Report, St Kitts, 1878, FCOL, p.194.
13 Quoted by David Carty, 'Address to Anguilla Archaeological and Historical Society', 31 May 1985, p.5, but without reference to source.
14. Misc. Colonial Reports, 'Anguilla: Report on Vital Statistics 1898', p.6.
15. Davy, p.449.
16. Ibid.
17. Colonial Report, St Kitts, 1845, FCOL, p.100.
18. Colonial Report, St Kitts, 1849, FCOL, p.47.
19. Colonial Report, St Kitts, 1860, FCOL, p.89.
20. Colonial Report, St Kitts, 1850, FCOL, p.103.
21. Ibid. p.107.
22. Colonial Report, St Kitts, 1863, FCOL, p.89.
23. Colonial Report, St Kitts, 1868, FCOL, p.88.
24. Colonial Report, Nevis, 1847, FCOL, p.139.
25. Colonial Report, Nevis, 1870, FCOL, p.150.
26. A.M. Willams, p.145.
27. Burns (1949), p.241.
28. Richards, p.8.
29. Brown, p.47.
30. Richards, p.6.

Chapter 17: Government, Justice and Defence

1. Boromé, p.37.
2. Colonial Report, Nevis, 1856, FCOL, p.124.
3. Colonial Report, St Kitts, 1856, FCOL, p.108.
4. Ibid. p.112.
5. Colonial Report, St Kitts, 1860, FCOL, p.77.
6. Madden and Fieldhouse, p.245.
7. Ibid. p.246.
8. Ibid. p.214.
9. Ibid. p.253.
10. Colonial Report, Nevis, 1866, FCOL, p.103.
11. Colonial Report, Nevis, 1868, FCOL, p.92.

12. Colonial Report, Nevis, 1870, FCOL, p.151.
13. Colonial Report, Nevis, 1877, FCOL, p.103.
14 Baird, p.93.
15. Colonial Report, Nevis, 1855, FCOL, p.169.
16. Hall (1971), p.169
17. Colonial Report, Nevis, 1882, FCOL, p.84.
18. Phillips (1985), p.116.
19. Colonial Report, St Kitts, 1867, FCOL, p.86.
20. *Anguilla: 25 Anniversary Magazine*, 1992, p.30.
21. Burns (1949), p.16.
22. Colonial Report, Nevis, 1857, FCOL, p.149.
23. Colonial Report, Nevis, 1856, FCOL, p.125.
24. Colonial Report, St Kitts, 1860, FCOL, p.80.
25. Colonial Report, St Kitts, 1862, FCOL, p.88.
26. Madden and Fieldhouse, p.240.
27. Colonial Report, Nevis, 1856, FCOL, p.126.
28. Colonial Report, Nevis, 1864, FCOL, p.131.
29. Burns (1949), p.265.
30. Davy, p.464.

Chapter 18: Towards a Modern Society

1. C.W. Day, vol. 2, p.218.
2. Colonial Report, St Kitts, 1860, FCOL, p.85.
3. A. Williams, p.60.
4. Anon., *The West Indies: General Information for Intending Settlers*, p.120.
5. Colonial Report, Leeward Is, 1948, FCOL, p.28.
6. Colonial Report, Leeward Is, 1955–56, FCOL, p.35.
7. Colonial Report, Nevis, 1855, FCOL, p.208.
8. Colonial Report, Nevis, 1879, FCOL, p.239.
9. C.W. Day, vol. 2, p.211.
10. Colonial Report, St Kitts, 1864, FCOL, p.124.
11. Colonial Report, St Kitts, 1852, FCOL, p.100.
12. Colonial Report, St Kitts, 1868, FCOL, p.87.
13. Colonial Report, St Kitts, 1880, FCOL, p.126 *et seq.*
14. S. de F. Day, p.87.
15. St-Johnston (1936a), p.138.
16. Ibid. p.149.
17. Colonial Report, Nevis, 1855, FCOL, p.203.
18. C.W. Day, vol 2, p.209.
19. Colonial Report, Nevis, 1856, FCOL, p.121.
20. Colonial Report, Nevis, 1862, FCOL, p.91.
21. Colonial Report, Nevis, 1876, FCOL, p.109.
22. Colonial Report, Nevis, 1877, FCOL, p.102.
23. Phillips (1991), p.73.
24. A. Williams, p.39.
25. Graves, p.182.
26. Glover, p.279.
27. Earle, p.41 *et seq.*
28. Berkeley, p.14.
29. Colonial Report, St Kitts-Nevis, 1910–11, FCOL, p.28.
30. Colonial Report, St Kitts-Nevis, 1928–29, FCOL, p.23.
31. Sutton (1990), p.146.
32. Blackburne, p.136.

Chapter 19: Progress in Health and Education

1. Colonial Report, St Kitts, 1847, FCOL, p.115.
2. Colonial Report, St Kitts, 1854, FCOL, p.149.
3. Colonial Report, St Kitts, 1856, FCOL, p.117.
4. Colonial Report, St Kitts, 1865, FCOL, p.91.
5. Ibid.
6. Colonial Report, St Kitts, 1885, FCOL, p.225.
7. St-Johnston, (1936b), p.51.
8. Macmillan, p.122.
9. Augier and Gordon, p.212.
10. Colonial Report, Nevis, 1856, FCOL, p.126.
11. Colonial Report, Nevis, 1868, FCOL, p.95.
12. Colonial Report, Nevis, 1870, FCOL, p.149.
13. Colonial Report, Nevis, 1860, FCOL, p.98.
14. Colonial Report, St Kitts, 1847, FCOL, p.115.
15. Colonial Report, St Kitts, 1853, FCOL, p.147.
16. Colonial Report, St Kitts, 1854, FCOL, p.138.
17. Colonial Report, St Kitts, 1870, FCOL, p.145.
18. Richards, p.5.
19. Colonial Report, Nevis, 1846, FCOL, p.58.
20. Davy, p.484.
21. Colonial Report, Nevis, 1855, FCOL, p.207.
22. Colonial Report, Nevis, 1856, FCOL, p.120.
23. Colonial Report, Nevis, 1862, FCOL, p.90.
24. Colonial Report, Nevis, 1866, FCOL, p.105.
25. Sutton (1990), p.152.

Chapter 20: The Development of Organized Labour

1. Colonial Report, St Kitts-Nevis, 1900, FCOL, p.43.
2. Watts, p.13.
3. Colonial Report, St Kitts-Nevis, 1910, FCOL, p.27.
4. H. Mitchell, p.169.
5. Colonial Report, St Kitts-Nevis, 1909, FCOL, p.28.
6. Colonial Report, St Kitts-Nevis, 1911–12, FCOL, p.30.
7. Colonial Report, St Kitts-Nevis, 1910–11, FCOL, p.29.
8. Colonial Report, St Kitts-Nevis, 1911–12, FCOL, p.27.
9. Lucas, p.374.
10. Turner, p.286.
11. *Union Messenger*, 23 November 1932.
12. *Papers relating to the Disturbances in St Christopher (St Kitts) January–February, 1935*, 1935, Cmd. 4956, p.4.
13. Ibid. p.8.
14. Ibid. p.9.
15. Ibid. p.5.
16. Ibid. p.6.
17. Ibid. p.12.
18. W.T. Browne (1992), p.13.
19. *Papers Relating to the Disturbances in St Christopher (St Kitts) January–February 1935*, 1935, Cmd. 4956, p.14.
20. Ibid. p.6.
21. Challenger took no further part in union affairs, but devoted the remainder of his life to historical research, dying in 2000.
22. W.T. Browne (1992), p.142.

Chapter 21: Constitutional Reform and Responsible Government

1. W.T. Browne (1992), p.288.
2. Blackburne, p.133.
3. Ibid. p.143.
4. Southwell, p.11.
5. Blackburne, p.143.
6. Colonial Report, Leeward Islands, 1955–56, FCOL, p.3.
7. Ibid. p.6.
8. Sealy, p.57.
9. *Report of the St Kitts/Nevis/Anguilla Constitutional Conference 1966*, White Paper, 1966, p.5.
10. Ibid. p.6.
11. Ibid. p.22.
12. Phillips (1991), p.118.

Chapter 22: The Anguilla Revolution

1. Petty (1984), p.23.
2. Address by the Premier to the formative meeting in London of the Organisation for the State of St Kitts-Nevis-Anguilla, 25 August 1967, transcript in the St Kitts Heritage Society Library, p.1.
3. See Petty (1984), p.24, and *Commemorative Magazine of the Anguilla Revolution, 1967–1992*, p.17.
4. Petty (1984), p.50.
5. Ibid. p.66.
6. Ibid. p.70.
7. Ibid. p.74.
8. Between 1983 and 1987 Anguilla received an average of £1,300,000 a year in aid from Britain (£167 per capita). During the same period St Kitts-Nevis received only £1,000,000 (£23 per capita).

Chapter 23: Moving Towards Independence

1. Phillips (1991), p.90.
2. Renwick, p.14.
3. O'Loughlin, p.19.
4. Phillips, p.95.
5. Payne, p.6.
6. Blackburne, p.144.
7. Crouse (1940), p.260.

Chapter 24: Independence

1. W.T. Browne (1992), p.390.
2. Where, up until 2002 at least, his body – just like those of Bradshaw and another stalwart of the Labour Party, Joseph France (who died in 1997) – lay in an unmarked grave, surely a peculiar and unbecoming situation with regard to the memory of all three men, considering the contribution each made while alive to the creation of the modern state.
3. Liburd and Bryant, p.18.
4. Ibid. p.20.
5. Ibid. p.38.

6. 'Address by the Premier over ZIZ TV and Radio, 13 January 1982', St Kitts Heritage Society.
7. *Report of the Saint Christopher and Nevis Constitutional Conference 1982,* White Paper, 1983, p.31.
8. Ibid. p.11.
9. Ibid. p.8.
10. Simmonds, p.4.
11. Inniss (1983), preface.

Bibliography

Alexis, F. (1984) 'British Intervention in St Kitts', *Journal of International Law and Politics*, vol. 16, spring, pp.581–600.

Andrews, E.W. (ed.) (1921) *Journal of a Lady of Quality: Being the Narrative of a Journey from Scotland to the West Indies, North Carolina and Portugal, in the Years 1774 to 1776*, New Haven, CT.

Andrews, K.R. (1978) *The Spanish Caribbean: Trade and Plunder, 1530–1630*, New Haven, CT.

Anon. (1818) *Case in Nevis, 1817*, London.

Anon. (1911) *The West Indies: General Information for Intending Settlers*, London.

Archibald, W. (1993) *Reflections: On an Epic Journey*, St Kitts.

Augier, F.R. and Gordon, S.C. (1962) *Sources of West Indian History*, London.

Ayearst, M. (1960) *The British West Indies: The Search for Self-Government*, London.

Baird, R. (1850) *Impressions and Experiences of the West Indies and North America in 1849*, Edinburgh.

Baker, P. and Bruyn, A. (eds) (1998) *St Kitts and the Atlantic Creoles*, London.

Beachey, R.W. (1957) *The British West Indies Sugar Industry in the Late Nineteenth Century*, Oxford.

Bennett, J.H. (1967) 'The English Caribbees in the Period of the Civil War, 1642–1646', *William and Mary Qtly*, 3rd ser. 24, pp.359–77.

Berkeley, T.B.H. (1881) *The Leeward Islands: Past and Present*, London.

Blackburn, R. (1997) *The Making of New World Slavery: From the Baroque to the Modern, 1492–1800*, London.

Blackburne, Sir Kenneth (1976) *Lasting Legacy: A Story of British Colonialism*, London.

Bolland, O.N. (1995) *On the March: Labour Rebellions in the British Caribbean, 1934–39*, London.

Boromé, J. (ed.) (1965) 'John Candler's Diary', *Caribbean Studies*, vol. 5, no. 4, pp.35–8.

Bourne, R. (1939) *Queen Anne's Navy in the West Indies*, New Haven, CT.

Branch, C.W. (1907) 'Aboriginal Antiquities in St Kitts and Nevis', *American Anthropologist*, n.s. vol. 9, no. 2, pp.315–33.

Bridenbaugh, C. and R. (1972) *No Peace Beyond the Line: The English in the Caribbean, 1624–1690*, New York.

Brown, J. (1961) *Leewards: Writings, Past and Present, about the Leeward Islands*, Barbados.

Browne, H.L.S. (1980) *Law, Power and Government in St Kitts, Nevis and Anguilla: Politics and Ambition Clash in a Mini-State*, St Kitts.

Browne, W.T. (1985) *The Christena Disaster in Retrospect: Error, Tragedy, Challenge and Hope (A Caribbean Story)*, St Thomas.

Browne, W.T. (1992) *From Commoner to King: Robert L. Bradshaw – Crusader for Dignity and Justice in the Caribbean*, Lanham, MD.

Buckley, R.N. (1979) *Slaves in Red Coats: The British West India Regiments, 1795–1815*, New Haven, CT.

Buisseret, D. (1973) 'The Elusive Deodand: A Study of the Fortified Refuges of the Lesser Antilles', *Journal of Caribbean History*, nos. 6&7, pp.43–80.

Burdon, K.J. (1920) *A Handbook of St Kitts-Nevis*, London.

Burn, W.L. (1937) *Emancipation and Apprenticeship in the British West Indies*, London.

Burns, Sir Alan (1949) *Colonial Civil Servant*, London.

Burns, Sir Alan (1954) *History of the British West Indies*, London.

Cabrera, J.M. (1851) *Paginas Históricas de la Revolución Hispanoamericana*, 5 vols, Caracas.

Cameron, T.W.M. (1934) 'The Early History of the Caribbee Islands (1492 to 1530)', *Scottish Geog. Mag.*, vol. 50, no. 1, pp.1–18 and 92–100.

Capadose, Lieut.-Colonel H. (1845) *Sixteen Years in the West Indies*, 2 vols, London.

Carr, F.B. (1994) *Nelson, Nisbet and Nevis*, Nevis.

Carty, B. (1993) *Anguilla: Beyond the Beaches*, Anguilla.

Clarke, C.G. (1971) 'Political Fragmentation in the Caribbean: The Case of Anguilla', *Canadian Geographer*, vol. 15, no. 1, pp.13–29.

Clarke, C.G. (1978) *Caribbean Social Relations*, Liverpool.

Coke, T. (1808–11) *A History of the West Indies*, 3 vols, London.

Coleridge, H.N. (1826) *Six Months in the West Indies in 1825*, New York.

Cox, E.L. (1984) *Free Coloureds in the Slave Societies of St Kitts and Grenada, 1763–1833*, Knoxsville, TN.

Cross, M. and Heuman, G. (1988) *Labour in the Caribbean: From Emancipation to Independence*, London.

Crouse, N.M. (1940) *French Pioneers in the West Indies, 1624–1664*, New York.

Crouse, N.M. (1943) *The French Struggle for the West Indies, 1665–1713*, New York.

Davy, J. (1854) *The West Indies, Before and Since Slave Emancipation*, 2 vols, London.

Day, C.W. (1852) *Five Years' Residence in the West Indies*, 2 vols, London.

Day, S. de F. (1899) *The Cruise of the Scythian in the West Indies,* London.

Dayfoot, A.C. (1999) *The Shaping of The West Indian Church, 1492–1962,* Jamaica.

Deerr, N. (1949, 1950) *The History of Sugar,* 2 vols, London.

Douglas, N. (1985) *An Amerindian Ceremonial Cavern on Anguilla,* Anguilla.

Dunn, R.S. (1972) *Sugar and Slaves: The Rise of the Planter Class in the English West Indies, 1624–1713,* Raleigh, NC. (English edn, London 1973)

Earle, K.W. (1924) *Reports on the Geology of St Kitts-Nevis, BWI, and the Geology of Anguilla, BWI,* London.

Edwards, B. (1793) *The History, Civil and Commercial, of the British Colonies in the West Indies,* 2 vols, London.

Ellis, J.D. (2002) 'Drummers for the Devil: The Black Soldiers of the 29th (Worcestershire) Regiment of Foot, 1759–1843', *Journal of the Society for Army Historical Research,* vol. 80, no. 323, autumn, pp.186–202.

Emmer, P. and Carrera Damas, G. (1999) *General History of the Caribbean Volume II: New Societies: The Caribbean in the Long Sixteenth Century,* Basingstoke.

Firth, C.H. (1900) *Narrative of General Venables: With an Appendix of Papers Relating to the Expedition to the West Indies and the Conquest of Jamaica, 1654–1655,* London.

Forbes, U. (1970) 'The West Indies Associated States: Some Aspects of the Constitutional Arrangements', *Social and Economic Studies,* vol. 19, pp.57–88.

Franck, H.A. (1920) *Roaming Through the West Indies,* New York.

Friedrichs, J. (1999) *British Regiments of the Line Garrisoned on Brimstone Hill, St Kitts, WI, 1670–1853/54,* St Vincent.

Frucht, R. (1977) 'From Slavery to Unfreedom in the Plantation Society of St Kitts, WI', *Annals of NY Academy of Sciences,* vol. 292, pp.379–88.

Gaspar, D.B. (1985) *Bondmen and Rebels: A Study of Master-Slave Relations in Antigua with Implications for Colonial British America,* Baltimore, MD.

Glover, Lady (1897) *Life of Sir John Hawley Glover, RN, GCMG,* London.

Goodwin, R.C. and Heymann, C. (1977) 'The St Kitts Archaeological Expeditions', *Explorers Journal,* March.

Gordon, S.C. (1963) *A Century of West Indian Education: A Source Book,* London.

Goveia, E.V. (1965) *Slave Society in the British Leeward Islands at the End of the Eighteenth Century,* New Haven, CT.

Government of St Kitts-Nevis (1976) *White Paper on the Acquisition of the Sugar Factory,* St Kitts.

Graves, C. (1965) *Fourteen Islands in the Sun,* London.

Great Britain: HM Government, *Report Exhibiting the Past and Present State of Her Majesty's Colonial Possessions,* London (1845–1885).

Great Britain: HM Government, 'Colonial Reports – Annual', London (1897–1919).

Great Britain: HM Government, 'Annual Report: Leeward Islands', London (1938–1956).

Gurney, J.J. (1840) *A Winter in the West Indies Described in Familiar Letters to Henry Clay of Kentucky*, London.

Hall, D. (1971) *Five of the Leewards, 1834–1870: The Major Problems of the Post-Emancipation Period in Antigua, Barbuda, Montserrat, Nevis and St Kitts*, Barbados.

Hall, D. (1978) 'The Flight from the Estates Reconsidered: The British West Indies, 1838–42', *Journal of Caribbean History*, nos 10&11, pp.7–24.

Harlow, V.T. (ed.) (1925) *Colonising Expeditions to the West Indies and Guiana, 1623 to 1667*, London.

Harlow, V.T. (1928) *Christopher Codrington, 1668–1710*, Oxford.

Harlow, V. T. and Madden, F. (1953) *British Colonial Developments, 1774–1834: Select Documents*, Oxford.

Harris, D.R. (1965) *Plants, Animals, and Man in the Outer Leeward Islands, West Indies: An Ecological Study of Antigua, Barbuda and Anguilla*, Berkeley, CA.

Higham, C.S.S. (1921) *The Development of the Leeward Islands under the Restoration, 1660–1688*, Cambridge.

Hoffman, C.A. (1973) 'Archaeological Investigations on St Kitts, WI', *Caribbean Journal of Science*, vol. 13, December, pp.237–52.

Horsford, J. (1856) *A Voice from the West Indies: Being a Review of the Character and Results of Missionary Efforts in the British and other Colonies of the Caribbean Sea*, London.

Hubbard, V.K. (1998) *Swords, Ships and Sugar: History of Nevis to 1900*, Corvallis, OR.

Hubbard, V.K. (2002) *A History of St Kitts: The Sweet Trade*, Oxford.

Hulme, P. and Whitehead, N.L. (eds) (1992) *Wild Majesty: Encounters with Caribs from Columbus to the Present Day*, Oxford.

Iles, J.A. (1871) *An Account Descriptive of the Island of Nevis, West Indies*, Norwich.

Ince, B.A. (1970) 'The Diplomacy of New States: The Commonwealth Caribbean and the Case of Anguilla', *South Atlantic Quarterly*, vol. 69, no. 3, summer, pp.382–96.

Ince, B.A. (1970) 'The Limits of Caribbean Diplomacy: The Invasion of Anguilla', *New World Quarterly*, vol. 5, no. 3, pp.48–57.

Inniss, Sir Probyn (1983) *Whither Bound St Kitts-Nevis*, St Kitts.

Inniss, Sir Probyn (1985) *Historic Basseterre*, St Kitts.

Jeaffreson, J.C. (ed.) (1878) *A Young Squire of the Seventeenth Century, from the Papers of Christopher Jeaffreson*, 2 vols, London.

Johnston, J.R.V. (1965) 'The Stapleton Sugar Plantations in the Leeward Islands', *John Rylands University Library of Manchester Bulletin*, vol. 48, no. 1, autumn, pp.175–206.

Jones, S.B. (1976) *Annals of Anguilla, 1650–1923*, Belfast.

Jones-Hendrickson, S.B. (ed.) (1988) *Interviews with Lee L. Moore*, US Virgin Islands.

King, G.H. (n.d.) *Brimstone Hill: The Gibraltar of the West Indies*, St Kitts.

Lanaghan, F.T. (1844) *Antigua and the Antiguans: A Full Account of the Colony and its Inhabitants*, 2 vols, London.

Liburd, J. and Bryant, F. (n.d.) *The Politics of St Kitts and Nevis: The Road to Independence, 1930–1980*, St Kitts.

Lindeström, P. (1925) *Geographia Americae with an Account of the Delaware Indians, Based on Surveys and Notes made in 1654–1656*, Philadelphia.

Lucas, C. (1923) *The Empire at War (Vol. II)*, Oxford.

McGuire, M.T. (1974) 'The History of the St Kitts Vervet', *Caribbean Quarterly*, vol. 20, no. 2, June.

Macmillan, W.M. (1938) *Warning from the West Indies: A Tract for the Empire*, Harmondsworth.

Madden, F. and Fieldhouse, D. (1991) *The Dependent Empire and Ireland, 1840–1900: Advance and Retreat in Representative Self-Government*, vol. V, New York.

Manchester, K.D. (1971) *Historic Heritage of St Kitts-Nevis-Anguilla*, Trinidad.

Marshall, B.A. (1972) 'Attempts at Windward/Leeward Federation', *Caribbean Quarterly*, vol. 18, no. 2, June, pp.9–15.

Marten, N. (1969) *Theirs Not to Reason Why: A Study of the Anguillan Operation as Presented to Parliament*, London.

Mason, K. (1993) 'The World an Absentee Planter and His Slaves Made: Sir William Stapleton and his Nevis Sugar Estate, 1722–1740', *John Rylands University Library of Manchester Bulletin*, vol. 75, no. 1, spring, pp.103–31.

Matheson, D.L. (c.1974) *The Thomas Warner Story*, St Kitts.

Matheson, D.L. (c.1986) *The Brimstone Hill Fortress: Brief History and Progress of Restoration, 1965–1986*, St. Kitts.

Mathieson, W.L. (1926) *British Slavery and its Abolition, 1828–38*, London.

Mathieson, W.L. (1932) *British Slave Emancipation, 1838–1849*, London.

Merrill, G.C. (1958) *The Historical Geography of St Kitts and Nevis, The West Indies*, Mexico City.

Mims, S.L. (1912) *Colbert's West India Policy*, New Haven, CT.

Mitchell, D. (1985) *Anguilla: From the Archives, 1650–1750*, Anguilla.

Mitchell, Sir Harold (1967) *Caribbean Patterns: A Political and Economic Study of the Contemporary Caribbean*, Edinburgh.

Moll, V.P. (1995) *St Kitts-Nevis*, World Bibliography Series, vol. 174, Oxford.

Munroe, T. and Lewis, R. (eds) (1971) *Readings in Government and Politics of the West Indies,* Jamaica.

Murray, D.J. (1965) *The West Indies and the Development of Colonial Government, 1810–1834,* Oxford.

Naipaul, V.S. (1972) *The Overcrowded Barracoon and other Articles,* London.

Newton, A.P. (1933) *The European Nations in the West Indies, 1493–1688,* London.

Niddrie, D. (1966) 'An Attempt at Planned Settlement in St Kitts in the Early Eighteenth Century', *Caribbean Studies,* vol. 5, no. 4, pp.3–11.

Oldmixon, J. (1708) *The British Empire in America,* vol. 2, London.

Oliver, V.L. (1910–19) *Caribbeana, being Miscellaneous Papers relating to the History, Genealogy, Topography and Antiquities of the British West Indies,* 6 vols, London.

O'Loughlin, C. (1968) *Economic and Political Change in the Leeward and Windward Islands,* New Haven, CT.

Olwig, K.F. (1993) *Global Culture, Island Identity: Continuity and Change in the Afro-Caribbean Community of Nevis,* Amsterdam.

Olwig, K.F. (1995) *Small Islands, Large Questions: Society, Culture and Resistance in the Post-Emancipation Caribbean,* London.

O'Shaughnessy, A.J. (2000) *An Empire Divided: The American Revolution and the British Caribbean,* Philadelphia, PA.

Paquette, R.L. and Engerman, S.L. (eds) (1996) *The Lesser Antilles in the Age of European Expansion,* Gainesville, TX.

Pares, R. (1950) *A West India Fortune,* London.

Pares, R. (1963) *War and Trade in the West Indies, 1739–1763,* London.

Pascoe, C.F. (1901) *Two Hundred Years of the SPG, 1701–1900,* London.

Payne, C. (2000) 'The Heroic Construction of St Kitts' "Papa" Bradshaw', *St Kitts and Nevis Country Conference Papers,* May.

Petty, C.L. (1984) *Anguilla: Where There's a Will There's a Way,* Anguilla.

Petty, C.L. (1991) *A Handbook History of Anguilla,* Anguilla.

Phillips, Sir Fred (1985) *West Indian Constitutions: Post-Independence Reform,* London.

Phillips, Sir Fred (1991) *Caribbean Life and Culture: A Citizen Reflects,* Jamaica.

Pitman, F.W. (1917) *The Development of the British West Indies, 1700–1763,* New Haven, CT.

Pope-Hennessy, J. (1967) *Sins of the Fathers: A Study of the Atlantic Slave Traders, 1441–1807,* London.

Ragatz, L.J. (1928) *The Fall of the Planter Class in the British Caribbean, 1763–1833,* New York.

Ragatz, L.J. (1931) 'Absentee Landlordism in the British Caribbean, 1750–1833', *Agricultural History,* vol. V, pp.7–24.

Ramsay, J. (1784) *An Essay on the Treatment and Conversion of African Slaves in the British Sugar Colonies,* London.

Rawson, G. (ed.) (1953) *Nelson's Letters from the Leeward Islands*, London.

Renwick, J.D.B. (1970) *Report on the Circumstances Surrounding the Sinking of the M.V. 'Christena'*, St Kitts.

Richards, G. (2000) 'Race, Labour and the Colonial State in St Kitts-Nevis, 1897–1922', *St Kitts and Nevis Country Conference Papers*, May.

Richardson, B.C. (1977) 'Political Changes in St Kitts and Nevis', *Geographical Review*, vol. 67, no. 3, pp.357–9.

Richardson, B.C. (1980) 'Freedom and Migration in the Leeward Caribbean, 1838–1848', *Journal of Historical Geography*, vol. 6, no. 4, pp.391–408.

Richardson, B.C. (1983) *Caribbean Migrants: Environment and Human Survival on St Kitts and Nevis*, Knoxville, TN.

Roberts, G.W. and Byrne, J. (1966–67) 'Summary Statistics on Indenture and Associated Migration Affecting the West Indies, 1834–1918', *Population Studies*, vol. 20, pp.125–34.

Robinson, J. (1999) *Nevis: The Last Hundred Years, 1900–1999*, Nevis.

Rubin, V. and Tuden, A. (1977) *Comparative Perspectives on Slavery in New World Plantation Societies*, New York.

St-Johnston, Sir Reginald (1933) *The Leeward Islands During the French Wars*, Antigua.

St-Johnston, Sir Reginald (1936a) *From a Colonial Governor's Note-Book*, London.

St-Johnston, Sir Reginald (1936b) *Strange Places and Strange Peoples*, London.

Saul, S.B. (1958) 'The British West Indies in Depression, 1880–1914', *Inter-American Economic Affairs*, vol. 12, pp.3–25.

Schomberg, I. (1802) *Naval Chronology; or an Historical Summary of Naval and Maritime Events*, 5 vols, London.

Sealy, T. (1991) *Sealy's Caribbean Leaders*, Jamaica.

Sebastian, Sir Cuthbert (2001) *St Kitts – One Hundred Years of Medicine*, St Kitts.

Sheridan, R.B. (1970) *The Development of Plantations to 1750: An Era of West Indian Propriety, 1750–1775*, Barbados.

Sheridan, R.B. (1994) *Sugar and Slavery: An Economic History of the British West Indies, 1623–1775*, Jamaica.

Shyllon, F. (1977) *James Ramsay: The Unknown Abolitionist*, Edinburgh.

Simmonds, Dr K. (1983) *Independence Address*, St Kitts.

Smith, V.T.C. (1992) *Fire and Brimstone: The Story of the Brimstone Hill Fortress, St Kitts, West Indies, 1690–1853*, St Kitts.

Smith, Rev. William (1745) *A Natural History of Nevis and the Rest of the English Leeward Caribbee Islands in America*, Cambridge.

Southey, T. (1827) *A Chronological History of the West Indies*, 3 vols, London.

Southwell, C.A.P. (1951) *The Truth about 'Operation Blackburne'*, St Kitts.

Stern, M.H. (1958) 'Some Notes on the Jews of Nevis', *American Jewish Archives*, October, pp.151–9.

Sutton, J.W. (1987) *A Testimony of Triumph*, Scarborough, Ontario.

Sutton, J.W. (1990) *Our Love Prevailed*, Scarborough, Ontario.

Terrell, M. (1994) 'The Jews of Nevis and their Synagogue', *Nevis Historical and Conservation Society Newsletter*, May, pp.4–7.

Truman, G., Jackson, J. and Longstreth, T.B. (1844) *Narrative of a Visit to the West Indies, in 1840 and 1841*, Philadelphia, PA.

Turner, M. (1995) *From Chattel Slaves to Wage Slaves*, London.

Walker, G.P.J. (1992) *The Life of Daniel Gateward Davis, First Bishop of Antigua*, St Kitts.

Wallace, E. (1977) *The British Caribbean: From the Decline of Colonialism to the End of Federation*, Toronto.

Ward, J.R. (1988) *British West Indian Slavery, 1750–1834*, Oxford.

Watkins, F.H. (1924) *Handbook of the Leeward Islands*, London.

Watts, F. (1905) *Report on the Sugar Industry in Antigua and St Kitts-Nevis, 1881 to 1905*, Barbados.

Wentworth, T. (1834) *The West India Sketch Book*, London.

Westlake, D.E. (1972) *Under an English Heaven*, London.

Williams, A.M. (1898) *Under the Trade Winds*, New York.

Williams, E. (1954) *The British West Indies at Westminster: Part I, 1789–1823*, Trinidad.

Williams, E. (1963) *Documents of West Indian History: Vol. I, 1492–1655*, Trinidad.

Williamson, J.A. (1926) *The Caribbee Islands under the Proprietary Patents*, Oxford.

Wilson, S.M. (1989) 'The Prehistoric Settlement Pattern of Nevis, West Indies', *Journal of Field Archaeology*, vol. 16, no. 4, pp.427–50.

Wilson, S.M. (1999) *The Indigenous People of the Caribbean*, Gainesville, TX.

Yorke, P.C. (1931) *The Diary of John Baker, Barrister of the Middle Temple, Solicitor-General of the Leeward Islands*, London.

Index

992-3750